OMNIBUS

For years Francis Clifford has been heaped
with critical praise for his novels of suspense;
and here is a collection of three that will show
why his reputation is so considerable.
From the pure espionage story (THE NAKED
RUNNER) through the story of suspense
(THE TREMBLING EARTH) to the story of
mystery and character (TIME IS AN
AMBUSH) he writes with beautiful style, with
great feeling for characterisation and with a
harsh awareness of the suspense writer's
main concern – to keep the reader excited and
interested. Often in the past he has been
compared to Eric Ambler, to John Le Carre,
to Graham Greene. These three novels will
show why.

Also by the same author,
and available in Coronet Books:

Overdue
A Battle is Fought to be Won
Another Way Of Dying
The Green Fields of Eden
The Blind Side
All Men Are Lonely Now
Amigo Amigo

Omnibus

The Naked Runner
The Trembling Earth
Time is an Ambush

Francis Clifford

CORONET BOOKS
Hodder and Stoughton

The Naked Runner
Copyright © 1965, 1966 Arthur Bell Thompson
First published in 1966 by Hodder and Stoughton Limited
Coronet edition 1967
Fourth impression (in this edition) 1975

The Trembling Earth
Copyright 1955
First published in 1955 by Hamish Hamilton Limited
Coronet edition 1970
Second impression (in this edition) 1975

Time is an Ambush
Copyright © 1962 Francis Clifford Productions Limited
First published in 1962 by Hodder and Stoughton Limited
Coronet edition 1969
Second impression (in this edition) 1975

Printed and bound in Great Britain for
Coronet Books, Hodder and Stoughton,
St. Paul's House Warwick Lane,
London EC4P 4AH
by Hazell Watson & Viney Ltd,
Aylesbury, Bucks

ISBN 0 340 19948 2

THE NAKED RUNNER

For John Attenborough
and Robin Denniston

All men dream: but not equally. Those who dream by night in the dusty recesses of their minds wake in the day to find that it was vanity: but the dreamers of the day are dangerous men, for they may act their dream with open eyes, to make it possible . . .

T. E. Lawrence: *Seven Pillars of Wisdom*

. . . a fear among fears
A naked runner lost in a storm of spears.

Arthur Symons

1

SAM LAKER watched his son serve himself with a second enormous helping of breakfast cereal then top it over with sugar and cream. Lord, he marvelled, how they can put it away at fourteen. And this was merely a beginning, he knew. Bacon and eggs, half a dozen slices of buttered toast, perhaps an apple to round off with—and sure enough the hunger-pangs would be back well before lunch. Only last week Mrs. Ruddick had said that when Patrick was home from Greynham it was like shopping for an entire extra household. Still, Laker reflected, he looks damn well on it, and that's the main thing. Big for his age, and chunky. Helen would have approved—except perhaps for the present state of his hair.

He folded the *Telegraph*, drained his coffee and smiled. "What's on the agenda for today?"

"The Planetarium."

"Oh yes, you told me. You and Tim Maxwell."

"That's right."

"And afterwards?"

"We thought we'd come back to the river. If the weather lasts, that is. Otherwise I'll probably go over to his place and listen to records or something."

"Didn't you do that yesterday?"

"Yes, but Tim's player packed in. He'll have had it fixed by this afternoon, though."

"I see." Laker paused uncertainly. "Well, you're all organised then?"

"Just about."

He rose, pushing away his chair. "The Planetarium ought to be interesting."

"Yes."

"Enjoy yourself, anyway."

"Thanks."

"And don't try anything too clever if you do go on the water."

"I won't. 'Bye."

They never seemed to speak much in the mornings. Patrick was invariably late down and Laker made a point of being at Gale and Watts by nine-thirty. Not that breakfast, even at the week-end, was an especially communicative time; but it often struck Laker that leaving the boy to his own devices five days a week throughout most of the school holidays was a routine act of desertion. It would have been different if he weren't an only child, or if Helen had lived, but regrets like that offered no solution. On the credit side, Patrick was nothing if not self-reliant. And, by way of amends, next week's trip to Leipzig and West Germany would help to balance things up a bit.

The mail had come. Telephone account, a picture-card for Mrs. Ruddick and a letter addressed to Patrick from Paris. *Patrick Laker, Esquire.* Laker opened the breakfast-room door and tossed the envelope on to the table.

"Just arrived. Which particular pen-pal would that be?"

"Gilles," Patrick answered, straightening it. "Gilles Leroux."

"Formal type, eh?"

"How d'you mean?"

"Esquire."

Patrick's eyes widened. "Oh, glory."

"Incidentally — "

"Yes?"

"Get your hair cut, will you?"

A grin from Patrick and Laker shut the door again. A minute or two later he looked into the kitchen.

"I'll be in at the usual time, Mrs. Ruddick. Around six-thirty."

"Very well, Mr. Laker."

"Patrick will be out most of the day as far as I can gather. Meanwhile he's busy taking on fuel."

"It's a wonder where he puts it, and that's a fact. But they're all the same at his age." Smiling, efficient, dependable Mrs. Ruddick. "You ought to see my nephew."

"By the way, there's a card for you," Laker said. "I left it in the hall."

Except for a few curled feathers of cirrus the morning was cloudless. Rain wouldn't come amiss, Laker thought, glancing at the roses as he cut across the lawn to the garage. He didn't fancy an evening's watering, but all the signs were that he was in for one. He ran the Humber out, locked the garage after him, then headed along the tree-lined avenue.

It was five miles to Gale and Watts and he had twenty minutes. He slowed at the intersection, waited for a line of cars to pass, then nosed into the main road that would lead him through Oatlands and on past the filling-station and into Weybridge. The trees and bordering hedges wore a bloom of late summer dust. He wound the driving-window all the way down, letting the air whoosh in. In Oatlands he veered out of the traffic's stream, switched off, and crossed to the tobacconist's for cigarettes.

"Morning, sir." From habit the man reached for the required brand and slid a pack of twenty across the counter. "Another lovely morning."

"Certainly is."

"We deserve all we can get, that's what I say."

Laker collected the change, nodded his thanks and stepped outside. Again and again he was to trace the nightmare back to that precise moment and wonder whether Slattery would in fact have got in touch if the next few seconds had never happened. But there and then he was aware only of the woman with the pram who was in the path of an oncoming truck. With abnormal clarity he saw the horrified expression of the driver in the high cab and the inevitability of disaster as the woman dithered between strides.

Instinct propelled Laker from the kerb. He sprinted, canted forward, going for the woman's waist, flinging himself at her in a rugby-tackle. She had begun to scream as his right shoulder crashed into her, and then she grunted, hands going up. In an overlapping blur of awareness he felt her moving with him and glimpsed the pram shooting clear and the bonnet of the truck shuddering towards them in a squeal of locked brakes that was merged with the hoarseness of a human voice somewhere in the distance. Then he was falling with the woman under him, rolling the instant they hit the tarmac, twisting away from the truck's towering bulk. With his eyes half-screwed he saw the red side of it loom vertically against the sky, going past him, the near wing brushing his clothes, and only then was he sure they were clear. The truck shook to a standstill with the cab-door immediately above Laker's head and the next thing he remembered with certainty was the driver staring down at him, eyes and face rigid with terror through sifting dust.

"You okay?"

Laker stirred. A wheel-hub was against his left calf. He tried to say "I think so," but there was a kind of dislocation between his brain and his tongue and all he could do was cough.

"*Jesus!*"

As the driver leapt from his cab Laker pushed himself on to his knees. The woman was stirring too, calling "Michael? . . . Michael?" in a dazed sort of way. Two or three people were between the truck and the pavement, righting the pram which had fallen sideways.

"Jesus," the driver said again to Laker, "they were goners but for you. You okay?" His face was the colour of zinc.

"Yes."

Laker stood up and helped the woman to her feet. She had a graze on her forehead and her eyes were frantic.

"*Michael!*"

The pram was upright now, the curly-haired child bawling but apparently unscathed. The woman ran to him, her voice breaking. All the voices seemed suddenly very loud, a little unreal. Someone said: "He had a bump, that's all. Just a bump when the pram hit the kerb and toppled over. He's frightened, that's all. He isn't hurt."

"They were goners," the driver was insisting. "She came

straight out from behind that parked van. Didn't give me a chance."

Laker went over to the pram. The woman had freed the child from its harness and was holding him to her, sobbing. She wasn't much more than a girl. Her yellow dress was streaked with tar and a man who'd apparently retrieved her shoes was offering them to her.

Laker said: "Can I take you home?"

He reckoned she scarcely heard him. He was only one of many; part of the babel. Somebody from a shop had brought out a chair.

"A doctor, maybe? My car's here."

She shook her head. A sizeable crowd had gathered. Laker looked at her. She'd be all right: no point in staying. He turned and made for the Humber, almost oblivious of the fact that the driver was asking: "Where's the fellow that pushed 'em clear? They'd have had it but for him."

He got into the car and drew away. His left knee throbbed and he was a shade light in the head, but it wasn't until he had nearly reached Weybridge that the reaction hit him in earnest. He pulled in to the side and felt the coldness blow through him and then the hot flush come. Everything went a greenish pink for a few moments and he rested his forehead on the wheel, eyes closed, blood and brightness beating together in his mind. A minute or two passed before the feeling of nausea began to ebb. Eventually, he broke the seal on the crushed pack of cigarettes and with trembling fingers lit up.

He'd scraped his knuckles, he noticed. He blew smoke against the windscreen, then took a deep lungful of air. Almost nine-thirty. Well, for once he'd be late. He wiped the chilly sweat from his face and sucked his knuckles, then prepared to drive on, a kind of disbelief possessing him as the scene began to run like a film across his natural vision. It had been close, all right, too close, and his nerves couldn't quite cope with it yet.

Gale and Watts designed and manufactured office equipment.

13

One of Laker's uncles, Charles Gale, had taken him into the firm soon after the war and for five years he served a kind of apprenticeship, "a grounding" Charles called it, first in the factory and then in the office, transferring periodically from one department to another. Accounts, Costing, Sales, Publicity, Organisation and Methods, Welfare — Laker duly went through the mill. On his thirtieth birthday, two years after marrying Helen, he had been elevated to the position of Frank Watts' personal assistant and when Charles retired on medical advice in the late fifties Laker was elected to fill the vacancy on the Board.

It was a small company, with something under eight hundred employees, and the neat red brick and white stone offices which screened the factory bays from the road stood back from the entrance gates behind a spread of shrubs and flower-bordered lawn. Laker ran the Humber into a space in the frontal parking-lot and got out, extracting his brief-case before locking up. He was one of those men who looked taller than his true height, which was five feet ten and a half inches, and he went to the scales around one hundred and ninety pounds. Like Patrick he was very solidly put together. His dark hair was on the wiry side, a trifle crinkly, and when he smiled it was a generous smile, radiating crow's-feet from the outer corners of his eyes and showing strong, even teeth that were his own. Guessing his age, strangers usually underestimated: he was, in fact, forty-three. "How d'you do it, Sam?" Baxendale, the sales director, had remarked only a couple of weeks earlier. "What's the secret? I break my back on the rowing-machine and do thirty-six holes every Saturday and Sunday, and what happens? All I get is a twin-sized paunch and a flabby chin."

Laker walked diagonally across the forecourt, the trace of a limp only slightly impairing his stride. MacDonald, the com-missionaire, offered a bright "Good morning, Mr. Laker" and held the door open. MacDonald had never really quit the parade-ground; he marched everywhere, his left arm scarcely swinging as if he permanently carried a rifle at the trail.

"Morning, John."

It was a pleasant entrance-lobby with half a dozen water-colours framed on pastel-washed walls. "No need," Charles Gale used to say, "for an office to look like a penitentiary." Laker nodded to the girl in Reception, unaware as he mounted the stairs that her gaze followed him curiously. Ten to ten. Carol Nolan, his secretary, was busy typing as he entered his second-floor office.

"Hallo," he said. "Had you given me up?"

"I was beginning to wonder."

"Well, I'm sure Gale and Watts is still solvent." His smile changed to a wince as he sat in the swivel-chair. "Any calls?"

"No," she said. "There's quite a post, though, and you've an appointment at eleven with Mr. Thornton of International."

Laker nodded, glancing at the orderly presentation of his mail and the files already flagged for reference. Carol was the best secretary he'd ever had, and by far the most attractive; raven-black hair, lively brown eyes and long slim legs. Baxendale was for ever suggesting that she ought to come to him when his own Miss Grigg retired, if not sooner. "She's just what's wanted on my front, believe me." And then, invariably, the corny crack: "To my mind Development can't do another thing for her."

"What's happened," Carol was saying now, "to your jacket?"

"Where?"

"The shoulder. No, the other one — at the back." She moved round the desk. "It's torn."

Laker craned his head. White padding bulged where the seam had come apart.

"And your hand. How — ?"

"That I knew about." He sucked the scraped knuckles again. "Get some tape, will you?"

"Did you fall or something?"

"Kind of."

She eyed him uncertainly. "Is that all you're going to tell me?"

"Let's say I had an argument with a truck."

15

"Whereabouts?"

"Oh, not far from home."

"Is the car damaged?"

"I wasn't in it." He shifted in the chair. "Look, be a good girl and get the sticking-tape, will you?"

She knew him well enough not to press him. When she returned from First Aid she said: "Can I have your jacket, please. You can't see Mr. Thornton if you're looking like that."

Laker gave it to her and she carried it away for temporary repairs. His suède shoes were smeared with tar across the toes, but they'd pass. Routine imposed itself. He got down to his mail, but it was quite a while before the day took shape in the way that others did, building upon their sequence of events and problems. His mind repeatedly fled to the woman in the yellow dress. It was a long time since he had been within a hair's breadth of danger or had his nerves stroked by anything worse than some minor, passing fear. Now, in retrospect, the incident had a curiously static quality, though once he shuddered dismissively as memory and imagination swept him with the vivid reality of every split second.

Carol brought his jacket back ten minutes before Reception announced that Thornton had arrived. He was a frequent visitor, so there was no need for Laker to have to apologise for the quality of the canteen coffee. He wasn't one for hanging about, either. As soon as they had studied the drawings and discussed the test reports on a new plastic sheeting requirement, he left. It was only then that Laker discovered he had lost his wallet. Dining-room accounts were presented on the last Tuesday of the month and, as soon as Thornton had gone, Carol was in with various additions to the paper-work together with the August account. And he always liked to settle on the spot.

"You didn't see it when you were mending my jacket, did you?"

"No," Carol said.

"Blast. Then it must have fallen out at Oatlands."

"Is that where you had your so-called argument with the truck?"

"Yes. Ring the police, will you? Don't go into details. Just report the loss. Someone may have turned it in."

No one had, she informed him a few minutes later.

He swore more forcibly.

"Was there much in it?"

"Driving licence, A.A. card —"

"Money, I meant."

"About fifteen pounds."

Carol made a pained face.

"Something from the Leipzig Fair people—flight particulars."

"*I*'ve got your plane tickets," she said. "And your Fair Cards and traveller's cheques and hotel reservations. Are you sure you started out with the wallet?"

"Sure," he said, then gave a resigned shrug. "We'll just have to keep our fingers crossed." Then again: "Blast it!" Helen had given it to him.

He lunched with Baxendale in the private room reserved for directors. Baxendale was in his most button-holing mood, unloading all the stories he'd heard at the golf club the previous evening including the one about the lama who unscrewed his navel only to find that his behind fell off when he stood up—a story so ancient that Laker could only imagine it must be going the rounds a second time.

"How's the delectable Miss Nolan today? On the ball as usual?"

"I'm happy to say."

"You ought to marry her, Sam. She's a guinea a box."

Laker laughed. "I thought you wanted her yourself to brighten your office."

"All in all, I'm the most generous of men."

"Where'd I find another secretary to come within a mile of her?"

"That'd be the last thing to worry me if I were in your shoes. Seriously, though, you ought to marry again. Margaret agrees with me. Mrs. Ruddick's a marvel and all that, but there's more to having a woman about the house than merely having a woman about the house." The boom years showed in Baxendale's thick flesh and pouchy eyes. "It'd be good for young Patrick, too—wouldn't it now?"

"I'll think it over," Laker countered lightly.

"My eye, you will. By the way, when are you two off to Germany?"

"Tomorrow week."

"Where are you going after you've done your duty at Leipzig?"

"The Rhineland. Ever been?"

"No."

"It was Patrick's idea. The house has been full of maps and leaflets for months."

"Well, I envy you. If Margaret has her way we'll never see anything except the bloody Costa del Sol. Oh, it's all right, I suppose, but it's too damned hot for golf unless you start before breakfast and the food's a bit off-putting. Those dreary paellas always look to me as if they've been regurgitated. Incidentally, what have you done to your hand?"

An incoming trunk-call summoned him away before he got an answer. Laker left shortly afterwards and went back to his office. Carol wasn't there, but she had pinned a note to the blotter. *1.10 p.m. Police rang to say crocodile wallet handed in. Thirteen pounds ten, A.A. card, driving licence, Leipzig letter and two photographs—C.N.*

Relieved, Laker mulled over the Minutes of the last Publicity Committee; he was due at the quarterly meeting at three. Apart from an occasional reminder either from his knuckles or his bruised knee the morning's shock had receded. If his thoughts wandered from the day's stint it was towards Patrick, wondering whether he was still in London or on his way back with Tim Maxwell. The weather had held, so they were probably bound for the river. Odd how one worried—out of a sense of inadequacy, he supposed. Yet Patrick did tend to be a shade

18

impetuous; someone more accident-prone would have learned his lesson by now.

"What did you tell the police?" he asked Carol on her return from lunch.

"That you'd call for it on your way home."

"Fine," he nodded.

She took letters from him for the next three-quarters of an hour. Baxendale's remarks kept echoing in his mind and once he caught himself looking at her almost as if it were for the first time. There was a bond between them—respect, trust, loyalty. Now and then he'd driven her home to Woking. She'd dined with him once or twice and he remembered her birthday religiously. But that was all.

At the door on his way to the meeting he asked suddenly: "How old are you, Carol?"

"Old?"

"That's right."

"Twenty-three," she said, colouring slightly. "Why?"

"I just wondered."

As if he didn't know. And Patrick was almost fifteen. But there it was; think an improbable thought and you got a very impractical answer.

The police-sergeant on duty asked if Laker could identify himself, then produced the wallet and turned the receipt book round for him to sign.

As Laker was checking the contents, the sergeant said: "A great thing you did this morning, sir. Quick thinking."

Privately, Laker had hoped that he wouldn't be associated with what had happened; but no such luck. He shrugged and countered: "Who handed the wallet in?"

"Horne's delivery boy." The sergeant consulted the book. "Said he found it in the gutter."

"Do you know him?"

"By sight, yes."

Laker put a pound on the desk. "Would you see he gets that?"

"I certainly will, sir. Yes, a fine effort on your part from what I've heard."

"How's the young woman?"

"Right as rain, I gather."

Curiosity got the better of Laker as he was turning to leave. "Who decided it was me, anyhow?"

"I think it was the tobacconist, sir. He's the one who recognised you. You didn't give your name or anything, you see. By the time one of our men arrived the fellow from the local paper had done his work for him, you might say. And then the wallet sort of confirmed things."

He ought to have guessed, Laker told himself, that the Press would latch on. There wasn't anything he could do except hope that some eager tyro wasn't going to overdramatise everything with the intention of catching the editor's eye.

On the way home he toyed with the idea of stopping off for a drink, but decided against it. At twenty-past six he ran the car into the garage and went through the side door into the house.

"Patrick showed up yet?"

"He just beat you, hardly five minutes ago." Mrs. Ruddick looked at him more carefully than usual. "Are you all right, Mr. Laker?"

He wasn't expecting her to have heard; not this soon, anyway.

"A reporter rang," she said. "A Mr. Case."

"Oh." That explained it.

"This morning." She had a trace of a Gloucestershire accent which gave warmth to her voice. "He wanted to get in touch with you, but I thought you wouldn't like to be bothered at the office so I told him you'd be away all day."

"Thanks. I'm glad you did."

"He mentioned what it was about, of course."

Laker found the admiring, slightly anxious gleam in her eyes embarrassing.

"What else did you tell him?"

"Nothing. Oh no, Mr. Laker. Once I knew you weren't hurt I thought it best to let you deal with it yourself."

"Thanks, Mrs. Ruddick."

He nodded and made for the cloakroom. It had been a slack day, slack enough to feel almost guilty about, but the evening was close, sticky, and a wash revived him. When he eventually entered the living-room Patrick was already there.

"Hallo," Laker said. "What did you make of the Planetarium?"

"It was great."

"Worth my going to some time?"

"I'd say so, yes." With the air of a conjurer disclosing his next prop, Patrick produced the *Evening Standard* from behind his back. "Seems to me you've been seeing stars yourself."

"Meaning?"

"Look," Patrick said, and gave him the paper, pointing to an item low down on the front page.

WAR HERO SAVES MOTHER AND CHILD
SCOOPED FROM LORRY'S PATH

Oatlands Village, near Weybridge in Surrey, was the scene of high drama at 9.15 this morning when a passer-by, Mr. Samuel Laker, flung himself in front of a heavily-laden truck to hurl a mother and her child clear of almost certain death.

The woman, Mrs. Edna Browning, was wheeling her eighteen-month-old son Michael across the road when the incident occurred. "She gave me no chance," lorry-driver Mr. Jim Smailes explained. "They would have been goners if she and the little kid hadn't been shoved out of the way. It was about the bravest thing I've seen in fifteen years' driving."

Mrs. Browning sustained slight bruising and shock. The child was completely unhurt. Mr. Laker, 43, who lives locally at Roundwood, Mill Avenue, was not available for comment. During the war he was awarded the Distinguished Service Order and the Military Cross. A widower, with one son, he is a Director of Gale and Watts, the office-equipment manufacturers.

"Oh, hell," Laker said quietly.

"Tim Maxwell spotted it. He was so impressed, in fact, that he paid the fares back."

"They make mountains out of molehills, you know that." Laker glanced at the by-line. *A Special Correspondent*: Mr. Case, no doubt. But whoever it was could certainly ferret.

Patrick was grinning like a Cheshire cat. "Come on, dad. Cheer up. It's not as if they've said anything awful about you. A million people will have seen what's there. Don't you think I'm entitled to the full story?"

Laker moved his shoulders. "They've made it full enough, flannel included." He dropped the newspaper on to a chair and started to pour himself a whisky. "It just happened—the way things do."

A million people. That Martin Slattery might have been one of them never so much as entered his head.

2

CASE, the reporter, didn't call back, but the telephone started ringing later that evening.

Baxendale was the first to get on to him ("You old dog, you, hiding your light under a bushel"), then Cranston from across the road, then Mary Armitage, another neighbour, then a cousin from Hampstead. As a consequence Laker neither finished watering the garden, nor gave Patrick all the time he'd promised him on the holiday intinerary.

He was in two minds next morning about dodging the tobacconist's and getting his cigarettes elsewhere, but doing so would have no more than staved off the inevitable. He endured the plaudits and the insisted-upon handshake only to find that there was no escape even when he arrived at Gale and Watts. MacDonald saluted him as if a guard of honour were drawn up awaiting inspection and on the way through to his office he collected more nods and 'Good mornings' than normally came his way in a week. Carol Nolan merely said: "You realise, I suppose, that you've destroyed the image I'd cultivated about myself outside of here? When I got home last night I was the one person who didn't know. The *one* person, mind"—and she clenched her fist at him on her way back to her desk. Then the private calls began again, about one in every three, and Laker found a formula to cope with them.

Slattery came through the following day, on the Wednesday. The thing was as good as over by then and there was suddenly a pile of work, like a seventh wave, to set Laker's conscience to rights about having had too easy a time earlier in the week. He was in the middle of a hastily-convened meeting with Wilson and Farrow, from Design Group, trying to unravel a particularly knotty problem, when Carol's buzzer sounded.

"Yes?" He was on the brusque side.

"There's a Mr. Slattery wanting you. I know you said you weren't to be interrupted but he insists it's urgent."

"What name?"

"Slattery. Martin Slattery."

Laker frowned, memory spanning the years.

"Shall I put him through?"

He glanced across at the other two. "Did he say *what* was urgent?"

"No."

"All right, I'll take it." He apologised briefly to Wilson and Farrow, then waited for the opening, "Martin Slattery here. Who's that?"

"Sam Laker."

"Sam! How are you keeping?"

"Fine."

"I'm delighted to see that your reflexes are as good as ever."

Even after so long a time the breezy, quick-fire delivery was instantly familiar.

"We must read the same paper," Laker said.

"Could be. Well, what's it been, Sam? How long?"

"I hate to think."

Farrow was pretending not to listen, whereas Wilson was making no bones about it.

"From the sound of things you're very much a tycoon these days."

"Hardly."

"Damned difficult to reach, anyhow. Almost easier to break into the Kremlin than get past your secretary." Slattery laughed, the dryish cackle Laker imagined he had forgotten.

"I'm sorry about that, but—well—I'm at a meeting."

"Then I won't keep you."

"Something urgent, wasn't it?"

"I wondered if we could lunch."

Laker raised his eyes to the ceiling. My God! "I'd like that, yes."

"Tomorrow?"

"Tomorrow's a bit sudden."

"I'm tied up the rest of the week, and most of next as well. Failing lunch, perhaps you'd dine with me?"

"Hang on, will you, while I look?" Reaching for his diary, Laker said: "Where are you? In town?"

"Yes."

"Still in the same business?" He was filling in.

"Not exactly."

Tomorrow was clear, Laker saw. But it was short notice all the same. At any other time he might not have felt so pushed to give an answer, but Wilson was surreptitiously glancing at his watch and muttering *sotto voce* to Farrow. Why was it that a first-rate designer like Wilson had to be such a difficult cuss?

"Let's make it tomorrow then."

"Splendid. Lunch?"

"Yes, lunch would suit me best." He could look in on International; two birds with one stone. "Where shall we meet?"

Slattery gave an address in Manchester Square. "The bottom bell. Don't pay any attention to the name. The bottom bell, yes? And how about twelve-thirty?" The last thing he said was: "It'll be really marvellous to see you again, Sam. A hell of a lot of water's gone down the Thames since we were within arm's length."

Laker hung up and looked across at the others. "Sorry," he smiled. "Now, where were we?"

He had met Martin Slattery in the penultimate year of the war, a few weeks after D-day.

One of Laker's more lasting memories of the Special Operations set-up in Grosvenor Gardens was the time they had spent together after his return from Italy. Slattery's office was in an overflow building not far from Victoria Station and Laker shared it with him, on and off, for a couple of months. Slattery had a limp then, the result of some accident on a grenade range, and what Laker particularly remembered was the homily framed behind his desk; he was word-perfect in it even now: *According to the theory of aerodynamics, and as may be readily demonstrated by means of a wind tunnel, the bumble-bee is unable to fly. This is because the size, weight and shape of his body in relation to the total wing span make flight impossible. But the bumble-bee, being ignorant of these scientific facts and possessing considerable determination, does fly—and makes a little honey, too.*

It was a bitter kind of honey, though. But amid the permissible murder of war those two months of waiting were quite unlike any other in Laker's experience. Office hours, bus queues, the tube, midday sandwiches and beer in the pub round the corner. He was even able to live at home in St. John's Wood.

Slattery was one of those responsible for briefing and de-briefing what were invariably described as 'foreign bodies'. Since Laker was due to be dropped into Germany himself as soon as conditions were right he was never present when these sessions took place: it was fundamental that field-operators remained in the dark as to who else was involved, and where, unless it directly concerned them. But while his own operation was delayed he was attached to Slattery, helping out with the collation of every scrap of general intelligence that came in, and there was a mass of it coming in around that time: the lean, scavenging years were over.

Sandwiched between the fury of Italy, with its naked violence and brutal hardship, and the gamble in store for him in Germany, an office had seemed to Laker an unreal place in which to find himself. He was never quite able to adjust his mind to the esoteric argot and the academic approach of head-quarters. But the work appeared tailor-made for Slattery. He would have been about thirty then; plump, red-faced and be-spectacled. Whether the homily about the bumble-bee was on his wall as a kind of self-justification for being chairborne, or whether it somehow pleased him for its own sake, Laker never could decide. Mentally, he was very alert, with a remarkable aptitude for being able to discard inessentials and to strip a report, no matter how garbled, down to its bare bones. Though he fought his war by proxy he fought it with a quiet intent that only once during Laker's contact with him, hinted at some hidden fury.

They'd have a drink or two most evenings before going their separate ways, but Laker didn't really get to know him. Not that he was in the mood for developing acquaintances then: he was too on edge with what was coming. But Slattery was with him when he received the call about the flying-bomb near Lord's and for some reason it was Slattery he rang from St. John's Wood to say that his parents and sister were dead and it was Slattery he walked with in Green Park a night or two later when, sodden with whisky and hatred, he swore what he would do when they let him loose in Germany.

And Slattery who said: "You do that, Sam. You kill the bastards. Kill every bloody one of them you can."

Which he did. And when it was all over and he finally came home to the ruins and the emptiness, it was to Slattery that he made his last report before he was eventually demobilised and taken under Charles Gale's wing.

Laker spent a useful half-hour with Thornton at Inter-national's enormous glass-and-steel rabbit-warren near Chis-wick before driving on through Kensington High Street and around the outskirts of Hyde Park. The midday traffic was sluggishly heavy and new one-way streets seemed to be cropping up every week. Even reaching Manchester Square was easier said than done and when he got there he couldn't park. In the end he found a vacant meter on the fringe of Grosvenor Square (*Eisenhowerplatz* Slattery used to term it; strange how the trivia stuck) and walked across Oxford Street into the comparative quiet of the Georgian environs of the Wallace Collection.

The address Slattery had given him was on the west side of the square. The bottom bell was marked *Curtis* but he pressed it dutifully, wondering while he waited why Slattery should choose to meet him here when there were half a dozen good restaurants and hotels barely a stone's-throw away.

Only a few seconds elapsed before the door opened. Momentarily, a stranger stood framed in the gap, a shortish, bulky, balding man who, as recognition dawned, Laker realised was Slattery. The spectacles and brick-coloured complexion outweighed any slight hesitation.

"I'm late, I'm afraid."

"Sam! . . . Come in, come on in."

Slattery encouraged him with a gesture, remaining where he was as if to avoid the direct sunlight. Only when the door was closed did he shake hands, enthusiastically, as if he were presenting Laker with an award.

"Good to see you again, Sam. You're looking marvellous, I must say."

"And you. Sorry about the time, but what with getting the car parked —"

"Oh, parking's murder around here. Murder." Slattery gestured again like a helpful shop-walker. "Go on through— first right."

They crossed a wide, tiled hall under a chandelier. There was a staircase with a filigree railing sloping up to the next floor. Laker entered a lobby which led into a small room with numerous sporting prints and miniatures on the walls and dustsheets over the furniture.

27

"Keep going," Slattery chuckled from behind. "Civilisation's just ahead."

There the room was spacious, bright, uncluttered. Striped paper, marble fireplace, deep brocaded chairs, rust-red drapes, a huge gilded mirror. One of the pictures might have been a Corot. Manchester Square looked misty beyond the window-length ninon.

"Would you like a wash or anything?"

"No, thanks."

There was a pause, a kind of mutual uncertainty, during which they were strangers again. Probing, Laker said: "You don't live here, I take it?"

"No. Cigarette? . . . No, it belongs to a friend. He lets me use it from time to time. No, as far as having an address goes, mine's in Kew. What will you have? . . . Sherry? Gin?"

"Sherry, please."

"It's a fino. Too dry?"

"Absolutely right."

Traffic rumbled vaguely in the distance, emphasising the quiet.

"Well, here's to you, Sam. It's certainly been a long time."

He hadn't changed much, really. Less hair, a slight looseness about his suit as though he'd shrunk a little; and he seemed shorter, somehow. But the face was unlined, almost cherubic, and his speech was as quick as ever. Behind the thick-rimmed spectacles his eyes were eagerly attentive. And the limp had gone.

They sank into the chairs and Laker said: "You stayed on, didn't you?"

"After the war?"

He nodded.

"Yes, I suppose you could say that."

"And you're still at it?"

"After a fashion."

"I guessed as much from the camouflage."

"This place? Oh, that's more habit than anything else." Beaming, Slattery crossed his legs. "Tell me about yourself,

Sam. Are Gale and Watts the people you joined when things folded up?"

"That's right."

"One of them was an uncle of yours, wasn't he?"

"Charles Gale, yes."

"I remember now. God," he said, "it's been a time, hasn't it?" He blew smoke. He was inclined to blink a lot. "You married, didn't you? I believe I heard that."

"Yes, but my wife died."

"I'm sorry."

"Eight years ago. Cancer. It was very sudden—mercifully so in the circumstances."

"I'm sorry," Slattery repeated.

"What about you?"

"Me? Oh yes, I'm married. Three children, what's more, all costing the earth."

They compared notes, the conversation flowing more easily when they touched on common ground. And there were names to fall back on—Ayres, Bill Maltby, McBride, Harry Castle, Gemmell . . .

"What ever became of Polglaze?" Laker asked.

"I rather fancy he went to the States."

"He and Harry Castle were always cheek-by-jowl in those days."

"They were, weren't they? Harry's a solicitor. *Very* prosperous. Who said that crime doesn't pay?"

"D'you ever see Thompson?"

"I read him from time to time. He writes, didn't you know? Well, you haven't missed much. Not surprising considering the reports he used to put together."

They laughed, Slattery tilting the decanter towards Laker's glass.

"There's a cold spread," he said. "D'you mind?"

"Sounds wonderful."

He watched Slattery bring the trolley in. So he was still at it, still in the game—whatever the game was now. Did it never go sour on him, corrode, rot? Or was it always fresh and complicated and worthwhile; beautiful, even? He'd admitted to that once.

Laker said: "Remember Erskine?"

Slattery paused, cocking his head. "Vaguely. Polish Section, wasn't he? . . . That's one I've quite lost touch with"—and there was something just sufficiently contrived about the denial to make Laker guess that Erskine was still in the game too. Not that he was particularly interested: *chacun son goût.*

An hour passed. It was a simple yet excellent meal: melon, cold lamb, a strawberry mousse with cream. Once or twice it crossed Laker's mind that he had come a long way merely to ramble over old times, but the claret and the pattern of their talk disarmed any lurking conjecture. And when Slattery eventually asked, "Is it next week you're going to Germany, Sam?" he let it drop like a stone.

"Yes." Then, looking up in surprise: "How the hell did you know?"

"I checked."

"Checked?"

Slattery nodded, quite unabashed.

"My God," Laker said. His lips curled in astonishment. "What are you? Some sort of eyes and ears?"

"We still keep tabs on—though doing so isn't my particular pigeon."

"Exactly what *is* your pigeon?"

Slattery avoided answering that.

Without hostility, Laker said: "D'you mean to tell me that anyone who happens to be visiting Germany is automatically —?"

"Of course not. But you're going to Leipzig."

"So?"

"Leipzig's in the Russian Zone." Slattery lifted his heavy shoulders. "Look," he then said cheerfully, leaning forward a little. "There's no mumbo-jumbo about this. When I read about you in the *Standard* the other evening I simply thought: that's Sam Laker. Why not get together? . . . So I called you."

"Having checked on me first?"

"I'm not apologising. Records are usually more rewarding than the *Directory of Directors*. It was just routine, Sam. You're an old pro, so you'll know how it is."

"I don't believe I do. Are you telling me that all this time, all these years, I've been under someone's beady eye?"

"Not in the way you're implying, no."

"But someone's kept tabs on—you said so yourself."

"Only certain tabs."

"Now you're talking in riddles."

"It's a rough world, Sam. Putting it at its simplest, Leipzig is behind the lines. That's the kind of tab I mean, the kind that sticks."

"I'm visiting the Trade Fair—about the largest, incidentally, and the oldest, in Europe."

"Which is precisely what's logged on the file."

"Your sources must be bloody good. All I've done is apply for Fair Cards and book a flight."

"They're good," Slattery said evenly. "Not perfect, but good."

Laker stirred his coffee. He couldn't help smiling. "Is Leipzig my only black mark?"

"D'you really want to hear?"

"Of course, I'm fascinated—and a little indignant."

"You've a boy, haven't you?—Patrick."

"Yes."

"Since May last year he's been in touch with an address in Rostock. Lenin-Strasse 32, to be precise."

Laker snorted derisively. "A pen-pal. He's got about six of 'em."

"A pen-pal in Halberstadt took the daughter of a certain Naval officer for a great ride a couple of years ago. Practically emptied her father's brief-case."

"There's nothing in mine worth having. Besides, all Patrick's contacts are thoroughly genuine. As often as not I see their letters myself. 'I am an East German boy, sixteen years old, and my hobbies are sailing, music and collecting postcards.' They're as innocent as the day's long."

"That's not the point, Sam. If you're using a net a whole lot of innocent fish swim into it."

"But you tab them just the same."

"As a matter of routine."

"You must employ an army," Laker said tartly. "What else have you got on me?"

"Not a thing."

"After so long?"

"There's the old stuff, of course. That's still there—in a class by itself."

"I must be a disappointment to you."

"It's only background, Sam. Don't get the wrong end of the stick."

"I haven't. But I'll be a damn sight more careful in future."

Part of him accepted the necessity of vigilance, part of him objected to the form it apparently took. On balance it struck him as pretty preposterous and he said as much.

"You wouldn't think that if you'd stayed on," Slattery replied.

"I wasn't cut out for staying on."

"Why not?"

"I couldn't have kept it up."

"Kept what up?"

"Oh, I don't know." Laker paused. "But I couldn't play it as a sort of everlasting chess, not on and on, world without end."

"Is that all you imagine it to be?"

"For want of a better comparison, yes."

Slattery said casually: "What kind of spur would you need, then?"

Laker hesitated. There was only one thing, one thing, but it was dead, thank God. Anyway, Slattery would remember; he was there in Green Park that night years ago.

He glanced at his watch. He didn't want a ticket on the car for overrunning his meter-time and it was quite a walk back to Brook Street. They talked more generally for a while, but the leads were tending to peter out. Once, the telephone rang.

Slattery merely said "Yes?" when he picked it up and "Yes" twice more before he put it down. Presently Laker suggested that he ought to be going.

"Must you?"

"I'm afraid so."

"It's flown, hasn't it? By the way, when are you off?"

"To Leipzig?"

"Yes."

"Surely a little detail like that hasn't escaped your notice?" Laker could still smile, though a trifle sourly.

"Refresh my memory."

"Wednesday. For forty-eight hours I'm picking other people's brains as regards office equipment, after which Patrick and I are spending about ten days in and around the Rhineland."

"Very nice." Slattery stubbed his cigarette, making an over-thorough job of it. "Sam."

"Yes?"

"I haven't been entirely honest with you."

"I think I understand."

"I don't mean that."

"What, then?"

"I had a particular reason for getting you to come along."

"Oh?"

"It was to ask a favour."

"What kind of favour?"

"I'm hoping you'll deliver a message for me."

"Where?"

"Leipzig." Then quickly: "There's no risk. Absolutely none."

So that was his pigeon. "Why me?" Laker said.

"Who better?"

"Have you run out of regular couriers, or what?"

Slattery blinked at him. "It's our availability, Sam. Plus the fact that you're totally uncompromised over there." The jargon hadn't changed. "In point of fact it's not such an exceptional request these days."

33

"A verbal message?"

"No. But that side of things will be taken care of."

"Isn't this wildly unorthodox?"

"Not with someone like you."

Laker looked away, watching a green car move towards Spanish Place through the sunlit fog of ninon.

"I'd rather not," he said.

"It would take about ten minutes of your time, Sam. Hardly more." Slattery waited, watching him. "You'll remember better than most what hanging on can be like. Well, there's someone hanging on now. And you could have them off the rack on Wednesday."

Laker kept his gaze on the windows. No, he thought.

"I'd more than hoped," Slattery said. "I was absolutely sure you'd agree." He spoke as if Laker owed him something. "It couldn't be more simple." With a ghost of a smile, he added: "No cloak, no dagger."

"I dare say."

"Think about it."

"If I must."

"Think about it and let me know."

"All right," Laker conceded.

"By this evening? It has to be by then."

"All right. Where do I phone you?"

Slattery gave him a Gerrard number. They started through the room where the dust-covers were.

"It's important, Sam. I wouldn't have put it to you otherwise. I know what's on your mind—Patrick, Gale and Watts . . . I can understand your hesitation. It's a lot to ask, but as far as you're concerned it will be as uneventful as stepping out into the street."

LAKER walked back to Brook Street, heeding the warning whispers. He hadn't collected a ticket, which was a relief. He sat in the car for a minute or two without attempting to drive, blind to the sauntering woman who slowed and offered a hopeful smile from the pavement.

It was a lot to ask, all right. And galling that he should have been asked at all. "An old pro like you"—Slattery seemed to consider this sufficient excuse. Once in the game, always in it, always an honorary member—that was his line. "When I read the file," his parting words were, "and where you were going, it was almost too good to be true."

Irritated, Laker lit a cigarette. What galled him particularly was the implicit suggestion that if he refused he was letting Slattery down. "There's no danger, Sam, absolutely none. I wouldn't have put it to you otherwise."

One way and another lunch had been an eye-opener. It was surprising enough to have learned that one's associations with Communist territories were so meticulously recorded. Granted it was a suspicion-ridden world. Granted, the bureaucratic net couldn't be individually selective. But when one's willingness to be used was apparently more or less expected if circumstances provided the need, and the opportunity—that jarred.

And the proposition itself was so damned vague. If Slattery had been more forthcoming it might have been easier to have reached an out-and-out decision before leaving Manchester Square. As it was Laker couldn't for the life of him understand why he should continue to mull it over. "A simple, straightforward person-to-person delivery . . . Ten minutes of your time." To whom? he thought. Exactly how and where?

Brooding, he switched on and went into gear; drew away. The old-pals act was a kind of blackmail. And nothing was ever one hundred per cent safe. Nothing. Slattery could say what he liked.

Park Lane sucked him into its flow. No, he thought again. But as he headed towards Knightsbridge and the Brompton Road his initial hostility to the idea began to fade. Against his will Slattery's anonymous contact in Leipzig weighed with him. There wasn't much worse than being cut off. He didn't have to stretch his imagination to know what it was to wait, and go on waiting. Day by day the certainty of having been abandoned gnawed at the nerves. Silence of that kind was the most agonising silence of all. He'd experienced it once, and once was plenty.

The airborne assault on Arnhem was already poised when Laker was dropped in. He went in alone more than two hundred miles east of the Rhine, touching down in wooded country to the west of Gardelegen. A reception party was there to hustle him away—Karl and Günter and the girl. If the punch through Arnhem succeeded the way to the heart of Germany would be open, and each and every bridge that could be kept intact across the Aller would be worth its weight in gold: that was the scheme. But Arnhem failed and their radio failed and Karl and Günter didn't return from a raid on an explosives dump at Klötze.

In case they'd been taken alive, Laker and the girl left the protection of the crumbling farmhouse and holed themselves up in a thick patch of spruce overlooking the Magdeburg–Uelsen road. Night after night long convoys moved north-east and aircraft droned across the autumn sky. It was cold and it rained a lot. Laker roofed over a hollow and at night they would lie in it. Every day the girl would go down to one or other of the near-by villages and somehow find food; once she came back with a blanket.

A week after Karl and Günter were lost he got the set to work again and began calling at the specified times. There was never an answer but he went on calling long after he was certain he'd been written off. He did it more to encourage the girl than anything. She wouldn't leave him. She was thin and freckled and about eighteen years old. She could have gone; she had an uncle somewhere in the south. But no. "You will starve," she said again and again. "Without me you will be finished."

They were to have linked up with another group to the north of Gifhorn, but without instructions they didn't know how. So they continued to wait, Laker vainly risking his call-sign three times a day. Twice they were forced to move. They waited in hunger and desperation. It grew colder and they clung to each other for warmth. "Sammy," she called him. They waited five days more, trying to deduce from the movement on the road what might have happened to the distant front. Eventually Laker decided their only chance was to travel west, but on the evening they prepared to start the girl became ill. He could hear her lungs bubbling as she breathed and her skin burned in the cold. By midnight her speech was rambling. He wrapped her in the blanket and carried her to an isolated house from which she had sometimes stolen eggs. He laid her on the ground where the light would fall when the door was opened, knocked hard and ran—stopping only to check when someone came: an old man.

Then he went back to the spruces again, kicked the set to pieces and retrieved his carbine and some grenades. It took him twenty-nine days to reach the Allied lines and on the way he conducted a private war, the full volume of his hatred released at last for what had befallen his parents and sister and out of grief and uncertainty for the girl. He killed where he could and when he could—an isolated sentry, two Luftwaffe corporals cycling together, all the occupants of a staff-car, the crew of a stranded tank. There were others, too; he lost count. He did it out of a haunting fury and because he could shoot marvellously well. And by the time he got through to the Americans he was as wild-eyed as a hunted animal and grabbed instinctively for the carbine when he awoke from his exhaustion and found a nurse bending over the bed . . .

There were things one never forgot.

*   *   *

After Hammersmith he took the less direct route back to Weybridge—Richmond, Hampton, Sunbury. It was always pleasant along by the river with the boats showing through the weeping willows and there was little traffic to distract his mind. Inevitably, as he passed through Oatlands, he was reminded of the woman in the yellow dress: if it weren't for her he'd have been spared the favour Slattery expected of him.

Chance had the longest, most unpredictable arm of all.

He had no illusions. It was a different kind of war now—more complex, more sophisticated, yet equally ruthless, equally deadly. No holes in the sodden ground, little overt violence. A different kind of war, yes; but hanging on would be no less desperate . . . Everything, nothing had changed. And Slattery, blast him, knew that he knew what hanging on was like; and that knowing would probably help to tip the scales.

He arrived at Gale and Watts shortly before four. Carol had dealt with most of the chores, but there was a fair amount demanding his attention. He cleared as much as he could in fast time and telephoned the two people Carol had listed for him. Baxendale looked in briefly, ostensibly to put him on to one of Piggott's rides next day but more obviously to indulge his fascination for Carol's legs.

It was after five when Laker asked for a line and dialled the Gerrard number. A woman answered without indicating where she was speaking from.

"Mr. Slattery, please."

"Who's calling?"

He told her.

"Is Mr. Slattery expecting you to telephone?"

"Yes," he said and waited for the click and Slattery's voice. "I'm at my office," he began.

"Go ahead."

"I'm not keen, but the answer's yes."

Slattery didn't exactly indicate enthusiasm. "Oh good," was all he said—rather as if Laker had found that he was free for dinner or something.

"If it's really that important and there's no one else."

"It is, Sam. And there isn't."

"And provided it's as elementary as you made out."

"It couldn't be more so."

"All right . . . What now?"

"I'll be in touch. Incidentally, about your watch —"

"My what?"

"Your watch. I'm most dreadfully sorry. It was entirely my fault. I'm arranging for it to be collected in the morning."

"In the morning?" Laker was a little slow.

"Sometime before noon if that's convenient."

"Oh yes . . . Very well." Suddenly there were a dozen questions welling out of last-second misgivings, but an open line made them impossible. "Is that all?"

"For the present, Sam. And thanks. I was banking on you, you know."

You bet, Laker thought. He fingered his watch, wondering how they would tamper with it; what it would carry. But at least he knew the means of delivery, and it wasn't difficult to guess how it was to be effected. The knowledge was curiously reassuring, underlining Slattery's insistence on the run-of-the-mill nature of what he'd agreed to do. Even so, how much of a fool was he to have committed himself?

He wasn't allowed to dwell on it without interruption. Carol plied him with a score of letters for signature and there was a joint report by Wilson and Farrow, suggesting a way out of the Design Group's difficulty, marked FOR URGENT COMMENT. Laker tried to concentrate on it there and then, but after a while he gave up. Leipzig kept intruding. Gale and Watts hadn't an export business worth talking about, so there was no possibility of doing them harm. And, as regards Patrick . . . Hell, if he started along those lines he'd better change his mind while he could. He was sufficiently lukewarm as it was without thinking in terms of a slip-up. Slattery had surely played his proxy game long enough now to have this aspect of it perfected. Behind the beaming smile and blinking, bespectacled eyes he was shrewd, a realist, and Laker's lingering doubts found

39

refuge in that. Scores of export executives carrying their brief-cases around Europe must have acted as unpaid postmen over the last few years—Slattery had said as much. And this was about what it came to—being a postman.

He stayed on for half an hour after Carol left, but the Wilson–Farrow argument still demanded more of him than he seemed able to give, so he decided to take it home. Patrick was there when he arrived, the maps spread out, a sentence in one of his tour leaflets underlined: *A cable car will take you high above Rudesheim to the Germania Monument, erected in the last century as a symbol of Bismarck's united Germany.*

"There's nothing in the papers," Patrick grinned mean-ingly, "but what exciting thing's happened to you since breakfast?"

MacDonald rang through from Reception sharp on eleven next morning.

"Person for your watch, sir. Shall I come up or will Miss Nolan come down?"

"Come up, John." Then: "No, on second thoughts ask *him* to come up."

"Right away, sir."

Laker's curiosity didn't reward him with anything out of the ordinary. A rather thin young man with a spaniel-like face and a neat brown suit presently put his head round the door. "Mr. Laker?"

"Correct. Come on in."

The suit was good; the tie instantly recognisable. It would have been interesting to know what he did with the rest of his time. For an absurd moment Laker thought of asking him whether he was in the habit of collecting watches.

"Do I get a receipt?"

"I'll write you one if you wish."

Laker shook his head. He unstrapped the watch and slid it into an envelope.

"Thank you," the young man said.

"That's all, I take it?"

"I think so, Mr. Laker. Good morning."

A minute afterwards Laker watched him from his window cross the forecourt and drive off in a plain, dark blue van. No one more casual entered the office throughout the day-long press of work; only the naked feel of Laker's left wrist kept sharply reminding him that the undertaking had moved a first stage from acceptance towards execution.

Slattery left him alone for twenty-four hours. It was noon on Saturday before he chose to telephone. Laker was in the book so it was no surprise to be caught at the house. But he said: "Another few minutes and you'd have missed me."

"Sorry, the week-end's always chancy, I suppose. Could we meet one evening?"

"When?"

"Tomorrow?"

"I'm playing bridge tomorrow."

"Monday?"

"It'll have to be Monday. Tonight I'm tied up and Tuesday's my last evening."

"All right, then. Let's say Monday. And to spare you the burden of all the comings and goings, how about meeting half-way?"

"Where?"

"The Mitre, Hampton Court. Nell Gwyn bar."

"Fine," Laker said.

He arrived a quarter of an hour before the agreed time, ordered a Scotch and waited. He had managed not to think about Slattery too much over the rest of the week-end. But on the short drive from Roundwood, and now, as he looked about him at the prosperous self-sufficiency of the bar's occupants, an undercurrent of uneasiness tugged at him. Oh, he'd do it. He wouldn't cry off at this stage. But the sooner Wednesday had come and gone, the better. And in—what?—less than six days' time he'd be shot of Leipzig and Patrick's carefully-planned side of things would have begun—Heidelburg, Mannheim,

Worms, Mainz, Rudesheim, Cochem, Coblenz . . . It was the boy's holiday, after all.

"Hallo," Slattery said, suddenly at his elbow. "Have I kept you?" He pulled a vacant chair from the next table and sat down.

"What'll you have?"

"A pink." He almost changed his mind. "Yes, a pink . . . I did explain, didn't I, that I can't stay?"

"You did."

"My wife's old father's been stomping round Kew Gardens all afternoon and he's dining with us. He's as deaf as a post and I'm the only one in the family whose voice has the right *timbre*, or whatever it is, so my presence is virtually obligatory on these occasions."

He leaned back, brushing his sparse hair with the flat of his hands, blinking from table to table as if innocently in search of friends.

"Good luck, Sam," he said when his gin came. "And thanks again."

Laker shrugged.

"Down to business?"

"I'm ready."

"How good are you on telephone numbers?"

"It depends. I remembered the Gerrard one. Try me."

"Double three, four two, eight six." Slattery repeated it. "Salt it away." He tapped his head.

Laker's lips moved.

"Got it?"

"I will have."

They were quite close; their voices sufficiently low.

"D'you know Leipzig?"

"I was once there as a kid, but it's all a blur now."

"What's your hotel?"

"Astoria."

Slattery nodded. "There's a jeweller's in the Luisenstrasse—a five-minute taxi-ride. The description's flattering, I admit, but that's beside the point. The name's Kromadecka." He spelt it out. "All right?"

"Yes."

"It's small, but you can't miss it. All you have to do is to ask them to fit a new watch-strap."

"Nothing more?"

"Nothing more." Slattery's smile seemed to be prompted by a memory. "I told you, it couldn't be more straightforward."

"When do I get the watch back?"

"There and then."

"From you, I mean."

"Sorry, stupid of me. I'll have it delivered on Tuesday evening, to your home."

"I see."

Slattery signalled a waiter. "Scotch, is it?"

"Please."

Neither spoke for a few moments. People were coming and going all the time. A girl laughed near by, content with the world she knew, safe. Leipzig seemed very remote. "Happier about things now?" Slattery beamed.

"You haven't raised any goose-flesh, I grant you that."

"Any questions?"

"Only why the hell I should be doing it."

Slattery laughed his ridiculous cackle.

"This place, Kromadecka —"

"Yes?"

"Doesn't it matter who attends to me?"

"The problem won't arise. There's only one person there."

"I don't need to furnish recognition aids or anything like that?"

"No. Merely ask for a new strap, wait while it's fitted, then push off. Get on over to the Fair and begin picking those brains you talked about. Start on your holiday, in fact."

"And the number?—where does that come in?"

"It won't." Slattery spread his hands almost apologetically. "Call it insurance, Sam. Wise-virgin common-sense. Has it lodged, incidentally?"

"Three three, four two, eight six."

"It's like the emergency handle on the train. It's a million to one against your having to use the thing but it's reassuring to know it's there." He matched Laker's gaze for a second or two. "Get me?"

"I get you," Laker said. He drew on his cigarette. There was always an element of risk, no matter how infinitesimal, and he'd made his own assessment of it. But he'd somehow have liked Slattery more if there hadn't been such smooth denials at Manchester Square.

"And I'll tell you this. You'll never hook me another time."

He smiled grimly and Slattery blinked back, fingering his glass.

"D'you want to recap?"

"Not really."

"What time d'you touch down?"

"Around noon. I've forgotten exactly."

"Do it that afternoon, will you, Sam? On Wednesday. Don't wait until the next day."

"I won't sleep on it, you can be sure of that. The quicker I'm through with being one of your acting unpaid supernumeraries, the better I'll like it, believe me."

"Good man," Slattery said. He drained his glass with a hint of finality. "Now I'm the one who's against the clock. What are you doing?"

"Going home."

They walked out together. After the artificial brightness the dusk seemed thicker than it was; the river air surprisingly cool. Beyond the wall and the trees across the wide road Hampton Court shaped the skyline. A man and woman passed, the woman carrying a small child, and the child was wailing out of weariness and the ancestral fear of what the gathering dusk might conceal.

Laker accompanied Slattery to his car—a grey Rover with a Royal Thames Yacht Club badge. The prefix to the registration number was UUU and Laker recalled a once-heard music-hall gag—"Three Volunteers". Slattery unlocked the door and

44

turned—to shake hands, Laker assumed. But he said: "There's something I haven't mentioned, Sam."

"What?"

A bus trundled by, and Slattery waited. Laker could hardly see his face.

"What?" he asked more doubtfully, suspicious of postscripts.

"At Kromadecka's. You mentioned recognition."

"Yes?"

Slattery cleared his throat. "You'll know who it is."

"How d'you mean—'know'?"

"The person who'll fix your watch-strap will be Karen Gisevius."

"Sammy," she had called him.

"Karen?" Laker echoed. "Karen?"

"That's right."

"But —" His thoughts seemed to be stumbling in several directions at once. He said stupidly: "She's alive, then?"

"Oh yes."

"My God." He could grasp so much and no more. Seconds elapsed. "My God," he said. "Why didn't you tell me the other day?"

"It wouldn't have been reasonable."

"Reasonable?" Laker frowned.

"To use her as a lever. It might have come to that if you'd refused in the first place. Happily, you didn't. But it's only right that I should put you in the picture now."

Slattery's head and shoulders were silhouetted against The Mitre's wistaria-covered, softly-lit façade.

"How long," Laker began, faltered, then started again. "How long have you known?"

"Known?"

"That she'd survived."

"Some time, Sam. A goodish time."

"Twenty years?" Something akin to resentment had entered Laker's voice.

"Ten's more like it." Slattery delayed for a couple to pass near by through the parked cars. "She was recruited in the mid-fifties but even then her name didn't ring an immediate bell. She's one of our best links. That's why it's so galling to have her out on a limb like this." He seemed to imagine that more was expected of him, because he went on: "There's been a misunderstanding. Not a slip-up. No one's been blown— nothing as serious as that. Otherwise I wouldn't be involving you. I can't explain, and you won't expect me to. But the result is that contact's been broken and it's imperative to make the damage good."

Laker wasn't really listening. His mind was on the house and the gasping, blanketed body abandoned in desperation to the mercy of whoever came in answer to his rap on the door, the years telescoping as he thought of that and a score of related things, one of them being the day he sat in Slattery's Grosvenor Gardens office for the last time and worded his report about Karl and Günter and Karen Gisevius and the failure of the gamble called Operation Extension.

"I could have been told," he said.

"Not once she was on our books."

"Unofficially."

"Hardly, old boy."

Slattery's silhouette moved as he shifted his legs. The dusk seemed to be shrinking all the time and the cars dipping over the bridge were jostling into position for the roundabout ahead. It was a ridiculous place in which to talk about anything, let alone this.

"Why not?" Laker persisted.

"It never crossed my mind, Sam. And we'd lost touch, hadn't we? Gone our own ways."

"Until it suited you."

"Until I read the *Evening Standard* last week."

"Oh balls," Laker snapped quietly.

He was confused, filled with wonder that Karen lived yet feeling cheated for not having known of it and disturbed at the sudden prospect of meeting her again. It was too much to take

46

at once and his mood compounded an unreasoning anger with Slattery that was shot through with distrust.

"If there's one thing I can't stand," he said, "it's being led by the nose."

"Sam —"

"Once a pro, always a pro. It's your claim, not mine. You can't have it both ways."

"I'm sorry. I had no idea —"

"Balls," Laker snapped again. "And another thing. D'you seriously expect me to walk into this place where she is and leave a handful of minutes later—just like that? Or have you forgotten you're dealing with people instead of little pins on the map?"

Judiciously, Slattery took his time. "You'd rather not do it, is that it?"

"I didn't say that."

"I don't think you've fully understood my position. The whole world might be making tracks to Leipzig, but I can't employ any Tom, Dick or Harry. *You* know that. It's a fluke if you like, about you and Karen, but these things crop up. And I certainly wasn't going to put pressure on you by mentioning her right away."

"Ten minutes, you said. Then push off, get back to the Fair . . . As uneventful as stepping out into the street . . . What sort of person d'you —?"

"I was merely underlining the extent of the commitment." Slattery spoke as if he were justified by a set of rules. "She'll be the judge of what's possible and what isn't."

Laker pursed his lips, still confused, still bitter. It was late in the day to have baited the hook. He glared at Slattery in the dusk. Karen, Karen Gisevius . . .

"She's one of our best, you know."

"I don't doubt it."

It bewildered him to realise they weren't speaking of the past, or of the dead. The use of the present tense kept ramming home the shock, awakening memories which time had grafted on to him so that the longer he listened to Slattery the more moved he became. Question upon question began to queue in his mind, but Slattery's answers increasingly had the quality of protective gestures.

"Listen, Sam—and don't get me wrong. I'm not running an international social-contacts bureau, nor am I holding a gun to your head. You're still at liberty to cry off. It's up to you, entirely up to you. It has been from the start. But now you know it's Karen, I rather thought you'd be especially glad to help."

"You make it sound like a good turn."

"Isn't it?"

Christ, Laker thought.

"Isn't it?" Slattery insisted. "Isn't that just what it is?"

Two worlds were overlapping as Laker drove back to Weybridge, thinking, thinking, sensing already that nothing could ever be quite the same again.

4

THE watch was brought to the house early on Tuesday evening. Laker had left the office before the usual time and was there to take it in. The small blue van looked as if it might have been the same one, but the man who came to the door certainly wasn't and he struck Laker as an unlikely accomplice—squat, middle-aged, untidy and badly out of condition if his shortness of breath were anything to go by. If Mrs. Ruddick had accepted the slim, brown-paper package it would have been odds on his getting a tip. As it was he simply asked Laker's name, nodded and walked away, his somewhat moody glance at the roses implying that, given the opportunity, he too could make use of leisure.

Patrick had gone upstairs to try and squeeze yet another afterthought into an already bulging suitcase and Mrs. Ruddick was quietly clattering in the kitchen. There was no writing or typed label on the package. Laker took it into the living-room and broke the seals, drew out the watch and examined the strap. Unmistakably, it was his own. Whatever had been done to it was completely invisible. They'd unstitched it, he presumed, but he couldn't detect the slightest trace of extra bulk or re-sewing. Slattery had been as good as his word on the score of technique ("Even you will doubt that you're carrying anything") and Laker had never been more than mildly curious regarding the details of the message he would be delivering at Kromadecka's. But from the moment Karen Gisevius was mentioned the project had taken on an entirely new dimension.

For a day and a night he had tried to convince himself that he had no reason to feel aggrieved at the way in which Slattery had played his cards. There was logic in his argument as to why he had avoided mentioning Karen until the last. But, knowing the potential of her name, it was naïve to imply that for ten years or more the thought of at least privately reporting her survival hadn't even crossed his mind. So was the specious nonsense about having lost touch when, only a couple of days earlier, he'd been quoting from Laker's file.

He wasn't easy to fathom, and renewed acquaintance had reminded Laker how slight their association ever was. Outside The Mitre his apparent insensitivity to everything except the main chance had injected anger into Laker's confusion, obliterating from the wake of the initial shock any purity of delight or astonished curiosity. These had emerged since, as Laker's resentment mellowed, and he tried to reason that Slattery was inhibited by a special code of laws and moralities. Slattery's parting words had been: "We'll meet when it's over, Sam." In the gloom he had fumbled a handshake like a Free-mason searching for the correct pressure-point. And only then, for the briefest possible duration, Laker had thought he de-tected the very slightest flaw in the bland indifference. "No hard feelings, I hope—now or at any time."

He gazed into the garden, thoughts focusing on Karen. She would be about thirty-eight, thirty-seven or thirty-eight. He could only picture her as she once was—thin, freckled and with eyes that burned with a gravity beyond her years. Everything else was conjecture, what they had shared being merely a spring-board for all the questions which filled his mind as he tried to imagine what might have happened between his leaving her at the house near Gardelegen and her now being at a jeweller's in Leipzig. He thought about her with a curious sense of unreality, as if he still couldn't completely accept that by tomorrow afternoon he would have seen her, vaguely concerned with the shape of his own life as much as with hers, drifting from one query to another, one problem to another, thinking about survival, dying, being chosen and not being chosen, recovery, living, about the war which had brought them together and the kind of peace that would do so again.

He had never been back: Germany was split from north to south even before he was out of uniform, with Gardelegen behind the wire and the freshly-sown mines. He wrote, though. He wrote to the Red Cross and other likely authorities, but they couldn't help. Twice he went as far as to send letters direct, addressing them as a child might—*Large Grey Stone House, 3 kms. South-West of Gardelegen* . . . But there was no answer and, in his heart, he had scarcely expected one. Europe was a place of ghosts and its desolation had swallowed her up along with the millions. She remained a memory, as vivid and deeply-branded as the murders he'd committed on his way out; dead, for all he knew, as dead as the hate that had made them possible.

He had to keep reminding himself that she wouldn't realise he was coming. It was useless to speculate on what had brought her back into the game, yet the watch on his wrist and the telephone number stored in the recesses of his mind were proof that tomorrow was first and foremost Slattery's business. But Slattery wasn't the only one to have lost contact and it was inconceivable that the Kromadecka shop on the Luisenstrasse would lead to an exchange of watch-straps and nothing more. Inconceivable, Russian Zone or no . . .

"Dad," Patrick was calling from the stairs, "what d'you think I should do? Load my camera now, or in the morning?"

It was an early flight: 8.55 from London.

Low slicks of mist threatened the approaches to the airport, but there was no delay. Exactly on time the Viscount soared into the overhanging blue. Laker and Patrick were forward of the starboard wing and Patrick had the window-seat; he'd only flown twice before and it was still very much of a novelty. As soon as Laker released his belt he looked over his shoulder along the tube of the fuselage; much as he'd expected there was hardly a woman passenger to be seen. The man directly across the aisle was already browsing through a glossy catalogue of toys and construction kits and the hum of conversation somehow lacked the normal defensive arrogance of English travellers on holiday; it sounded more in keeping with any expense-account Pullman.

They were to put down at Amsterdam and Laker's guess was that ninety per cent of those aboard would transfer to the Leipzig connection. He eased back into his seat and stared past Patrick's profile at the mottled drift of Surrey and Kent. By the time the grey-and-pink encrustation of Canterbury was discernible on their left the morning's collation had been served, the flight particulars passed along and Patrick's concentration on the view was beginning to wane. He grinned at his father and fished out a German phrase-book.

"The postillion," Laker said, "has been struck by lightning."

"That one's not here."

"I honestly doubt if it ever was."

"'Where can I obtain a good phrase-book?'—that is, though."

"I don't believe it."

"Cross my heart."

Laker chuckled. His own German was excellent. "What's 'The Trade Fair'?"

"*Die Messe.*"

He took the book, opening it at random. "How about 'How do we get to the museum?'?"

Patrick screwed his face. "*Wie komm man —*"

"*Kommt. Wie kommt man . . .*"

"*Wie kommt man zu dem Museum.*"

"Full marks. They must be teaching you something at Greynham after all. Now . . . 'Is there a price reduction for students, singly or in groups?'"

"Ouch."

"No?"

"Definitely no."

"Try 'Are there any jelly-fish or dangerous currents?'"

Patrick deliberated, then retrieved the book. "I'd better stop while I'm ahead. Anyway, who's swimming?"

"You never know. We'll be over the sea any minute."

"Pessimist."

Except for the eyes Patrick didn't much resemble Helen, but in this respect they were memorably alike—blue, with thick dark lashes. "Look after him, Sam," she had whispered that afternoon before they put her under for the unavailing operation. No one had told her, but she must have sensed it was hopeless. "Look after him for me, won't you?" Laker glanced away almost guiltily, fingering his watch, torn between the slight yet ineradicable malaise that recurred every time he considered what he had undertaken on Slattery's behalf and the eagerness with which he anticipated the chance it had given. In the room looking out on to Manchester Square his rejection of the proposition had been quite automatic. No, he'd thought, the amateur in him instinctively on guard—and again as he'd brooded in the car in Brook Street. And then, somehow, by a series of mental stepping-stones which he couldn't precisely retrace, he had found himself swung over, unenthusiastic yet willing, arguing away the risk he might be running the further he committed himself until, finally, Karen dominated every aspect of the assignment.

"Did you know," Patrick said, flicking through a leaflet now, "that Bach was Cantor at the Thomaskirche in Leipzig?"

"If I did I'd forgotten."

"I wonder if the Liverpool guides will mention The Beatles in a couple of hundred years' time?"

Laker winced theatrically.

"It's quite a thought, isn't it?"

"Everyone will be going to the moon by then," Laker said.

A quarter of an hour passed. Toy ships floated in the wrinkled expanse of sea. Soon the coast of Holland showed, brown and wandering, flanking their line of flight. It was barely ten, but in a heavy Dublin brogue the man across the aisle asked the stewardess for a Jameson, and seemed genuinely put out when informed that Irish wasn't available: he settled for Scotch and two hundred cigarettes instead. Construction kits, Laker reflected, must be doing all right.

Presently a girl's voice clicked on, brittle with courtesy. "In a few minutes we will be landing at Amsterdam, ladies and gentlemen. Would you please extinguish all cigarettes and fasten your seat-belts . . ."

There was the best part of an hour's hanging about at Amsterdam. The transit-lounge was resonant with disembodied announcements and the occasional whine of aircraft. Outside the day was fine; the sky still cloudless. Patrick bought a Coca Cola from a machine and, through the windows, fired off a couple of shots with his camera at a Caravelle disgorging its load on the hard near by.

"By the way," Laker said, "I'd be careful about using that thing while we're in Leipzig."

"Even at the Fair?"

He shrugged, aware that he was being absurdly inconsistent. "It's the Russian Zone, after all." Aware, too, that he had suddenly sounded like Slattery. "Better check what the form is first."

They flew on in a piston-engined aircraft operated by Czech Airlines; it looked like the old Dakota. After the Viscount's smoothness it was a bumpier, noisier ride, though the furnishings were a good deal more ornate: the windows had tasselled velvet curtains and the seats were covered in scarlet velour. "Wow," a bald-headed man in front exclaimed as everyone was settling in, "it's like a whore's parlour," and his companion said drily: "You ought to know, George."

No flight-maps were provided, but Patrick had brought the B.E.A. one along and it wasn't difficult to make an intelligent guess at their route. To begin with they headed into the sun, east, and they were low enough to interpret the shifting view— the metallic-looking Rhine, the industrial haze of the Ruhr far to the south; later the Ems with what could only be Munster dragging under the port wing.

Laker had been right: most of the London passengers were still with them. More names for Slattery's files—it was an odd and still unacceptable thought. Laughter, over-enunciated English to the stewardesses, voices raised above the engines' din: Spurs might have been playing in the European Cup. The person nearest to him caught his eye and asked: "Didn't I see you last year?"

"In Leipzig?"

"Yes."

"I wasn't there."

"First time, eh?"

"Yes."

"Odd. I could have sworn we'd met. What's your line?"

Laker told him.

"You're starting the young man early, I'll say that." This with an amiable nod towards Patrick. "My name's Black, incidentally. Dargle and Tait, Ilford . . . Optical Goods."

Laker wasn't in the mood for shop, and to his relief the man seemed more or less content to let it go at that. Patrick was saying: "D'you reckon that's the Weser?"

"Could be," he answered, peering.

"It must be."

"You're the navigator."

It was impossible to block out the past. His first time to the Fair, yes; but he'd flown this way before, in cloudy moonlight,

54

with a diversionary raid on Magdeburg to distract attention, and he suddenly remembered the dispatcher, a New Zealander, leaning back from the intercom and bawling: "Skipper says we've passed the Weser. Hanover to starboard. Two-fifteen and not a mouse stirring . . ." And then he remembered another time, days later, when he lay with Karen in the covered depression among the spruce trees. Huddled close, her breath warm on his face yet frosting in the air, she had said: "D'you know what I'm thinking, Sammy? I'm thinking how normal tonight is for millions of other people—at home, out dancing, at the theatre maybe, sitting somewhere by a fire, having a bath, cooking, feeding the baby, making love . . . When is it going to be normal for us, Sammy?"

He closed his eyes and let the darkness in. No need for qualms. He was a postman. Only fools were picked up; fools and those who risked the deep water. For all he knew Leipzig would be swarming with front-and-cover organisations. Intelligence had become a major post-war industry. Getting rid of the strap would be child's-play. But meeting Karen again wasn't something that could be conducted across a counter in the space of a few brief minutes.

Surely, he thought, it was going to be possible to see her after that?

Clouds began to obscure the land. Towards noon they turned south-east, canting over, the sun swinging. They were due in at twelve-twenty. Patrick had put the map away. The white scar of an autobahn made itself visible and other gaps in the overcast offered tantalising glimpses of minor roads and railway-tracks spidered between towns and villages clustered about the grey-green countryside.

"D'you know what?" Patrick said. "I'll send a card to Hans Meiner. That'll shake him."

"Which is Hans?"

"The boy in Rostock."

"Ah." Slattery was inescapable. "What about the others?"

"Oh, I'll do them too. Gilles, Paris; Erich, Hanover; Jenny,

San Francisco; Manuel Chapi, Barcelona . . ." Patrick ticked them off on his fingers.

"Only one girl?" Laker smiled. "What happened to that glamorous thing who used to write from Athens?"

"I wish I knew. She was a bit square, though."

"Don't forget Mrs. Ruddick."

"And Tim Maxwell. Still, the point is to get one off to Hans when I'm on his side of the fence. You know—wish you were here; having capitalist time."

Patrick laughed, pleased with his joke, and Laker fisted him playfully on the shoulder. Once, a year or so ago, when they were searching the store-room at Roundwood, Patrick had come across the box containing Laker's decorations and medal ribbons, but there was no mention of Karen in the citations and Laker had never spoken about her. What would he tell him now, supposing they all could meet? "A friend," would he say? "Someone I worked with during the war, long before you were born, before I even knew your mother, someone I believed I would never see again . . ."

The stewardess with the severely swept-back hair and the trained smile that could have masked contempt had started along the gangway, signalling everyone to fix their belts. They were lower already, the vibration more marked, wallowing a little on the up-currents.

Cloud streamed like mist past the windows and, quite suddenly, the outskirts of Leipzig slid obliquely into view like a multi-coloured street-map, Instinctively, Laker pointed. The aircraft seemed to search for a line, then chose one and held it, slanting in, wheels down, flaps down, throttled back, flattening out as the runway rose abruptly out of a smear of crops and hedgerows.

"Dead on time," Patrick said like a seasoned traveller as soon as the jolt was over.

The airport formalities weren't prolonged. An announcement, first in English, then in French, greeted them as they filed indoors: "Passengers are requested to present their passports and Fair Cards at the Immigration Bureau. Facilities are also available for currency exchange. All enquiries regarding the Trade Fair should be addressed to the Information Department in this building or to the Foreign Visitors' Centre at the New Town Hall . . . Thank you."

They had to queue at Immigration, but there were no difficulties. Returning to Dover after a day-trip to Calais couldn't have been easier. A page of their perforated Fair Cards was stamped and detached; a nod and they were clear. Perhaps because the Customs official hadn't expected Laker to answer in German he chalked squiggles on their luggage without asking for anything to be opened and even went as far as to wish them a pleasant stay in the German Democratic Republic. Then they were free to move into the high, echoing Arrivals hall and pass under the flags and welcoming banners which draped the exits.

Outside, another queue waited for taxis. Theirs, when it came, was a Skoda, newish, with a photograph of Ulbricht stuck on the windscreen like a talisman and a driver who wore a black plastic cap with a duck-bill peak.

"Astoria Hotel," Laker said.

He was sweating thinly, and Patric remarked on it. He shrugged: "It's a bit stuffy." But he glanced at the rear-view mirror all the same, deriding his caution even as he did so, aware only then of the effort the Customs had cost him. And yet they'd waltzed through. He watched Leipzig straggle towards them, alien and unrecognisable. Roundwood, Gale and Watts, Mrs. Ruddick, Carol Nolan—all at once they seemed immensely remote, in time as well as distance.

The city took shape, graceless and functional, the heavy Russian style of the outlying tenement blocks and the more central commercial area only partially redeemed by the temporary rash of decorative bunting. The treeless squares were as drab as parade-grounds and there was a heavy sprinkling of uniforms on the thronged pavements. Laker had forgotten who had recommended the Astoria, but he'd booked weeks in advance and even then it meant Patrick sharing a room with him. As they entered the foyer the Irishman from the plane was already on his way out, giving them the thumbs-down sign as he passed.

"Mr. Laker?" a plump woman-receptionist inquired, studying the hotel's letter of confirmation he'd produced. "Mr. Laker and son?" She pronounced it "Larker", but he let it go. He nodded and they waited. The décor was confused, modern pastel incongruously burdened with Edwardian gilt; and the place seemed packed. When the woman spoke to them again it was in English. She hadn't much charm but she was certainly efficient. "Yes, that is in order, Mr. Larker. You have a reservation for two days. You will both complete and sign the register, if you please."

They did so, and she said: "Your room is number fifty-four." She couldn't manage the 'r' and it sounded like 'womb'. Then she pinged a bell and a cadaverous porter collected the key and their luggage. The elevator whined them up to the third floor.

"You're busy," Laker remarked to the porter.

"Busy, yes. Oh yes. Fair-time is always busy." He looked as if life had tried to crush him, and might do so yet. "The whole world visits Leipzig for the Fairs." When it came to a tip he asked for cigarettes instead of money.

The room was on the small side, but adequate. Twin beds, a handbasin, a single wardrobe. The atmosphere seemed heavy, as if peat were burning somewhere. Patrick opened a window and they stared out. Beyond the immediate solidity of the neighbouring façades there were vacant, rubble-heaped lots and bomb-truncated ruins. Nearer, a poster implored housewives to collect scrap. Everything looked grey and it had begun to spit with rain.

"Well," Laker said. "What d'you think?"

"It's different."

"From what you imagined?"

"No. Just different—like the old news-reels. Does that make sense?"

"After a fashion."

Patrick unslung his camera and tested one of the beds. "Still, the womb's all right."

Laker smiled. Fourteen, he thought.

"Shall we lunch now? I'm starved."

"Right away." But he delayed at the window, wondering where the Luisenstrasse was.

It was a reasonable meal. The dining-room was loud with the collision of voices. Laker recognised at least three of the London passengers scattered about: Black was one of them and he seemed to be fraternising to good effect. He waved vaguely in Laker's direction.

Laker took out the folder into which Carol had put all the Fair particulars and glanced through them. There was no reason why they should go to the Foreign Visitors' Centre; he'd changed twenty pounds at the airport and had no desire to "meet and converse with trade partners in your particular sphere of interest," as one of the leaflets worded it, either at the New Town Hall or at the Messedienst—"a must for information and assistance in the advancement of international Fair business."

He wasn't there for that, or for the junketing. From the first his intention had been to make a couple of visits to the Fair itself, one general, one more specifically on behalf of Gale and Watts, and to fill in with some routine sightseeing for Patrick's benefit. A few hours' snooping round the Business-Systems section was the most he'd envisaged and even before he was hooked by Slattery he had decided to leave that side of things until the following day. The general tour of the Fair could start after lunch, so nothing had changed—nothing, that was, except having to leave Patrick to his own devices for a short while.

He said: "I'll have to duck away for a bit this afternoon. You know—business. It would only bore you."

"For how long?"

"Not so long. We'll get over to the Fair as soon as we've unpacked and then, say about four, I'll leave you to browse on your own for a while. Okay?"

59

He was restless now, wishing the damn thing off his wrist; but not on that account alone.

They had the choice of a dozen or more exhibition buildings and the overall effect on Laker was rather as if Earls Court and Olympia and the old British Industries Fair had been lumped together in the city's centre. Once off the streets and confronted with the panoply of the various trade displays it was hard not to forget that, in Slattery's phrase, they were behind the lines. Plush carpeting, ingenious presentation, subtle dioramic lighting—it was the same shop-window world with the same eye-catching gadgetry, the same kind of product demonstrators, the same extrovert bonhomie of the salesmen with the same smoky stuffiness, the same sort of voices and earnest gropings. Jerry Baxendale would have been in his element.

Laker went through the motions of showing interest, but his mind was elsewhere. The television and musical-instrument section was like the Radio Show in miniature and it seemed the best possible place in which to leave Patrick. Time was getting on: time to go.

"You'll be all right?"

"Sure."

"It's almost four now. I'll be back before five. But just in case I'm not, or you get bored around here, push off to the hotel."

"Okay."

He handed Patrick some money. "Don't blue it all on records."

Patrick grinned and he left him, suddenly uneasy, regretting the necessity. At the exit he turned and looked back, as if the scene would somehow offer reassurance, then made his way into the street. It was still spitting with rain. He found a taxi-rank under some plane-trees at the corner of the first block and asked for the Luisenstrasse.

"Whereabouts?" the man said. "What number?"

"Twelve," he answered, guessing, not wanting to give the name or to be vague.

He sat on the edge of the seat. Fair directions were everywhere but he had no idea which way they were heading. "A five-minute ride"—though that was from the Astoria. Off to the right he glimpsed a railway-station, then a square dominated by an ungainly piece of statuary. Thereafter the concentration of flags and banners began to peter out: there was another Leipzig and it came quickly, more nakedly drab, the hoardings no longer proclaiming a welcome.

EVERY INCREASE IN OUTPUT IS A NAIL IN ERHARDT'S COFFIN . . . WE ARE LEARNING FROM SOVIET SCIENCE, THE MOST PROGRESSIVE IN THE WORLD . . . DO YOUR SHARE AND STRIKE A BLOW FOR THE GERMAN DEMOCRATIC REPUBLIC . . .

Bicycles were everywhere. Lights delayed them and Laker watched the passers-by: they were cosmopolitan no longer and their faces showed evidence of the hard life. Some stared, as if a taxi were a novelty, and the stares gave him a disturbing sense of isolation, of having strayed out of bounds. This was far enough, he kept thinking, far enough. And then, as if in obedience to his silent urging, the taxi made an abrupt right turn and cruised to a halt in front of a second-hand clothing shop.

It was an unlikely destination to have chosen. He climbed out and paid the man off, then made a pretence of tying his laces, giving the taxi time to draw away. The rain had stopped. There were shops on both sides of the street, two-storeyed mainly, a run-down look about them: a queue of women gossiped outside a baker's opposite. He lit a cigarette and started walking. It was a hundred yards or more before he saw Kromadecka's—just as he was beginning to have an awful feeling that he must have come to the wrong place. It was diagonally across the street, narrow-fronted, the name lettered in black on a yellow ground. In the minute it took him to reach it, he twice looked over his shoulder. He would have felt less exposed amongst a crowd, but the Luisenstrasse had none to offer. Apart from the queue it seemed almost unnaturally quiet —few people, no cars, hardly a cyclist.

He walked at an even pace. "Nothing to it, old boy . . ." He had talismans of his own. "Couldn't be more elementary . . ." But there was more to this than actively taking sides in a war and, despite the tension, he was strangely elated. Ten yards away he slowed, keeping to the outside of the pavement so as to widen his view of the shop. A clock centred in the window showed that it was a little after a quarter-past four. There was a hand-written notice in German taped to the inside of the glass.

WATCH REPAIRS
ESTIMATES FREE
PRICES MODERATE

It greeted him like an invitation, something meant for him personally, and he reached for the door, eager to make an end of being manacled to Slattery and effect a beginning of his own.

5

A BELL above the door tinkled as he went in. The place was small, cluttered, glass cases forming a counter on three sides. Through a curtained opening he could see the base of some stairs leading out of a back room.

"A moment, please."

It was a woman's voice; soft, quite cheerful. Time had blurred how Karen had sounded, but it could only be hers— Slattery had said so—and Laker heard the intensified thud of his heart above the irregular ticking of several clocks. The walls were hung with them. In the cases were cutlery sets and a

62

few pieces of silver plate, embossed pottery, tankards and some glass; after the lavish sophistication of the Fair everything looked pitiable. He wiped his face and waited, suddenly caught between anticipation and a kind of dread, staring about him, wondering. There was a selection of watches in a wall-cabinet and an old square safe screwed to the floor in the opposite corner.

A truck ground past just as he heard her on the stairs. Before she came through the curtains she was saying, "I'm sorry, sorry." And then she was there, the curtains closing behind her. "Good afternoon. Can I help you?"

Perhaps it was vanity, but he thought she hesitated when she saw him. For a second or two it seemed as if her face clouded with incipient disbelief, her brows knitting slightly as she moved behind the counter. But, for his part, he had no need to rack his memory; reality matched the basic image. He would have picked her out in the street, in a restaurant—anywhere. The gentle freckling, the broad mouth, the blonde hair; above all, the eyes—as brown and grave as he'd remembered.

"What was it you wanted?"

He mastered emotion. Again, momentarily, he believed he detected the beginnings of a frown of recognition.

As dutifully as a boy on an errand he said: "A new watch-strap."

If she felt anything she didn't show it. She gave nothing, absolutely nothing, away. "Any special kind?"

"Something like the one I'm wearing will do."

He took the watch off and handed it to her. She had dropped her gaze now.

"It's an English strap, isn't it?"

"Yes," he said. "I got it in London."

She nodded and reached for a batch of cards, each displaying a choice of samples. She was very calm, very practised.

"I can't give you leather. Imitation is the best I have; the alternative would be plastic."

She wore a darkish orange costume of tweed-like material and a white bead necklace. Her lips were only lightly reddened

63

and her hair curled softly away from the forehead. The skin was a fine, delicate colour. When she placed the cards in front of him he saw how slender her fingers were. There was no ring, he noticed.

"Imitation will be all right."

And suddenly it seemed beyond reason that he should continue his part of the masquerade. He couldn't be bothered with the cards. He said quietly: "Don't you remember me, Karen?"

If she bore scars at all they were in her eyes. Now, as she lifted them to his, he saw for a fleeting instant not merely wariness but a whole background of apprehension, like an illness she had learned to live with.

"Sam," he said. "Sam Laker." Then, as if it were a code-word: "Sammy."

There was nothing then but the sound of the clocks. For a long time that was all. He thought her stare would never end.

"Sammy?"

Smiling, he watched her expression as she made the leap in time, her eyes widen a fraction, the line of her mouth alter. He didn't know what he expected—delight, wonder, incredulity; any or all of these. The incredulity was dawning, but there was something else as well: dismay, perhaps—he couldn't decipher it. She lifted a hand to her throat.

"No!" she said. "Oh, no!"

"Am I so different?"

She didn't answer.

"Am I?"

She shook her head, staring still, searching his face. Slowly, she began: "I didn't expect —"

"How could you have done?" He leaned nearer, Patrick forgotten, Slattery forgotten. "You look fine, Karen. You haven't changed." Matured, filled out, but not changed. "As soon as you came through the curtains —"

"I . . . I can't believe it," she said. She shook her head again, closing her eyes momentarily. "Sammy Laker"—and now when she used his name the wonder was there.

"You frowned when you saw me. I thought perhaps —"

"It was the light," she said. "You were against the light."

"You didn't guess?"

"No."

"And now?"

"There's no need to guess now." Her lips trembling.

"I thought you were dead, Karen—until forty-eight hours ago, that is, when they asked me to do this."

Laker gestured towards the watch lying between them; they were safe here. Thoughts a million times faster than speech were racing through his mind. He began to talk about the Red Cross, about the letters to the house near Gardelegen, very moved suddenly, and all the time she gazed at him as if certainty hadn't quite enveloped her yet. Little by little she seemed to be shedding her dismay or whatever it was he imagined he saw; but there was no smile.

"How long have you been in Leipzig?"

"Since 'forty-seven."

"And in this shop?"

"Twelve years. It was my uncle's. When he died I kept it going."

"Do you live here?"

She raised her eyes to the ceiling. "Upstairs."

They paused then. She had hardly touched the watch.

"I wondered about you," Laker said.

"So did I," she said. "I wondered, too. Many, many times." A kind of tremor seemed to pass through her. "I still haven't grasped it, Sammy . . . You."

He nodded. "And they say miracles never happen." He offered her a cigarette but she refused, with a fluttering gesture. "Tell me about yourself."

She shrugged.

"Were you ill for long?"

"At that house?"

"Yes."

"Not so long. They were very kind."

He had the feeling that she couldn't give her mind to what

65

had happened all that time ago. Biting her lower lip she stared at him, denied in some way the ease to let her wonder live and grow out of the passing moments. They both faltered sometimes, lost for words. Behind Laker's back a clock whirred and struck the half-hour. He'd almost forgotten what had brought him there. Even in the silences he seemed to be re-discovering something about her. He wasn't sure whether Karen asked him or not, but he found himself telling her what he had done since the war; about Helen. She must have asked, otherwise he would hardly have been speaking about Helen so soon, but he was confused himself, split by many emotions.

"There are children?"

"A boy—Patrick. Not that he's a child any more. He's with me in Leipzig, incidentally." Another clock was chiming. "Are you married?"

"No," she said.

"Were you?"

"No."

Someone went by in the street, a woman wearing a headscarf, blinking in the light from the window as she passed. Karen glanced quickly that way and he realised how tense she was.

"You will have to go," she said.

"Not yet."

"Soon." Slattery's comment echoed in her tone—"I'm not running a social-contacts bureau, Sam."

"You've got to fix my strap first."

She picked up the watch and reached into a drawer for a pair of sharp-pointed pliers.

"How many years have you been fixing straps?" he asked. "Straps from London?"

She frowned over the watch, probing with the pliers, but refrained from answering.

"Or shouldn't I ask things like that?"

Without looking at him she said: "You have never done this before, have you?"

"Does it show so much?"

She nodded.

"There's a whole lot more I want to ask."

"There won't be time."

"I'm here until first thing Friday morning. At the Astoria. Couldn't we meet there?"

"It would not be wise."

"Tonight, for dinner?"

"No, Sammy."

"Why not?"

"You know why."

"But, hell —" he began, the amateur in him hurt. He thought of Black, Black who could fraternise openly in the hotel's dining-room, and the score of animated meetings he'd witnessed during that self-same afternoon. Leipzig was packed with foreigners, its arms flung wide in the interests of trade. Openly, in the Astoria's bar, with Patrick, and then to dine, the three of them—where was the harm?

He tried to put it to her, but she only shook her head.

"I can't."

"Do you want to?"

"Of course," she said. "Of course."

"But you won't?"

"It's not a risk I can take." She looked at him. "Believe me, please."

Once she had risked so much, survived so much. They both had. Suddenly he remembered that other time, and her saying: "When is it going to be normal for us, Sammy?" Suddenly he realised that in a few minutes he would be out in the street. One wing of the strap was already detached and she had started picking at the fastening of the other. Slattery loomed once more. The Mitre, the flat in Manchester Square and the plain blue van. "She's one of our best, Sam . . . There's been a mis-understanding. You can get her off the rack."

Laker stubbed his cigarette. "I can phone you, surely?"

"No."

He stared at her, striving to accept that her coolness towards him wasn't wilful.

"I can't just go," he said. "I can't just walk away. Not after twenty years. I can't just say 'Good-bye' and not see you again."

"You must."

"Can't you suggest something? Isn't there a park, or a square, or a café —?"

"Don't push me, Sammy. It's no good." She unclipped the other wing of the strap, more clumsily than before, her movements showing signs of stress. "Don't you understand?"

"I do, but —"

"Already you have stayed too long."

"Ten minutes?"

"They must have told you how it would be."

He said nothing.

"I didn't know you were coming." Now, all at once, she was near to tears. "I didn't know *who* was coming, or even when it would be. I'm not expected to know, I'm not expected to ask. That isn't my part of it." Her eyes burned, brown and huge; yet her face still held its fine colour. "I thought you were dead, Sammy. And not until forty-eight hours ago. Until just now . . . It's harder for me—can't you see? I didn't know it was going to be you standing here." Her lips trembled again. "Oh, God," she finished wretchedly.

"I'm sorry," Laker said. "I'm sorry, Karen." He seemed tongue tied. Impulsively, reaching forward, he touched her on the cheek. For a moment she didn't draw away, but suddenly she stiffened.

"No."

Her voice was sharp. She pulled back and bent her head over the watch. Outside, there was the drag of footsteps.

"Vopos," she whispered tersely.

"Who?"

"Vopos."

The light faded as the window was partially blocked. Out of the corner of his eyes Laker saw two members of the People's Police, one taller than the other, and the taller of them was leaning forward as he peered in, hoisting his shoulder-slung carbine.

68

"Which strap have you chosen?"

Karen's tone had utterly changed: the cards shook slightly as she held them in front of him.

Laker pointed. "I'll take that one."

The light swelled again as the figures moved. He thought they were going away, but he was wrong. When the door-bell tinkled his neck prickled coldly. They came in, heavy boots gritting on the worn linoleum, and stood behind him, close because of the lack of space. For an awful moment that seemed quite interminable he remained woodenly at the counter, expecting them to speak, to challenge him even. The two wings of his old strap lying on the glass looked frighteningly conspicuous.

Karen finished unfastening the new one from the display-card before addressing them. "Can I help you?" It amazed Laker that she should have the ability to smile.

One of the two cleared his throat. "You have a brooch in the window."

Over his left shoulder Laker focused briefly on to a fleshy, constipated face under a green fore-and-aft cap, a young face with thick lips and snub nose. Then he turned his head away.

"Would you like to show me which one?"

"I will wait."

"It's no trouble. You can be making up your mind while I finish with this gentleman's watch."

Karen moved to the window; the Vopo who had spoken followed suit. "There," he said. "There, yes, that's it."

She returned to where Laker was standing without so much as glancing at him. In his relief he marvelled at her control, but there was lead in his heart. A kind of angry dejection filled him as she began fixing the new strap into position. It was almost unendurable to wait to be dismissed, unable to speak with her again, let alone to make one more plea that their reunion shouldn't end in such a fashion. Behind him the two Vopos muttered over the brooch. "What d'you think?" one of them said. "Will it do?" and the other answered: "Do? She'll fall for it. Look, if I hold it you can see it better." As if

69

mesmerised Laker stared across the counter, watching Karen's small-boned hands fold the last clip down with the pincers.

Then she was saying: "There, sir . . . I think you'll find that's satisfactory."

Sir . . . He took it from her, vainly hoping to hold her gaze if only for a second, aware that she was facing the Vopos, yet hoping despite that. "Thank you."

There were a thousand questions, but nothing was possible. He paid with a note. The till was on a shelf fixed to the wall and as she turned she casually picked up the pieces of the strap and dropped them into the open drawer, for all the world like a woman for whom tidiness was everything. And when she spoke to him again, counting out his change, he might have been exactly what he was meant to be—a stranger.

"Thank you, sir. Good afternoon."

The sound of the door-bell seemed to mock him as he walked away. Yet the resentment locked within his feeling of deprivation wasn't directed against her. The Vopos had served to remind him of the dangers. Until they came the shop had seemed quite safe: Slattery's game—her game—a shade unreal, undeserving of extreme caution. But now that alarm had brushed his own nerves he more fully understood the high wire on which she existed, and it was this that he hated—its discipline and its denial.

For what? Yes, for what?

He crossed the street, his mind whirling, selfishly grateful that she had almost reached the brink of tears. The past meant something, then. He hadn't nurtured an illusion or romanticised a memory.

It was getting on for a quarter to five. An enormous effort was required to bring his thoughts to bear on where he had arranged to meet Patrick. He walked briskly, heedless of his surroundings, hoping to find a taxi. There was a telephone booth at the first intersection. She had insisted that he mustn't call but he went in and looked for Kromadecka in the tatty directory, scribbling the number, the number only, hurriedly in his diary. He wouldn't use it for a while, perhaps never; but he couldn't accept that he had seen the last of her. Tomorrow, perhaps, he might return to the shop, ostensibly to buy something. He would have to think what to do, what was best—weighing the possible risk to her against what the last fifteen minutes had aroused in him.

He walked with his shoulders hunched, embittered by the irony of the situation, unable to think very clearly. After several hundred yards he found himself passing a bookshop. ART IS A WEAPON, the window-display proclaimed. Inside, he asked where he could get a taxi and the assistant, speaking slowly as if unsure of Laker's command of the language, directed him to a rank a couple of blocks away. The driver at the head of the rank accepted him without enthusiasm and crunched through the gears on his way to the Astoria. Patrick would almost certainly have gone back to the hotel; it was as near to five as made no difference.

The streets spread themselves as they approached the area of the Fair. Under the bunting and the banners there were crowds again, people moving with varying degrees of purpose, the stiffening of uniforms amongst them. He was in the clear now, a postman no longer, so the uniforms conveyed no sense of personal threat; yet they were the outward and visible reason for care before he made a second move towards Karen.

He recognised the Ring-Messehaus, with its fringe of flags hanging limply after the rain, but he failed to see the railway station he had passed on the previous journey. Vaguely, he suspected the driver was giving him a tourist's run-around and soon he leaned forward, saying "Astoria" in such a way as to indicate that he knew his Leipzig, only to find that he didn't. Hardly had he spoken than they were drawing up outside the hotel, scraping the kerb.

He suffered the driver's smirk, paid, and turned towards the steps. The heavy peat-like scent enveloped him as he entered the foyer. There was no sign of Patrick. He hesitated, wondering whether to wait for him there or to go on up to their room.

71

And, as he hesitated, a man in a light raincoat rose from one of the tables near the entrance and approached: a shortish man with a slightly lopsided face.

"Mr. Laker?"

He didn't use the broad 'a'. With affected ease Laker said: "That's right."

"Mr. Samuel Laker?"

"Yes."

"I have some unfortunate news, I'm afraid, Mr. Laker."

"Oh?"

"There's been an accident." He stuttered slightly. "I'm sorry to say that your son has —"

"Accident?" Scalp tightening, Laker snatched at the words. "What happened?"

The man started on some rigmarole about stairs, a fall, but Laker couldn't wait for him to finish.

"Is he badly hurt?"

"He was unconscious when they put him in the ambulance."

"Where is he?"

"At the University Clinic."

"God!" Laker said.

He wheeled blindly for the doors, isolated by the shock, unaware that he was followed. But on the steps his arm was grabbed.

"This way, this way . . . I have a car."

He remembered being guided to an old grey Mercedes and getting into the back seat, the man in the raincoat lurching against him as the door was slammed. Another man was already at the wheel and they started to move almost immediately, nosing into the traffic.

"When did it happen?"

"Half an hour ago."

"How's he injured? Is it his head, or what?"

"I couldn't say exactly. But don't alarm yourself too much. I don't think you will find his condition too serious."

"Unconscious, you said."

"Yes, but —"

"Did you see him?"

"Not personally, no."

"Was it at the radio-and-television place?"

"Yes, yes; that's right."

"God!" Laker said again. He felt sick; stunned. "I left him alone for a while because there was some business I had to attend to and I thought it would bore him. I wondered at the time whether I was making a mistake. But his German's not bad, d'you see, and he's normally quite capable of looking after himself." Anxiety, self-reproach spilled over. The streets blurred past. "How far's the hospital?"

"Not too far, Mr. Laker."

His hands wouldn't remain still and he brought them together, the knuckles bone-white. He heard himself say: "It's very good of you to help like this. I appreciate it." By talking he could at least keep his imagination under control. "How did you recognise me?"

"Please?"

"How did you know me? Or that I'd be at the Astoria?"

"Your son said you would be there."

Laker frowned. "He *was* able to speak, then?"

"I understand so. To begin with."

He found himself looking at his companion as if for the first time. The man had a hat on now, a brown trilby. The person at the wheel was bareheaded, wearing a black leather jacket; around the cropped blond hair-line his neck was inflamed with boils. "Take a left," the one with the hat said, and Laker felt the centrifugal tug as the tyres snickered. Since the shock hit him he had been in a daze, apprehensive of what awaited him, oblivious of the distance they were covering. The minutes passed. He couldn't for the life of him understand how Patrick had come to pitch down a flight of stairs, but his questions increasingly drew a blank, a shrug. Suspicion was some way from taking hold, but his wits were thawing a little and it struck him that the man was losing interest, more concerned with their route and issuing directions. Twice in succession they bore right. There was less traffic and the streets had narrowed: it

73

was the other Leipzig again, cheerless and gaunt with factories squatting amid old untended scars.

Laker said urgently: "What's the hospital called again?"

"The University Clinic."

"Are we nearly there?"

"Soon."

But there was no indication of it. On edge, he said: "Wasn't there anything more central?" He glanced at his watch. Time suddenly took meaningful shape. Where were they? They were moving fast and the city was running more and more to seed.

"Who are you?" he said, alarmed by a wild doubt.

The man shifted position, but didn't answer. Small, bright eyes; a crease-bracketed mouth.

"Look, where's my son been taken? Where's this hospital?"

"Keep quiet, Mr. Laker."

Laker stiffened, heart missing a beat.

"There is no hospital and there has been no accident." The slight stutter emphasised the injection of menace. "Keep quiet and don't try anything foolish."

"What the hell are you talking about?"

"I'm talking about you, Mr. Laker. Do as I say and you will come to no harm."

As casually as if he were about to offer a cigarette the man withdrew his right hand from inside the raincoat. Dropping his gaze Laker saw an automatic pistol.

"Otherwise," the man said, "I will have no alternative but to kill you."

6

LAKER stared at the gun with incredulous dismay. Fear crawled clammily over his skin.

"Is this a joke?" he managed thickly. "Some kind of a joke?"

"No joke, Mr. Laker."

They must have covered a quarter of a mile before another word was spoken and throughout that time his thoughts spun in chaos.

Karen, Kromadecka's.

He achieved that one coherent deduction before the confusion regained its hold. With as much control as he could find he said: "What's the meaning of this? Just what d'you think you're doing?"

Except with his eyes the man ignored him.

Laker licked his lips, desperately seeking to pacify himself, not to bluster. "Look," he said, "I don't know who you are, and I don't care, but you've made a mistake. A bloody silly mistake." But it was hopeless and he already knew it. Something had gone wrong, terribly wrong; the gun and the two men and the story about Patrick were an integral part of disaster.

"Where are we going?"

No reply.

"What about my son? Where's he?"

"In good hands, Mr. Laker. Safe and sound."

"Where?" he shouted. Then he tried again, more persuasively. "I'm a British subject. This is ridiculous. Intolerable"—echoing the protests of all those who had ever walked into a trap; and again, even as he formed the words, he knew the futility of them. Appeals, bribes—these were out, too. He'd fallen for the oldest trick of all and it was twenty years since he had been within reach of a weapon, twenty years since he was trained in the unarmed skills that might have led to a physical break. Pressing against his side of the car he felt unable to move, held by the gun and the other's eyes, his groping relief that Patrick was uninjured whirled away by apprehensions so tortured that they amounted almost to a physical pain.

"Who are you?" he demanded. "Police?"

"We aren't kidnappers, Mr. Laker."

"Who, then? And what am I supposed to have done?"

"You will find out." A joyless, off-centre smile. "But, if it is any comfort to you, my colleague and I have official blessing."

They were leaving the fringes of the city; numbly Laker was

aware of a smear of crops behind the man's head, trees dotted about an untenanted green slope. For a moment or two his thoughts seemed to reach a state of appalled calm, but before he could attempt to reason the confusion began to renew itself, repeating his mind's instinctive cry of dismay when he first saw the gun. Patrick was at the heart of it, Patrick and Karen and Slattery. And there were others, others who were involved in that they were a part of the pattern of his life, faces and places near and far, all frenetically scrambled together, kaleidoscopic images sweeping him as if he were drowning.

Christ, he thought. Oh Christ.

He started feeling for his pockets, but the man checked him.

"I want a cigarette," he said.

"Use these."

A pack was tossed across together with some matches. Laker lit up clumsily, fingers shaking, narrowing his eyes against the smoke. Another weakening rush of panic surged through him. There had been nothing to arouse his suspicions, no evidence of being followed, no feeling the weight of another's scrutiny. Lies, denials; he must cling to these now. Karen would and so must he. They'd have picked her up as well; everything pointed to the inevitability of that. It couldn't be him without her. Her without him, yes, but not him without her.

Oh Christ, he thought again.

Pines stood along each side of the road. "Where are you taking me?" he asked a second time, but he might have been talking to himself. The sun flickered like a signal-lamp through the trees and the driver grunted, reaching to retrieve dark glasses from the empty seat beside him.

They were heading north-east and it had passed the half-hour. A sign pointed to Berlin and Laker felt an inner cold blow through him, chilling him in the marrow. Minute after minute he was stumbling around in his mind for a clue to what might have betrayed them, yet his most desperate anxiety was still for Patrick.

"What d'you mean by 'in good hands'?"

"Exactly what the phrase implies, Mr. Laker."

"But where is he? . . . What's he been told? I was meeting him at five."

A shrug.

"He's fourteen. Fourteen—a kid. And he's only once before been away from England."

He waited, but there was no answer.

"Are you deaf?" he suddenly raged through his distress. "Why the hell can't you explain what this is all about?" Then, finally, in English: "You bastard. Whoever you are, you sodding bastard." And he saw the man's eyebrows contract and knew he'd understood.

An autobahn crossed their path like a dyke. They took the looping underpass and gradually the trees straggled back to fence the road. They must have been seven or eight miles from the outskirts of Leipzig before the driver cut his speed. A track led off to the right. They nosed clear of the tarmac and headed into the pines, the car slewing a little as the wheels shuddered in and out of some ruts. Laker stared about him, sensing the journey was almost at an end yet baffled by the sudden change of route. The pines hemmed them in. After about half a mile the track branched and they bore left, not far, debouching eventually into a small clearing in which there was a log-hut. If Laker had anticipated anything beyond the certainty of an interrogation it wasn't this.

"Listen," the man in the raincoat stuttered quietly. "No foolishness. Get out and remain still. Don't move. Don't do something you might regret."

Laker obeyed woodenly. The driver had beaten him to it. Until his companion had rounded the back of the Mercedes he stood close to Laker, close but not too close, as watchfully as a wrestler. Blue specks were sand-blasted into the coarse facial skin and the mouth was sullen. Over Laker's shoulder he must have received a signal because he nodded and turned towards the hut.

"Follow him, please." This was from behind.

Three wooden steps led up to a door. There were several windows, none of them curtained. A board fixed to the nearest

77

side of the hut stated in red on white FIRE CONTROL. B SECTOR. The driver fished a key from his leather jacket, unlocked the door and pushed his way inside. Laker entered as cautiously as the pistol at his back allowed. Everything seemed dark for a moment or two and then, as his vision adjusted, he found himself in a squarish room in which was nothing except a table and a few hard chairs. Another door led out of the room, but this was closed. A single bulb with a white enamel shade hung from the central rafter.

"Sit down." The man in the raincoat elbowed the door to, then removed his hat, motioning with the automatic as he did so. "Sit at the table and empty your pockets." What passed for a smile pushed his features askew. "Everything, mind."

Laker glared at him, risking stubborness. "Who the devil are you? Just what authority have you got?"

"This." The gun. "This will do for now. And if you think I wouldn't use it you are very much in error."

The room was resonant and their voices bounced off the bare walls. Laker emptied his pockets slowly, the only show of defiance remaining to him. Wallet, pen, nail-clippers, comb, handkerchief, cigarettes and lighter, some loose change, diary . . . Panic could still block his thoughts to reason and, as he put the diary on the table, he remembered with a prickle of alarm that it contained the Kromadecka number.

"Anything else?"

"No."

"It would be wise for us to make certain, don't you think? Take your overcoat and jacket off. And your trousers." There was a pause, during which Laker did nothing. "You have no option, Mr. Laker. Hurry now."

The driver went over them as minutely as if he were looking for lice. All he found were a couple of old cinema-ticket stubs, but the seam which Carol Nolan had re-sewn on the right shoulder of the jacket interested him. He produced a clasp-knife, slit it open and explored the wadding, ignoring Laker's protests. Eventually, after a shake of the head, he tossed the clothes on to the nearest chair.

Laker put them on again, his anger as impotent as his desperation. "What did you expect?" he bellowed. "Look, this is monstrous. I demand an explanation. I'm in Leipzig for the Fair, a *bona fide* visitor, and my son's expecting me at the Astoria Hotel. You've made a mistake, I tell you, and the sooner —"

"If there has been a mistake, Mr. Laker, you will be entitled to, and will receive, the fullest amends. Meanwhile we can only wait and see."

"Wait?"

"Wait, yes."

"How long, for God's sake? What for?"

"I mentioned, didn't I, that your arrest had official blessing?"

"Arrest? Now look here —"

"The last half-hour has perhaps been a little unorthodox. However, Colonel Hartmann will be here at six and he, better than anyone, will be in a position to judge whether a mistake has been made. Colonel Hartmann, you see, is head of S.S.D. —the State Security Service."

With that the man picked up the diary, crossed his legs and began to turn the pages. "Watch him," he said, and Laker saw that the driver had a pistol, too.

Again the milling confusion of mind descended. And again Slattery was there—"No one's been blown; nothing like that . . ." Well, Karen was blown now, and he was linked with her. The two Vopos? . . . No, no. How, then? He still couldn't think straight. There was an awful feeling of emptiness in him, as if his strength had been sapped.

It was ten to six, and the sun was splintering lower through the pines. He went to the nearest window and stared out. The immediate landscape wasn't irrelevant to his fears. Why had they brought him here instead of to some urban headquarters? He turned nervously, in need of another cigarette, but the driver warned him away from those he had left on the table and threw him one of his own instead.

"Mine aren't poisoned," Laker said bitterly, but the man only cleared his throat and rubbed the barrel of his automatic on his sleeve. You lout, Laker thought. He looked at the one leafing through the diary, and as if he had been given a cue the man said: "I see your son's birthday is the same as mine— June 14th."

Laker glared, hating him. It was imbecilic to have noted the Kromadecka number, yet it would be equally mad to deny having been in the shop. He would have admitted that in any case. They knew, anyway. Karen was the focal-point of what had happened and for him to be here at all could only mean that she must have been under suspicion long before he set foot in the Luisenstrasse. Why else had he been hi-jacked? And so promptly? If only he could calm his mind . . . He smoked about half-way down the cigarette, weakness returning like a fever. Then the one in the raincoat rose and dropped the diary on the table. He had given no indication of having noticed the number; in fact he'd appeared to be more interested in the London underground map than anything.

"You were a busy person, Mr. Laker," he remarked. "You lived a full life back there in England."

He said it as mildly as a priest reproving a common vice. At any other time Laker might have fastened in alarm on to the use of the past tense, but for some inexplicable reason he was suddenly aware of the correct pronunciation of his name. The receptionist at the Astoria had called him "Larker", but this man had never made that mistake. Not once. He had been right from the very beginning ("Mr. Laker? . . . Mr. Samuel Laker? . . ."), and the only other person in Leipzig who'd addressed him accurately was Karen.

A terrible possibility entered his head. He tried to shove it aside, attributing the accuracy to Patrick, but it insisted, boring in. With an almost convulsive movement that tore skin from dry lips he snatched the cigarette from his mouth, searching his memory for Slattery's exact words outside The Mitre— "A misunderstanding. I can't explain and you won't expect me to. But contacts have been broken . . ." In disbelief he then remembered something else. "No!" Karen had said when she recognised him. "Oh no!"—and with a sense of derangement he found himself interpreting her look of dismay as one of guilt. Had she been aware of what was going to happen? Could it be that she was blown *before* Slattery ever approached him; her shock principally that of discovering whom she was forced to expose? "Oh God," she had uttered finally. "I didn't know it was going to be you standing here . . ."

It was unbelievable that he should be thinking of her as if she were a kind of enemy when only an hour ago he had been moved by her very closeness. Yet the fact remained that within fifteen minutes of his leaving Kromadecka's the Mercedes was at the hotel, *waiting for him,* along with the lies about Patrick and this devastating, slowly burgeoning seed of Laker pronounced as it should have been . . .

If she had been under duress he was sunk. He heeled out the cigarette on the floor, subsided on to a chair and for barren moments afterwards rested his head in his hands. He didn't hear the car coming. The others did, and the man in the raincoat went outside. But after perhaps a minute he was conscious of voices, the one that stuttered and the one he didn't know, and the clatter on the steps.

He was expecting someone in uniform, but he was wrong. Hartmann was wearing a dark brown belted overcoat and a black velour trilby, the brim of which was turned down back and front. He was tall, lean, older than Laker, and his eyes had a slightly fixed stare, like a ventriloquist's. He paused when he saw Laker, looked at him for a long moment, then motioned to the driver who had stopped leaning against the wall and was suddenly at attention.

"I'll use the other room." The voice was throttled, as if he had had laryngitis.

"Yes, colonel."

The driver opened the communicating door and snapped on a light. The other two went through and the door was shut, leaving Laker and the driver alone. Laker sweated, listening to

81

the murmur which reached them through the partition, protest and apprehension compounded. Several minutes elapsed before the door opened again and the man in the raincoat emerged.

"All right," he said, and jerked his head.

It was a similar-sized room, with a table and only two chairs, but the whole of one side was stacked with buckets, bags of sand, coiled lengths of hose and long-handled birch brooms. All but one of the windows were obscured, so the electric light was necessary. With a renewal of bewilderment Laker questioned why he had been brought to such a place. He felt scared, scared and irresolute, as if he sensed that he wasn't far from the border-line of nightmare.

"I understand you speak German."

"Yes."

"Very well. Sit down."

They faced each other across the empty table. Hartmann's swarthy complexion seemed to emphasise the blueness of his eyes. Narrow nose, straight grey hair. His hat had left a pressure-weal angled across his forehead and he rubbed it gingerly.

"The two in the other room aren't the only ones who are armed." The strained voice, the ventriloquist's stare. "Is that clear?" He didn't wait. "Now tell me something about yourself, Mr. Laker." The 'a' was correct again, feeding Laker's new-found conclusion.

"I want to know why I'm here first."

"We'll come to that."

"I want to know now. And I want to know what's become of my son." He was like an actor with no faith in the weight of his lines. "If you can't tell me I insist on being taken to someone who can."

"To whom, for instance?"

"I don't give a damn as long as I get some answers."

"And an apology, I suppose?"

Laker shifted position.

"What would you expect this apology to cover?"

"My God," Laker snapped. "What d'you think?"

82

"False arrest? Or is your objection to the manner in which it was carried out?" Hartmann seemed amused. "There was no violence, was there? If you cast your mind back you will realise that my colleagues employed the Judo technique of using their opponent's muscles."

Laker leaned towards him. "I was told my son was at the University Clinic. But since I now know that was a lie, where is he? Who's looking after him? What kind of explanation's he been given about this . . . this nonsense?"

"The story is that you've been called away."

"He won't accept that."

"He really doesn't have any choice."

Laker clenched his hands. "Where am I supposed to have been called to? For what reason? And for how long? . . . I've a right to know. And I've a right to be told on what grounds, what possible grounds —"

"We aren't here to discuss your son. And rights, you will discover, begin and end with me." Hartmann paused to rub the diminishing weal. "You should have taken his welfare into consideration before you came to the Democratic Republic."

"I don't follow."

"No?" The tone was almost conversational, but his eyes never once left Laker's face. "You will, though. I am certain you will . . . Now, what brought you to Leipzig?"

"I came for the Fair."

"On your own account?"

"No."

"What line of business are you in?"

"We design and manufacture office equipment."

"'We'?"

"My firm. Gale and Watts."

"In London?"

"No."

"Where, then?"

"In Weybridge, Surrey."

"I see . . . And have you found our Fair worth the visit?"

"What I've had time for, yes."

"How about your particular trade section?"

"I haven't been to it yet."

"When did you arrive?"

"This morning."

"By air?"

"Yes. I applied for Fair Cards at your Agency office in London two months ago—for myself and for my son."

"Never having been here before?"

"Not since I was a child."

Hartman nodded. "How did you and your son spend this afternoon?"

"On a general look-round." Laker tried to match the stare. Now the crux was coming.

"A general look-round at what?"

He moved his shoulders. "Sports goods, photographic equipment, radio and television —"

"So you didn't visit the section you specifically came to Leipzig to see?"

"We're on holiday as much as anything and I gave the boy his head this afternoon. Tomorrow, though —"

"Where else did you go, Mr. Laker?"

"Personally?" He hadn't meant to stall, but he couldn't seem to help himself.

"Personally. What decided you to separate from your son?"

"I went to get something done to my watch."

"What, exactly?"

"It needed a new strap."

"And where did you go?"

"To a shop in the Luisenstrasse."

"The Luisenstrasse?"

"Yes."

"And the name of this shop?"

"Kromadecka."

Another skilful, demoralising pause. The overhead light seemed to burn brighter.

"Why there?"

"How d'you mean?"

"What made you choose that particular shop?"

"It was recommended."

"Oh yes?"

"I broke my old strap on the plane. One of the passengers suggested I ought to go to Kromadecka."

"Mr. Laker," Hartmann said, "there are half a dozen places which you could have gone to within walking distance of the Astoria Hotel."

"I wasn't aware of that. I haven't been in Leipzig for over thirty years."

"So the distance to the Luisenstrasse surprised you?"

"Yes—I suppose it did."

"You went by taxi?"

"Yes."

Hartmann rested his chin on his knuckles. "Your only reason for going to Kromadecka was to have your watch attended to—am I right?"

"Quite right."

"There was no other motive?"

"No."

"You would swear to that?"

"Certainly."

For a lunatic moment Laker thought it possible that there was some sort of hope. But almost at once this died.

"When did you write the Kromadecka number in your diary?"

"On the plane."

"Why not the address?"

"I wasn't given the address." Suddenly he was floundering.

"A telephone number only? By a stranger in an aircraft?"

"Yes."

"You expect me to believe that?"

"It happens to be true."

Seconds elapsed. Then, gazing across at him with what could have been pity, Hartmann said. "You are very much a novice, Mr. Laker. Those people who sent you —"

"Gale and Watts?"

"The people who sent you to Kromadecka . . . Didn't they tell you the cardinal rule?"

He stood up, walked to the door and opened it. The man in the raincoat was there, like an eavesdropper.

"Bring the Gisevius woman in," Hartmann said, and Laker's heart plummeted as he spun round.

Apart from the first frightened glance she would not look at him. She was dressed exactly as when he saw her last except that the white bead necklace had gone. Her hair was slightly disarranged. She came in as if she had been pushed, then halted abruptly, swaying a little, terribly pale.

"Do you know this man?" Hartmann asked.

"Yes."

"Explain how you know him."

"He called at my shop." It was a whisper, almost inaudible, but there was no hesitation.

"When?"

"This afternoon."

"For what purpose?"

"To renew the strap of his watch."

Laker had got to his feet. Wheeling on Hartmann he protested desperately: "I told you. I told you this."

Hartmann's face was expressionless. "What was sewn into the old strap, Fräulein? The one he left with you?"

"Microfilm."

An insect pinged against the light. Hartmann glanced sidelong. "You see, Mr. Laker? Or do you still insist that your arrest is without cause?"

"I don't know what the hell you're talking about."

"No?"

"No," Laker shouted, dismay absolute.

"Are you making out that we have confronted you with a liar?"

Laker choked back the instinctive assent. Karen's eyes were averted from him. Hartmann allowed time for an answer, then nodded to the other man.

"Very well. Take her away."

She went without prompting, as if she wanted to run from the room, but in the doorway she turned suddenly and met Laker's gaze, sobbing, defeated. "I'm sorry . . . I'm sorry . . ." The man in the raincoat shoved her into the other room. Laker heard them cross to the outer door, heard it opened and slammed. The grass killed their footsteps after that but the sound of her crying seemed to go on and on, bitter and broken, matching his own wretchedness.

And Hartmann's throttled voice was saying: "Spare me, please, the story that you were merely doing a friend of yours in London a favour. I have heard that one before, and there is nothing more tiresome than repetition."

For perhaps another quarter of an hour Laker denied everything except having visited Kromadecka's; either that or he met Hartmann's leads with a dogged silence. In a mood of heart-break and recrimination the ragged edges of his mind isolated themselves from the reality of Hartmann's presence and turned in hostility upon the mainspring of disaster, Slattery—Slattery who must have been aware that, at best, Karen was on thin ice and that anyone sent to contact her was running an abnormal risk. *Must* . . . So he should have been told, warned; instead of which he'd been criminally misled. And now, as at Gardelegen years before, he was as good as written off, Slattery's get-out number as useless as the wireless-set which wouldn't work. And this time he was trapped, without choice of action, run to earth on behalf of an organisation he didn't know or belong to and which would almost certainly disown him.

Whose game *was* this? Whose war? . . . Not his. Not Patrick's.

Hartmann had just said: "You are either an unfortunate fool, Mr. Laker, or a benighted idealist. The Gisevius woman is clearly the latter—though in her case, since she is a German, such a phrase is a euphemism." The ventriloquist's stare was there again. "Which are you, Mr. Laker?"

Laker looked through him.

"Did it not occur to you that this might happen? How much did they tell you in London before they borrowed your watch?"

He didn't answer. They knew more than he did. Karen had branded him from the doorway, and the remembered sound of her voice sent a pang through him as stunning as grief. She must have been as powerless as he was now. Chance had worked against them both, lain in wait for them after half a lifetime, and London would have ditched her as well. Nothing he said could help her. And he owed Slattery nothing, absolutely nothing. His first loyalty was to himself and to Patrick and it was better to stick to the lies and protestations than offer one word too many. Co-operation wasn't a way out. What was on the microfilm? What kind of postman had he been?

"I want to see my son," he cut in on Hartmann.

"That will not be possible."

"Why not?"

"There won't be time."

Time? Time? "I want to write to him, then." He licked his lips. "A note. I'm . . . I'm trying to be practical. He's got no money, to start with, and —"

"That side of things has been taken care of."

"Who by?"

"By my department."

"He's fourteen," Laker said, veins swelling in his temples. "If there's a spark of sympathy in you —"

"I'm aware of the boy's age."

"He hasn't done anything."

"I'm aware of that, too. But, as I said earlier, we didn't meet to talk about him. And remember this, Mr. Laker. You are a long way from home. What's more, your country does not recognise the German Democratic Republic. This, as you will discover, is greatly to your disadvantage since it means that what are sometimes called your interests cannot be safe-guarded."

Again, for a fleeting moment, Hartmann's face seemed to

register a hard-held pity. Then, abruptly, as if he had come to a decision with himself, he got to his feet and went out, taking his hat, leaving the door open. Laker heard a muttered conversation in the other room. Craning round, he saw the driver framed by the doorway, arms crossed, watching him. Half a minute later someone left the hut—Hartmann, he presumed—and presently he heard a car retch, roar, then purr away.

He moved to the solitary window, thoughts churning frantically. It was small, too small, the frame heavy. Daylight still held in the clearing and long shadows were printed across the grass. Why here? he questioned again. And what would follow? What happened to the others?—those one read about? A People's Court? . . . He couldn't understand why Hartmann had left without pressing him further, but his mind had been stretched beyond conscious usefulness and he could find no answers—to that or to anything else.

They left him alone for a few minutes. Presently the driver came to the door, the automatic like an extension of his right arm, and ordered him out. The man in the raincoat followed and the three of them walked across the clearing towards the Mercedes. The air seemed cold and Laker shivered involuntarily. A stained wash of clouds patched the gaps in the pines. Far off, a train rattled. He slowed as he neared the car, but to his surprise the driver said: "Keep going." Puzzled, Laker started to round it, imagining that he was expected to get in from the far side, but the driver waved him on. When he hesitated the other one stuttered: "Into the trees, Mr. Laker."

Alarm entered him then. "Why?"

"Into the trees. Go on—move."

He obeyed, tightness gripping his stomach. Perhaps thirty paces brought them to the edge of the pines and his panic mounted with every step.

No, he thought. No. They couldn't.

The driver was three or four yards behind. "Where are you taking me?" Laker demanded, but there was no answer. The light faded as he entered the trees. The ground was springy, deadening their footfalls. The trees were well-spaced. He stopped again.

"What's the idea?"

Their faces confirmed his fears. Unnerved, he stared at them. *Jesus* . . .

"Hurry, Mr. Laker."

He seemed to have lost the ability to move. Suddenly the nightmare was on him, insanely improbable, yet happening, actually happening. He started to say something but his lips stuck to his teeth and a kind of leer resulted, dragging the corners of his mouth.

"Walk," the driver snapped. "Turn round and walk. Otherwise you can have it here."

Laker made about ten paces, a withering contraction shrinking his insides, numbing him through and through.

"Stop."

Almost immediately a rope was flipped over his shoulders, pinning his arms. He struggled as if an icy douche had restored his senses. The man in the raincoat stood with the pistol pointed at Laker's chest while the driver looped the rope round the nearest tree, then hauled so that Laker stumbled back. He began to bawl at them, demoralised, swept by a kind of frenzy, fighting against the rope, kicking, dread and disbelief compounded into an electric terror.

From behind, the driver fastened the rope across Laker's ankles, whistling tunelessly as he did so. Then he stood up, fumbled inside his jacket and brought out a thick brown paper bag. The last things Laker saw before the bag was shoved over his head were the blond hairs poking through the driver's chin and the smoke from the other's cigarette hanging on the air like ectoplasm.

The sugary smell of the bag and the acrid stink of his own sweat enveloped him. He stopped shouting, jerking his head, trying to toss the bag away. The driver was backing with the alacrity of someone who had lit a fuse; Laker could hear the crushing of pine-needles. Light blurred through a small hole on one side of the bag. It wouldn't shift. Now, straining his ears, he tried to stifle the monstrous hammer-blows of his pulse, desperate to identify the slightest sound.

His guts seemed to be liquidising. Stiff against the tree, fingernails digging into the bark, teeth beginning to chatter.

No! . . . No! . . .

Silence.

Where were they?

A bird twittered somewhere in the branches. A cough, several yards away, its hoicking rasp muffled by the bag. A whisper. A metallic click . . . Time seemed to run to a halt. Laker screwed his eyes, images sweeping in raving disorder across the throbbing, blood-red darkness—Patrick, Slattery, Helen, Patrick, Hartmann, Karen . . . Patrick . . .

Body arched, the back of his legs beating a flabby tattoo against the tree, bladder beginning to empty.

Silence.

A tiny thread of awareness made him understand that time was moving on again. He cocked his head.

Nothing.

Then a sound, slow and deliberate. The soft crunch of someone walking. Half right. Coming closer. Laker held his breath. His lips moved, but nothing escaped them. His wits were resurrecting, clinging to life. The footsteps approached casually. Two or three paces from him they stopped.

Another silence that seemed to last as long as the spinning, recollected years. He flinched from whoever was there, whatever was happening. Finally the man in the raincoat spoke.

"Not today, Mr. Laker." It came with a rush as the stutter broke. "We'll forget about it this time."

And Laker vomited into the bag.

THEY helped him to the car, linking him in an underarm grip. One of them gave him some rag to wipe himself and afterwards, when he had slumped into the back seat, a metal flask was pushed into his hands.

"Cognac."

He shook his head.

"Cognac. You need it."

Through a blur of awareness he tilted the flask. The cognac caught at his throat and he started coughing. He pushed the flask away, bending over, heavily gasping for air. Then he slumped back again and closed his eyes, horror beating through him.

"Let's go," he heard.

Icy ripples were moving everywhere over his skin. The car lurched as it met the ruts and he swayed with it, limp and unprotesting. Shivering, hugging himself, he had no control over the reflexive spasms which occasionally twitched his body, nor could he unlock his jaws. He could smell the bag still and the foulness of his soiled clothes wafted up at him, reviving the tidal-wave of terror and release that had buckled his knees and made him sag on the rope.

Several minutes must have passed before the violence of the trauma began to ebb a little. After a while he opened his eyes and stared glazedly through the window, dimly conscious of speed, cars flicking the other way, the rubbery lick of tyres. The sun had dropped below the horizon and the slopes were darkening below their gilded rim, but this didn't register. Questions were drumming a shaky tattoo against his senses, demanding an explanation. One thing and one thing only was clear—he wasn't alive because of any sudden change of heart. What had happened had been intended to happen.

A feeling of vertigo assailed him. Something else was in

store, but it was beyond his powers of recovery to grapple with what it might be. He wound the window down and raised his face to the draught, ashen, oblivious of the driver's curiosity reflected in the quivering rear-view mirror or the other's sideways glance.

They corkscrewed under the autobahn. Soon, Leipzig began to fashion itself, the scattered fringes rising out of the shrinking dusk.

"More cognac?"

The stutter, more than the voice itself, seemed to summon the enfeebling nausea. Laker groped forward, a gargling noise in his throat, but nothing came.

"Pull over, Hans. I don't want him messing the car."

They slowed and the man in the raincoat watched him as anxiously as a parent.

"All right?"

Laker nodded, threads of spittle hanging from his lips, wondering how much longer he was to be toyed with, cat and mouse, and to what end. Solicitude was as much a part of the nightmare as survival.

Where he was taken he didn't then know. It seemed to be the back of a building towards the city's centre. A narrow entrance, a dozen or so stone steps and then a small rope-operated elevator which moaned them up to about the second floor. Several right-angle turns brought them to an expanding metal gate which snapped behind them. The driver didn't accompany them beyond the gate, but the other one directed Laker along a short, ill-lit corridor. Nobody else was in evidence. They passed a number of plain grey doors, each with an exterior observation shutter. At the end door on the left Laker was told to halt. The man produced a key and tossed it to him, taking no chances even here, the pistol bulging his right-hand pocket.

"Inside, Mr. Laker."

There was a steel bunk, a wooden table and a galvanised slop-bucket; nothing else. Walls and ceiling were whitewashed. High up, set in a chute, a small barred window framed a square of near-darkness. Two lights burned, one above the bunk, the other from a plug directly below the chute.

As soon as Laker stepped inside the door closed and he heard the lock go on. Without as much as looking round he flung himself on to the bunk. For what seemed an immense amount of time he remained motionless, as if he had been pole-axed, staring blankly at the opposite wall, chained to a succession of appalling cameos that flitted across the surface of his consciousness. When he eventually gazed along the length of his body and saw what he had done to himself he lacked any sense of shame. Thoughts stirred and eddied, shying from the edges of reality. But there was no refuge, no escape from whatever unfinished crisis chance and Hartmann had chosen for him, and the question-marks continued feebly in the background with disordered insistence.

Soon after eight he heard movement in the corridor. He sat up, muscles rigid by the time the door was opened. Someone he had never seen before came in, a youngish, dark-haired individual with a long penitential face who wore a white shirt and black trousers that could have belonged to a uniform. He was carrying a plastic bowl in one hand, a towel in the other.

Putting the bowl on the table he said impatiently: "I want your clothes." Then, as the towel landed on the bunk: "Your clothes. I haven't got all night."

Laker stripped to his shirt and underpants without a word, defiance bludgeoned out of him. There was warm water in the bowl and a cake of brown soap wrapped in the towel. When he was alone again he washed, then pulled a blanket over his shoulders and sat huddled on the bunk with his back against the wall, desperately trying to still his mind and to get a grip on himself.

"Not today, Mr. Laker . . ."

Whatever was coming he could find no basis for hope. Pencilled on the wall to his left were someone else's initials together with a year-old date, and there were others when he looked for them, half a dozen or so, one spidered into the brickwork as if with a thumbnail, the date more recent. From the depths of shock Laker wondered who these people were and whether secrecy and half-truths had erupted into madness for them, too.

Towards eight-thirty the same man kneed the door open and brought in a tray on which were soup, a hash of some kind, coarse dark bread and a mug of coffee. On his way out he delayed to drop matches and a pack of cigarettes on to the bunk, but Laker was beyond the reach of surprise. The sight of the food almost turned his stomach; he couldn't touch it. He drank the sharp black coffee, though, and lit up, inhaling so fiercely that it made him dizzy.

Patrick, Karen, Slattery—his mind revolved endlessly. It was absolutely quiet except for the small sounds of his own making and these seemed to increase his isolation. A star or two glittered in the dark square of the window. The hash formed a wrinkled skin as it grew cold. For what might have been hours he relived what the day had done to him, travelling again through expectancy charged with tension, tension with action, action with dismay, dismay with that awful escalation of fear; and now the savage, impenetrable remorse.

God, what a fool he'd been. What a blind, uncalculating fool . . .

But it wasn't hours: when he next heard movement in the corridor he saw that it was only ten-past nine. The man entered again, this time fully uniformed in black, carrying Laker's suit draped across his arm. His eyes, his expression, conveyed nothing.

"Put it on," he said, and waited.

The suit had been sponged and pressed; the tear in the right shoulder re-sewn.

"Where am I going?"

"Colonel Hartmann wants you."

Laker had guessed as much, but he was too exhausted to care. When he started to walk his legs felt as though he'd been bed-ridden for weeks.

To reach Hartmann's office they descended a spiral iron staircase to the next level and made their way through a maze of windowless, yellow-brick corridors that smelt of disinfectant. Again they passed no one, saw no one. Presently they reached a door with a green light glowing on the lintel. The man ordered Laker to stop, then motioned him in, not following, closing the door as soon as Laker had passed through. And Hartmann was there, behind a desk in the centre of a largish room, waiting for him with the choked, unforgettable voice.

"Sit down, Mr. Laker."

There was a chair on the near side of the desk and Laker went to it, dry in the mouth. Hartmann studied him in silence, reverting at once to this particular weapon in his armoury, using it now almost as if he hoped it would produce a reaction: hatred, perhaps.

"How d'you feel?"

Laker swallowed.

"How was it in the pines with a bag over your head?"

No reply.

"An experience, eh? To be remembered?"

His shoulders were so square that he might have had the chairback under his jacket.

"To be remembered?"

"Yes."

"Not pleasant, eh? Not willingly gone through again?" He tapped the desk. "Answer me."

"No."

Framed behind his narrow head was a colour print of a healthy-looking Ulbricht. The desk was empty of papers. Glass ashtray, blotter, two telephones—that was all. Some filing cabinets lined one of the walls; slatted blinds shut out the night. But Laker's gaze didn't wander far.

"Why d'you suppose you continue to be alive, Mr. Laker?"

"I don't know."

"Have you wondered?"

"Of course."

"Have you also wondered how it came about that you were ever taken into the pines?"

"Yes."

96

Hartmann cleared his throat to no effect. "With more success?"

"I can only think that you must imagine me to be somebody else."

"Somebody else?" It seemed to surprise him.

"Yes."

"Who, for instance?"

"Somebody more important."

"You aren't being very logical. The Gisevius woman identified you."

Laker gestured weakly. He would have tried to shield her once, but that was hours ago. Lies, denials, pretence—these were pointless now. She was sunk, too. There was no one to betray. "In which case," he said, "you've thrown her away on account of a nobody."

"'Thrown her away'?"

"As far as using her's concerned."

"Is that what you are? A nobody?"

"Yes."

"You're too modest. I wouldn't say that. I wouldn't say that at all." Hartmann leaned back, crossing one leg over the other. "In time I shall explain." He swung his free leg and let the silence settle for a few moments. With a kind of admiration he then said: "You are remarkably resilient, Mr. Laker. Not many could sit there and be so self-possessed so soon after what has happened. It was an outrage, was it not?"

Laker clenched his jaws.

"An outrage," Hartmann repeated as if he found pleasure in the word. "And I shouldn't like you to think anything so drastic is normal practice. The S.S.D. and its agencies have certain responsibilities, certain functions, within the Democratic Republic. I won't bother you with what they are. But, in the usual way, when a courier is intercepted he—or she—is most rigorously interrogated. How rigorously I am sure you can imagine. In your case, however, interrogation has been kept to a bare minimum. This is not because the Gisevius woman has volunteered all we might have wanted to know about you. Far from it. The fact is that, for once, we aren't particularly interested. All that interests us is your being here." He flicked a speck of dust from the blotter. "Does any of this make sense?"

"No."

"We have plans for you, Mr. Laker. You are about to work for us . . . Oh, yes. There is a job to be done. A very special job. It will mean your being taken from here and set free."

Laker frowned.

"I assure you. Tomorrow you will be on your way. And you will do the job as surely as a puppet dances when the strings are pulled."

"I don't understand."

"Soon you will. First, though, I want you to get used to the idea."

"And if I can't?"

"You are not in a position to object. You're as good as dead, Mr. Laker. Don't tell me your memory's that short."

Now it was Laker who paused. "You said I would be released."

"That is so. By tomorrow evening you will be in Copenhagen."

"*Copenhagen?*"

Hartmann nodded.

"Why? What for?"

"To kill someone."

"*What?*"

"To kill someone," Hartmann repeated evenly. "Does it shock you so?"

He was met with an appalled stare. Laker heard himself say: "You must be mad."

"We're talking about you."

"I couldn't do it."

"You could, Mr. Laker. And you shall." Hartmann leaned on the desk. "I can read you like a book. I can almost see your mind working—do you know that? Copenhagen, you are thinking. How will he make the puppet dance at such long range? I will have a frontier behind me. He can't control me then. Why should I kill anyone for him? The idea's preposterous."

Laker dropped his gaze.

"Am I not right?"

"You underestimate me if you believe I'm so naïve." Suddenly there was a trace of venom. "I thought you would be quicker to appreciate the situation. Must I explain what will operate the strings?"

A fearful possibility had begun to dawn, but Laker couldn't bring himself to utter it.

"Why do you think you were made to stand against that tree? . . . No? All right, I shall enlighten you. Imagination is a poor substitute for experience, Mr. Laker. You were put there so that you would know exactly what your son will experience if you fail in Copenhagen. The only difference being that, in his case, there will be no last-second reprieve . . . Have I made myself clear? From the moment you are liberated until you complete this assignment it is going to be—how shall I say?— zero hour for him."

Hartmann watched the blaze of horror in Laker's bloodshot eyes.

"This is the crudest form of blackmail, I admit. However, I can assure you that the old-fashioned pressures are far and away the best. A few hours ago you were terrified in the marrow of your bones—and who can blame you? This is not to say that you wouldn't offer to be taken into the pines again to spare your son. It would be a natural enough gesture. Unfortunately for you, *I* choose who goes there and who doesn't."

Laker's voice shook. "You can't mean that." The nightmare had reasserted itself with the same demented improbability. "You can't . . . You wouldn't dare. He's innocent."

Hartmann blew through his lips. "I'm not concerned with that. But you are, which is as it should be."

"He's a schoolboy. A schoolboy, d'you hear? On holiday. He was keeping me company, that's all. After tomorrow we were going back to the West, to the Rhineland." The protests spilled over, words, words. "You can't mean this, any of it. You *can't*."

But he did. Oh Christ, he did.

"I want to see someone else." Panic brought Laker to his feet. "Where am I? Where is this place?" Desperately he struggled to control himself. "Who are you to decide what becomes of us. Look . . . listen to me. I want to speak to someone else. All I've done —"

"There *is* no one else—not for you. Contrary to what you may believe the Soviets give us a very free rein in certain matters. Now sit down. This is between you and me, Mr. Laker."

In vain Laker searched for the glimpse of pity he had once detected. But Hartmann's fixed blue stare was implacable. He looked very sure of himself, as if he'd inhabited this room for a long time, proposed such things before. Even as his thoughts reeled and blundered Laker knew the futility of pleading.

"Where's my son now?"

"Unaware that he is under discussion, I promise you."

"That's not an answer."

Hartmann half-smiled, as if a thought had that moment struck him. "All this has come at you very quickly. How much of it do you doubt, I wonder?" He reached for one of the telephones and dialled a number, unhooking the ear-piece extension as he did so and pushing it in Laker's direction.

Laker lifted it in time to hear: "Astoria Hotel, good evening."

"Reception, please." Then, when they were connected: "I'm enquiring about two of your guests. They are British, and the name is Laker . . . Laker, yes. L,A,K,E,R . . . Can you tell me if they are still with you? The room number is fifty-four, I believe."

Hartmann's fingers drummed the desk. A hum throbbed along the line. Muffled voices sounded in the background—sane, unaware.

"Are you there, caller?"

"Yes."

"The people you are inquiring after checked out earlier this evening."

"Thank you." Hartmann hung up. "You see, Mr. Laker? . . . I have your luggage, incidentally. Only yours, of course. Your son has kept his own."

Laker swore at him.

"You can say all you wish, but it will change nothing. And you have only yourself to blame. Deep waters are for those who can swim. You should have reckoned on the possibility of getting beyond your depth. Now, for want of a better phrase, you are an instrument about to be put to practical use. And, human nature being what it is, you will take every care to see that you operate with maximum efficiency."

Silence and heart-break closed in on Laker. "You're asking the impossible."

"I think not."

"You've got the wrong man. I'm not a murderer."

Hartmann pressed back in his chair. "You are old enough to have been in the war. Were you in the war, Mr. Laker? A soldier, perhaps?"

"What's that got to do with it?"

"Killing was a duty then. A daily duty."

"I wasn't in the S.S."

Hartmann coloured slightly. "All it needs is provocation. Provocation or necessity. Listen very carefully. If you change your mind and don't go through with this, your son will never rejoin you, safe and sound. And if you try, yet fail, the result will be the same. Either way I promise you that on whatever you care to name as sacred."

Laker closed his eyes, what remained of his spirit crumbling.

Hartmann was saying: "The psychology is soundly based. I am quite certain you will give me your fullest co-operation. We're continuing with the Judo technique, d'you see? Everything has been most thoroughly considered. On the face of it you will be your own master. You will go to Copenhagen, you will take certain actions, and you will ensure that the job is successfully completed. Then, and then only, will you and your son be reunited."

"How can I be sure of that?"

"You have my word."

Clutching at straws now, Laker said thickly: "If my son were harmed in any way there'd be an outcry. What you've done already is a violation of every international —"

"Listen, Mr. Laker. Keep listening. I've no qualms about the story you'll tell London when you eventually return there. But do you suppose the people who sent you will care to broadcast it to the world at large? Two years ago something went badly wrong for a certain Mr. James Wyatt. Were you, as a member of the British public, ever made aware of Mr. Wyatt's objectives or what became of him? Was there an outcry then? Have you ever heard of him, in fact? . . . No. And why not? Because, unless the circumstances are exceptional, outcries are an embarrassment to those who make them. They should have told you of this in London. In effect, Mr. Laker, you and your son have ceased to be public property. Here, in this room, you may well be of the opinion that there is no such thing as justice. But you will find it doesn't exist where you come from either. Sympathy there may be; generosity, no doubt, if your silence has to be bought. But if your son suffers as a result of your failure in Copenhagen the world will never be allowed to know. London will see to that. They have too many skeletons in too many cupboards. They'll go along with our account of an accident; accept our post-mortem certificate. You yourself will know it's all a lie and so will they. But an outcry? . . . No, Mr. Laker, particularly in view of the seriousness of what we can level against them and the degree of your involvement."

Laker looked away, overwhelmed by the imagery of vicarious terror, trapped and committed by it. A shudder racked his shoulders.

"Now do you understand?"

He didn't answer.

"You have no choice, d'you see?"

Laker ungummed his lips. In a low voice he said: "What am I to do?"

"I told you. You will go to Copenhagen and kill a man."

"Who? How shall I know him?" Christ, he thought hysterically, what's happening to me?

"We have photographs. Have you ever been to Copenhagen?"

"No."

"Denmark?"

"No."

"We will brief you before you go, both as regards the city and the person concerned. We will speak about the details tomorrow. You will be given every possible aid. But the timing must be yours and yours alone. And you must not fail—remember that should freedom affect your judgement." Hartmann yawned almost theatrically. "Now, though, I suggest you sleep on it. There has been enough for one day, wouldn't you agree? Unless, that is, you have any questions?"

He was cold, ruthless, perfectly equipped for the business of murder. And yet, when he indulged what could only amount to a sadistic pleasure, there was something contrived about his manner as if at all costs he wanted the satisfaction of Laker's hatred before he was done.

"Do you believe it yet?" he tilted his head. "Or do you imagine it all a joke? An elaborate, unforgivable far-fetched joke?"

Laker dug his nails into his palms.

"Like this evening's charade in the pine trees, perhaps?"

"No."

"What, then? . . . This room, S.S.D. headquarters, you who were so very nearly dead—and the talk is of Copenhagen and your son and London and an assassination." His leg swung back and forth, back and forth. "It's not a dream, d'you suppose? A bad dream that morning or some other awakening is going to wipe away?"

"No," Laker heard himself answer. "It's not a dream."

IN the labyrinth of empty corridors that led back to the cell Laker's despair was like darkness, like night, and when the lock crunched home, shutting him away, he lay on the bunk in the grip of an awful stillness.

The enormity of the blackmail was too appalling for reasoned thought. He kept telling himself that, given time, he would find a way out—tomorrow, the next day. But now he was weak with the assault of weariness and shock, hollow, a sensation that was mental as well as physical, and while it lasted he numbly accepted that his will was tied.

The wall close to his face and the scrawled initials and the barred window reinforced reality. He fell asleep and woke and fell asleep again, over and over. Always when he woke the lights were burning. Sometimes a dream broke into his sleep like an intruder, once bringing him out of it in a fit of shaking, propped on the bunk, hearing the tail-end of his own voice. There was a time when he found himself running along an echoing passage vainly searching for a door; another when he was talking to Karen and Slattery in the forecourt of Gale and Watts, looking across Karen who was at the wheel of the blue van with Slattery sitting beside her, and Slattery beamed: "Tell me, Sam— what's Hartmann like? What trick d'you fancy he might have up that S.S.D. sleeve of his? . . . Incidentally, I warned you about him, didn't I?"

No! . . . No!

Towards five he surfaced once more and remained awake. He chain-smoked despite a fierce thirst, the intimidation and the purpose of it as devastating as before, his mind back on the treadmill. He couldn't even begin to make a coherent assessment of what might be possible until Hartmann told him more. Disbelief was stone-dead. Yesterday's terror had hammered acceptance into him. He was being sent to murder someone.

Who? . . . How? . . .

In desperation he drove his thoughts elsewhere. Jerry Baxendale, Carol Nolan, Mrs. Ruddick, Roundwood, the Humber in the garage, Mill Avenue, Oatlands, the woman in the yellow dress with the pram . . . They had receded, yet always, always, they drew him back to Slattery and what had followed since and the monstrosity of what was still to come. He watched the new day beginning to fill the small, high window, wondering where Patrick was, thinking of him with terrible grief and guilt, thinking of Helen and the last time, other times, Karen, vainly trying not to be confronted with the question of how he could ever bring himself to kill in cold blood and what was promised if he failed.

His suitcase was in the cell, unopened. He was in his pants and shirt. For the fifth time within an hour he lit a cigarette. Presently he put his shoes and suit on, then either walked up and down or sat on the edge of the bunk, fretting for someone to come and take him back to Hartmann so that he could know all there was to know.

He was fed first—black bread, some mottled slices of cold sausage, the same sharp, gritty coffee. This was around seven-thirty. The man who brought the food didn't speak, either then or when he returned to take the tray away. Laker found his razor in the suitcase; plugged it into the socket below the window-chute, shaved, then sluiced his face in the bowl of water the man had brought when he removed the tray.

Another hour dragged by after that. Death and violence were commonplace when he had found it possible to kill. The whole world was at it then. But he had grown, learned to pity, acquired sentiment, softened. Jesus, how could he go about it now—even for Patrick's sake?

There were no more cigarettes. He put his head in his hands and stared at the floor, trembling.

Hartmann was seated behind his desk in the same attitude as when Laker had last seen him, for all the world as if he hadn't moved. It was just nine o'clock. A grey brick wall showed through the open blinds.

"Did you sleep well?" Hartmann asked with soft hoarseness.

"I slept."

"And so, I understand, did your son. That will be a relief to you, I'm sure." The taunting smile. "When did you last handle a gun, Mr. Laker?"

"What kind of a gun?"

"Any gun."

"In nineteen forty-five."

"Not since then?"

"No."

"You don't possess one—privately?"

"No."

"Then the first thing on this morning's agenda will be for you to get some practice. I told you, didn't I, that you would be assisted as much as possible?" He glanced at his watch. "However, there is a little time yet . . . I have no doubt you've given the proposition plenty of thought. Who wouldn't, in your shoes? So I ought to touch on something which must have crossed your mind." He paused briefly. "Rid yourself of any idea of approaching your Embassy in Copenhagen or telephoning your associates in London. Inevitably, they would take steps to see that the person in question is removed from harm's way. And that, in the circumstances, is precisely what you cannot afford to have happen. D'you follow? This is between you and me, Mr. Laker. Until everything is over you have no alternative but to keep it so."

"When will that be?" That Laker could even ask was the measure of the hold on him.

"By Saturday. The moment we have confirmation that you have successfully completed the assignment your son will be on a London-bound plane." Hartmann studied his finger-nails before glancing up. "It's an ugly business isn't it, Mr. Laker? Medieval one might say—without the medieval sanctity, that is."

Saturday ... Two days. Two days from now.

Hartmann went on: "We'll come to the person's identity presently—after you've practised at the gallery. But in case your imagination is running away with you, let me tell you now that I doubt if you will ever have heard of him. He isn't the Mayor of West Berlin, or the American Secretary of State, or the Secretary-General of the United Nations. The history books won't be interested." He glanced at his watch again, like a man who calculated every move. "What kind of marksman were you, by the way?"

With sudden dread Laker burst out: "Why me? Why've you picked on me?" All at once it had struck him that there might not be a loophole after all. Incredibly, everything was pointing to his doing exactly what Hartmann had planned. "You want a killer, an out-and-out killer ... a professional." His voice cracked. It was the nearest he came to abasing himself.

Hartmann stood up, smoothing his jacket. "You suit me very nicely, Mr. Laker. When the time comes I am certain we will find that you excel yourself."

They rode down in the elevator, as close as friends, as silent as strangers, then descended the flight of stone steps. An official on duty at the exit into the street saluted as Hartmann approached. A dark green saloon was drawn into the kerb. The official hurried out and opened the near-side door. Hartmann motioned to Laker to get in, then joined him, rounding the car and squeezing behind the wheel.

The street was narrow, one way. They swung into a crescent-shaped thoroughfare with tall buildings on one side and a railed enclosure on the other. Only yesterday, watching the flocks of pedestrians, Laker had presumed of their joylessness natures corrupted and made stone-hard by promises and exhortations; and pitied them. But now, as the car threaded through heavy bicycle traffic into the world of posters and statues and other bolsters of hope, a crushing envy filled him for the sheer drab normality of their lives. From nowhere, ringing in his mind as if it were an echo-chamber, he remembered the girl in The

Mitre laughing happily while he and Slattery sat together and he said: "You haven't raised any goose-flesh yet . . ."

Hartmann turned left and right, then left again. Laker glimpsed a string of lettered bunting forming the word TEXTIL and some coloured direction indicators, but the Fair and everything to do with it seemed utterly unreal. Except that they appeared to be leaving the city's centre he hadn't the least notion where they were. PEACE IS OUR PROFESSION a hoarding announced. Within five minutes they were crowded by warehouses and the gaunt shards of some derelict buildings. Soon afterwards Hartmann nosed into a cobbled street and brought the car to rest outside what looked as if it might have been a bowling-alley.

"We have numerous rifle clubs and galleries in the Democratic Republic, Mr. Laker. Shooting is a very popular activity —in the schools, among factory organisations." Hartmann spoke like a guide. "Mainly it is the responsibility of the Association for Sports and Technology, but this particular gallery is administered by the Leipzig Division of the State Security Service. I think you will find it more than adequately equipped."

They got out. The entrance was round a corner. Half a dozen steps led up to a reinforced glass door. Hartmann let them in with a key. A cloakroom led off the tiled lobby and there was also a door marked GUN-ROOM. The enclosed air had the stale tang of expended cordite.

Hartmann said: "Normally a caretaker would be here, but on Thursdays the gallery is closed. There are two ranges, one for recruits, one for those who are more advanced. It would be sensible—don't you agree?—to treat you as a beginner."

Laker didn't reply. It was all a nightmare.

"No stupidity, Mr. Laker. I'm armed, remember—though that isn't the real deterrent. You're a marionette already, as you surely know."

He opened the gun-room, selected two rifles from the racks and took some ammunition cartons from a drawer. Emerging, he pointed: "That way." Laker walked along a short passage which brought him to another door. "Go on through," Hartmann said, flicking some switches, and Laker found himself in the intense brightness of what looked to be about a twenty-five-yard range.

There were fibre mats for six firing-points on a low, planked dais. The walls were a light grey except for the far one, which was black, and this was spattered raw above the sand-bagged, boxed-in target area. The air's bite was very strong, catching the throat. The door padded behind Hartmann who went immediately to the control-panel and started extractor-fans humming. He placed one of the rifles and a carton of ammunition on the dais, returned to the panel, fiddled with it for a few moments, then raised a small, ringed target on the butt numbered 3.

"Get down on the mat and load. I've given you a Walther ·22. It's single shot and the magazine holds a clip of eight. The catch on the side releases the magazine." Hartmann moved round behind Laker. "One last thing. We aren't expecting the impossible of you in Copenhagen. Average ability will suffice and this is your chance to bring yourself up to that standard ... Now, take your time."

Laker made a deliberate botch of thumbing a clip home, muddled snapping in the magazine, then settled into position on the mat. Even after so long a time the rifle had an easy, natural feel, but he made a show of awkwardness. With what he believed was cunning he aimed interminably before snatching at the trigger. Nothing happened and he tried to look puzzled.

"Push the safety-catch forward."

He did so, aimed slightly off and fired. Sand spurted.

"Again."

Another miss, well wide.

"Again," Hartmann said tartly.

Laker missed six times in succession before Hartmann told him to stop.

"You aren't that incompetent."

"I am. And I always was."

"Try once more. Finish the clip."

The target remained untouched.

"What kind of idiot are you, Mr. Laker? Don't you value your son's life?"

"Not everyone can shoot," Laker gritted.

"All but the blind can do better than that. Get this into your head, once and for all. You've a job to do. In terms of skill required it won't be so difficult. And I've given you the best incentive I could think of."

"Why me?" Laker shouted once more. "Why not do your own filthy work?"

"A wise dog never fouls his own doorstep, Mr. Laker."

"What's that supposed to tell me?"

"You'll find out. Now—reload and try again."

Laker obeyed, anger filling him; helplessness. He took a sighting shot and squeezed the trigger, shutting his mind to thoughts of bone and muscle, flesh and blood. The electrical device above the target area recorded an inner at two o'clock.

"That's more like it," he heard Hartmann concede.

He fired again, cutting the black edge of the bull on approximately the same radial line.

"Good . . . Good."

With sudden contempt Laker emptied the magazine at speed, the crack of each shot punctuated by the trickle of ejected shell-cases on the floor beside him. Five clear bulls and one just clipping the line were recorded. He heard the hiss of Hartmann's indrawn breath.

"Good. *Very* good." For once there was neither threat nor mockery in the voice. Hartmann crossed to the control-panel and switched the extractors off. "You make a poor actor, Mr. Laker. How long is it since you used a rifle?"

"I told you."

"Twenty years?"

"I told you."

"It's hard to believe."

"I don't give a penny damn what you believe."

"Isn't it a relief to you that your son's future may not be so precariously balanced after all? It certainly is to me. Come—I want to see how you make out on the other range."

In size, colouring and layout the second range was a duplication of the first. They reached it through a pair of communicating steel doors. This time Laker was given the other rifle.

"It's a Russian weapon," Hartmann said. "It has recently been superseded as a standard infantry issue, but it will serve your purpose very well and approximates in calibre and velocity to the one you will use. Make yourself familiar with it for a few moments. Then at five-second intervals, I shall raise a selection of random targets."

Laker got down on the mat, legs splayed. He was shackled by a situation that was foul and crude and utterly compelling. Whatever chance there was of breaking free of it lay in the future, and the future was unmapped territory which his mind shrank from examining too closely lest he became convinced that it would offer nothing but the same hopeless subservience. He could not, dared not, think about it.

"Are you ready?"

He nodded, propped on his elbows, waiting, the catch off. Hartmann pressed a button on the control-panel and a small white pear-shaped metal cut-out sprang up to the right of the butt's centre. Laker fired and missed; nothing showed on the electric indicator-board. Hartmann grunted. The cut-out was already on its way down when Laker fired again, and this time he clipped it, taking Hartmann by surprise. Almost immediately another target appeared ten degrees or so to the left, identical but higher, wobbling on its arm. Laker scored a hit. The rifle was beautifully balanced, the recoil hardly noticeable. He missed the third cut-out, got the next, drew a blank on the indicator with the fifth, then put in two shots at the sixth, scoring both times, five seconds already seeming an over-generous exposure.

"Try again," Hartmann said. "Reload and be ready for a three-second interval only. And a different target order."

Laker scored seven hits. He was a born shot, relaxed, controlled, rock-steady, and he used the rifle now as if what remained of his pride depended on it. After he had emptied the magazine he loaded another and, on instructions, took the cut-outs from a standing position, Hartmann mixing both their order and the duration of exposure. When the last puff of dust erupted from the protective wall of sandbags a full eight hits had been registered.

Hartmann nodded approvingly. "Remarkable, Mr. Laker. Quite remarkable. I would say you are exceptional. Chance isn't always so obliging. It was a fortunate day for me when you decided to go to the Luisenstrasse." He smiled. "We have a saying; perhaps you know it? If you start with certainties you can end in doubts. But if you start with doubts, and are patient with them, you can end in certainties . . . I don't think we need continue with this, do you? The most useful place for both of us is back in my office."

They were there by ten-thirty. It had begun to seem to Laker that there had hardly been a time when he hadn't faced Hartmann and met or avoided the pale-blue stare, hardly a time when his mind hadn't hovered between dread and loathing and despair.

"Now," Hartmann said, lighting a cigarette. "About this person of ours in Copenhagen."

A thin stream of smoke flattened and spread as the desk deflected it. He withdrew a pink folder from the drawer in front of his stomach. Opening the folder he tossed a photograph towards Laker: it was about half-plate size.

"There," he said. "As I told you, the history books won't be interested. You won't achieve fame, Mr. Laker. It won't be like Dallas, Texas."

Laker picked the photograph up. A broad, heavily-jowled face confronted him. Bushy hair, thick eyebrows, nipped-in ears, bulbous nose with flared nostrils, large mouth with a slightly pendulous lower lip.

"Who is he?"

"Rudolf Frenzel."

The eyes looked more Slavic than German. And surprise was

112

in them, alarm, as if they had begun to flinch from the flash or even from the upward movement of the photographer's hands.

"If you were a student of the Democratic Republic's affairs, Mr. Laker, you would recall that Frenzel was once a member of the Politburo of the Socialist Unity Party. Four years ago he defected to the West. Until quite recently he hid himself away. But at last he has ventured out of his hole. He has become a sort of errand-boy—in which connection doesn't matter. What does is that tomorrow he visits Copenhagen."

"How d'you know?"

"We know," Hartmann said, and the manner of his saying it somehow reminded Laker of Slattery. "We know where he will have travelled from, the time of his arrival, the time of his departure. And we also know where he will be most exposed during his stay."

He seemed to think that Laker would ask him where this was, but Laker was staring at the photograph. "Did you hear me?" The tone was harsh again. "When you arrive in Copenhagen yourself you will realise that we have given you what help we could. Nothing can be perfect, of course, but fear can remove mountains, I assure you." He raised a finger as if he were at an auction. "The photograph, please."

It skidded across the desk and fell to the floor, but Hartmann didn't bother to retrieve it. Laker's expression seemed to gratify him.

"You will be supplied with another picture before you leave, more convenient for your pocket. It would be rash to rely too much on your memory. After all, when you are about to kill a man it is important to be certain you have picked the right one—isn't that so?" Hartmann opened the folder again and glanced at some typewritten notes. "Our friend has a reservation at the Metropol Hotel and my information is that he has been allocated room sixty-eight. When you are contacted in Copenhagen you will realise the significance of this."

"Contacted?"

"Your passport photograph has been copied and prints sent in advance. You'll be recognised, don't worry." He picked up the typewritten sheet and passed it over. "It would be better if you looked at this while I explain." He might have been discussing a sales campaign, a holiday schedule—anything; anything except the preliminaries to a murder.

Laker read:

Axel Bar, Tivoli. Thursday 20.30
Copenhagen-National, Sunderspladsen. Friday 10.00–15.00:
17.00–18.00
Metropol Hotel, Halmstergade. Friday 18.00–Saturday 14.00.

"This afternoon," Hartmann said, "you fly to Copenhagen via Schönefeld, Berlin. You will be there—in Copenhagen, that is—around seven. Contact will be made at the Axel Bar at eight-thirty tonight. Not only will you find that accommodation has been provided for you, but once you have taken your bearings you will discover also that it is directly across the street from where Frenzel will be staying. A narrow street—no wider than the range where you have so reluctantly demonstrated your skill."

He paused. He was talking about a real place, a real man. And Laker could not hold his gaze.

"Frenzel arrives tomorrow, on an S.A.S. flight from Paris, due at six in the evening. He leaves again next afternoon—on the Saturday. That means you will have a maximum of twenty hours, during a proportion of which he will be as close as I can bring him to you. Across a street, Mr. Laker, a narrow street. Third-floor window to third-floor window. His will be the one directly in front of yours. With a telescopic sight it will seem almost as if you are prodding him."

He paused again, stubbing his cigarette in the glass tray. "You see there is reference to Copenhagen-National."

"Yes."

"Copenhagen-National is a bank. We have rented a safe deposit for you in the name of George Marshall. In it a rifle is waiting to be collected. The rifle is in a special case and no one will raise an eyebrow. The fact is that you will be in no personal danger until the moment you decide to put an end to Rudolf

Frenzel's existence. Then, of course, your real difficulties will begin. But you can be down a fire-escape and on a bus or in a taxi within three minutes of pressing the trigger. It has been timed, Mr. Laker. We gave it what we call a dry run."

He kept using 'we', but as far as Laker was concerned there was no one but Hartmann. And every time Laker's mind moved he was there to block it.

"You can't afford to fail; I hope I have made that crystal clear. By three o'clock on Saturday afternoon, at the very latest, we will know whether you have succeeded or not, and I won't labour the consequences. We want Frenzel dead, Mr. Laker. Dead at all costs—even if it means jeopardizing your own chances of escape. If time begins to whittle down or there are other difficulties it may be that you will have to abandon the role of sniper and seek him out—cross the street, go to his room. These will be things for you to decide. But remember this—the Danish police are very efficient. The more you expose yourself the greater will be the risk of their laying hands on you. And—should that happen—I cannot warn you strongly enough not to open your mouth until you have been advised by your colleagues in London what to say. They will think of something, Mr. Laker. What is more, they will expect to be given the opportunity. Never forget that. They used you in the first place, after all. They will have something at stake too, remember."

A muscle was jumping in one side of Laker's face. "When will I see my son?"

Hartmann consulted the folder. "Assuming all goes well his plane will reach London at eleven o'clock on Saturday night. Incidentally, there is a letter for him here which you have to complete."

He pushed it across. It was typed, bore yesterday's date and was headed Leipzig Airport.

I'm terribly sorry. After I left you this afternoon I got caught up in some urgent business which has made it essential for me to travel to Copenhagen immediately. I tried to find you, but couldn't. The only thing I could do was to ask Mr. Rauter to keep an eye on you while I'm away and he has kindly agreed to do so. He suggests you ought to stay at his house rather than at the Astoria and this of course you will be doing before this hurried letter reaches you.

Expect to see you by Saturday at the latest. If I can't manage to rejoin you by then I have asked Mr. Rauter to put you on a flight to London that evening. Then we'll be able to start for the Rhineland and pick up the planned schedule. Once again I'm very, very sorry, but it couldn't be helped. Mr. Rauter will have explained.

Enjoy yourself meanwhile. I've had to dictate this, by the way.

"Who is Rauter?"

"A family man. He has a pleasant apartment, a homely wife, two children of his own. As long as your mission is successful I can promise you that your son will have nothing but happy memories of his time in Leipzig." Hartmann gestured. "Sign the letter, Mr. Laker. We've done our best not to alarm him, and you of all people should approve of that. Sign it, then listen."

Laker fumbled for his pen. *Dear Patrick,* he wrote; then, *Your affectionate father* and his initials.

"Listen," Hartmann said. "Your own flight is at 14.40. Your passport is in order. You will be provided with ample funds. Before you leave Leipzig you will have memorised the details on that piece of paper—the Axel Bar and so on. Above all you will have memorised the deadline."

He waited, watching, always watching.

Laker ran his hands over his face. A full minute must have elapsed. Faintly, from the street below a horn blared like a cry of pain. He felt stunted, smashed. Mercy was what men wanted most; quarter. And Hartmann was able to offer it—at a price.

"If I do this —"

"Yes?"

"What can you promise for Karen Gisevius?"

"Who?"

"Karen Gisevius."

Hartmann leaned forward, one eyebrow raised. "Why should she interest you?"

"I know her."

"Naturally."

Laker shook his head. "During the war. I worked with her. I haven't seen her since. Until the other day I thought she must be dead. She . . . She was . . ." And suddenly he couldn't go on. All he could do was to stare and see Hartmann slowly dissolve, solidify.

Through a blur, as if from a long way off, he heard: "You have enough to worry about."

"What will happen to her?"

"Does it matter?"

"Yes. *Yes.*"

"Then I am sorry for you."

Once before Hartmann had come to an abrupt decision with himself, and so it was again. He pressed the buzzer on the desk and rose.

"That's all, Mr. Laker. Go and memorise those Copenhagen details. In—what?—something over three hours your plane will be leaving. On it there are likely to be businessmen. But not one of them, I assure you, will be *en route* for home with a contract more binding than yours."

9

LEIPZIG AIRPORT sank below. Soon it was smothered by clouds—the ragged fringes of the city, too; everything.

Laker pressed back in his seat. The last thing Hartmann had said was: "There's no way out, Mr. Laker. Racking your brains won't help. The longer you live with the situation the more you will realise that you have to go through with it to the end. One word to anyone—*anyone*—and you know what that will mean. We have our reasons for wanting Frenzel killed just as you have reasons for making sure that he is. Until then this is between you and me. Always remember that. You and I have become partners." And in the shadows of Laker's mind his narrow face presented itself, half-smiling, eager for drama, looking for it with eyes for the most part empty of anything except a cold, lonely light.

The twin-engined aircraft was about three-quarters full but mercifully the seat beside Laker was vacant. He couldn't have coped with a stranger intent on trivialities about the Fair. He had clung to the hope that once he got away he would somehow be able to detach himself from the dementia of the past twenty-four hours, continuing to cling to it long after he knew in his heart that freedom would alter nothing, clinging to it even now when doing so was no more than an act of despair. Hartmann held the strings. Distance was irrelevant. He had two days in which to go about Patrick's salvation, two days in which the memory of yesterday's terror in the pines was to goad him into becoming an instrument of vengeance.

He shook his head. Things like this happened to others; never to you and yours.

Behind his back someone was saying in a flat, Midlands' brogue: "I found 'em charming. Couldn't have been friendlier. It's dreary there, God knows, but they're all right. If you ask me there's a damned sight too much drivel talked about the Curtain and all that. I'm not denying it's a fact, any more than I'm saying there isn't a flaming great wall across Berlin. But what I *am* saying is that the whole political thing doesn't make the sense it once did . . ." The knowing voice insisted through the engines' roar. "The tension's easing all the time. We aren't at each other's throats any longer. If we imagine we are it's largely the fault of the Press and the television people. They need news, that lot, so they balloon every trivial little incident in the hope it'll burst and make a bang. That's my view, and I've been here twice now. Seeing's believing after all . . ."

Laker opened his eyes and fixed them blankly on the empty

sky. Patrick, fresh from some junior book of instant knowledge, had once said: "People think the sky's blue, but it isn't, not really—did you know that, dad? When you get beyond a certain point it's black, pitch black."

It seemed fantastic that he should be scared to make a move when he was within arm's length of people who could pass a message for him. Inaction seemed a crime, yet it was part of the measure of reality. He was even nervous of being spoken to; when the stewardess offered him coffee he was brusque and dismissive, as if he were under surveillance from somewhere in the rear.

He thought of Frenzel, Frenzel with his hours already counted. Frenzel was the lynch-pin. Warn him, spare him, fail to get him—and Patrick paid; those were the equations. "An outcry, Mr. Laker? Oh no. You and your son have ceased to be public property. You should have asked more questions than you did before you so casually set out for Leipzig ... And another thing. We'll want proof about Frenzel. Nothing short of a 22-carat job will do, and we have means of telling whether you will have undertaken it honestly or not . . . I'll know, Mr. Laker."

He was in quicksands, trapped. And if he struggled or called for help they would close over Patrick's head, not his. The more he strained his mind the more scared he found himself, the more crammed with useless hatred. And, deep down, he was aware that if the nightmare persisted, if he lived it through in puppet-like obedience, self-disgust would be the final horror.

The man behind was still ploughing on: "East Germany's all right. And it's got a tremendous market potential if only the British Government would take its finger out over the recognition business. The people I met were touchy about that, and no wonder. Still, I got nothing but courtesy wherever I went, and I'm damned certain no one comes to any harm nowadays unless they deliberately go looking for it . . ."

Laker stared at the sky's immaculate blue, lost in bitterness and abandonment.

*   *   *

It was a short flight to Schönefeld; forty minutes. They were down punctually at three-twenty, down through the clouds, and everything was grey again. The accents were different, but the uniforms were the same.

There were almost three hours to wait for the Copenhagen connection and to Laker they seemed interminable. He sat in the peeling transit-lounge along with a score of people, men mostly, some of them bleary from lunch and liquor who sprawled on the couches and dozed. Every half-hour or so a cafeteria trolley was wheeled round. On and off he paced the floor, submerged within himself. If he didn't contact London he felt he would go mad before the next forty-eight hours were over. But he seemed to have lost any capacity for trust, in Slattery most of all. Slattery had bungled where Karen was concerned, miscalculated—and he might again. By comparison with Hartmann he now seemed a child, an amateur, a dabbler; but there was nobody else to bring pressure to bear. He might have strings of his own . . . *Might*.

And Hartmann was there at once to push the pendulum the other way—"One word to London and, inevitably, Frenzel will go back into his hole. You can't afford to have that happen."

Laker's throat burned from incessant smoking. He couldn't remain still for long. Sometimes when he glanced at his watch he thought it must have stopped. The new strap, the wad of Kroner in his pocket, the safe-deposit key, the deckled edges of the photograph he dared not look at—there was no refuge. Tides of panic ebbed and flowed as his thoughts swung between Slattery and Hartmann. Slattery would have no choice but to act, and act quickly. Patrick was his responsibility. Or was the situation so insane that he would be forced to yield to Hartmann's stranglehold himself?

One moment such a thing seemed inconceivable, the next a terrifying probability. Hartmann had been so sure, so cast-iron sure, as if he knew exactly how far London would be prepared to go. "There are unwritten rules in this business, Mr. Laker. And one of them is to be wary of having your own dirty washing blown into the scandalised face of the world. London, believe me, has more than a fair share on its hands and they will guard it more jealously than you would think possible. They'll muzzle you when the time comes—quite shamelessly if their treatment of Mr. Wyatt's unfortunate widow is anything to go by. Meanwhile, Frenzel is valuable to them and they won't willingly allow him to be obliterated. London, I suggest, would only confuse you. So keep away from your Embassy, Mr. Laker. And don't ring anyone—I'd take it as a sign of weakness, d'you see?"

But he would. He must.

And yet . . .

The Copenhagen flight was called at ten to six. Along with thirty or so others Laker trailed across the oil-slicked hard to a turbo-prop Ilyushin. With the resignation of the powerless he belted himself in and gazed out at the red-black-and-gold flags fluttering lazily along the rim of the airport buildings. The nightmare had been many things already; now, once more, it took the form of finding himself surrounded by people whose lives were wholly normal.

He wanted to shout at them, to protest, to shake their smugness, their boredom, to confide. Above all, to confide. There were files in London, he wanted them to understand, in which the names of every one of them armed with a British passport were automatically recorded once they ventured to this side of the Curtain. And there were men like Slattery who would use them if time and opportunity provided a need and they were fools enough to acquiesce. And there were men like Hartmann who could manipulate them to such a degree and with such cold certainty that they could find themselves inhabiting the same world as everyone else yet secretly terrorised, unable to cry out, committed to something that, only hours before, they would have considered utterly impossible.

With a whining crescendo the Ilyushin lifted off, graceful and buoyant, the violence of the noise and the feeling of thrust diminishing. Second by second the horizons widened. Berlin tilted like a display model beyond the port wing and every head turned. Then the clouds intervened and spread below like crusted pack-ice.

The thick-set crew-cut man beside Laker was galloping through a Swedish translation of Fleming's *Casino Royale*. Laker shut his eyes. Hartmann's stare and throttled voice, the sound of Karen's sobbing as she was taken from the hut, Patrick's parting grin as he left him, the ghastly stutter muffled by the paper bag, Slattery's bland elusiveness, Frenzel, Rudolf Frenzel—all were there again to torment and tear at his mind and his heart together with the remembered feel of the rifles and the smell of cordite in the shooting-gallery and the prospect of a strange city and a rendezvous at the Axel Bar at eight-thirty. And then ...

The palms of his hands were unnaturally moist. Twice he lit a cigarette only to stub it out after a few nervous draws. The man in the next seat smiled and turned yet another escapist page. Time passed. Coffee was served again, but Laker ordered a cognac and drained his glass in a single gulp. After a longish while he heard someone say, "Rostock, I reckon." Peering down he saw an amoeba-like sepia smudge at the centre of a radiation of lines and scratches and the apparently motionless sea pressed against the map of the coastline. "Having capitalist time, wish you were here"—Patrick's joke echoed brutally. Then Slattery claimed priority: "Since May last year he's been in touch with an address in Rostock: Lenin-Strasse 32, to be precise"—Slattery who knew so much, so bloody much, Slattery of the homily about the bumble-bee, of the time before and after the Gardelegen débâcle, Slattery of The Mitre and the room in Manchester Square and the talk of helping out—"No risk, old boy. Absolutely none . . ."

Never-do-it-yourself-Slattery. What match was he for Hartmann? As an ally he'd diminished, yet who else was there?

The Ilyushin made short work of the Baltic. Copenhagen was under them several minutes before the scheduled seven o'clock. The tanned young Customs officer who eventually dealt with Laker said, "Holiday or business?" as a brisk preliminary to letting him go and Laker answered, "Business", at the mercy even of a chance word.

He slumped in the coach that would take him to the terminal. A B.E.A. Trident screamed in while they waited for the coach to fill and the sight of it made London seem closer suddenly: attainable. Why delay? There were telephones in the Arrivals building . . . The pendulum started swinging again. But he was suspicious of freedom, suspicious of everyone in the immediate vicinity. Wait. Lose everyone first. Wait until they all reached town; scattered. And then . . . Should he? Christ, should he? The power of decision was draining out of him.

Anxiously, as the coach began to roll, he glanced at his watch: seven-twenty. "How far's the terminal?" he asked a stout woman beside him. Fifteen minutes . . . There'd be time enough to call London—yet what if Slattery made another balls of everything? And he could. One rash move, one hasty indiscretion, and Hartmann would complete the equation. But would Slattery believe that? Could he make him understand— quickly, and on a public line—how desperate the balance truly was? . . . Panic renewed itself the nearer he came to chancing it. If he didn't, now or later, there was only one alternative.

Copenhagen's outskirts scarcely made a mark on his mind. A bridge and the evening glint of water, some laden coal barges— not much else registered. A man near by remarked as if he'd seen an old friend: "There's the Europa"—but Laker didn't even look. He stared straight ahead, rehearsing what he would say, compressing it, trying to keep Hartmann's threats at bay. "Listen, Slattery. They were waiting for me. Kromadecka's was blown before I got there. They picked all three of us up— Karen, Patrick and me. I'm in Copenhagen now and this is why, this is what's happened . . ."

The light was still good. He noticed trees; a verdigris-covered spire. Some of the passengers were already getting to their feet. Two minutes after the half-hour . . . The coach turned right and veered towards the kerb. "Is this it?" somebody asked as movement ended. Laker took his turn at the door. Neon blinked and cascaded palely around a large square. He collected his suitcase then walked away, anywhere, anywhere, it didn't matter. Several times he glanced back, but singled no one out. He left the square and crossed a street, passed through an arcade, then turned left, mingling, one of many, moving faster than most though not conspicuously so.

After a few minutes he paused in a shop doorway; there was a post office opposite with telephone booths flanking the entrance. Several people passed, one with a brown dog on a lead, and the dog sniffed at his ankles. But there was no other interest taken in him, nobody loitering to keep their distance. He delayed for some cars to go by, then went over to the post office, certain he wasn't followed. Inside at the counter, he asked the cost of a call to London. The clerk, who spoke English, changed two 100-Kroner notes for him. There were booths along the facing wall but the clerk said: "We close at eight. I suggest you use those in the street. You may have some delay on a call like that."

Laker nodded and went outside. One of the booths was occupied. He stepped into the vacant one, put his suitcase down and studied the English version of the procedure instructions. The booth was glassed on three sides. He looked all round; no one watched or waited, yet the back of his neck prickled. A moment's hesitation, then he dialled.

"I want to make a person-to-person call to London . . . London, England, yes . . ."

A click and a different voice, slightly sing-song, very precise. He gave the Gerrard number, repeating it twice, touched by a sudden alarm that Slattery might not be there at such an hour.

"Is there a delay?"

"I don't think so. There wasn't half an hour ago. What is your number, please?"

Laker read it out.

"Have you the right money?" The girl quoted the tariff.

"Yes."

"What is the name of the person to whom you wish to speak?"

Laker ran a hand through his hair. "Look," he said urgently, "I don't want it person-to-person, after all. I want a straight call on the Gerrard number."

"Not person-to-person?"

"No."

His alarm grew. Say no one was there? Suddenly everything had narrowed down to this. All he could remember was that Slattery lived in Kew.

"Hold the line, please."

He straightened, moving his feet. Turning slightly he glanced out. A short, hatless man was leaning against the post-office wall, reading a newspaper. For a second or two Laker had no qualms. Come on, he urged, as the wire crackled. Come *on* . . . Then he realised that the man was looking at him over the top of the page.

A tentacle of suspicion fastened around Laker's heart. He tried to drag his eyes away, but couldn't. For what seemed an impossible length of time he stared back. Then the man lowered the newspaper, making no bones about his purpose, and with a chilling stab of dismay Laker recognised him. He had been on the plane from Leipzig, in the transit-lounge at Schönefeld, on the Ilyushin. In the toilets at Schönefeld they'd been alone, just the two of them, shoulders almost touching . . . Suddenly Laker was certain. His brain seemed to stall as the man prolonged the blatant warning, pushing away from the wall and moving nearer.

"Have your money ready, please. I will have London for you in a few mo—"

Laker's nerve broke then. He slammed the receiver down, grabbed his suitcase and backed out of the booth. And he ran— as if something were yapping at his heels. Only when he found himself in the square where the coach had deposited him did he slow to a walk. He rested against a lamp-standard, sucking in air. Despite the fading light he attracted attention: somebody stopped and spoke to him, hand on arm. Laker shook his head and walked on, frightened still, very frightened. Leipzig was three hundred miles away, behind the Curtain. But he wasn't free, he couldn't choose. Hartmann had as good as twitched the strings to prove it.

The dark was coming. Blocks of light fell from expanses of plate-glass window and the pulsing neon took a more gaudy hold. It was five past eight and his legs ached. Someone was still on his tail; he could sense it. He hadn't tried to lose himself again. Sick in the stomach he had stayed with the crowds; conformed. "Don't allow Copenhagen to affect your judgement, Mr. Laker . . ." Hartmann kept pace with him like a second shadow, Hartmann whose mind was sharp with years of suspicion and who wielded the power of life and death. "I'll know if it does, you see. I'll know for sure."

Near a bicycle-park Laker hailed a cruising taxi. "Axel?" the driver queried. "Tivoli?"

It was only a short ride. He was put down at one of the entrances to the Gardens. The driver tried to explain something, pointing, but the Danish defeated Laker. He went to the arched gateway where he spoke to an attendant. "Axel Bar?" he asked uncertainly and was rewarded with a nod. He paid to pass through the turnstile. There was a restaurant immediately to his right, the Wivex, and he heard the throb of music. Pustules of coloured lights bordered a choice of paths between avenues of brilliantly-lighted trees. A direction-arrow showed him which to take. Couples strolled hand in hand under the faery glow, animated, dreaming, the world shut out for a while. Presently he passed an open-air stage where a clown was performing on a trampoline before a seated audience. Some scattered applause startled him, reminding him that he was different from everybody in this place, from everybody in Copenhagen, and again he felt the swift breeze of fear in his belly.

Lugging his suitcase he walked perhaps another hundred yards before he saw AXEL in electric blue on the fascia of a small, low building. As he approached he wondered if the same man would again disclose himself. Some of the tables were alfresco, spaced about a hedged enclosure, and others were roofed over behind a glass screen. He chose not to go inside. A waitress with a pink beret came for his order. He didn't want anything but he asked for a beer. Then he lit a cigarette, apprehensive, heedless of the sauntering passers-by, suspecting that his contact was already present.

A military band played in the tinted distance. He sat alone with the suitcase beside him, fingering the chequer-board cloth. Again and again he checked his watch. Eight-thirty . . . Eight-thirty-two . . . Eight-thirty-five . . . No one yet. But there would be. Someone was waiting to show him where his room was, biding his time before closing in. There was beginning to be a dreadful inevitability about everything now.

"Can you manage a light?"

It was a girl's voice, the accent transatlantic. Laker jerked round, taken off-guard. Unknown to him she had seated herself at his table.

"A light?" she said.

Dark eyes, dark hair, white teeth, a mouth redder than blood—his glance was cursory. He nodded and fumbled in his pocket. She looked like a tart. As the flame spurted he held it to her cigarette and she steadied his hands, fingers touching his. Fawn coat, collar up.

"Thanks."

The smoke swirled. He was turning his back on her.

"The picture didn't do you justice."

He frowned.

"You were very punctual, I'll say that."

Now he stared, pulse quickening. "Aren't you making a mistake?"

"Hardly." She smiled. "Shall we go? I don't want a drink."

He didn't move.

"It isn't far. And it's getting chilly here." She smiled again. "Yes?" she prompted.

He emptied his glass. They rose together. As they moved away under the lights she said: "Tivoli closes next week for the winter, did you know?" But she was talking to someone who wasn't altogether listening.

10

WHEN they reached the exit by the Wivex he asked if they needed a taxi, but she said they didn't. It was the only time he spoke to her on the way. They walked for about five minutes, her heels clacking briskly as she strutted by his side. Familiar names occasionally showed amid the indecipherable welter— PETER O'TOOLE . . . CARLSBERG . . . ELIZABETH ARDEN . . . SHELL—but to Laker they seemed to belong to some other stage of his existence.

They turned a couple of corners; crossed a tram-clanking street. The crowds thinned out; soon they were almost alone. They were passing a line of shops when the girl stopped by a door next to a delicatessen.

"Here we are."

Opposite were more shops with five or six rows of windows above. Laker glanced at them quickly before following her in. There was a small hallway with stairs leading up. She went first, slim calves level with his face. On the first landing she said: "Are you fit? There are two more yet," and again there was that smile. Already Laker was confused. He had expected an anonymously-rented room, bare perhaps, and then to be left alone—watched and followed only when he went out. But he was wrong. On the second landing he suspected it, on the third he was sure. He wasn't to be trusted for a minute.

Even so he asked: "D'you live here?"

"Of course."

She let him in, surprise in her tone. He found himself in a comfortably-furnished bed-sitter. Doors opened off to either side of a curtained window. Quilted double divan, a radio, some framed photographs, a square table with some bottles on it, a couple of deep, soft chairs—these were among his first impressions.

She tossed her coat on to the divan and bent to plug in an electric fire. A wild doubt took Laker to the window. He pulled back the curtains.

"Where's that place?"

"Across there?"

"Yes."

"The hotel, d'you mean?"

"What's it called?"

"The Metropol."

He turned, the enslaved part of his mind bewildered, unable to grasp that these terrible hours were to be shared. There had been no mention of it in Leipzig.

He said: "Are you here all the time?"

"Of course," she said again. "Where else?" And then she said: "My name's Anna. What's yours?"

He didn't answer.

"Knowing it will make things easier."

"David."

David would do. In one respect he'd been right about her. Men came here in search of an hour's safety, an hour's trust, release, a breath of comfort. But Laker had forgotten what desire was. He studied the room again, his thoughts racing a full round of the clock ahead, entering a new dimension of uncertainty.

"Are you tired? You look tired. There's Scotch if you want it." She chuckled softly, kicking off her shoes. "It's all paid for. Everything is—so make yourself at home. Everything's paid for the two days—so that's out of the way."

"Who paid?" He was cautious.

Again she seemed surprised. "I could describe him."

"When?"

"This morning."

He poured a whisky. There was no sign of a telephone.

"Where do those doors go?"

"Bathroom there. Kitchen there." Sitting on the divan she watched him check. Her lips curled. "Why not look under here as well?"

129

He shrugged. He felt caged.

"Are you English?"

He hesitated, unsure to what extent he was bound, not knowing whether to lie, how much would be reported back, what mattered and what did not. Hartmann had left such details in the air.

"Well, are you?"

"Yes, I'm English." Then, probing once more: "What about you?"

"Oh, I'm a local girl."

"Not German?" She could have been. The transatlantic veneer camouflaged another, more basic, accent.

"No."

She laughed, tossing her hair, and the laughter mystified him. She seemed so at ease, so indifferent to why he had come. Yet the Metropol was across the street and tomorrow he was expected to bring a rifle here; kill from here. She knew that, she must know that . . . He pulled the curtains aside once more, peering at the window directly opposite. It was in darkness, but several others were lit and in one of them, a floor down, he could see a maid turning back the bed-covers. She was close, all right; against his will the fact registered.

"When are you going to relax?"

He swung round, facing the unfamiliar room. The girl was putting a match to a cigarette. As if for the first time he noticed that she was wearing a green skirt and a white, frilled blouse. Twenty-five or -six; it was hard to tell. She proffered the pack.

"D'you want one?"

He shook his head.

Her eyes lacked something; the mouth, too. Whore's eyes, hard yet friendly, bold yet cautious, never quite certain. "What's your work?"

"Office work."

"In England?"

He avoided answering. He drank, haunted by others, further confused, wishing he were alone. He hadn't reckoned on this. Nothing was constant except the guarantee of climax.

Desperation could drive him in search of another telephone; he could even take a plane to London—somewhere, sometime, he'd already considered that. Yet what would Slattery *do*? What *could* he do? . . . That was the ultimate uncertainty. Hartmann had been in no doubt, and he believed Hartmann; the clearing in the pines and the bag over his head encouraged him in whom to believe. "A joke, Mr. Laker? A dream? . . ." Neither; Jesus, no. Something filthy instead, filthy and cowardly and merciless. Something he didn't know the half of, yet which had him by the throat whichever way he turned.

"Have you eaten?"

"I'm not hungry."

"It's no trouble to fix something. *Smørrebrød*, say? Yes? . . . I'm going to the kitchen anyway."

"All right."

He was curt. She was linked with Hartmann, paid by Hartmann, and that was enough to stoke what he felt. He went to the window for the third time, thinking distractedly. No one, as far as he could tell, stood in a doorway or in the bars of shadow between the shops on the other side of the street, but he was past being deceived or deceiving himself. They had warned him off Slattery once and the moment he left this room they'd be told; she would see to that.

He poured another whisky, numbing a little of the crisis within him and the stark chill of many fears. He moved nearer the fire. A tear-off calendar on the wall carried a thought for the day, attributed to Ibsen: '*I*' *is the capital city of the underworld in which all things happen to us.* Close by there was a coloured print of the Matterhorn framed in black passe-partout, and over the divan a beach-scene with the girl in a bikini waving at the photographer: *Klampenborg, August* was scrawled in ink across one corner.

She was singing quietly in the kitchen. They would have made plans for her; there was no other answer. For him there was a fire-escape—off the landing, probably: three minutes to a bus or a taxi . . . He remembered everything, every word. They'd done a dry run, timed it. So she was aware of what was to happen—and she would hardly wait to be a witness. She would go while the going was good, before a light showed where it mattered across the way, before six tomorrow evening when Frenzel was due. Surely . . . .

His thoughts jerked on and on. Yet she lived here; it was a home. Clean, cared-for. His eyes travelled over the pictures again, the furniture, the strewn magazines, the bright dressing-table with its glass top, the amassed trivia, the long mirror facing the divan . . . Would she abandon it all? He was mysti-fied still—and frightened simultaneously that he should be thinking this way, weighing only this, as if he knew in his heart of hearts that for him there might be no option.

"Switch on the radio, will you?"

The whisky in him obeyed. He went to the table and poured another glass, then sat down, staring at the coiled red bar of the fire. Presently he took out his wallet and extracted the picture of Frenzel, studying the startled eyes, the flared nostrils shad-owed by the flash. "One of those for whom the world will never be safe, Mr. Laker. And it shows, don't you see?"

"There," the girl said, emerging with a tray. "Was I long?"

He shoved the photograph away like someone found out. She set the tray down on the table which she then drew closer to the chairs and the fire.

"I made coffee," she said. "Okay?"

Her face was conventionally attractive, well-boned, a fringe of dark hair low on her forehead, her skin ivory smooth. The eyes were green, he saw now, not black as he'd supposed them to be under the Tivoli lighting. He tossed back some more whisky, feeling its dull glow. She reduced the radio's volume to a background throb, then settled into the other chair, legs curled up.

"Better?" Smiling, she took a plate from the tray.

"Better?" he countered.

"When you came in you were wound up like a spring." She held herself stiffly. "Like that—you were, you know."

She baffled him. What she had brought him there to do would incriminate her if he went through with it. Unless he could wriggle free, devise something—either in conjunction with Slattery or alone—she was involved up to her slim white neck. Yet she was there to prevent him from doing just that, a jailer, ready to report on his comings and goings.

He said: "How long have you lived here?"

"A couple of years."

"D'you rent it?"

"Uh-huh." She was eating.

"So everything in the place is yours?"

"Except the bath and the wallpaper. D'you want a bath, by the way? The water's hot."

He shook his head.

"Aren't you going to eat?"

There was ham garnished with lettuce and shrimps on light rye bread. He munched without really tasting anything. He was beginning to feel so weary that everything was muted—the play on his nerves, the gnawing sense of dread, the mental confusion. She didn't look like a fanatic or someone on the eve of drama. She looked slim and young and unconcerned and well content. This was where the abandoned rifle would be found, but she didn't seem to care. He couldn't fathom her; couldn't think properly.

She sipped her coffee. "Tell me about yourself."

He was silent.

"You're quite a way from home."

Oh God, he thought, caught on a backwash of panic.

"Don't tell me nothing interesting has ever happened to you. Interesting things only seem to happen to interesting people, and you're interesting. Very."

The sensation of madness seemed to touch him again. He rose from the chair and went to the whisky bottle. She more than most would know what it was to receive confidences: men must have fed her with them, unloading their complaints, their failures, sure of sympathy, buying that too. Yet he dared not speak about Frenzel. Hartmann's warnings to stay mute couldn't apply where she was concerned; she'd already been bought—with one specific thing in view. So why not have it in the open? There was so little time. But he could not. He had doubts about her, and they were growing. Once, when a back-fire in the street made him start, she chuckled: "Easy. You've too much imagination. This is a quiet neighbourhood." Right or wrong he was ready to consider that she didn't know about Frenzel after all. Somewhere in the tired depths of his mind he was finding reasons to believe that she might have been lied to, misled. For all he knew she had been deceived about him and would be sacrificed when the time came. It was possible. Nothing about her was clear-cut any longer except the certainty that she expected him to share the divan, make love, sleep, wake and perhaps make love again when morning came. It was part of his right, paid for, but he was far from sure to what extent she had sold herself. Yet precisely because she had made the Axel rendezvous and had brought him to where Hartmann had promised it was dangerous to assume too much. Either way he couldn't trust her, couldn't ask whether there was a tele-phone in the building, couldn't chance the offer of a bribe or think of pleading.

The whisky spun his brain. If he broached the truth and dis-covered that she was, in fact, ignorant of it, disaster could ensue. She would turn him out, call the police, warn the Metropol—any or all of these. When he thought of her as someone tricked and used like himself he read into her a capa-city for horror and instant action. Frenzel would survive, but there would be another victim; Hartmann had left him with the certainty of that and it governed him.

Some of the time he matched her small-talk, sometimes not. She seemed to fence when he questioned her obliquely as to what she knew, yet she warmed to him with explorations of her own as if anxious—and grateful—to be spared for once some hasty, wolfish stranger. She laughed frequently, juggling almost coyly with words and meanings, but her eyes, her ges-tures, made it plain that she would ease his nerves, deaden whatever tortured his mind, whenever he wanted.

Eventually she turned off the radio. Laker put down his glass, seeing nothing, never so alone. And weary beyond words, exhausted by everything the endless day had done to him. He gazed at the ceiling as if he were suffocating. Tomorrow he would think again, balance everything, think and decide which gamble to take, with her, with Slattery.

"Have a bath and freshen up." She was calling him "David" now. She came to where he sat and knelt in front of him. "Yes?"

He shook his head. It had gone ten-thirty: when he glanced at his watch the new strap claimed his thoughts, dragging them back through the nightmare's web.

"Bed, then?"

He shrugged. She took his hand, leaning closer, smiling, enjoying the unaccustomed luxury of play.

"There's nothing like it."

He got up again, abruptly. She watched him confidently. He drank another whisky, as if he were in a hurry, then went to the bathroom. His reflection greeted him in the wall-mirror and he stared at it as if amazed by the sanity of his appearance. He washed his hands and face, then returned to the room. All the lights were out except the one beside the divan. Without surprise he saw that the girl was wearing only pants and brassière and he remembered thinking how full her black-cupped breasts were. But he felt nothing, not even when she released the brassière, turning expectantly as she did so. Nothing. He took off his jacket and slung it on a hook on the kitchen door, then pulled the two soft chairs together.

"What are you doing?"

He didn't answer.

"David!" She made it a complaint.

"I'm sorry," he said.

She came towards him, silhouetted. "Don't joke."

"I'm not."

"Nonsense." A little laugh. "Nonsense."

"I mean it." He punched the cushions. "I'm sorry, but there it is."

For a moment he was prepared for an outburst, but it didn't come. For what seemed a long time as he softened the cushions

135

he was aware of her standing close, aware of a tiny part of him numbly crying for comfort and escape, aware of her lips parted in astonishment.

"Truly?"

Then she knew it was truly.

"Are you married?"

"No."

"Why, then?"

He shook his head and started unknotting his tie, still expecting anger, scorn—he wasn't sure what it would be. But, instead, her mouth twisted.

"Well, that's the first time ever. I'd like you to know that— the first time ever."

She went to the divan, pulled back the covers and tossed a blanket at him before flouncing between the sheets, indignation in the violence of her movements. But she said nothing more. Laker heeled off his shoes, got out of his trousers, then fitted himself on to the chairs and covered himself over.

The girl switched off the light almost at once. The sodium-white blur of the street-lamps softly filled the room through the curtains. And Laker lay heavily on his side, huddled as if in protection against the coming day of obligation.

Karen whispered: 'Sammy? . . . Sammy? . . .' She was clinging to him in the hollow and the cold was like death. Even in the shadow-play of the dream he knew that the memory would brand him throughout his lifetime; that heart-break would come of this. "When will it be normal for us, Sammy?" He held her tight, close, their breath like ghosts, her face pinched and freckled, her eyes burning with the onset of fever. "We'll have to go," he said. "We'll have to work west. It's no good waiting. They've given us up. We're no use to them any more." She was coughing already. "You know best, Sammy." He gazed down at her, moved, frightened for her. She'd never make it. There were planes droning in the sky. "Now?" she asked. "Right away?" But he shook his head. "When it's dark."

The picture fragmented. For a while he seemed to be no-where, floating, not cold. He felt his body heave. He heard the crack of his carbine and saw a helmeted figure double up, saw another opening the lid of the stranded tank, aimed quickly, fired and ran. Then he was floating again, aware of the stench of decay, of destruction. And Slattery was saying: "And then, Sam? What happened then?"—Slattery blinking across the desk in the Grosvenor Gardens office, tapping his teeth with a silver pencil. "How many did you get, Sam?"

Then everything was changing once more, dissolving, focus-ing anew. "A favour, old boy, that's all. Nothing to it. I wouldn't be asking you otherwise . . ." In a voice that didn't sound like his own he heard himself answer: "I couldn't do it. I couldn't. Besides, Patrick will be with me." Slattery beamed: "Do what?" There were stars now, darkness, a child wailing. "Kill anyone. That's what you're asking, isn't it?" Slattery had vanished, though Laker could still hear him—"You did once, so why not again?" He began to shout back: "I had a reason, the only reason. I hated them then. *You have to hate*." And all at once it wasn't Slattery any more, but Hartmann, Hartmann with his head tilted, saying: "Either that or you need an incen-tive, Mr. Laker. And I've seen to it that you've been given the best there is."

The dream went out of him with a rush. He was mumbling, grinding his teeth. It was night and he knew where he was, remembering the room, the girl, the reasons why—everyone, everything.

"What is it?"

He grunted, twisting on the chairs.

"What's the matter?"

The lamp clicked on and he squeezed his lids together. He could smell her scent, the room's stuffiness. Gradually his eyes took the brunt of the light. Sitting up, she was holding the sheet across herself, alarm making her seem prudish.

"Were you dreaming?"

"Time." He licked his lips. He was in a sweat. "What's the time?"

"You scared me."

"Huh?"

"You were saying things. Shouting."

"What?"

"Names."

"What names?"

"Frankel."

He stared.

"Frankel, Frenzel—something like that."

"Frenzel?" he said thickly.

"Yes."

He paused, then tried it. "Who's Frenzel?"

"God knows. It was your dream." She frowned. "Are you in some kind of trouble?"

"Is that what you were told?"

She shook her head. "I'm guessing."

"What *were* you told?"

"That you wanted a girl."

"Just that?"

"Just that. I must have got the story wrong, though." The hurt was still there. She gazed at him for several seconds without speaking. "Is it bad? Something bad?"

He lay back. So she didn't know. That at least was clear. He believed her. His briefing had been incomplete. Hartmann hadn't warned him she would be a stumbling-block.

"I thought you were in town for some kind of conference."

"That's right," he lied.

But she wasn't satisfied. "What is it, then?" she said after a pause.

"Nothing."

"You sounded terrified. And now you look like death. And when you first came in tonight you were—"

"It was a dream," he said.

He wiped the sweat from his face, suddenly afraid that she might not be prepared to harbour him. Her anxiety didn't sound as if it were altogether unselfish. And he'd wounded her pride as it was. Yet it was vital to stay. He must. This place was his last resort. Indeed, he might have to get her out of here—and keep her out.

"Nothing worse than that?"

"No," he forced himself. "Nothing."

He could feel her eyes on him. Inwardly he groaned. "The old-fashioned pressures are still the best, Mr. Laker." He turned away from her. God, oh God. He didn't hate Frenzel.

11

THEY must have slept again. A whimper of tyres in the street finally made Laker stir. He awoke quickly, tense at once, reality boring in. He got up immediately and went to the window; looked across. In the dullness of morning the window facing him seemed almost opaque: he couldn't see to any depth beyond the open slats of the blinds. A pigeon perched itself contentedly on the sill. Peering right he noticed that the entrance to the hotel was at the corner of the block. It was early for crowds, and those who walked moved briskly, intent on destinations, unaware of Frenzel, of Patrick, of Hartmann, buying their newspapers from a shop away to the left, glancing at the headlines as they hurried out, informed of violence and disasters and tyrannies around the globe, but ignorant of what fear was doing to someone above their heads, what tomorrow's editions might carry.

He let the curtain swing back and pulled on his trousers, then lit a cigarette. The girl was still sleeping. He gazed at her for a moment, then took his razor and a towel from the suitcase. The sharp click of the locks roused her. She rolled lazily on to her back, the sheet slipping from her breasts as she stretched.

"How long have you been up?"

"A couple of minutes."

"Is it late?"

"Five to eight."

She yawned and made a long arm for the radio. He entered the bathroom, shaved and washed. He ached from the chairs. He sat on the edge of the bath when he'd finished. Hartmann's remote control guiding the rabid course of his thoughts, endlessly warning him, daring him. After some time the girl thumped on the door and he opened it. She was in a pink housecoat. "I reckoned you must have made camp," she said tartly, brushing past. He was drawn to the window again, held there as if by a magnet. The light had improved and now he could vaguely discern the interior of Frenzel's room-to-be—a cupboard, part of a mauve-covered bed . . . But there was a point beyond which his mind refused to go.

He turned away sharply, a tightness in his chest. Yesterday's date had been torn from the calendar. *Do not men die fast enough*, he read, *without being destroyed by each other?* Friday . . . Almost with disbelief he realised that he and Patrick were to have been *en route* to Heidelburg. "Lucky mortals," Baxendale had said. "Heidelburg, eh?" It seemed a lifetime ago.

He looked out on to the landing. It was squarish, the walls papered in silver grey, the carpet dark blue and showing signs of wear. There were two doors, one presumably the entrance to another apartment. The second was in the angle of the stairs. He went to it quickly. There was no lock. It opened outwards on to an iron platform and he saw the steps leading down, wire-meshed on both sides and roofed with corrugated sheeting. Below were garages and the service-yards to the ground-floor shops; beyond, a tangle of buildings, the partial view of a back street where traffic crawled as if in obedience to a promise. Three minutes? . . . Instinctively, the query lodged.

He returned to the girl's sitting-room and a calypso jerking from the radio. She emerged from the bathroom shortly afterwards and dressed in front of him with complete indifference, once asking "Hungry?" but saying nothing more. They ate in the small kitchen—boiled eggs, toast and coffee. Her mood had changed. He was wary of her, sensing that her doubts about him were unallayed. The green eyes, a little puffy now, bleary, wanted no problems, no trouble. But at least he could be open about one thing.

"Where's the nearest telephone?"

"In the shop—the delicatessen."

"Not downstairs?"

"No." Her tone was surly. "Will you be at your conference today?"

He nodded, remembering.

"What time?"

"Ten."

"Where?"

He named the place where the bank was, Sunderspladsen, and she repeated it, correcting his pronunciation with a touch of scorn. Last night she would have teased him, but she'd made a bad bargain and her feelings showed.

"And then?"

"Then what?"

"What will you do?"

"I don't follow."

"You won't want to come back here."

"Of course." Alarm chilled him. "Of course I will," he repeated.

"Why?"

"Why not?" he stalled.

"What's wrong with the Metropol?" She tossed her head. "You look across there often enough."

"This place is fine."

"For what?"

"It suits me."

With difficulty he held her gaze.

"On a couple of chairs?" she said. "You get a bed in a hotel."

He tried to laugh.

"There's no need to go on with it. Mistakes happen. How were they to know you didn't want a girl? You'd be better off elsewhere."

"I like it here."

"But I don't. It's . . . it's stupid. If you're sick or something, okay. Let's forget it ever happened." More than pique was niggling her. "Or is there another reason—one I haven't been told about?"

He snapped: "You took the money, didn't you?"

"That was yesterday."

"And tomorrow I'll have gone."

"I'm counting the hours."

She ground her cigarette in the saucer and went into the other room. Laker ran his hands over his face, dreading the depths of self-discovery to which he might yet be dragged. He had to keep a foothold here. And then, if need be, take the place over. God alone knew how. The imperatives controlling him made her presence unforgivable. Because she menaced an act that stabbed his mind with horror she prompted a terrible malice in him. He was too far gone in desperation to appreciate the irony. All he knew was what Hartmann had done to him, what Hartmann wanted, what was at stake.

The girl was straightening the crumpled divan when he left the kitchen. As if from habit he glanced towards Frenzel's room, the marksman in him automatically noting snags, thinking in terms of fleeting opportunity.

Nine twenty-five . . . Eight and a half hours before Frenzel's plane touched down; ten, say, before he was installed. So there was time yet. Time and Slattery. For too long he'd discounted Slattery. More and more he needed him, despite the risks, the misgivings. Alone he would crack.

"Have you got a spare key?"

"I'll be here," the girl said.

"Say you aren't?"

"I will be."

He didn't press it. He took his coat from its hook and went out on to the landing. In case she listened he walked all the way down. There were glass panels to either side of the front door and he studied the street through one of them. Nobody obviously waited for him, but he was taking no chances. He opened and shut the door loudly enough for the girl to hear, then went quietly up the first flight of stairs to the fire exit.

Again there was no evidence of being under observation. The fire-escape put him down by an outside lavatory at the rear of the delicatessen. The yard was stacked with wooden crates and a delivery van was parked close to the wall. No one was about. Laker walked between the crates and entered a storeroom where a woman was loading shelves with jars of pickle. She didn't notice him. He elbowed through a door into the shop, surprising an overalled youth on a ladder at the near end of the counter, but drawing no comment. It was a long rectangular shop. Half a dozen customers were either being served or waiting their turn. A solitary telephone-booth stood in an alcove. Laker checked his mass of small change, then stepped inside. A light clicked on as the door thudded. He paused before dialling, staring blankly at the activity behind the counter, the cheeses, the cooked meats, the patés, the hung salamis and knackwursts, isolating himself, visualising Slattery, putting his trust in him.

"London?" a voice echoed. "A moment, please."

And when it began again, the repetition, the waiting, the rising tension. "No delay for London. Shall I book the Gerrard number?"

Three minutes after the half-hour. Someone would answer. Someone would be there. Laker closed his eyes, willing it, praying for it. The wire hummed, clicked, gabbled unintelligibly. An assistant sliced ham on a machine, a customer loaded her shopping-basket . . . If Slattery wasn't available they would tell him where he could be found. He'd make them. And Slattery would have a solution, institute counter-measures . . . Hope fed upon hope.

Every second lengthened, every minute. The booth was stifling. Outside, a man pointed at some mortadella, nodding, lips moving soundlessly. All the time people were either entering or leaving the shop.

"Hold for London, please."

He had the money ready on a ledge, a pencil to hand. Aloud

he urged: "Hurry, please . . ." Another pause, another clash of tongues. On instructions he thumbed a succession of coins into the slots, waited, hands restless, eyes fixed, whispers like the sea filling his head. All at once there was silence, a moment's complete silence, before he heard the Gerrard number quoted. He hesitated, somehow unable to release himself from an intolerable strain.

"You're through, caller," the operator prompted.

He swallowed. "Mr. Slattery, please."

"Who's calling?"

It sounded like the same person, the woman who'd answered when he rang from Gale and Watts. He told her, adding "It's urgent." But she stuck to her careful drill.

"Does Mr. Slattery know you?"

"Yes."

"Is he expecting you to telephone?"

"Yes," he snapped.

He waited again, trying to prepare his mind. Then, following a final click, Slattery was there at last, incredibly clear, seemingly in the booth with him, as close as ever he'd been. And cautious.

"Sam?"

"Listen —"

"Where are you?"

"Copenhagen."

"*Where?*"

"I'm in trouble. Bad trouble . . ."

It came in a spate. He was never able to remember where he began or exactly what he said once the initial rush spilled over. He knew it was vital to be precise, chronological, absolutely accurate, but Slattery's interpolations confused him from the start—"Hang on, Sam . . . Hold your horses . . ." He ignored them for a while, blundering on, but they became more frequent, louder, sharper, eventually cutting him off between words.

"You're on an open line, man. *An open line.*"

"I've no choice."

"Then use your head. Scramble. Wrap it up."

"How can I?"

"Try."

"To hell with that. Listen —"

"I'm warning you."

Laker bit back another retort.

"Do it my way," Slattery said. "*My* way."

"Very well."

"Question and answer."

"All right."

The sound of Slattery's breathing raced along the line. "You dropped in at K's?"

"Yes."

"And found you were expected?"

"Yes."

"After which they had a talk with you?"

"Yes."

"Who did the talking?"

"Hartmann, S.S.D."

"About Patrick?"

"In part."

"Patrick's stayed on, I take it."

"Yes."

Slattery delayed for a second or so. He hadn't missed much. "I didn't get the other person's name."

"Rudolf Frenzel . . . He flies out of here tomorrow afternoon, at two."

"Is he there now?"

"No. Tonight at six. From Paris."

"And it's a case of either, or. Either, or—is that the proposition?"

"Yes."

Silence.

Very quietly, Slattery said: "Christ."

"What are you going to do?"

"Give me time."

"I tried to get to you last night, but they objected."

"From Copenhagen?"

"Yes."

"Someone's with you?"

"Not at the moment. But I may not be able to contact you again."

The wire spat. Laker licked his lips, staring as if mesmerised at a shop-assistant weighing cheese.

"Slattery?" he asked sharply, frightened by the lack of response.

"I'm here. Got my thinking-cap on . . . Is Patrick aware of the situation?"

"He's been told he's with friends of mine."

"When did it come to a head?"

"Wednesday afternoon."

"At K's?"

"After I left. Karen's been arrested. I saw her —"

"Easy, Sam."

"She was blown. They knew I was coming —"

"Simmer down!"

Laker glared, seething. "Get Patrick back and I'll simmer down."

"All right, all right. But —"

"I'm not asking a favour. It's a matter of life and death. No one's playing a game at this end."

"Look," Slattery said. "I'll alert Paris—that's the first thing. Our friend won't fly, d'you understand? He won't arrive."

"That's no help."

"It'll take the pressure off you while we —"

"It won't, it won't." Frantically, Laker beat a fist against the coin-box. "He's got to be here. *Got* to be. Don't stop him coming, for Christ's sake. They threatened me about that. He must arrive. Must, d'you hear?"

"To be an Aunt Sally?"

"It's him or Patrick."

He began to talk about Hartmann, the words pouring from him again. He couldn't stop himself, straining desperately to convey the terror to which he had been subjected, the certainty

146

that Hartmann wasn't bluffing, quoting him, restating the equation. Slattery seemed to have given up trying to interrupt.

"I haven't any choice, don't you see? Unless you intervene I've got to do what he wants."

"You couldn't."

"Put yourself in my position."

The operator cut in to say that his time had expired. Urgently he asked for an extension, for Slattery to accept the charges, and Slattery agreed.

When it sounded as if they were once more alone Slattery said icily: "Listen, Sam. I've got the message. If you go off the rails like that again I'll hang up—is that clear?"

"You wouldn't dare," Laker snapped. "You got us into this. Now get us out."

"That's easier said than done."

"Why?" He was trembling. "If anything happens to Patrick I'll raise the roof. You'll have to answer for it—I'll see to that. You, personally. So think of something. And it had better be effective."

"Such as?"

"How the hell d'you expect me to know? But you aren't powerless, are you?" He paused hopefully, but there was no answer. "Are you?" he echoed.

"I'll do what I can. It's tricky, though."

"Can't you offer anything more than that?"

"Not off the cuff, no."

Laker gazed wildly at the continuing mime in the shop. A woman in a fur coat waited near the booth. Slattery was saying something about "Playing it by ear". Despite his blandness he sounded harassed and the jargon had a terrible sterility. In utter dismay, Laker shouted: "What are you going to *do*?"

"Good God," Slattery retorted. "What d'you expect? I can't promise miracles. And even if I could I wouldn't be fool enough to broadcast them."

The woman was tapping on the glass. Laker turned his back on her.

"Don't side-track Frenzel," he urged Slattery. "I want him here—tonight."

"Look —"

"He's the only safeguard I've got."

"Sam, listen —"

"You listen," Laker shouted, beyond himself. "Leave Frenzel alone."

A frizzling noise filled the line. Through it Slattery was saying: "I'll be in touch."

"How?"

"Ritchie Jackson, at the Embassy."

"I can't go there. Haven't you got the picture yet?"

"Can't you telephone?"

"I'm not sure I can risk it."

The woman tapped on the glass again, harder now.

Almost hysterically Laker flung out: "Hartmann said that Patrick and I had ceased to be public property. He said that because of circumstances I don't know about you'd be unwilling to lift a finger. Well, if you won't or can't, I will. I'll have to go through with it—and don't try and stop me. Leave word at the Metropol. The Metropol. If there isn't something by six tonight I'll know where I stand. And, so help me, I'll lay the whole bloody issue at your door when the time comes, whatever happens . . ."

He went on, goaded towards a kind of dreadful bravado. But after a while he was aware of a dribbling sound in his ear; he was talking to himself. Like someone betrayed he hung up and backed out of the booth. "*Tak!*" the woman said with heavy sarcasm. He stood amid the bustle and sudden chatter of the shop in a daze of anger and confusion. Whatever hopes he'd had had dwindled. But the upstairs room, the problem of the girl, the rifle awaiting collection at the bank—these were certainties, as real as the shoulders that jostled him.

Behind the counter an assistant cocked his head "Nothing," Laker muttered. "Nothing." Turning away he wished to God he'd had the sense to withhold Frenzel's name.

He went out through the back, crossed the yard and mounted the fire-escape. Then he walked down to the front door and let himself quietly into the street. After a few paces he paused to light a cigarette, glancing both ways as he did so. Once again no one caught his eye, but this time the feeling of menace was there. Where the block ended he waited for the lights to change before going over to the Metropol. It was shaped like a blunt V with traffic flowing along both sides. He made his way past the cars squatting in the forecourt and entered the deep-carpeted foyer.

The tall blonde on duty in Reception smiled politely, waiting to discover what language she was expected to match.

"I'm enquiring after a Mr. Frenzel."

"What name?"

"Frenzel. Rudolf Frenzel."

She consulted a list, running a scarlet nail down the side of the type. "Frenzel," she said, reminding herself.

"That's right."

"There's a Mr. Frenzel expected. He has a reservation from this evening."

Laker could see the number against her finger-nail: 68. And Hartmann loomed as if to remind him that one more thing had been proved; one more guarantee honoured.

"Mr. Frenzel would hardly be here yet, sir. Overnight visitors do not vacate their rooms until midday, but I can have him paged if you wish."

"No, thank you."

"Will you leave a message?"

"No." Laker shook his head. "Thank you," he repeated, then walked away.

She would remember him, but he had hardly begun to concern himself with hazards of that sort. He was still trying to assess Slattery's tone, his attitude, still dismayed that his reaction hadn't been more appalled, more encouraging. Incredibly, his main concern had seemed to be for Frenzel. Nobody else could twist Hartmann's arm, and unless that were done there could only be one end. And Hartmann had been

149

certain what that end must be; confident. "I wouldn't care to be in London's shoes, Mr. Laker. No one likes humiliation, London least of all. But then, if I *were* in London's shoes, I wouldn't be aware of the situation, would I? You wouldn't have been stupid enough to tell me about Rudolf Frenzel, would you?"

For a while Laker walked aimlessly, blinkered by old and new fears, willing Slattery to act, to better Hartmann in some way, yet dreading a blundering, helping move which would result in catastrophe. For a day and a night he had never quite abandoned faith in Slattery's ability, but he was nearer to it now than ever before. Yet his hatred was for Hartmann, Hartmann who knew the lethal fury to which a person could be driven and who chose the victims and set a zero hour. Hartmann deserved what he meted out to others.

Thirty to forty yards to the rear a man in a dark overcoat kept his distance. He looked like the one who'd been in the foyer of the Metropol, but Laker wasn't sure about him and he didn't experiment. But he thought: All right, all right. So you know why I went there . . .

It was after ten and the banks were open. He would collect the rifle; he must. He was a puppet still. Nothing had changed.

A taxi brought him to the Sunderspladsen, a neat cobbled square centred on a fountain with a church filling most of one side and what Laker took to be municipal offices on the other. They had crossed a bridge to get there. The Copenhagen-National branch occupied a corner position. He paid off the driver and went in, affecting unconcern, as George Marshall requesting access to his deposit box. Once again the stepping-stone was ready and waiting; there were no snags. A clerk accompanied him down to the strong-room, used his master-key on Laker's locker, then discreetly withdrew. Hartmann's key opened the steel door. Inside was a narrow black case, about three and a half feet long and ten or twelve inches high. It wasn't new; the rexine covering was worn along the edges and slightly scratched. Laker slid it out and took it to one of the cubicles at the end of the room. To his surprise the case was secured only by catches. He sprung them simultaneously, then lifted the lid.

The weapon nestled in a bed of yellow velvet—the stock, the barrel and the telescopic attachment, each separate. Laker didn't touch them. They looked immaculate; the polished wood, the thin film of oil on the blue-black metal, the protective caps over the sight's ends, all gleamed dully under the overhead strip of light. In a recess at the top right-hand corner was a brown fibre box and he opened that, discovering what he expected—rimless ammunition packed in cotton-wool. A dozen rounds or so; he didn't count. There was an envelope taped inside the lid; 'Key' was written on it in German. He removed this and shut the case, locked it, putting the key into his hip-pocket as he left the cubicle.

The clerk said: "Are you taking the case with you, Mr. Marshall?"

"Yes."

"I see." He was inclined to fuss. "And are you continuing to rent your compartment?"

"Yes."

"Very good." He pushed the door to. It snapped shut and he turned the master-key, giving Laker a conspiratorial smile. There was nothing to sign, but the clerk entered the date in his ledger against the locker number.

"Thank you, sir."

They walked up to the ground floor together. A nod, another smile, and they parted. Laker was sweating slightly, his face set. The case was heavier than its slimness suggested. He stepped out into the quiet square, armed now, equipped, yet as unremarkable as a musician on his way to rehearsal or a salesman hawking his particular brand of samples.

It was barely half-past ten. Only the waiting and the hoping remained, but he couldn't go back to the room so soon. He must use up a few hours first. The girl was the major flaw in Hartmann's planning. And as he walked from the bank he once more began to realise how much hinged upon his ability to handle her—the lies, the blandishment, the persuasive wheedling that might be necessary; even the violence. But he had to have that room.

12

HE couldn't make up his mind whether anyone tailed him or not, but he took no deliberate avoiding action. It was strangely inefficient tailing, crude, apparently spasmodic; either that or immensely skilled. After a while he found himself on a tree-lined embankment overlooking a stretch of water in which the morning's white, ribbed clouds were mirrored. He paused there, the case at his feet, studying his wavering reflection.

Slattery would fail him; the feeling grew. For the hundredth time he went back to their meetings in Manchester Square and at The Mitre, appalled again by the amateur enthusiasm and cheerful understatement which had roped him in. If only he'd refused him at the outset, never learned of Karen's existence, been spared that aching wound along with the blackmail and its merciless inducement. Karen was already in the net by the time he was recruited, as helpless as he and Patrick were now. And Slattery should have known it; the secret wastes beneath the surface of daily living were his province.

It was futile to theorise, yet the question-marks persisted, throbbing through layers of hostility and desperation, blaming the years of deceit which had blunted Slattery's once sharp-eyed keenness for detail and his almost reflexive ability to read between the lines. At the very least Karen's position must have been suspect. Yet all he had thought necessary was to throw in a Leipzig telephone number—and that almost apologetically, as if it really weren't done even to imply that anything could go wrong.

Laker gazed into the water. The rhythmic clatter of a train reached him, making him raise his head and stare blankly at the buildings opposite. How glib Slattery had been. "Wise-virgin common-sense, Sam . . ." That was then; and just now he was cagey, slightly flustered, not shocked enough, as if he still didn't fully understand what he'd started, what Hartmann would finish. *Not shocked enough.*

Laker moved on, scared again as his thoughts clipped nearer and nearer to Frenzel, picturing the hotel window with its slatted blinds. Say they were kept closed? Would he be forced to go to Frenzel's room—confront him? The sense of panic was never far off, and now it swept him anew. Aloud, almost dementedly, he heard himself ask: "Why me? . . . Why me?"—and a couple passing on the embankment glanced at him with surprised amusement.

Intermittent sunshine cast his shadow on the paving-slabs; that of the case looked out of proportion, elongated. He crossed the road, a prisoner within himself, unaware of the car forced to swerve and the driver who shouted. Soon there were shops to either side. He went into a café and ordered a cognac, needing its fire, its strength. For a while as he sat there his mind fastened wildly on to the possibility of somehow entering into collusion with Frenzel, enlisting Jackson at the British Embassy, the Press and the police, between them faking a story and a photograph that would fool whoever waited to inform Hartmann of what had happened. But the idea withered like others before it.

The self-sufficient chatter at the neighbouring tables filled him with an extraordinary viciousness which presently drove him into the streets once more. He paused outside a newspaper office, its windows filled with enlargements of a military parade, the King and Queen arriving at the ballet. "One word to anyone, Mr. Laker. *Anyone* . . ." The throttled dictum stayed with him, warning him that Slattery was hamstrung, too—"An outcry, Mr. Laker? Public outrage? . . . Oh no"—reminding him all over again that Frenzel and Patrick were privately in the balance and must remain so. Yet hope could be stubborn.

He dared not chance another personal visit to the Metropol, but under the pressure of stress he impulsively waved a cruising taxi into the kerb.

"D'you speak English?"

"Some. Where you want?" Cropped hair, blue eyes, a jaw like a boxer's.

"The Metropol."

"Okay."

"Go there for me. Ask at the desk if there is a message for Laker. Then come back here."

"A message?"

"For Laker." He spelt it quickly.

"You don't come?"

"No."

A frown. "You stay here, is that it?"

"Yes."

"Okay—but for twenty Kroner."

"All right."

"Twenty Kroner first."

Laker paid, repeating the name, the hotel.

"Okay," the driver said. "Five minutes."

He drew away, grinning, and Laker waited nervously. He wasn't clever, but it was the best he could do. For what seemed a very long time he gazed into a window where a model of a black bull, pinned with paper banderillas, blinked electric eyes at him amid a display of sherries. He watched the traffic's flow in the glass, convinced he wasn't watched in turn. But he fidgeted, on edge, then paced up and down. Just as he was beginning to conclude he'd allowed himself to be robbed, the taxi slid in from behind a grinding tram.

"No message."

"Are you sure?"

"Sure. Nothing for Laker."

A muscle flicked by Laker's mouth. It was early yet, only ten to twelve. Even so . . .

"Thanks," he said.

154

"Okay." The driver grinned again. "Perhaps she send word another time, eh?"

Laker decided to give Slattery another couple of hours. Meanwhile there were practical things to be done, preparations to be made. He couldn't cling indefinitely to straws.

He found his bearings, then explored the area to the rear of the delicatessen, timing himself over the distance between the service-yards and the nearest taxi-rank, walking briskly towards the street he'd seen from the top of the fire-escape earlier in the day. It took him almost six minutes, but that included mistakenly entering a cul-de-sac. The second trip took under five, the third, cutting corners, only a fraction over four. And this was walking; against that there were three levels of fire-escape to be negotiated. It was an all-night rank, he noted.

Eventually he took a taxi and was driven to the B.E.A. office. There were several flights to choose from and he booked on one leaving for London at four-thirty on the Saturday afternoon, two and a half hours after Frenzel's own proposed exit from Copenhagen. That part of him which had already lost confidence in the chances of a reprieve was dismayed by the gap between the unpredictable moment Frenzel was going to be squarely in his sights and four-thirty on Saturday. It might amount to hours, half a day, perhaps a night as well. There were so many imponderables. Where would he go after that headlong rush down the fire-escape? The Embassy? His mind wouldn't stretch that far. Self-preservation was the least of his concerns.

He chose a place to eat within a stone's-throw of the Tivoli. It was small, crowded, and he shared a table with a middle-aged man with a voracious appetite who read a newspaper and whose feet kept coming into contact with the gun-case. Twice Laker moved it, apologising. He wasn't hungry. He was killing time. He could only toy with the food, but he drank three large whiskies and several cups of black coffee. At a quarter to two he pressed some Kroner into the waiter's hand and asked him to ring the Metropol. The reply was the same: nothing, no message. Anxiety hounded him into the streets again, the weight of the case insisting that the nightmare was going to run its prescribed course after all, all the demented way.

He followed the route he and the girl had taken the previous evening. As he neared the delicatessen his eyes went up to her third-floor window and the one directly opposite. The sun glinted like gold on Frenzel's.

"Fear can remove mountains, Mr. Laker . . ."

He pressed the door-bell and thought of Patrick.

"Oh," she said when she saw him. That was all—"Oh," without inflexion.

She let him in and he followed her up the steep stairs. The room seemed to have shrunk since he was last there. A cigarette burned in a tray beside the divan and the covering was pulled back, the pillows dented. He put the case down at the foot of the divan and tossed his coat over it. She was wearing dark slacks and a striped sweater and there was a pale-blue velvet band across her hair. Last night she'd been bright, talkative, eager to draw him out and have him relax, to have him laugh. But he'd put paid to that and the grudge still showed.

He muttered something about a wash: "Please yourself," she said and curled on the divan, reaching for the magazine.

The bathroom window was narrow and rather high. Laker moved the plastic curtain aside and gazed across the street. It surprised him how much of Frenzel's room he could see now that the sun was behind him, streaming in. He could even pick out the light-switch by the white door through which Frenzel would come and go. He wouldn't inevitably be deciphering shadows, then. And, sometime or other, Frenzel would surely attend to the blinds—close them, open them; it didn't matter much. A couple of seconds would be long enough, a couple of heart-beats. Four windows to the left a plump, bald man was at that instant polishing his spectacles and Laker drew an imagined line on him. It would be easy, given the occasion, given the chance of maintaining a vigil.

He felt no relief; every fibre of him ached to be spared. In an hour or two, somehow, he would check with the Metropol again. Meanwhile he must consolidate his position and make the vigil possible. Everything hung on what was said, how it was said. He sluiced his face from the cold tap, then looked at himself, in the grip of his own helplessness. His vision seemed to cloud. He was a businessman, a widower with a house in Weybridge. Weybridge, Surrey . . . England. Who was Frenzel?—Frenzel who would never know Patrick and whom Patrick would never know? What had Frenzel done except to change sides? . . . But he mustn't start thinking about Frenzel —not as a man, not like that. Only of what he must do and how to cope with the girl.

He finger-combed his hair and joined her in the room, mastering his nerves. She glanced up from her magazine, then went on reading.

"Have you been out?"

"No."

"You're missing a fine day."

She shrugged. He sat in the chair nearest to her and fastened his shoe-laces. Money might interest her, but first he had to establish rapport. She had gone cold on him; the glance just now was full of surly surmise.

"Where did you learn your English?"

"Huh?"

"Your English. It's good."

"At school. Here and there."

"It's good," he said lamely.

"I was with S.A.S. for a while. That helped."

"Flying?"

"For a while."

She sounded bored, as if she had been asked these things a thousand times. Laker watched for a smile, some softening of her features, but there was none. He asked about her flying, the places she'd been, in what aircraft, where she liked best, not caring what her answers were, not interested, his mind in the employ of a situation three hundred miles away. If she warmed to him it was barely noticeable. He got up and went to the table where the bottles were, the lava flow of doubt and anxiety endlessly pressing through him.

"D'you want one?"

She shook her head. He poured himself a whisky, deliberately avoiding looking towards the window, seeing in her green eyes a lurking background of suspicion. Given time she would probably relent; tenderness was her professional stock-in-trade. If he had been hungry for her he would have had confidence in his ability to thaw her out. He carried the glass back to the chair and sat with his fingers locked round it, trying to hide his thoughts, afraid of showing that he was afraid.

"How was the conference?" she asked.

"All right."

"Isn't there an afternoon session?"

"No."

"Don't tell me you came to Copenhagen just for a morning's meeting."

"We started yesterday," he lied.

"On what."

"Business efficiency."

It was twenty to three. He began talking again, about her, working for a return of the smile which would be a beginning. Hartmann's funds weren't exhausted and he had traveller's cheques of his own; together they totalled around two hundred pounds. She could have the lot if need be. For money like that she might be willing to leave, stay the night somewhere, allow him the run of the place until the following afternoon. It was possible. It would be tempting. Two hundred pounds and no questions asked—yes?

He finished the whisky, reached over and switched on the radio. She arched an eyebrow, measuring him with a look while he struggled to mask his nerves, his tension.

"I'm sorry about last evening. I . . . I'd had a hard day—you know how it is."

She didn't answer. He lit a cigarette, the hard core of his mind intent, the rest uneasy, uncertain. If he couldn't buy her absence he would somehow have to keep her prisoner—that or quit the room entirely and haunt the Metropol until Frenzel arrived and could be tackled squalidly at close quarters. For two days now he had existed in loneliness, anguish burning into him, destroying hope and pity and self-respect. It was worse than fever, worse than hysteria. Yet he was absolutely clear as to what the issues were, feeling Hartmann's corrective tug whenever he asked how it could possibly be that he was committed to a killing while the world went by outside and neither he nor Slattery could let it know. "There are rules to this game, Mr. Laker . . ." Memory never let up.

"Anna," he said.

He moved to the divan and sat beside her. She turned her head on the pillow, wary still. He took the magazine, sliding it from her grip, and tossed it aside.

"What's become of that smile?"

"It's not my smiling day."

"Why not?"

She shrugged again, lifting her shoulders like a piano-player, narrowing them.

"Come on," he said.

She grimaced, lips pressed together.

"Is that the best you can do?"

"I'm not a tap," she said.

"I'm sorry about last night."

"I heard you the first time."

He still believed it was only a matter of patience. He touched her callously, as if he were just another man for whom machine-like response would suffice. "Anna," he said, despising himself, reduced to this so that she might feel sorry for him, glad to be necessary, and then be ready to listen, more willing to consider what he had to propose.

"What's got into you?" she said flatly.

She was stiff, unyielding. He ran his fingers over her white neck and into the softness of her hair. He felt no thrill, no excitement. He was using her, or seeking to. They would find the rifle here, but he didn't care. The contract permitted no stab of regret. Only the end mattered, and she was in the way of Frenzel's mortal danger.

She didn't move. Her eyes seemed harder, as if he were one of those who haggled when everything was finished.

"Where's this conference of yours?"

"The Sunderspladsen."

"Where in the Sunderspladsen?"

"Where?"

"Where, yes."

"Near the bank."

She glanced away from him. The radio was pulsing out a staccato beat. Laker should have been warned, on his guard; but no. Ruthlessly he traced the line of her lips.

"You're lying," she said after a few moments.

"Lying?"

"There is no conference."

"Nonsense."

"Not in the Sunderspladsen."

"Of course there is." He forced a laugh.

"I checked," she said.

He saw the spiky glint of anger as she pushed his hands down. He sat back, alarm knotting in his chest.

"Look," he began, "this is ridiculous."

"No, it isn't."

"What's a conference got to do with us?"

"There isn't any conference."

"All right. Have it your own way. But how does that matter?"

"It matters."

"Tell me how."

She twisted off the divan and reached for a pack of cigarettes, fumbled one loose and lit it. He watched her, thoughts in turmoil. Later, time and again, he was to recall how she looked at him then.

"I want you to go."

"Why?"

"I do, that's all."

160

"Listen —"

"You can have the money back."

"It's not mine."

"The one who laid on your fun, then." Her nostrils flared. Instinct was warning her, it could only be that, warning her not to allow herself to be involved in something she sensed yet did not understand. "I don't want you here any more."

He got up. "You're being stupid."

"Perhaps."

"You are."

"That's my affair."

"Anna," he said desperately. He took hold of her, making one last try, fondling her roughly in the way she knew best, his mouth finding hers. "You must be out of your mind."

She wrenched herself free. "I mean it." She reached for a bundle of notes on the mantelshelf. "Here," she said furiously.

"I'm staying." His voice had thickened. "You can't turn me out."

"I can and I will."

She flung the money at him and started for the door. He caught her by the arms as the notes scattered about his head.

"Be reasonable, for God's sake."

"Let—me—go!"

Even then he could hardly believe that disaster was land-sliding down in a cheap brawl. If she hadn't struggled he might have been able to control himself, quieten her—at least quieten her. But she was vicious, kicking at his shins, her voice rising all the time and the sound of it sliced into his brain like a knife. He slapped her, horrified by what she was doing, knowing that it had to be stopped. She spat at him, kicking again.

"Don't be a fool!" he shouted. "Don't be —"

She was strong, absolutely wild. They crashed into the table and all the bottles went over. He freed a hand and slapped her a second time, hard, full on the cheek-bone. She screamed. He tried to drag her towards the divan but she broke away, her gaping red mouth destroying Patrick—in panic he could think of nothing else and in panic he went after her, thrashing round the cluttered room. With a convulsive movement she grasped one of the bottles. He closed, warding off the expected blow, but before he could check her she hurled the bottle through the window. For a moment they both stared, panting, silent until the sound of the brittle smash below reached them and a yell came from the street. And then she ran to the broken window and screamed piercingly again, with her hands clenched beside her head.

Laker seemed unable to move any more. Aghast, he watched her retreat from the window and sink on to the arm of the nearest chair, shaking, sobbing now. He felt as if the whole of his stomach was going to come up.

"Go away," she moaned. "Go away."

Vaguely he was aware of a noise in the street; feet thudding on the stairs. Stunned, he couldn't think. He heard himself say: "D'you know what you've done? Oh Christ, d'you know what you've done?"

Someone banged on the door. The girl scurried to open it. A uniformed policeman came in, then another, big men who seemed to fill the room. There was a brief interchange between them and the girl before they motioned Laker out. He could understand so much, but no more. He thought he was merely being ejected and he picked up the gun-case and his coat and the suitcase. With a hand to her swelling cheek the girl flinched as he drew level. He paused, staring into her uncomprehending face, trying to speak; but words wouldn't come.

The taller of the policemen pushed him on to the landing. It was only then and on the way down the stairs between them that he realised they were taking him with them.

13

In a daze Laker leaned against the side of the wagon jolting him away. There had been people on the landings, people around the street doors, people outside the delicatessen—all watching as he was bundled across the pavement. He hadn't protested; he seemed to have been deprived of his strength, his will, his wits. And now, sitting between the two policemen in the enclosed back of the wagon, he was still beyond reasoning, the girl's screams still vibrating in his ears. "Where am I going?" he kept asking, but either they didn't understand him or they weren't disposed to answer.

When the wagon stopped, the rear doors were opened and he lurched out, clutching his coat and the two cases. One of the policemen attempted to grasp him by the arm, but he shook the hand away, beginning to react at last.

Stone steps led up to heavy double doors. Inside was a brightly-lit lobby with corridors branching left and right. He was taken past a railed barrier and brought to a standstill in front of a counter where his escorts conferred with the grey-haired policeman on duty.

Without fluency this one asked him: "What is your name?" A sheet of paper was briskly torn from a pad. "Name?"

Laker stared at him, shattered, thoughts beginning to race. He was sweating.

"Name?"

"Laker."

"Other name?"

"Samuel."

"English? American?"

"English . . . Look," Laker blurted, "you aren't thinking of keeping me here, are you?"

"Passport?"

"What?"

"You have passport?"

Laker drew it from his inside pocket and the photograph of Frenzel nearly came out, too. Glimpsing that startled expression again all but overwhelmed him. The light above his head was clinical and fierce and he was suddenly unnerved lest someone decided to examine what was in the black case.

"Will there be a fine?"

The policeman pursed his lips and turned the pages of the passport, studying the visa stamps with earnest, puckered eyes.

"I'm in a position to pay if there's a fine. Or if there's any damage to be made good."

Laker faltered, every moment of the brawl fresh and stark; frantically asking himself how it could conceivably have happened. There hadn't been reason enough; she'd almost manufactured it. He wiped his face, obsessed by what she had cost him in terms of angles and opportunity; what she might cost him yet. A clock behind the counter showed a minute or two past three.

"There was a misunderstanding." He pressed against the counter. "A misunderstanding. The window was broken by accident . . ." He swallowed. "If you'd only listen I'd like to explain —"

Ominously, the passport was set to one side.

"You wait," the duty man said, then corrected himself. "You *will* wait."

"What for? . . . For how long?"

"Long?"

"When can I go?"

"Not to go. Wait."

"Yes, but for how *long*?"

There was no answer. "Look here," he exploded, then stopped, warned by a hint of exasperation in the other's stolid glance. More quietly he managed: "Am I being charged—and, if so, what with?"

"Charged?"

With as much calm as Laker could dredge he said: "If there's any question of my being held I insist on being put in touch with the British Embassy—a Mr. Jackson. A Mr. Jackson at the British Embassy, is that clear?"

It didn't seem to be. He leaned across the counter and snatched up a pencil; swivelled the pad round. *Mr. Jackson*, he wrote, *British Embassy*.

"Yes?"

The man nodded. "Understand," he said. "But now you wait."

Laker fought down another distracted protest. With his coat draped across the gun-case he went where the escort directed, turning into a corridor, entering a room the door of which was opened for him. The window was barred, but it was more like an interview-room than anything, with a trestle-table and some tubular steel chairs, cream-painted walls, red lineoleum. Outside, cars were parked in a courtyard. He put the cases on the floor and sat at the table, trembling so much that he could hardly light a cigarette, reliving the swift crescendo of words and scuffling which had ruined Hartmann's basic plan, still flushed and sweating ice and fire.

He had botched everything. He'd never set foot in that room again, so there was only one course left—sickening even to contemplate, yet imperative, Hartmann's threat more urgent now than ever. He shuddered. Once he got out of here he would have to go on, on, with his senses gutted and his mind like that of a hunting animal, deprived even of the sop to his conscience which the width of a street, the impersonal pressure on a trigger, might have given.

They hadn't locked the door; he tried it after a while and looked into the corridor. But he wasn't tempted. It would be madness to cut and run; the exits were sure to be guarded. What was more they had his passport. And he needed to contact Jackson—not merely so as to smooth his release but because Jackson was his link with Slattery, perhaps the only one now.

Less than three hours remained to Slattery: six o'clock was his dead-line for producing a formula. And, if he couldn't, if there wasn't one, Frenzel was as good as dead. This was what terror did to you; what Hartmann had achieved by threat and argument and what he'd known could be sustained on the strength of a promise.

Nerves several times propelled Laker to the door during the next half-hour. Once a girl passed carrying some files, and she smiled at him, interested. Shortly afterwards what he took to be an officer went by with a couple of civilians; these all ignored him. At twenty to four a policeman came into the room with a cup of tea. Laker was too eager to talk with him to be surprised. "Have you been in touch with the British Embassy? . . . Is Mr. Jackson on his way? . . ." But he got nowhere. Even when he followed the man into the corridor in an attempt to persuade him to fetch someone with a better understanding of English or German he failed to extract more from him than a series of gestures, shrugs and one repeated word—"Soon."

But for the rifle he would have stormed back to the counter in the entrance-lobby. There was nothing to stop him, yet he was afraid of incurring official enmity by creating a scene. If they took it into their heads to retaliate by checking his luggage, his pockets, inevitably he would find himself the focus of attention. Instead of being left to cool his heels there would be questions, questions he couldn't satisfactorily answer, and he might be held indefinitely, pending further enquiries. A sordid little shouting-match with a tart was one thing; explaining away a sniper's rifle would be a very different matter.

He left the door open to minimise the feeling of being cut off. Four o'clock gradually came and went. He couldn't settle. His thoughts grass-hoppered interminably between past and future. At ten minutes after the hour the same man returned to collect the cup. "Soon," he said when Laker tackled him.

"Soon what?"

"Yes."

A nod and he left. Jesus . . . Another thirty minutes elapsed, inflaming Laker's despair, stretching his control almost to breaking-point. It was nearly five before anyone else acknowledged his existence. Then an officer put in an appearance, a blond giant with protruding ears and an unexpectedly amiable manner. Laker hardly gave him a chance to shut the door.

"How long am I to be detained like this?"

"That is what I have come to explain." At last the English was excellent. "It depends."

"Depends?"

"On whether the young woman decides to take action against you."

"Prefer charges, you mean?"

"Exactly. Unfortunately, she has gone out. So far we have not been able to check with her."

"But that's ridiculous. I've already been here two hours."

"I realise that."

"Am I under arrest?"

"No."

"What could she charge me with?"

"Assault."

"Say she did—what then?"

"You will be released on bail pending the hearing. And we will continue to keep your passport."

Laker somehow kept a grip on himself. "I asked at the desk for a Mr. Jackson at the British Embassy to be contacted."

"That has been done."

"Is he coming?"

"I could not say, but he has been informed."

The officer turned to leave. Laker could feel the veins bulging in his temples. "You can't hold me indefinitely."

"Not indefinitely, of course."

"Overnight?"

"I should not think that would be likely."

"Can't you be more precise."

"I have told you—it depends. The woman should have been brought here at the same time as you. That is the normal practice. She would then have had the opportunity of asserting her rights and you would have been spared this rather unfortunate delay." In the doorway he paused as if anxious to show that he wasn't without sympathy. "However, it may be for the

167

best. She might not want her pound of flesh—is that what you say, her pound of flesh?—once she has calmed down. Her sort rarely do."

A meal was brought to him around seven. Earlier a young policeman came with a tattered copy of *Reader's Digest*. They meant well. Laker touched neither. Imperceptibly the sky darkened. The lights were put on. Most of the cars in the court-yard drew away. Twice, imprudently, he quit the room and went to the entrance-lobby asking for news of the girl, of Jackson, once insisting that the Embassy was telephoned in his presence, and the imperturbability of those on duty, their stubborn adherence to a petty technicality, seemed more and more like a grotesque conspiracy.

Frenzel was installed in the Metropol by now. And Slattery had failed, failed even to respond, Slattery who outside The Mitre had said: "No hard feelings, I hope, Sam—now or at any time." Jackson was a dead loss, too. It was unbelievable; unforgivable. Laker rocked back and forth on a chair with his eyes hard closed, wishing to God in a kind of delirium there had never been any woman in a yellow dress with a child in a pram and a lorry bearing down on them all that distorted life-time ago.

With an enormous effort he gathered himself together, know-ing the futility of questioning anything, steeling himself to be patient, trying not to dwell on what he was being patient for. Yet he took Frenzel's picture from his pocket and stared at it, feeling hollow, drained, asking why either of them had been born.

Jackson arrived at twenty-five-past eight. Laker guessed who it was from the slightly drawled "This way?" that heralded his approach along the corridor. And then he was there, about Laker's age, slight, sandy-haired, a dinner-jacket showing beneath his unbuttoned overcoat. "Thank you," he said to the accompanying policeman. "Thank you very much."

He stepped into the room offering a well-trained smile and a seemingly boneless handshake.

"Ritchie Jackson . . . I'm sorry to have been so slow. I gather you've been kept dangling for quite some while."

"Since three o'clock."

"As long as that?"

"At least."

"I really am sorry. But I didn't get your message, d'you see? I wasn't in my office during the afternoon and it was only just now, half an hour or so ago, that the Embassy switchboard knew where they could catch me—glass in hand, as it were."

Laker didn't know whether to believe him; not that it mattered. Tersely, he said: "They're holding me on an idiotic technicality. I'm not under arrest and yet they say I can't leave—not, that is, until they know whether or not a complaint —"

"It's all fixed," Jackson cut in smoothly. "I've had a word with 'em."

"I can go?"

"Yes. They're feeling quite a little guilty—and no wonder. They really didn't need much persuasion. They reckon the, er, other person concerned has had every chance, so they've agreed to forget there was ever any trouble. It was pretty much a storm in a teacup from what I hear, anyway. So —"

He spread his hands, smiling like a magician awaiting the applause. Laker's relief was minimal. He was searching for an indication that Jackson appreciated he wasn't rescuing just another tourist who'd run out of money or gone off the rails. But there was no sign of it, no hint that Jackson realised what was at stake. He closed the door.

"Slattery told me to ask for you."

"Oh yes—I was coming to that."

"Well?"

"He wanted you to know he's doing everything he can." Jackson paused. "Everything he can, unquote."

Laker's mouth dragged at the corners. "Is that all?"

"As far as I know. The switchboard passed the message on,

169

d'you see, while I was drinking the Italian Ambassador's health."

"When was it received, for God's sake?"

"About five, I understand."

"And there was nothing else?"

"No . . . Does it make the sense it should?"

Laker was incapable of answering. Desolation ploughed through him. For an awful nauseous moment a part of him recoiled from what now seemed inevitable. All day he had clung to one last shred of hope, and it was part of the nightmare that Slattery's uselessness should be conveyed at second-hand, casually, with gin on the breath and small teeth bared in an anxious little smile.

"Does it?" Jackson repeated like a fool. "You fellows always —" And then he stopped, on the fringes of the game and keeping there.

Dumbfounded, Laker picked up the two cases and his coat. Jackson opened the door and they walked the corridor's length to the counter, where the grey-haired policeman interrupted booking a drunk to give Laker his passport.

"Can I drop you somewhere?" Jackson asked. "My car's round the corner—unless it's been pinched, that is."

The night air was cool. Jackson drove with a flourish. He was wearing a hat now, its angle slightly jaunty. When Laker recognised the square where the airport coach had put him down the day before he said curtly. "This'll do," and Jackson edged into the side.

"Sure?"

"Quite sure."

"You don't want a hotel?"

Laker shook his head. Neon jazzed through the windscreen.

"Well, if there's nothing else," Jackson said, holding out a hand and smiling the smile he did best, "I'll be off to claim my wife before all that Italian charm bowls her over. Glad I was able to help. A police-station's no place to spend one's time and I'm only sorry I couldn't get to you earlier. Still, better late than never I suppose."

170

Laker got out. From the kerb, he said: "How soon can you get word to Slattery?"

"Practically right away."

"Tell him I had no choice, no choice at all."

"Just that?"

"'No choice at all'—will do."

"There's more."

"Yes?"

"Tell him also that if Patrick suffers as a result of this, I want him to know in advance that my name isn't Wyatt . . . James Wyatt."

Jackson frowned. "You can't enlarge a bit, I suppose? Or will that be clear to him?"

"It'll be clear," Laker said.

His voice shook, yet he was unnaturally calm. He watched the car ease into the traffic, then began to walk. It had ceased to concern him whether he was tailed or not. Hartmann had all-but won. Shrink from murdering Frenzel and Patrick vanished, fail to murder Frenzel and Patrick vanished . . . Nothing had changed; nothing *could* change. He now realised he had asked the impossible of Slattery. The blackmail embraced them both. But he'd never excuse the callousness of almost total silence, the apparent indifference, the continued implication that once a pro always a pro and that, as such, he must fend for himself.

From the girl's room Laker would have been forced to take the first chance that presented itself, not knowing if another would follow. If she hadn't screamed him out of there Frenzel might have been dead already, the hunt in full cry. But he could delay now, choose his time—and pay the price in terms of horror. He walked slowly, on the lookout for a telephone, mentally leap-frogging forward to the moment when Patrick would touch down at London Airport tomorrow night, trying to reconcile everything with that.

It was nine when he found a public booth. Three hours had elapsed of Frenzel's twenty. He got the Metropol's number from the book, then dialled.

"Reception, please." When he was connected he said: "Have you a Mr. Frenzel with you? Rudolf Frenzel? . . . Yes, that's correct."

He waited, beginning then to screw himself up for what would follow this preliminary reconnaissance. He could hear a rustle of papers; somebody coughing in the background.

"Did you say the name is Frenzel?"

"Yes."

Another crisp rustle.

"No, caller, there's no Mr. Frenzel booked here."

"There is," Laker retorted. "I checked earlier in the day."

Alarm was slow to spiral. The plane must be late. Frenzel had delayed booking in . . . Yet he was saying urgently: "Mr. Frenzel has been allocated room sixty-eight. Rudolf Frenzel— from Paris."

"When did you check, caller?" The voice was helpful.

"This morning."

More rustling; a mutter. Then: "Ah yes, I see it now. Frenzel, sixty-eight . . ."

"Thank you."

And then it came.

"But since then, caller, the reservation has been cancelled. Mr. Frenzel relinquished his booking at four o'clock this afternoon."

It must have been five minutes before he could get a taxi. He had no recollection of hanging up or quitting the booth. In a frenzy of disbelief he signalled every passing cab, bawling at them through the traffic's rumble until at last one acknowledged him and took him to the Metropol. And there, by a quiet-spoken woman with blued hair who met the full force of his distress with impeccable politeness, his despair was made absolute.

He turned from her with a dead, beaten stare. By the Enquiries desk he stopped and asked if there was a message for him, doing so with the numbness of a person whose mind had congealed beyond sensible usefulness. And there was one. He snatched it from the man who took it from the pigeon-hole, capable as he did so of assuming that Slattery finally had a germ of hope to offer, guidance, instructions, even an explanation that the miracle had been achieved and Frenzel kept out of harm's way as a precaution.

He fumbled open the folded slip. *You should not have contacted London.* And the sender's name leaped at him—*Hartmann.*

14

HE moved blindly out into the night, oblivious of the flow of people, the gaggles of traffic, the guano-green fairy-tale roofs above the floodlit buildings. He felt his legs would give and he entered a bar and sat there staring, motionless, leaving untouched the whisky he never realised he ordered. Then he walked again. Finally, on a public bench under a street-lamp, he extracted the slip of paper which was crushed between his fingers and the handle of the gun-case and gazed at the scrawled writing of whoever had taken the message down. *Message for:* Mr. Samuel Laker. *Received by:* Telephone. *Time:* 16.50. The printed headings were in three languages. *Message:* You should not have contacted London. *Sender's name:* Hartmann.

He read it over and over, protest groping in the stupefied darkness of his brain. And every time it turned in agony on Slattery for what had been done Hartmann was there to intervene, claiming priority, inviting the hatred he had seemed to relish from that initial meeting in the hut.

"Between you and me, Mr. Laker. Always remember that . . ."

Laker crumpled the paper into a ball, split beyond control,

guilt and rage beating behind his eyes. He should never have given Slattery Frenzel's name. Slattery could wait, though. Slattery was a reckless incompetent and would answer for it. But Hartmann was a destroyer, the begetter of horrific sins for whom mercy was a word, pity a word. "Then I am sorry for you," he had said when Laker pleaded for Karen—and sorrow was a word, too.

"You and me, Mr. Laker . . ." So be it. There was another kind of equation now and it had Laker silently in tears. He felt an urge like lust, ugly and savage, demanding satisfaction, deeper than the will to live or preserve life.

He was going back to Leipzig.

He nursed the hatred, letting it fester, drawing on it to drug his grief. He put on his coat, picked up the cases and walked until he reached another bar; and this time he drank, blinkered by the fierceness of his intent, numbing what he could of a hundred other memories. He drank until the place closed at midnight; heavily, effectively, but he was steady on his feet when he left.

It would be morning before he could make a move, nine o'clock at the earliest before he could set about getting himself another Fair Card, nine before the air-line ticket-offices opened. Despite the drink, and the pain that drink could never tranquillise, he saw the essentials clearly. He wandered into a park at one time, alone by a small lake except for some furtive lovers. The streets were emptying now; more and more he had them to himself. Nobody kept that careful distance and the fact showed that Hartmann had finished with him—emphasising what this meant, what it could only mean. He believed Hartmann. All along he'd believed him. He'd have made himself kill for Hartmann, so there was no chance of not believing him now. "On whatever you care to name as sacred, Mr. Laker . . ."

Only revenge was left, and he felt the lust for it grow in the sodden depths of his spirit as he walked the night.

Sometime in the small hours he found himself passing the air-line terminus. He entered and sank on to a vacant couch,

174

aching in thighs and calves, surrounded by a scattering of passengers waiting for dawn flights. The effect of the whisky was wearing off and he knew how close he was to breakdown. His jaw-muscles quaked as if a fever threatened. He shut his eyes, clinging to hatred as once he had to cling to hope, bolstering himself with it. The place filled up. People moved back and forth, bored, expectant, their hand-luggage labelled, carrying guide-books and magazines, about to venture somewhere new, returning home.

Home. Jesus, what could home be now?

He watched a coach-load depart. An indefatigable porter came to take his cases for weighing-in, but Laker stopped him.

"What is your destination, sir?"

He shook his head. Perhaps he looked ill, lost, incapable; perhaps he'd been there overlong.

"Do you know your flight number?"

"I'm all right," he retorted hoarsely. "All right."

He searched the leaflet-racks. S.A.S. listed a Czechoslovak Ilyushin at 12.15, arriving Schönefeld 13.20. The fact registered dully. S.A.S. would confirm the time of the Leipzig connection when he bought his ticket. He'd be there before evening. The temporary visa that went with the Fair Card would see him through. There was one unavoidable hurdle, but he would face that when it came.

He urged the time away so that he could make a start. There was a discarded newspaper on the couch: the *Express*, yesterday's. He dragged it towards him distractedly. HELICOPTER SNATCH OFF BEACHY HEAD . . . 'I WON'T BUDGE': FRANCO . . . RECORD POOLS WIN . . . His eyes glossed over the headlines, the centred wedding picture, the Lancaster cartoon, and it all seemed totally unreal. ALBRIGHT HERE, MOSCOW SAYS . . . *Matthew Albright,* he read, *the Sino-Soviet expert missing for several months from the U.S. State Department was today officially admitted by Moscow to be in the Soviet Union. This is the first time Russia has disclosed Albright's whereabouts, though the West has known since May that he had defected. As in the case of Pontecorvo, Burgess, Philby . . .*

Names, names.

A smudge of dawn was showing in the street. Laker stared at it, thinking of Frenzel whose ghost would haunt him to the end, Frenzel who had once defected too, earned a paragraph, if that, and whose life had been balanced against Patrick's.

He took up his cases and went stiffly into the morning's pearly chill. "Provocation or necessity, Mr. Laker; they're the two incentives. You're an instrument about to be put to practical use."

Not any more. Of his own free will, of his own choice—as at Gardelegen all that time ago, before Patrick ever existed.

He ate breakfast in a café where labourers and tram-crews apparently began their day. It was a quarter to seven when he paid the bill and left; eight before he found a barber's open and got a shave. A poster in a travel agent's window enticed the world to visit the Leipzig Fair. At half-past eight he was in the Farimagsgade, waiting for the Fair's office to start business. Sharp on nine he was admitted and by twenty minutes past he was out again, the forms completed, his passport details logged, the fee paid, the Fair Card in his wallet.

The S.A.S. booking-clerk was no less obliging. The Schönefeld flight connected with one for Leipzig at 14.40; Leipzig arrival time was 15.10. Would that be satisfactory? A traveller's cheque? Certainly . . . She bore no resemblance to the girl who yesterday had seemed to have loosed disaster upon him, but the S.A.S. uniform and a certain similarity of speech dragged his mind back to the room and the window opposite and what he had prepared for then, what had bound him then. Watching her make out the flight-ticket he pieced the broken jigsaw together once again, and with the clarity of hindsight he saw a pattern of inevitability in what had happened, step by step, Slattery's use of him and Hartmann's use of him sucking him down into the dark mouth of this funnel of vengeance.

He rode in a taxi to the airport. He was there with more than an hour to spare. A dozen times on the journey he must have tested the locks on the black case, yet his trust in them diminished as his luggage was weighed and heaved out of sight. But it was early yet to worry on that score; the hazards were still three hundred miles away. He went into the departure lounge and wrote a bitter cable for Slattery, but even the most vicious phrasing was inadequate and, in the end, he sent nothing. Nothing to Gale and Watts either. Nothing to Roundwood. Nothing to anyone, lest in doing so he should somehow weaken and waver, remember friends, sanity, remind himself that he would never get back.

When his flight was called he filed out with only a handful of others, fifteen at the most, and about half of them seemed to consist of a delegation of some kind; they all knew one another and solemnly filled a block of seats just aft of the wings. Except for a woman wearing a headscarf who sat immediately in front of him Laker was quite alone. He had never seen a plane more empty. He felt exhausted, yet his thoughts were measured, held by the savage fatalistic mood.

He watched the runway blur beneath him, the airport sink below, the green earth bank and wheel and level off. Presently he took out the Fair Card and thumbed it through, drawing what encouragement he could from it, keeping his anxiety about the coming Customs' confrontation battened down. Over the Baltic he dozed fitfully, never quite under. A stewardess startled him when she served coffee and from then on he was wide-awake, staring down at the broken German coastline dead ahead, then at the slow slide of the land itself.

The weather was clear as far as Berlin and for some of the time he looked westward in the direction of Gardelegen and the River Aller, recalling how his father often used to say that when a man turned his back on something it usually got him again before the end, seeing a resemblance between that wartime gamble and this, that prolonged bout of murderous rage and this, gazing out on the country once openly trampled and fought over which was now the hunting-ground of back-room entrepreneurs who'd devised their stealthy games of blackmail and death, catch-as-catch-can, their own dirty laws, their own ethics. And hating them for it, each and every one; but Hart-mann above all.

They whined into Schönefeld within minutes of the scheduled time. They had flown south, yet it was colder; on the walk to the airport buildings Laker felt a nip in the air. Along with the delegation and most of the others he was herded into the transit-lounge, the same peeling place he'd waited in the other day with the same waxen-faced woman trundling a trolley round and the same take-away Fair leaflets scattered on the tables between the couches along the wall. *During eight centuries the servant of peaceful trade and understanding between the nations . . . A many-sided event, much more than the normal Trade Fair, set in a city where the hospitality of its inhabitants has become a byword throughout the world . . . Meet and relax in Leipzig . . .* Through the window he glimpsed his first Vopos—a pair of them patrolling the perimeter of a half-empty car-park—and another kind of chill fingered him. He'd almost come full-circle.

The delay was quite short. A juddering piston-engined air-craft punctually lifted them off, bucking on the up-currents after it had gained height and set course above the overcast. There was no passenger service now, no drinks, no cigarettes. Laker didn't unclip his belt. He sat alone, more closely hemmed about than before but insulated from the alien chatter by a steadily-generating tension. He had only the sketchiest of plans, and he couldn't grapple with what lay beyond the next thirty minutes or so. They would be down by then and every-thing would hang on some anonymous official's whim. That was part of the gamble, the part over which he had absolutely no control. From the first he had known it, accepted it, and now it was coming. But without the rifle he would be harmless: im-potent.

The minutes passed, elongated by stress. He listened to the change of tone which marked the start of the descent. Scarves of cloud streamed over the wings. "Fasten your seat-belts, please..." With a pang he remembered the previous nosing in; Patrick's "Dead on time" as the wheels touched—and now it was beginning again, the plane's shadow racing across the tarmac to join them, the bump, the throttled roar, the ponderous run towards the hard, the final lurch and the silence.

The doors opened and the steps were angled into position. Laker took his turn, head buzzing with the sensation of continued movement. WELCOME TO LEIPZIG was emblazoned across the front of the Arrivals building. Inside, the metallic greeting of the public-address system vibrated in his altitude-clogged ears—"Passengers are requested to present their passports and Fair Cards at the Immigration Bureau . . ." Beneath Ulbricht's blown-up, stony stare he completed the formalities and changed his money. There were fewer passengers to be attended to than before and the queues were shorter, but nerves made everything seem more prolonged. The thin person in cadet grey who studied Laker's passport took his time, squinting carefully at the dates of the smudged visa stamps.

"You were here earlier in the week." It was a statement, but an answer was expected.

"Yes."

"On business?"

"Yes."

That was all, but there was a dragging sensation in Laker's stomach. He walked into the Customs bay, wondering which of the knot of waiting officials would pronounce sentence on him. To claim the black rexine case when the baggage arrived called for a feverish brand of courage. He picked it up and set it on the bench beside his suitcase; clumsily lit a cigarette. In a state of terrible fascination he watched the nearest official's technique with the person next to him. Farther along someone's luggage was being rummaged. Then it was his turn: two hands descended on the cases.

"Both yours?"

"That's right."

Small brown eyes held Laker's as he struggled not to bluster; held them but told him nothing.

"You are here for the Fair?"

"Yes."

The man looked down; stroked the suitcase leather admiringly. Then he tapped the other one.

"And here you have —?"

"Samples." Laker could feel the sweat breaking like pins-and-needles in his neck hair. "Trade samples."

"Such as?"

"Precision instruments."

A gesture, a chalked hieroglyph, and he was dismissed. He nodded and backed away; moved into the crowded Arrivals lobby. He was trembling violently. There was no sense of triumph. He pushed out into the open and stood on the steps. For a full minute he paused there, trying to give the impression that he couldn't make up his mind whether or not to join the taxi-queue; then, with a gesture meant to indicate to an observer that he'd that moment remembered something, he swung on his heels and returned inside. But no one seemed in the least interested; he knew the feeling now.

The delegate group was being officially greeted by a trio of smiling men with identification-tags in their square-cut lapels. Laker passed them all by, making for the battery of telephone-boxes in the far corner of the lobby. For hours he had known what he was about to do. He selected the centre one of three vacant booths and pulled the door across; grimly fumbled for change.

Double three, four two, eight six.

"Like the emergency handle on a train, Sam. Long odds against your having to reach for the thing, but it's reassuring to know it's there . . ."

He thumbed in the coin. After that blinding decision back in Copenhagen this had been the first practical idea to come to him, and it had come effortlessly. And the awful irony was with him again as he dialled—that Slattery had his uses at last.

"Salt it away, Sam . . ."

. . . eight . . . six.

He waited then, fingers drumming a tattoo, mind riveted by the repeated bleeps.

A woman answered with a marked Saxonian accent, almost adenoidal. For some reason he hadn't expected to hear a woman. He hesitated, then spoke the introductory phrase that had been buried in the retentive pit of his brain along with the number.

"Peter told me you have a room to let."

"Who?"

"Peter. I was told you had a room."

There was no change of tone. "That is correct, yes."

"Would it be convenient if I called to see it?"

"Of course. How soon will you be coming?"

"In about half an hour?" he suggested.

"Very well."

She enunciated the address carefully, like a school-mistress dictating to a backward pupil. Laker hung up. As he slid the door open he found the exit blocked by someone in the black uniform of the S.S.D. and a spasm of fear gripped him. Self-control demanded a tremendous effort. But almost at once he realised that the man had stepped aside and was giving him the right of way. He brushed by, muttering thanks. Badly shaken, warned, he went outside and joined those waiting for transport.

At least he had somewhere to go, some kind of sanctuary. Next he needed information; more than that he couldn't expect. But he had to discover what had happened, exactly how, precisely where and when. What he did then was his concern, no one else's.

And Hartmann had armed him for it; the irony had no end.

15

THERE were a few isolated spots of rain, as heavy as bird-droppings, before Laker reached the head of the queue. A converted Wartburg saloon picked him up. He didn't give the address, only the street, and he took his cases into the back with him, his eyes on sentry-go as they pulled away.

They went nowhere near the centre of the city, turning right once they were past the outlying tenement blocks, dog-legging through the scruffy wilderness of the suburbs. But it wasn't a long run: fifteen minutes, if that.

Laker walked for a while after settling with the driver, then made his approach. It was a sombre residential street and the house was as drab as its neighbours, of blemished brown stone and with tall windows draped with lace curtains: in the one to the left of the front door a 'ROOMS' notice was propped against the inside of the glass and Laker guessed it had been placed there for his benefit. Some children squabbled on the pavement; a white cat fled from the steps. Chimes ding-donged softly when he pressed the bell and the door opened almost before he had glanced both ways.

The woman was in her middle fifties, dumpy, greying, red-cheeked, with an apron over a flowered dress. She was wearing slippers.

"Was it about the letting?"

He nodded. The smile was cautious, but it welcomed him in. She remarked on the weather. Wiping her hands on the apron, she showed him into the front room, an overcrowded place in which the air seemed absolutely motionless, as in a museum. A horse-hair settee, a weighty table as a centre-piece with carved straight-back chairs, china cabinets, decorative plates around the walls. In the window, flanked by aspidistras on brass stands, was a caged macaw.

"Isn't he beautiful?" the woman remarked, removing the paste-board notice.

She seemed a highly unlikely ally. The macaw clambered on to the side of the cage and tried its great beak on the woman's proffered knuckles.

"How long would you require the room?"

"I'm not certain."

"I let by the week." She quoted the rate, explaining that this was inclusive of meals. "Would you like to see it?"

"Thank you."

She wagged a finger at the macaw. "Naughty," she smiled, then took Laker upstairs. It was a back room, small, with an iron-framed single bed and an old-fashioned marble-topped washstand. They were there for only a minute or two. Downstairs again she asked if he thought it would be suitable, and there was something disturbingly ordinary about the whole business, as if Laker had made a fantastic mistake and arrived at the wrong house. There was no indication that he hadn't. As he counted out a week's money she told him that soap and towels would be put in his bedroom and explained various domestic details about hot water, times of meals, the lights on the upper landing. He wasn't really listening. Having to pay worried him. Did you pay for a bolt-hole?—for that was what this was. Surely. "Just in case, Sam . . ."

"I imagine you'll be staying in for the time being?" the woman said.

"Yes."

"There'll be a key if you want one later."

"Thank you."

"You have only to ask." She took the money from the baize-covered table. The macaw eyed them beadily through the bars. "Don't you stick your little black tongue out at me," she repri-manded it. "And be nice to the gentleman. He's our guest— remember that."

She smiled at Laker, only then dispelling his anxiety. "Some-one will come," she said.

"When?"

"Before too long." And with that she left him.

After a little while he heard her go upstairs and come down again. He went up himself then; towels and soap were on the washstand. He slid the catch on the door, then went to the window. The room wasn't overlooked. Walls jutted out to either side and there was a narrow view towards the rear of some other houses which were partially screened by trees. Beyond them was the silvered dome of a gas-holder. He unlocked the rexine case and took out the dismembered rifle; fitted it together. It was only the second time he had looked at it and he remembered how the first had destroyed the last flimsy shreds of hope that he was somehow at the centre of a vile, unfathomable hoax.

All the markings had been obliterated. He wiped it clean of the film of oil, slotted the telescopic attachment into position and removed the protective end-caps. It was a precision instrument, all right: self-loading, single-shot. He didn't fill the magazine, but he reckoned it would take six. The balance was perfect and the shaped cheek-rest fitted snugly against the side of his face. Standing well away from the window he sighted on the lopped end of one of the branches of the nearest tree and the magnification brought it in from about fifty yards to what seemed to be no more than arm's length, so close that he could see the growth rings in the exposed wood. For perhaps twenty minutes he acquainted himself with the rifle's handling, selecting an occasional snap target—a bird, a man at work on a distant roof—and every alignment amazed him with its apparent shrinkage of distance, the hair-line accuracy at his command. Frenzel wouldn't have had a chance.

He broke the weapon down and re-packed it in the velvet recesses; put on the locks. The house was very quiet, though once he thought he heard the woman talking, perhaps on the telephone. It was a quarter to five. He lay on the bed, wondering who would come, thinking. The unrelenting fury smouldered like a coal. But he seemed to have absorbed fatigue and mostly his mind was sharp and clear, no longer fogged with stupefaction, not so frantic. Time was at a discount now. He'd got back; found shelter. The rest would follow—somehow, somewhere.

He smoked a cigarette and watched a drizzle begin to blur the panes.

The door-bell chimed soon after five. He got off the bed at once. He could distinguish voices, pitched low—the woman's and a man's. After a short while footsteps padded softly on the stairs and someone knocked.

"Come in," he said.

The man was shorter than Laker, and older, perhaps ten years older. He was wearing a dirty raincoat. His face was long and heavily lined, pallid, and his mousy hair was cut short, like a soldier's or a prisoner's. The blue eyes seemed to lack any capacity for surprise.

"Good afternoon." His grip was like a vice. "Is the room satisfactory?"

"Thank you."

"There's no need to confine yourself to it. You can use the living-room if you wish. I'm sure my wife mentioned that." There was a wine-coloured birthmark on one side of his neck just above the collar-line.

"She did, yes."

"Shall we go down? It is more comfortable there."

"All right."

A bicycle had been wheeled into the hall and there was a cloth bag slung on the cross-bar. Perhaps he was a plumber. Askew on the front of the cage the macaw clucked at them drily as they entered the room.

"D'you want names?" Laker asked.

"The fewer the better."

"Mine?"

"No."

The man shook his head. They continued to stand.

He said: "When did your friend Peter recommend us?"

"Earlier this week."

"Never before?"

"No."

"So this is your first time?" The glance implied that beginners usually made their own trouble.

"Yes."

"And you arrived . . .?"

"On Wednesday."

"When did anything go wrong?"

"That afternoon."

"Three days ago?"

"Yes."

"How wrong?"

"I was arrested."

"By?"

"The S.S.D."

"When were you released?"

Laker shook his head. "It wasn't like that."

"I'm sorry, but I don't understand. Where have you come from?—today, I mean. Now."

"The airport. Copenhagen."

The man frowned. He motioned towards the settee and they sat down. "Tell me," he said. "Tell me from the beginning."

"And then?"

"We'll see what can be done."

"You don't know what I want."

"Tell me, and I shall."

It didn't take long. Laker phrased the story carefully, selectively. He mentioned only Patrick and Hartmann by name. Kromadecka and Karen he left out of it; Frenzel too. He didn't once refer to Slattery or to London. The man listened in silence, without interrupting, poker-faced; mostly he stared at his grimy finger-nails. It was a mercy to be able to talk at last, like a letting of blood. Laker said nothing about the girl either. He kept to the essentials, beginning with the mock-execution in the pines and ending with the cancelled reservation at the Metropol which had brought despair and hatred to a white heat. And as he underlined the pressure put upon him and the promised consequences of failure he felt that he was speaking

186

to someone who understood the realities of living—the potential terrors, the springs of desolation that only one in a million were aware existed. Whoever he was he looked a person who had suffered, for whom pain and violence weren't abstractions.

Laker finished and the man glanced up at him. For a long moment he was quiet, then nodded several times, lips pressed tight.

"You say you came on Wednesday?"

"To start with, yes."

A pause, "Kromadecka?"

"Yes."

"Ah." He had it now; Laker watched him: it was all of a piece. "Ah," he said and nodded again. Then he muttered: "Bad, this is bad," and his breath made a long sigh.

"Can you help?"

"With regard to your son?"

"I have to know what happened."

"Of course, of course." He got up, rubbing his birthmark, his attention seemingly held by something in the street. "How did you return—on a Card visa?"

"Yes."

"You'll never get out the same way—you realise that?"

Laker shrugged.

"Not even if you tried to go now, not in view of what you've told me. The machinery isn't slow to function. They'll have the shutters up already."

"I dare say."

"Something can be arranged, though. It can be done, but not before Monday." The man turned and studied him. As if it were a duty he said: "Don't pin your hopes for your son too high, my friend. I have to say this. Don't hope too much."

Laker made no reply. He didn't need telling, but to hear it said fell on his heart like a blow. He squeezed his hands together, looking down between his knees.

"Forgive me," the man said gently, "but I know Hartmann.

I know the kind of person he is. He is warped; there is a flaw of honour in him. Himmler had the same kind of flaw. In his case he was incorruptible where money was concerned. Hartmann's flaw is that he keeps his word."

"For what?" Laker burst out. "He could force me to do what he wanted, but once I'd failed, once that booking was cancelled . . ."

He choked to an end, Hartmann's image looming in his mind. The macaw skittered amiably about the cage. The man went to a cupboard and filled a glass.

"Here," he said. "*Schnapps*. Take it." He sat beside Laker again, his lined face very grave. After a while he said: "I can help in two ways. I can find out about your son. I can also get you across the frontier." He waited, then went on: "What more is there? You can't stay here, not indefinitely."

Laker drained the glass. At last he had someone to rely on— at last, and too late. He rose from the settee.

"There's a third thing," he said thickly.

"Yes?"

"You can tell me where Hartmann lives."

"He has an apartment at S.S.D. headquarters."

"Nowhere else?"

"No."

"Where he goes, then. What his movements are."

The man regarded him quizzically.

"I want to know," Laker insisted.

"What can you do? What can you do with your bare hands? . . . It would be suicide, my friend."

"He provided me with a sniper's rifle."

"In Copenhagen."

"I brought it back."

"Here?" At last there was surprise.

"Here, yes. It's upstairs."

"My God," the man said slowly. "Now I have heard every-thing." He stared, as if making a reappraisal of the forces at work in Laker. "You carried it with you—openly?"

"Yes."

"My God," he said again, this time almost in anger, "the risk you ran. Do you realise the risk you ran?"

An obsession diminishes perception. With infinite weariness Laker lifted his shoulders, let them drop. "I've been out on a limb for three whole days and no one's lifted a bloody finger—not until now. You're the first." He hadn't meant to say this, but his voice had a steely edge. "London led me by the nose, then dropped me. Three days ago I was just another business-man. I was beginning a holiday with my fourteen-year-old son. There was also someone I knew—Karen Gisevius . . . And now? . . . Who am I now? What am I?" There was no self-pity; only the terrible emptiness, the unquenchable loathing. "I'm entitled to take all the risks I choose."

The man hadn't moved his eyes from him. "I can get you out," he repeated, the anger, the alarm, quickly gone. "Remember that."

"I want Hartmann first."

"But say your son is alive. Say, for once, Hartmann hasn't —"

"I don't believe he is."

"But you must have proof. At least you must wait for that."

"I know. I know." Laker's vision blurred. "I was told he was staying with someone called Rauter. I . . . I signed a letter, explaining my absence. He wouldn't have believed it, though. I don't write letters like that . . ." Again he didn't finish, sick with the numbness.

"I have a friend who will know where to enquire."

"How soon?"

"I can't tell. It depends. But I will go and see him."

"When?"

"Now. Immediately." The man started to button his rain-coat; he hadn't taken it off. "Rauter, was it?" He tightened the frayed belt.

"That's right."

At the door he turned, and Laker saw a look of pity which was akin to another he'd glimpsed somewhere back in the nightmare—whose he had forgotten. "My wife will be here," the man said. He made an attempt at a smile. "You'll find her an excellent cook if you want anything."

Laker heard him cross the hall; a muttered exchange—in the kitchen, he supposed. Then the front door opened and he saw the man wheel the bicycle out and pedal away, shabby yet nondescript, along the drenched, dusky street.

Almost at once the woman entered the room. She pulled the curtains carefully before switching on the lights, as if a blackout were in force. Normally they had supper at nine, but if he was hungry . . .? Some coffee and biscuits, perhaps? . . . No; Laker thanked her and went upstairs, threw himself on the bed. Hope was spent. There was nothing left to revive. He was sure about Patrick already, absolutely sure. All day he'd been sure; all night. Hartmann had conditioned him. Hope had shrivelled and died in the Metropol's foyer in one chilling moment of certainty.

The room darkened; the last of the daylight vanished. He thought a thousand things, confusedly, without sequence, in the way the drowning are said to do—except that there was no rush, no panic-stricken compression. Strangely, it was the memory of Patrick's penfriends which moved him most, as if only now he had discovered there must have been loneliness.

"Look after him for me, Sam . . ."

It had gone eight when he heard the chimes and the woman slop in her slippers into the hall. His pulse quickened sluggishly, but he didn't move. He listened to the steps approaching on the stairs, on the landing, and even before the knock sounded he knew exactly what he was going to learn. He was resigned to it, ready, and the man's reluctance to speak was proof in itself.

Yet he said: "Well?"

"It is as you feared, my friend."

Laker closed his eyes. There was silence.

Then the man said awkwardly: "Shall I put on the light?"

"No."

"There is a paragraph in *Neues Deutschland*."

"What does it say?"

"D'you want me to read it?"

"Yes."

The man leaned into the wedge of light that came from the landing and peered short-sightedly at a clipping.

" 'A foreign youth, identified from papers on his person as Patrick Laker, last night received fatal injuries believed to have been caused by a motor vehicle in the Walder Platz. He was dead on arrival at the University Clinic. Enquiries are proceeding.' "

Silence again, longer. "London will go along with our account of an accident, Mr. Laker. They'll accept our post-mortem certificate . . ."

"I'm sorry," the man was saying. "Very, very sorry."

He didn't seem to know what to do with his hands. He came to the side of the bed and, in the gloom, put the cutting on the table there. Then he went back to the door where he paused, his face strained.

"What can I say? . . . Such an act is senseless. Meaningless . . . Is there nothing I can do?"

"No."

"When it suits you we will talk some more. Any time . . . When you wish it."

No answer.

He closed the door behind him, shutting the darkness in.

An hour must have passed before Laker went downstairs. The man and woman were eating in the kitchen and he joined them, the worst of his agony shed. There was cold meat, bread and soup, and he ate a little. The other two didn't speak much; when they did their voices were subdued. Laker drank a good deal of wine and afterwards he and the man went into the front room.

The first thing he said was: "I won't involve you. It's my affair. You've got something to lose." He was quite calm. "All I want is information concerning Hartmann's whereabouts."

"That won't be so easy. He doesn't parade himself." The

man slipped a dome of green baize over the macaw's cage. "And that's what you're asking for, isn't it—a sitting target?"

"I'll take what offers."

"Listen. I know something about abominations, my friend. Both of us do in this house, believe me. But we also know something about survival—and the way your mind is now you will never see London again. What's more, you *would* involve us— inevitably, and that would mean our involving others. A chain-reaction would start. Few of us are ever as strong as we pray to be. A litre of castor-oil, electrodes against the genitals, ice-cold immersion—the threat alone is often quite sufficient. I hardly need explain what fear can do to a man."

A car was splashing through the wet. He cocked his head, his eyes following the sound along the street.

"We operate an escape route, my wife and I. People come here in order to survive, to get clear and lick their wounds in safety. That's our function." He drew in his breath slowly. "We tell ourselves it's a worthwhile occupation."

He opened a drawer in one of the china cabinets and extracted a map. "You've misunderstood me."

"I don't think so."

"I haven't said I won't help. But I *am* insisting on conditions." He glanced earnestly at Laker, and again there was that built-in pity. "I can't stop you from leaving this house whenever you choose. But they're on the lookout for you. And they'll pick you up before you even get wind of Hartmann, let alone squeeze a trigger." He was spreading the map on the table, flattening the creases. "I can't stop you. But I can argue with you. I can make the point that you weren't given this telephone number in order to endanger others on account of a personal vendetta."

Laker gazed with suspicion at the grey, cadaverous face. "What conditions?"

"One, that you're patient. Two, that I decide what is possible, and relate it to the problem of getting you back where you belong." A bruised finger-nail stubbed the map. "You're a hundred and fifty kilometres from the frontier. Even if you managed to get that far—alone—you'd never cross the death strip."

"How patient?"

The man shrugged. "Getting out may be secondary to you, but it isn't to me. I want you off our hands, my friend." He offered Laker a cigarette. "You aren't the first to have wished Hartmann dead. But yielding to instinct won't achieve it. If you're going to succeed you need more than a few scraps of information and advice. I'll give you all there is, and practical help as well, but you must accept that it will have to be tied in with getting you away."

He coughed. "Besides, I should imagine you have good reason for wanting to return to London. From what you tell me I'd say they also have something to answer for."

It was almost midnight before they finished. Laker was so weary by then that he could scarcely employ his mind, but he had a dread of being alone again. Towards the end he was using the man as a safety-valve, unburdening himself, as confiding as a solitary drinker in a bar. The woman came in eventually and offered him a couple of sleeping-pills. He took them and the session ended. At the foot of the stairs he said to the man: "Don't try and fob me off, that's all I ask. You'll be wasting your breath."

"I won't, my friend. I promise you"—and Laker gripped his bony arms in a spasm of emotion.

The cutting was beside the bed and the gun was in its case. But oblivion came fast and, mercifully, there were no dreams.

16

Twice next morning Laker heard the telephone. The first time it woke him to the waiting desolation; the second took him to the bedroom door, listening. But he deciphered nothing: on both occasions the woman was speaking. He lay in the bed until ten o'clock, then slowly shaved and dressed. While he was in the bathroom he thought somebody used the front door, but he wasn't certain.

There was a place set for him at the kitchen table. The woman greeted him with the same ingenuousness as when he'd first arrived. "I thought you'd like to rest," she said, clattering at the stove. "Did the pills help?"

"Thank you."

"You can get over-tired, can't you? They're useful then."

"Yes."

"It looks like rain again. And we had a lot in the night, too."

The perfection of the lie she was living never varied, somehow raising an echo of the blatant disbelief that had unsuccessfully tried to hold Laker in the moment of waking. When he asked where her husband was she said: "He's just gone to the shops for cigarettes. He won't be long"—and he wondered how much she really knew, how much her red-cheeked smile masked a longing for peace and safety.

He finished her strong, ersatz coffee and went into the living-room, restless already, watching the street. Last night, sprawled on the settee, he had talked with an abandonment that was rare for him, wretchedness loosing his tongue. It had come piecemeal, in no chronological order, yet it had made a kind of whole—mainly about Patrick, but about Helen too, about Weybridge, Gale and Watts, Roundwood, about the war and Karen Gisevius; all that. And now, remembering some of the things he had said he also remembered how the man had listened and how his sympathy had once or twice mounted almost to visible distress so that his willingness to assist in dealing with Hartmann grew like a bond between them. In the hall, when they were about to go upstairs, there had been a glint in his eyes which had reminded Laker of that night in Green Park half a lifetime before when Slattery had suddenly burst out: "You kill the bastards, Sam. Kill as many of them as you can."

Just one this time. Just one to clean something out of his mind, out of his heart, out of his insides. And then, with what was left over, to face Slattery.

No, he hadn't done with London; the man was right. If it were possible Slattery wasn't going to get away with it either.

Half an hour elapsed before the familiar figure cycled shabbily into view along the street. The lack of haste wasn't encouraging. The macaw squawked and fluttered excitedly when the front door opened and again when the man entered the room: simultaneously the telephone rang. He hesitated, ready to go, ready to stay, waiting tensely as the woman took the call.

"Yes, he's here," she said, and the man returned to the hall. "That's right," Laker heard. "Yes . . . With pleasure . . . Certainly . . . But not for two or three days. On Wednesday, perhaps. May I call and discuss it with you? . . . Very well . . . Yes, I'll do that. I will be in touch. Without fail."

He was smiling grimly when he rejoined Laker. "A lady wants her kitchen painted."

So that was his cover. He tossed his cap on to the table. He hadn't shaved and he looked tired. "It's early yet. Don't expect too much all at once. It's going to be like walking in long grass for a while . . . Did you sleep well?"

Laker nodded.

"How good are you with a rifle?"

"According to Hartmann, exceptionally good."

The man savoured that quietly. "You'll need to be. You won't find him hanging about, asking for it."

"Where is he now?"

"At headquarters. At least, his car's there."

"A green one? Dark green?"

"A Moskvitch, yes."

He took a folder from his breast-pocket and shook it open—a street-map of Leipzig. "Hopeless," he said. "Hopeless. You wouldn't stand a chance in the city. Yesterday, for instance, he was here . . . and here . . . and then here, in the Alte Markt." He used his hands dismissively. "Hopeless. Impossible. You're going to have to wait until he travels farther afield."

"When's that likely to be?"

"Perhaps days."

"For God's sake!"

"How should I know?" He seemed on edge. "I'm not a prophet. But I am a realist, and what might suit you tactically might not suit me. Be reasonable . . . Yes, reasonable," he repeated tartly. "Don't expect me to produce Hartmann for you like something out of a hat. I shudder when I think what has been done. Words are inadequate. But what you are asking has to be planned, thought about, worked on. Without help you'd achieve nothing except the certainty of disaster for others. So save up what you feel, my friend. Be patient."

The morning passed. The man left the house around noon, on foot. Laker hadn't asked what his sources of information were, and he didn't want to know. But the restraint, the frustration, were almost unendurable. He went up to the bedroom for a while, assembled and practised handling the rifle. Somehow he hadn't bargained on a lengthy delay. On a base, yes; but not on caution, not on being cooped-up, not on marking time. In the demented haze of his return he had imagined something reflexively swift, unaided, a snarling pent-up release that would find satisfaction in seeing Hartmann crumple and go down. Now he must wait for it; curb himself. He recognised the necessity. But grief was like a wound; the real pain was slow to come, and it was still spreading, raw now, giving existence to depths of him long since insensible.

And this was Slattery's territory; that worried him. Already Slattery would be wondering where the hell he'd got to. He would have begun to check and counter-check—and even a fool like Jackson would very soon find out. If Slattery put two-and-two together it was possible that he would attempt to warn the local network off. Almost certain, in fact. Karen had been lost to him already and he wouldn't want any more casualties. As a side issue he might approve of Hartmann's death, but not if it meant jeopardising his listening-post, his contacts, his go-betweens—all those who earned him dividends, showed returns. Someone would replace Hartmann, anyhow. The game would go on, Hartmann or no Hartmann, and for people like Slattery the game was the thing. In that ivory-tower of his what mattered was to keep his pins firmly on the map . . .

Stay out of this, sod you, Laker thought. You've done enough—or haven't you heard yet?

He hung about the living-room, anxiously watching the street.

The man was soon back, but only to shrug. Nothing yet . . . Towards one o'clock the telephone rang and he grunted cryptically several times into the mouthpiece, but all he said to Laker afterwards was: "Still at headquarters."

The three of them ate together in the kitchen. It was strange, but when the woman was present it was as if Laker and the man shared a secret from which she was excluded: the masquerade took over. But this time, as they were finishing, she suddenly remarked: "You didn't mind about the money, did you?"

Laker frowned.

"The rent."

"No." He fingered his glass, puzzled, dragging his thoughts away from where they swarmed. "No."

The man leaned forward. "My wife always insists that the labourer is worthy of his hire, no matter what the circumstances. But we aren't mercenaries, my friend, and if she has given you that impression she does herself less than justice." Quietly he said to her: "Show our guest your arm . . . Go on."

The woman slid back the right sleeve of her blouse. Three or four inches above the wrist a six-figure number was crudely tattooed on the pink skin. Laker had no need to ask what it signified or when it had been put there.

"Ravensbruck," the man said. "And memories are just as indelible. I told you, we know something about abominations." He gestured. "Perhaps our willingness to help you is more understandable now. London would hardly approve, but that is neither here nor there. They spin the webs, but they don't live in them . . ."

It was as if he had been reading Laker's mind.

He went out again presently, on foot once more; where, why, he didn't say. He never said.

There was little movement in the street—an occasional cyclist, a scooter or two. A dog barked periodically from the broken railings on the other side and a handful of people walked by, women mostly, sometimes pausing to gossip. Laker's agitation reached a new peak; drove him upstairs. From the window there the dome of the distant gas-holder had sunk from view; almost twenty-four hours had frittered away since he first saw it. He lay on the bed, but soon got up and returned to the living-room. There was no sign of the man and the telephone remained silent. Gone three . . . The macaw ground its beak furiously on the cage-wire; the clash of crockery sounded from the kitchen.

Half-past three. He'd never stand another day of it. Another day chained like this and something would snap. For the second time that afternoon he returned to the bedroom and lay there smoking, staring at the ceiling, watching the sagging grey sky, his face recording ugly inner journeys.

It was twenty to four when the telephone rang. He listened, head cocked, but for all he could tell it was another false alarm. Then he heard the woman on the stairs and he didn't wait for her to knock.

"Yes?"

She might have been coming in to turn the bed-covers down, or change the towels. "My husband asked me to tell you to be ready in five minutes."

Laker's heart lifted urgently. He nodded. "Very well."

"With both your cases. And would you please wear these."

She dropped some old blue overalls on to the end of the bed.

"All right."

He didn't question why. She left him and he put them on, dry in the mouth, his pulse quickening. The overalls were tight under the arms, but otherwise the fit was good enough. After a momentary indecision he folded his topcoat and pressed it into the suitcase, then hurried downstairs.

"Would you like some coffee?" The woman amazed him to the end. "It's on the stove."

"No, thanks."

He followed her into the living-room where she remarked to the macaw: "Our guest is going. Aren't you sorry to lose him?" The bird clawed clumsily round the cage. She stroked its gaudy head, but her eyes were on the gap in the draped lace curtains. Very soon she said: "This is him now," and Laker saw a small battered open truck rattling along the street.

"Stay here," she said, a soft command in her tone for the first and only time. "Let him come in first."

The truck shook to a standstill and Laker watched the man get out and saunter towards the steps. The woman waited for the bell before she went to open the door. "Is he ready?" Laker heard, and her quiet "Yes." He moved into the hall. The man looked at him and nodded meaningly. The two cases were at the foot of the stairs. Laker picked them up, but the man took the suitcase from him. "I'll attend to this."

"Good-bye," the woman said. "Good-bye. I'm pleased to have met you."

She would baffle anyone, Laker felt, even under blinding lights.

He shook her by the hand, moved suddenly. "Good-bye."

The man went first. He slung the suitcase into the back of the truck and covered it over with a square of perished tarpaulin. Laker clambered into the driving-cab, shoving the black case between his knees. It was a rickety vehicle, the blue-grey paint chipped and scored and patched with rust; the off-side wing was badly concertinaed and Laker could see the ground through a hole in the flooring.

The man climbed in behind the wheel, fastening the door with a twist of string. He had left the engine running. With a crunch of gears they drew away. Laker didn't look back; never saw the woman again.

"Well?" This before they'd shuddered twenty yards.

"He's gone north, towards Dessau."

"How far's that?"

"Seventy, eighty kilometres. But he'll be turning round at the district border, which is only half as far, and coming south again. And he's had a fair start, so we're against the clock." They swung left, clipping the kerb. "He'll be on the autobahn, understand?"

"Travelling?"

"Travelling, yes."

That meant anything up to a hundred miles an hour; perhaps more. Daunted, Laker screwed his eyes, doubts and protest rising together.

"Listen," the man said loudly above the clatter. "At one point the south-bound slow lane is under repair. There are warning notices out. Traffic's down to about half-speed over a longish stretch."

Sixty, say. Even so . . . It could be lunacy. Laker bit his lips, questioning his companion's judgement.

"You might wait a week and never have as good a chance. There's a party on its way from Berlin and Hartmann's taking over escort duty at the district border. It isn't often that he strays so far from home."

They were rattling between drab rows of suburban shops.

"How's the time?"

"Four," Laker said. Then, uneasily: "I hope to God you know what's possible and what isn't."

"You want everything guaranteed, don't you?" Suddenly the man was nettled. He wrestled the wheel, glowering. "You want the work done for you, the risks all —"

"No, but —"

"Wait and see, then." He dabbed the brake-pedal to avoid a cyclist; swore. "I made conditions, remember. There are other necks at stake besides yours. I tell you Hartmann's as vulnerable as ever he'll be, but more important as far as I'm concerned is what happens afterwards."

Laker was silent.

"I can get you away," the man said, calming again. "And that matters. Any fool can commit suicide. Tonight you'll be over the frontier. We aren't waiting for Monday."

They were nearing the city's centre, the Fair's flags and streamers, the Sunday afternoon crowds. LEIPZIG—ANOTHER NAME FOR HOSPITALITY . . . Laker felt exposed, the overalls no protection against the attention attracted by the truck's racketing progress. A siren wailed behind them and his heart-beat thudded; there was no rear-view mirror. For an awful moment it seemed as if the man were pulling into the side, but he was merely getting out of the way. An ambulance slid past, and Laker's skin crawled with relief.

"There's a map under the seat," he was told.

Traffic-lights delayed them as he groped. A black saloon drew alongside and its uniformed passenger stared broodingly at the truck from a distance of three feet.

"National People's Army," the man muttered from the side of his mouth. "General." Then, when the lights changed and they had jerked into the car's wake: "We're taking the Halle road . . . Halle, got it? Through Schkeuditz."

"Yes."

"We hit the autobahn after leaving Schkeuditz. It's marked E6. The slow section I mentioned is about four kilometres north of the junction. That's where I'll put you down."

"And then?"

"The details don't make sense until you've seen the ground. But west of E6, running parallel, there's a minor road."

Laker peered, trying to steady the map. "About a kilometre west?"

"That's the one. We'll rendezvous there."

The man's voice was taut, authoritative. He was allowing

Laker no choice. His plans were made, but they had the vagueness of something hurriedly thrown together. Laker managed to hold his uneasiness in check, focusing his mind on an imagined stretch of autobahn, picturing a vehicle at speed, thinking about angles, height, time, distance . . . It was going to be now or never.

"How will I know which car is his?"

"That's taken care of. I'll explain when we're on the spot." A clock showed four-twelve. They passed the Ring-Messehaus and its frontal gardens, then the Astoria where the nightmare had begun with stuttered explanations from a stranger in a raincoat, then the square where Hartmann had driven to the shooting-gallery.

Laker needed no reminders. He pressed his calves against the rexine case, keeping it steady. A few storm-drops struck the windscreen and he willed the sky to hold off, clenching his hands as he squinted upwards.

"Time?" the man asked hoarsely.

"Four-fifteen."

They were heading west now: a sign pointed to Schkeuditz and Halle. All the din in the world seemed to be concentrated inside the draughty cabin as they passed through a succession of cobbled streets. Shops, houses, factories, a ruined church, more factories, wasteland, rubble—gradually the city fell away. A stream meandered in to flank them on the left and there were meadows to either side, dotted with oaks and larches. The road was mostly straight but the truck swayed dangerously, buffeted by a gusty cross-breeze, and the man crouched at the wheel, working the loose steering. They covered the distance to Schkeuditz at a kilometre a minute, slowed there to the permitted maximum, sweated out a traffic jam, then picked up speed again, steam issuing from the radiator. The countryside widened, more thickly wooded, slightly undulating. Northwards, slanting cords of rain darkened the horizon.

"How long have we got?" Laker shouted.

"You ought to be in position by five."

"That rain will be on us by then."

The man risked a sideways scowl and grunted. He looked drawn and the creases in his forehead glistened. The grunt was his only comment.

Five kilometres brought them to the autobahn's approach. The road climbed a shade, veering right, then topped a low crest, and all at once the autobahn was there, as wide as an airport's runway, split by a humped strip of grass. Tucked in behind an ancient Porsche they filtered into the first lane and the man opened the throttle again, steam flattening continuously over the shaking bonnet.

Hartmann would be coming south. South, on the other carriageway.

The traffic there was light, unevenly spaced. Laker singled out two or three of the faster cars, watching them swell from the size of toys and flash past, blurring as they went. Short white markers were planted at intervals along the far verge, behind which was a post-and-rail fence and then a broken fringe of pines. He was going to need cover and it looked as if he'd get it twenty or thirty yards from the carriageway; but the speeds had shaken him—even allowing for the fact that he was trying to assess them while the truck was flat out in the other direction.

A slightly-banked curve and the entire autobahn changed course, heading towards the blue-black clouds along the northern rim. As they roared beneath a bridge the man suddenly pointed half left. "There . . . There," and beyond the humped divide Laker saw the beginnings of a long line of red-and-white tar-barrels which sealed off the opposite outer lane. They drew level; continued on by. The obstruction lasted a full two kilometres and the traffic was noticeably slower. The bulldozers and cement-mixers were idle: Sunday. Beyond the heaps of sand and steel mesh and broken concrete and the gangers' huts a bank sloped up to the perimeter fence and the trees.

It would be there, then. Somewhere over there.

The man had the accelerator against the floor. Twenty to five. They continued north for another couple of minutes, then looped off, spiralled, crossed the autobahn, looped down and rejoined it, heading south. The warning-signs began almost at once. ROAD WORKS . . . REDUCE SPEED . . . TWO LANES ONLY . . . NO OVERTAKING . . . Then the first of the barrels was in sight. ROAD NARROWS . . . SLOW . . . SLOW . . . Brake-lights blinked dutifully on the saloon ahead of them. Angled trestles squeezed them into what was normally the centre lane and the man eased his foot from the throttle. They cruised for about a third of the obstruction's length before he chose a gap between barrels, nosed through and came to rest in the lee of a covered tarring-machine.

"Now," he said immediately. "Now what I tell you will make sense. Get out and pretend to look at the engine with me. For once she has boiled to order."

They climbed down. He lifted the bonnet. Steam rose in clouds from the spitting radiator-cap. He nodded towards the crossing they had just used.

"That's where I'll be—on the north-bound shoulder. I'll be pulled off with the bonnet up, the same as now. Hartmann's escorting two other cars, so they'll come together, the three of them in convoy. I've some binoculars here which I'll give you in a minute. Keep me in view from wherever you locate yourself. Watch me all the time. When Hartmann comes through the underpass you'll see me slam the bonnet down and prepare to drive away. Is that clear?"

Laker nodded.

"There will be three cars, remember. I'll give my signal immediately they emerge from the underpass. You can't possibly make a mistake. You'll see them all the way from here. And the green Moskvitch will almost certainly be in the lead."

Laker nodded again. A lorry whined by, wet, wipers still working. Speed and rain—it would be touch and go. A chill moved through him.

"Hartmann has a driver," the man said, "so he'll be riding in the back seat."

"What else should I know?"

"Afterwards go due west. Through the trees. Keep going

until you reach the minor road you saw on the map. Then wait there. Wait until we pick you up."

"We?"

"I'll have switched to a car, but I can't say what kind it will be. Possibly a Volga. Just wait, that's all. And get rid of your overalls."

"All right."

The man leaned under the steering-wheel and brought out a pair of binoculars. Laker shoved them into a pocket and pulled the black case from the cabin. Air beat over them from a passing car.

"Now it's up to you," the man said. "I've done the best I can. Select your position, then watch for me on the shoulder by the underpass. I'll be there in five minutes." He clamped the bonnet shut, heaved himself aboard and switched on. The engine raced. Pulling away he wound the window down and pumped his arm to indicate urgency. Above the roar he shouted: "Good luck, Mr. Laker."

Laker didn't reply. He cut between the tarring-machine and a stack of steel pipes and loped up the grass slope towards the fence, bending low as if he were under fire. The grass was soggy, sucking softly at his shoes. He climbed the fence and made for the trees, a kind of nausea welling up. And as he ran he began asking himself how the man had got to know his name.

He went a short distance into the wood, then dropped on to one knee and snapped the case open. In the couple of minutes it took him to assemble the rifle the query persisted.

How? . . . Last night, when distress and fatigue had made him talk so much—had it slipped out then? He didn't believe so. And there was more. The man had known what name to look for in *Neues Deutschland*. Only now this other fact struck him, now when action was all that mattered.

He must have told him. *Must* have done . . .

He broke open the carton of ammunition and loaded the magazine, thumbing the rounds in separately. He put in four against the pressure of the spring, hesitated with a fifth, decided against it, and rammed the magazine home. Two was about all he'd be able to use and an over-full magazine could jam; from twenty years ago he remembered. He stood up, pivoting on his heels. He was deep enough into the trees for the autobahn to be almost invisible. The sound of the traffic was pierced by a bird singing somewhere overhead.

"Good luck, Mr. Laker . . ." It wasn't a time for question-marks.

He left the case where it was and moved to the edge of the cover. He was ten yards from the fence and the fence was about fifteen from the white markers along the carriageway's border and those, in turn, were ten from the line of tar-barrels. There were better places: he was quick to decide. Off to his right the trees receded up the slope, then spread down again almost to the fence. He ran there, slithering on the carpet of pine-needles, impelled by a devil of instinctive obedience that was unleashed at last—like the time he'd kicked the radio-set to pieces and started his own war, skill and hatred fused, all the layers by which he recognised himself stripped away, peeling away now as he came to the fence and studied the line of fire the new position gave him, possessed by the same terrible hurt as then, the same elemental lust as then, except once it had been for Germans, any Germans, faceless, anonymous enemies, and now it was solely for Hartmann, Hartmann who had asked for this from the moment they first met.

Laker went prone behind the fence. Perhaps three-quarters of a mile separated him from the underpass; a quarter from where the south-bound carriageway narrowed. He was about eight feet above road-level with an uninterrupted view between a steam-roller and one of the deserted gangers' huts. SLOW . . . NO OVERTAKING . . . SLOW—over his right shoulder he could see the warnings repeated behind him along the whole length of the obstruction. He took out the binoculars and fixed them on the underpass: there was no sign of the truck, but the rain had spread nearer, blue and obliterating.

Five o'clock exactly . . . The ground was uneven so he

wriggled back a few feet, angling his body about fifteen degrees from the fence. Emerging from the underpass the cars seemed to crawl. Where the slow section began they rocked minutely in tell-tale fashion from a touch on the brake or a sudden easing of the throttle, yet when they were about two hundred yards away the head-on effect rapidly diminished and it appeared as if they were actually accelerating as their individual detail loomed and they bore obliquely past with a rubbery whine.

The truck crashed along the north-bound track as he was slipping the end-caps off the telescopic sight. He watched it, the query renewing itself, niggling, the man's willingness to be an accessory suddenly suspect.

Disturbed, he sighted on an approaching Skoda, splaying his legs. It was sharp and clear when he picked it up at three hundred yards. For about four seconds the hair-line cross centred on a heavy face in the dark V cleared by the wind-screen wipers; then the swift traversing movement began and Laker couldn't hold the aim without slewing. He took a line on the next two cars, concentrating on the rear seats through the spattered side windows, coldly, expertly, a culmination coming, the scent of the near-by pines a needless mnemonic of fear, manipulation and murder.

If the rain held off he had a sixty-forty chance. But would it? Christ, would it?

The truck had limped on to the shoulder just short of the underpass and the man had the bonnet up: the binoculars made him seem within shouting distance. Six minutes after five . . . Laker's mouth was as dry as a kiln and the truck moved in and out of focus with every hammerstroke of his heart.

Why such risks for a stranger? . . . What had been plausible an hour ago, a day ago, was increasingly in doubt. Who else could have disclosed his identity?

A solitary lorry crept through the underpass.

Slattery?

Sweat dribbled from Laker's eyebrows and he blinked it away.

Slattery?

A couple of cars, abreast. A light flurry of rain. And the growing confusion, the whirling suspicion that, even now, he was somehow being used.

The man was going through the motions of tinkering with the engine. The binoculars trembled in Laker's hands. With the distrust of the abused he tried to ask himself if it could possibly be that he was still a puppet, Slattery's now, led unknowingly as if he were in his sleep to settle some score that wasn't his. And as he groped for an answer that made even a freakish hint of sense he knew that such a thing was inconceivable. Patrick was dead; the score was his and his alone. "Between you and me, Mr. Laker . . ."

Nothing through the underpass.

Frenzel was alive and Patrick was dead. The equation was Hartmann's, *the weapon was Hartmann's.*

Another lorry, another gap, then an old grey saloon. In ten minutes the rain would have engulfed the underpass.

Five-twelve.

Laker eased his weight from one elbow to another, fiddling the binoculars into sharper focus. As he did so he saw the man suddenly drop the truck's raised bonnet and three cars come out of the underpass in line astern, the Moskvitch in the lead.

His scalp tightened. The overalls split at the armpits as he reached for the rifle. Three-quarters of a mile . . . A deluge of noise was filling his ears. He pushed the safety-catch forward, not hearing the click, deaf to everything except the crescendo of the blood-beat inside himself. Vaguely he was aware of the truck moving off the shoulder and heading the other way but his stare was riveted to the convoy: the cars were still small to the naked eye, like models, one green and two black, seeming to inch clear of the underpass.

He shifted position slightly, tensing, raising the rifle. The grey saloon had swept by where he lay. At half a mile he saw the nose of the Moskvitch dip as it approached the warning-signs and he knew it was cutting speed. Six hundred yards . . . Nothing but the noise in his head, no conscious thoughts, no last-second spurt of rage, everything instinctive.

Five hundred . . . He nestled against the cheek-rest and took preliminary aim. The car was shedding a misty spray. Wipers going, peaked cap behind the wheel, Hartmann in the back, alone, blurred by the smeared side-windows. A peep-show, crossed by the hair-lines, enlarging . . . First pressure already on the trigger, the squeeze beginning. Another second. The angle widening, the apparent acceleration. An infinitesimal moment more —

Now!

Laker felt the jolt, saw the glass splinter and the simultaneous clutching movement inside the car. In an intensity of awareness he fired again, the aim held, the window frosting a hand's-width from the first point of impact, the figure slumping, hat askew—all this he glimpsed in the identical jarring instant, all at telescoped distance.

Then the lightning traverse to the right began and his chance of a third shot had gone. And he was stumbling to his feet, discarding the rifle, running.

He ran with his head down. The trees hid him almost immediately. The roar in his ears cleared for a moment, like enormous bubbles bursting, and he heard the savage whimpering of tyres. After a short distance he stopped and looked back through a gap in the pines. The three cars were at a standstill, askew on the track, men leaping from them. The driver of the Moskvitch had opened the near-side door and Laker could see the overcoated figure sprawled head and shoulders on to the carriageway, motionless.

He didn't wait. One glance was enough. He turned again and ran on, a choking sensation rising in his throat. The sounds of the autobahn receded. After a little he slowed, but the possibility of pursuit kept him going. The pines gave way to fields and he felt rain on his face as he moved into the open. Six or seven minutes brought him to the road, the self-same scenes flickered vividly across his vision. The road was sunken, unsurfaced, narrow. He stripped the overalls off and tossed them into a clump of bushes, then climbed some barbed wire and clambered down the bank. The rain was intensifying. He sheltered against the trunk of a huge beech, breathing hard, mind churning, an exultant shiver once racking him like an ague.

It seemed a long while before he heard something coming. Fifty yards away the road cornered gently and disappeared from view. He quit the protection of the tree and started to move in the direction from which the promised car was approaching. He'd taken about ten paces before he saw it, a mud-flecked Volga. He raised a hand in greeting and stopped. It came quite fast, in low gear, almost filling the width of the road. Several people seemed to be in it, but the rain hid their identities. As it braked to a standstill Laker started forward again, thumbs up. In the same moment doors opened on either side and the front-seat occupants got out. And with a blow of incredulous dismay he recognised the blond, black-jacketed driver and the man in the raincoat with the lop-sided face who'd been his captors once before.

For a lifelong moment he was rooted where he stood. Then he turned and fled, mind and body temporarily dissociated— the one stunned, the other in a paroxysm of movement.

"Mr. Laker!"

He sprinted along the road. A stuttering voice repeatedly bawled at him to stop. Doors slammed and he heard the car start after him. With a despairing effort he flung himself up the bank, expecting a shot. He clawed his way up frantically, reached the top as the car drew level below, then went to vault the barbed wire. The post he grabbed for support broke off as he was in mid-air; one foot caught the topmost strand of wire. Falling, he felt the sickening impact as his head clubbed against an outcrop of stone and everything exploded into darkness.

They had him in the car and the car was moving. He heard someone moan, not realising it was himself. In the dim beginnings of revival he struggled, fighting the hands that seemed to be holding him down. Through swelling pain he babbled defiantly: "I got him, anyway . . . I got him!"—kicking, straining against whoever was there.

"What d'you think?" someone asked a million miles away, but not of him, and someone else replied: "Perhaps you'd better."

He felt his jacket being dragged off, his left sleeve being pulled up, then the prick and deep slide of a needle in his flesh. Almost immediately the blackness started to lump and tumble into the featureless landscape of renewed unconsciousness.

"You should have told him about his son," another voice was protesting. "You should have told him that."

It was the last thing to register and he took it under with him, bewildered even then. For it was Karen who had spoken.

17

HE floated in the darkness, sometimes totally unaware, sometimes with his mind beset with problems which had been with him since childhood, sometimes swept by eddies of weakness that seemed to suck him down to where it was darker still. In the delirium of this darkness people touched him, shifted him, talked to him and about him and several times a whisper echoed round the resonant cave of his skull—"Patrick's all right. Can you hear? . . . Patrick's all right."

How long he floated he pieced together afterwards. But a moment came when he felt himself once more being lifted, cradled, borne slowly upwards towards actuality. In a daze of vagueness he opened his eyes, then clamped them shut, stabbed by a blaze of light that seemed to start his head hammering as if a switch had been thrown. For an incalculable period his thoughts streamed away in ribbons of jumbled pictures, the thudding in his temples like a pile-driver. Then, fearfully, he began to blink, his hands to wander.

He was in a bed. A shaded light on a glossy wall beyond the hump made by his feet, a chintz-covered window, a silver-grey door, a silver-grey cupboard, a table . . . Gingerly he felt his head, discovering bandages; dully, he noticed that he was wearing his own pyjamas. The fevered condition of his mind prevented him from guessing where he might be, or even reflecting that it was different from what he ought to have expected. He called out, a hoarse croak, but no one came. His watch had been taken from his wrist, so he had no idea of the time. He felt sick and closed his eyes, yielding to the heavy drag on his senses, remembering the autobahn, the Moskvitch, Hartmann in his sights and Hartmann inert, sprawled like a rag-doll on the tarmac; remembering the narrow road and the Volga and the shock of who was in it, remembering running, knowing that something had gone horribly wrong—all that part very clear. And then remembering the darkness in which, impossibly, Karen Gisevius had existed and another voice had gently whispered lies to him about Patrick.

He slept again before the chaotic wandering took hold.

Now the curtains had been pulled aside and daylight was furring the edges of the window. He stared at it for what seemed a long time without fully realising he was awake. The pile-driver had been replaced by a lazy throbbing and he sat up cautiously, surveying the room, mystified. A vase of bronze chrysanthemums stood on the bedside table and his watch was there beside it.

Eight-fifteen . . . Monday? An enormous effort was required: his mind was sore, as if it had been kicked. Impulsively he started towards the window, but he swayed when he got to his feet and sank back, dizzy.

From the bed he could see the top of some trees. He pressed against the pillows, struggling to make sense of the neat room, the flowers, the comfort. A flask of water was also on the table and he started pouring some into a tumbler. As he was doing so the door opened and a dark-haired nurse looked in. The crisp headgear, the white crossbands over the lilac blouse, the starched cuffs and apron—none of it rang a bell with him.

"Where am I?"

He spoke in German. She hesitated fractionally, then entered, closing the door behind her.

"Where is this place?"

To his astonishment she answered in English. "I haven't passed my colloquial yet, but if you're asking what I think you're asking the answer is the British Military Hospital in Hanover."

"*Where?*"

"Hanover, Germany. And I'm from London, England." She smiled pertly, looking down at him. "Have you been awake long?"

Hanover: it wouldn't sink in. "How in the hell did I get here?"

"I wouldn't know," the nurse said. "I only came on duty at eight."

"What's today?"

"Monday." She was feeling his pulse. "How's the head?"

"Spinning."

"You've got six stitches in it, so no wonder. D'you feel you can cope with a visitor?"

"Who?"

"I wouldn't know that either. I'm just responsible for your well-being. What d'you think? Yes or no?"

"Yes," he said.

"It's up to you." She studied him clinically. "Are you sure?"

He nodded.

"Very well. I'll get him."

She went away with a starchy rustle. A minute or two elapsed before the door opened again, and in that time Laker's mind moved sufficiently fast through its labyrinth of bewilderment not to be entirely surprised to see who came in.

"Sam."

Slattery tiptoed across to the bed as if he were in church.

"How are you, Sam?" The brick-red complexion, the smooth-as-glass manner.

Laker spurned his offered handshake. "Where the blazes have you sprung from?"

"I've been waiting along the corridor. They gave me a cubby-hole in which to park myself. I wanted to be with you the moment you surfaced."

"Is that so?"

"There's something you must know, Sam—right away."

"Go on."

"I talked to you during the night, and you answered after a fashion. D'you remember?"

"No."

"About Patrick." Slattery couldn't seem to manage it first time. "He's come to no harm, Sam. He's safe and well, here in Hanover."

All his life Laker was to remember that tremendous leap in his heart. The delirious whispers echoed—"Patrick's all right ... All right ..." Yet, staring at Slattery, he heard himself say: "I don't believe you."

"It's true. As true as we're together."

"It can't be. *Neues Deutschland* —"

"It is, Sam."

"Prove it." Oh my God, he thought. Oh Jesus.

"I shall. But take it easy, take it easy."

"Where is he?"

"With friends, on the other side of town."

"Bring him over. Let me see him."

"Just as soon as I can. But give him a chance, Sam." A tentative smile. "He probably hasn't had his breakfast yet."

"Let me talk to him, then."

"Are you up to it?"

"My God," Laker said. "Where's the telephone?"

He started to scramble out of bed, beside himself with wonder and excitement, but Slattery checked him and went to the door, opened it and called the nurse.

214

"She's fetching one," he said, returning. "You're in no state to be walking about."

Laker closed his eyes. He was trembling. His voice had thickened. "There was a paragraph about him in *Neues Deutschland*. It said he'd been killed in a street accident."

"It was false, Sam. A lie. You'll see."

Laker sucked in air. He needed time. Time. "How did you manage it?"

"Manage what?"

"Getting him out." Incredibly, they were talking about the living.

"I'll put you in the picture presently."

"Now."

"Presently."

"And me . . . What about me? I was picked up by a couple of —"

"Let it wait, Sam. First things first."

Slattery raised a finger to his lips as the nurse entered to plug in a telephone. Only when he'd thanked her and she'd gone did he speak again.

"There's just one thing before you have a word with Patrick. He's swallowed the business-trip story, and as far as your being *hors de combat* is concerned the line is that you had an argument with a door at the airport last night. There shouldn't be any awkward questions, but play it by ear."

Laker nodded. His mind was being asked to make too many somersaults all at once, but he was too relieved to be thinking clearly, too muddled, too grateful. A miracle had happened; at the moment he could forgive everything. He ran his hands over his face while Slattery gave the operator a number.

"There's quite a tale to tell, Sam." The smile was still a shade uncertain. "But this is what matters now."

Slattery hung on, twisting the telephone cord in his fingers, blinking away behind his spectacles.

Laker exclaimed: "Why did *Neues Deutschland* carry a false report, for God's sake? I shot Hartmann on the strength of it."

215

He looked sharply at Slattery. The nightmare wasn't done with yet. "Hartmann's dead. I shot him with the rifle he supplied me with to kill Frenzel."

But Slattery had turned aside. "Yes?" he was saying. "Is Patrick there, please? . . . It's his father." And whatever reaction Laker had looked for in Slattery was forgotten as he grabbed the telephone.

"Patrick?"

"Hallo, dad. I hear you've been in the wars again."

"It's nothing."

"I was expecting you last night. I wasn't told until first thing this morning that you'd been carted off to hospital . . . How are you?"

"Some stitches in the head, that's all."

"Did you have a good trip?"

"Fine, thanks . . . I'm sorry about Leipzig. It couldn't be helped."

"That's okay, dad. Mr. Rauter explained."

"Rauter?"

"Your associate. He fixed it for me to come over to Hanover."

"Who've you been staying with?"

"Erich Meyer."

"Erich?"

"You know, dad—Erich Meyer, one of my pen-friends."

"Yes, yes; of course. Stupid of me, but I'm still a bit woolly . . . Have you had a good time?"

"Great. Mr. Rauter said you'd settle with him about the money and all that."

"Of course . . . When are you coming over here?"

"Just as soon as I can."

"A colleague of mine will send transport for you."

"Oh, good."

"In about an hour, probably . . . All right?"

How he controlled his voice he never knew. He was sweating when he hung up. Joy quivered through him, a kind of weariness

216

in its wake. Slattery was at the window, gazing out, and Laker asked him for a cigarette.

As the smoke swirled Laker said: "I don't understand. Rauter was the person . . ." Then: "Christ, I'm so confused. So bloody confused. When did you get him over? And how? He spoke as if —"

"We'll start unravelling it, Sam." Slattery pulled a chair across to the bed. "When you're ready we'll unwind the whole thing."

"The last I can remember is being in a car after I'd tried to jump some wire. Two of Hartmann's men were there, the same two who'd arrested me previously, the two who'd given me the firing-squad treatment . . . When I went back to Leipzig I made use of that last-ditch number of yours. It was the fellow at the house there who produced the *Neues Deutschland* cutting—and he believed it, too . . ."

Haltingly Laker attempted to feel his way.

"Hartmann was travelling south on the Berlin-Leipzig auto-bahn. Afterwards I went west to a side road as arranged. Then something went wrong . . ." He frowned, trapped by another memory, another echo. "I was sure Patrick was dead, d'you understand? I got a message from Hartmann in Copenhagen which said as much, and then there was this *Neues Deutschland* confirmation . . ."

He shook his head. "That car," he said suspiciously. "Karen was in that car."

Slattery's lips began to curl.

"Karen Gisevius," Laker insisted. "Wasn't she?"

"Yes."

"How the devil —?"

"She came over with you. You crossed near Duderstadt. And it wasn't easy, the state you were in."

"But what about Hartmann's pair? Who squared them?"

"No one. They laid the crossing on."

Disbelief narrowed Laker's eyes.

Slattery leaned forward. "I told you the other day that Karen was one of the best contacts we had. Well, she'd be the first to admit that Hartmann knocks her into a cocked hat."

"*Hartmann?*"

Slattery nodded.

"You're not serious?"

"Very much so."

Stunned, Laker ejaculated: "He's dead. I shot him."

"No, Sam."

"I got him twice. He was in a green Moskvitch —"

"Not Hartmann. Not Hartmann, Sam . . . You got the one we wanted you to get."

And with the sudden hindsight of one too long deceived Laker began to see the rough outline of the whole appalling fraud.

It didn't matter to him at the moment who the other person was. All he could grasp was that he had been terrorised, debased, manipulated, led with a ring through his nose from beginning to end, forced to grieve, made to hate, sited to kill . . . All to order.

His brain seemed to writhe. Shaking, he pressed back on the pillows. A full minute must have passed. And then, in a low voice, he said: "Who was he?"

"A very elusive gentleman."

"Tell me," he flared.

"Matthew Albright."

"Who?"

"Matthew Albright."

He hadn't needed the reminder. *Sino-Soviet expert missing from the U.S. State Department . . . Known since May to have defected . . . ALBRIGHT HERE, MOSCOW SAYS . . .* A key turned sharply in his mind, but there had been too many shocks for another to register. And that it was Albright wasn't the awful thing.

Woodenly he said: "He was in Hartmann's car."

"Hartmann switched him when he took over the escort role at the Leipzig district border. For safety's sake, d'you see?

218

Ostensibly there was a rumour of an attempt on Albright's life."

Slattery beamed without restraint.

"Albright was the Russians' prize piece. More precious to them than half a dozen nuclear physicists. He was *the* outstanding expert on Sino-Soviet relations and virtually the whole of the West's economic and military strategy in the Far East is based on his prognosis. Moscow was a long way from picking him clean, even after three months or so; he'd have been invaluable for plenty of time yet, particularly with the see-saw rocking as it is now. We had to get him, and the sooner the better. The Americans asked what we could do to help, and— thanks to you—our scheme paid off." Slattery lit himself a cigarette. "We knew where Albright was, but he couldn't be touched while he remained tucked up inside Russia. But directly we heard of this trip of his to satellite Party centres there was just a chance. I'm not a Kremlinologist, so why he was making the grand tour I couldn't say; perhaps Moscow has a *nouveau riche* compulsion to show off its assets. It's happened before—Burgess, Pontecorvo; they and others made the rounds. But in Albright's case the Russians were certain to be ultra careful—and so it proved. In Warsaw, for instance, they hardly let a chink of natural light fall on him. About the only time he was going to be at all vulnerable was when he was being shunted, and even then . . ."

Slattery went on, engrossed with the background, Slattery who had once had the gall to say: "No hard feelings I hope, now or at any time." And when he next paused Laker found his tongue.

"You bastard." He dragged it out. "You bloody bastard."

Slattery blinked as if to ward off Laker's murderous glare. "There wasn't any other way, Sam."

"No one has the right to do what you've done."

"A duty, though."

"Balls. Oh balls to that."

"I could give you precedents, chapter and verse."

"To hell with precedents. I want an explanation."

"You're getting it."

"Am I?"

"I had you listed for this days before you got your name in the *Evening Standard*; that was a coincidence, pure and simple, though it couldn't have happened at a more convenient time as far as I was concerned." Slattery blew smoke and tried another tack. "Look at it my way. If I'd asked you to dispose of Albright, d'you think you'd have agreed? Of course not. But I especially needed you. In the first place you were the finest marksman I've ever known. And whoever took on this job would have to be a whole lot better than good."

"I undertook to deliver a message—no more, no less."

"And you finished by killing a man."

"Thanks to you."

"Not entirely. Nobody made you."

"Oh no?"

"Nobody made you, Sam."

"I was put against a tree with a bag over my head. I was told Patrick was dead . . . And you sit there and split hairs about who's responsible —"

"Listen. There's a second reason why I needed you. I haven't forgotten what you were like in Green Park that night during the war or the way you were when you got back from Gardelegen. No one who knew you in those days could ever forget. And we don't change, Sam—not underneath, not where it matters. Given the circumstances the chances are we'll conform. So"—he spread his hands—"we set a sprat to catch a mackerel. And Hartmann couldn't be mealy-mouthed if he was to bring out what I knew was in you."

Coldly, Laker said: "Is this the way you work?"

"If need be."

"Without thought for those you exploit—not caring what it costs them?"

"Albright had to be removed. It was vital."

"You didn't answer the question."

"The circumstances were exceptional. We put you through the hoop, I don't deny, but you qualified on that score, too.

220

You're as tough as nails, Sam. You always were." Slattery beamed again, and his look implied: but not the smartest, not the most cerebral. "Fear and hatred are the best tools in the trade. It was a gamble, even so. You might easily have let us down."

"*You* down!" Laker rolled his head, seething. "I wish to God I had."

"At the moment, perhaps. But not at the time, not while you were waiting for Hartmann's car. You wanted him then as badly as we wanted Albright. And you made sure you got him, as I guessed you would."

There was silence. Laker took a deep, shuddering breath and put his hands to his throbbing temples. He still hadn't grasped how completely he had been stage-managed.

Slattery said: "I expect you've tumbled to it—Frenzel never existed. A dozen things could have gone wrong, but not that." With a kind of relish, as if he were explaining a sequence of chess moves, he began to reconstruct the pattern of events. "It was all relatively straightforward as far as Copenhagen. We tried to keep the pressure on you there, though Ritchie Jackson tells me the tailing was a bit too erratic. You were hardly expected to land up with the police, of course, though that was a minor matter—and it helped in a way. After Ritchie telephoned the Hartmann message to the Metropol it was a question then of wait and see. That was *the* crucial period, and later it was also touch and go whether you'd bite on that Leipzig number. What made everyone grey, though, was your going back with the rifle. We hadn't reckoned on that. Your friend with the macaw would have equipped you, d'you see?" He stubbed his cigarette. "He was in a quandary about telling you who would pick you up on the side road for the getaway. We certainly hadn't anticipated your knocking yourself out and having to be bundled across the frontier like a sack of coals . . . However, by and large it all worked very well."

He was speaking about a certain operation which had been carried out in a certain way, for all the world as though Laker hadn't been involved and there had been no private agonies.

Laker studied him, amazed and contemptuous. Even Hartmann had been unable to contain a fleeting show of feeling.

"That cutting from *Neues Deutschland* —"

"We had it specially set, Sam."

"Your idea?"

"After a fashion, yes."

"Then sod you."

"We have to do these things."

"Don't try to justify yourself. For Christ's sake don't start that—not to me."

"There's a war on, Sam. No one likes to admit it, but there is. For some of us it never ended. We fight it out how and where we can." Slattery looked almost pained. "I thought you'd understand, I really did."

"Say I'd failed?"

"We'd have tried something else."

"Used someone else, you mean."

"If necessary. We'd have found a way."

"God forgive you."

Slattery got to his feet. "You're tired," he said. "But all's well that ends well. Ease off, Sam. A lousy trick—all right. A lousy, shabby, underhand trick, and I apologise for it." He was still smiling. "But only you went through the hoop. Patrick was never in the least danger and we had your own safety at heart all along the line. For instance, there was no message in that watch-strap of yours."

Near the door he turned. "By the way, I gather you'll be fit enough to travel tomorrow. A word from you in the office downstairs and they'll see that you and Patrick are whisked off to Heidelburg or wherever you decide." He paused, as if to receive thanks. "There are just two other matters, then we can call it a day. Hartmann's stayed on. He's sticking it out, and he might get away with it. But Karen's been wanting to cry off for a longish while now, and finally she has. It's too hot for her there anyhow. Remember this, though, when you see her. She was almost as much in the dark about what was afoot as you were. All she was told was that someone would call at at Kromadecka.

She had no idea who it would be and she had no idea why —though when she did she hated every part of it. In fact you could say that we used her, too."

Slattery cleared his throat.

"And—lastly—there's the fact that you're in a privileged position. You know too much, but that's the price I had to pay. I can't gag you. You can blow your top if you like. We'd deny everything, naturally—though that wouldn't prevent a few heads rolling over there in Leipzig. I can also appeal to you, though in your present mood I doubt if doing so would cut much ice. So I can only stress one unpalatable truth. You're a killer, Sam. Given the circumstances you're a killer. That, *inter alia*, is what's on the files, but don't brand yourself publicly as such; people wouldn't understand, not in the midst of their peace and plenty. Let's keep it between you and me."

"Go away," Laker grated.

"I'm going, Sam. Good-bye. Look after yourself."

Ten minutes before Patrick arrived the door opened again. It was Karen.

"Sammy?"

She moved swiftly across to the bed. Laker held out his hands, taking hers. Tears, bright and shining, filled her eyes, and as he drew her towards him he knew that she wasn't crying for him, or for herself, or even out of happiness, but for what men had always done to one another in the endless collision of their dreams and would go on doing by way of lies and violence and dedicated cruelty until the world burned itself to a cinder.

THE TREMBLING EARTH

For D. again
for the same reason

Extract from a newspaper report of last year:

VALENCIA, August 5: A sharp earth tremor was experienced early this morning in part of the coastal area of the Valencian province of Castellón.

The centre of the disturbance seems to have been a few miles inland in the region of the two small villages of Alquena and Valandorra. A certain amount of minor damage was caused to property, but first reports indicate that there has been no loss of life among the local populace. . . .

WALKING slowly away from the altar towards the iron-studded, half-open sacristy door, Father Robredo had a strange, inexplicable sense of dread. It came so suddenly and his mind was so confused while it lasted that—for the moment—he had no opportunity of reasoning it out. It was almost as if time had stopped and was being sucked backwards. For a fraction of a second he imagined he must be unwell, for there was a peculiar rumbling sound in his ears. Then the small, tousle-haired boy who had been serving him at Mass glanced over his shoulder, and the look of bewildered apprehension on his young face told the priest that he, too, had heard the noise.

At most it was ten yards from the centre of the altar to the sacristy door; fifteen or so decorous paces. But Father Robredo began to think he would never get there. The queer sucking-back of time seemed to increase in intensity; the rumble rose to a hollow roar, and through it he believed he heard a woman cry out from the far end of the little church. Though he nodded encouragingly to the boy he felt his nerves grow taut as the first spasms of fear took hold of him. He wanted to turn his head so that he could see the congregation, but he found himself incapable of doing so. The door held his attention. Getting there had become immensely important, but they seemed to be nearing it in a fantastic sort of slow motion. Then, with terrible abruptness—as if something had snapped—time started to roll forwards again and the red-tiled chancel floor began to shake.

He was never very certain of what happened immediately after that. He half-remembered taking a couple of quick paces and stabbing out an arm to reach for the white stone frame of the door; of feeling it shudder under first one hand, then two, as he clung to it for support; of screwing up his eyes and standing like a drunkard while the floor twitched and everything seemed to spin. He was quite unable to think properly. A tiny part of his brain scurried feverishly around in search of a prayer, but the rest of it was rigid with the din and the violent movement under his feet and hands and a ridiculous obsession that, at all costs, he must keep his vestments from getting soiled. Nor was he very certain of how long he stood there, clinging to the door frame as if tied to a whipping post. But at last—it might have been seconds or hours later for all he knew—the floor and the thick stone walls were suddenly steady and the only things that were shaking were his legs and arms.

A moment of incredulous relief followed, mingled with the return of his original suspicion that he had been taken ill, but soon he was aware of the shouting from the body of the church, the clatter of running feet, and—close by—the soft whimpering of the boy. Only then did his brain thaw sufficiently for him to guess at what had happened, and as the most obvious solution dawned on him he realized that he felt slightly sick.

When he opened his eyes the air was white with powdery dust. The boy was crouched on the sacristy floor, shielding the back of his head with podgy, locked hands.

'Ernesto!' the priest called. 'Are you hurt?'

The boy lifted his head. 'No, father,' he squeaked uncertainly.

'Are you sure?'

'Yes, father.' His sallow face had gone a zincy grey; his lips trembled. 'What was it?'

'An earthquake.'

The significance of what he had said freed the priest from the sensation of unreality that still gripped him. 'An earthquake!' he repeated, and this time his voice was louder, full of shocked surprise and alarm. He pushed himself away from the wall and almost ran into the centre of the chancel, not knowing what he expected to find.

Through the white cloud of dust he could see a score or more people wedged in the west door as they struggled to get outside. They seemed vaguely remote, but their shouts filled the church and, once again, fear brushed lightly over his nerves. He looked wildly about him, caught sight of the swinging sanctuary lamp and hurried across to steady it—partly because his fear found expression in action, partly because the lamp's gentle circular motion increased his feeling of nausea. As far as he could tell the church was intact. The tabernacle—that had been his first concern—was undamaged and, astonishingly, the altar candles were still in place, their small yellow flames round and unwavering. But the panicky voices from the doorway forced into his mind the realization that the village might have been less fortunate. Until that moment he had not thought of the village. While it lasted the earthquake had been something intensely local, shared solely by him and the boy. Later, immediately it was over and the mounting clatter from the back of the church began to make sense, his confused understanding of what had happened widened only sufficiently to include the congregation in the experience. Now, for the first time, he wondered what damage had been done outside and he started to run anxiously down the narrow centre aisle.

He was still only half-way along it, the stiff, white chasuble partly concealing the agitation of his movements, when the last of the people jammed in the door escaped into the open. Their disembodied cries, trailing behind them into the dust that clogged his screwed-up eyes and half-open mouth, drummed on the priest's imagination as he ran down what seemed the longest aisle in the world. And when, suddenly, he burst out into the strong dazzle of sunshine, his whole body was tensed as if he had just awakened from a bad dream and still doubted that what he saw was reality.

The church stood a little above the level of the village. From the west door the nearest roofs appeared to slant out of the contour of the hillside. Away from them, spreading downwards and to either side—along the line of the main street—others projected in a jumbled patchwork like small, evenly-ploughed terraces of bright red earth. Here and there rectangular sections of white and blue and ochre-coloured walls showed up. A black splodge of tuft-headed palms in the centre marked the location of the square. And beyond the final ragged fringe of houses and roof-tops the ground bumped and sloped gradually into the early morning haze towards the sea.

Father Robredo brought to the scene a sense of amazed disbelief. During his seemingly unending run from the chancel he had automatically braced himself against the terrible spectacle he imagined would greet him when he got outside. But what he saw was apparently so normal that his mind insisted that it must be a deception. As he blinked at the village his thin body alternated between bouts of nervous rigidity and a heaving struggle to drag some fresh air into his lungs. Then, with a jerk of his head, he switched his attention to the disappearing remnants of his congregation.

The most agile had already vanished. A few had reached the point between two houses where the path descended to the level of the street. In the moment of his turning to look at them an arm gesticulated, heads and shoulders bobbed right and left—then they, too, were gone. All that remained was an untidy trail of six or seven old women hobbling frantically down the slope.

Pity flooded through the priest as he saw their drab, familiar figures struggling away from the church like a troupe of badly-manipulated marionettes. He started to hurry after them, suddenly indignant at the way in which they had been left to manage for themselves, his own agitation momentarily calmed by the competing rush of fresh emotions. But he had scarcely gone a couple of yards when he caught sight of Rafael Arias, the sacristan, coming bow-legged up the path towards him.

Like the women going in the opposite direction the sacristan was also old, but he could move with the speed of someone half his age if the need arose. He had just proved it, though it was for another reason that he had run with the others. Along with them he had panicked; and now, as he lumbered heavily past the frightened, wide-eyed women, he had recovered his wits sufficiently to reproach himself for it.

That was not like me, he thought; not like me at all. I am a fool to have run with the rest of them. I should have stayed at the church.... He shook his head rue-fully and clicked his tongue.... I never imagined I should live to see the day when I would act with such stupidity.

He continued to grumble at himself all the way up the path, but he knew in his heart that he would have felt less badly about it if Father Robredo had not been there waiting for him to return. He wished very much that he could have got back without the priest knowing where he had been.

Perhaps, his thoughts went on, perhaps it would never have happened if I had not stood at the church door when everyone burst out. I was going to hand them pamphlets after the service, but I forgot about that when the shock came and the rush started. All I remem-ber thinking was that I must get to the village with everyone else. Stupid, very stupid.... He shook his head again.... If it had not been for them I would probably be at the church now—and spared this humiliation.

He was a simple old man, still a little dazed, and his natural pride unconsciously sought to excuse his be-haviour. Less than a minute ago he had found himself dithering in the street—neither knowing what he was doing there nor where to go next. Then, glancing back, he had seen Father Robredo dash from the church into the open. The sight of the priest seemed to smooth the jagged edges of his mind and he had turned quickly to retrace his steps, suddenly embarrassed by an acute awareness of what he had done. And by then it was too late for anything but shame and self-reproach.

Father Robredo started the questions when he was at least twenty yards away. 'What has happened in the village?'

'It was an earthquake,' Rafael answered defensively.

'I know; I know. Is there any damage? Anyone hurt?'

'Not that I saw.'

'How far did you go?'

'To the end of the path.'

'Is that all? You cannot see much from there.'

Rafael's face was beaded with sweat as he came to a halt in front of the priest. To be chided for not going far enough was the last thing he had expected. 'I thought I should return here, so I did not go further.'

'As far as I could tell the church is safe,' Father Robredo said, nervously sweeping dust from the corners of his eyes. 'In any case there is nothing that needs to be done immediately. But the village is another matter: we must go there at once.'

He was moving before he had finished speaking. Rafael jogged obediently beside him. The pamphlets were still clutched in his left hand and, as soon as he realized it, he bundled them hastily into his coat pocket. From somewhere far along the street a man shouted. The last two black-shawled old women still hobbled between the flowering bushes towards the end of the path. Rafael knew Father Robredo was angry that nobody had stayed behind to help the women, and he wished he could hit upon a face-saving explanation which would justify his having run with the others. He badly wanted to do so before he and the priest overtook the stragglers, whose slow, limping progress seemed to nag at his conscience. But it was difficult to think quickly of any plausible reason. Then, to his relief, he noticed something that brought him to an abrupt halt.

'Your vestments, father,' he blurted out.

'What?'

'Your vestments. You are still wearing your vestments.'

Father Robredo stopped dead, lifted his arms a little and gazed down at his dusty chasuble with obvious surprise. 'So I am,' he said. 'So I am.'

He did not seem to know quite what to do, and Rafael saw the look of indecision on his narrow face. The sacristan felt uncomfortable in the priest's presence; much more concerned with his own sense of guilt than with what the earthquake might have done to Alquena, and—for once—he was sharp enough to see his opportunity.

'It is perhaps best for me to go on ahead and for you to follow as soon as you can,' he suggested.

'Yes.' Father Robredo nodded doubtfully. He had just remembered that he had not said his after-Mass prayers. 'Yes. You go on. I shall only be a few minutes....'

He stared beyond the stocky old man as he spoke, glancing from side to side at the gaudy splash of the village as if to reassure himself that there was no great urgency; that the apparent tranquillity of what he saw was genuine. But his ears still echoed with the scared hubbub from the jam in the west door of the church, and he felt suddenly that it would be wrong if he went back without first finding out if he were needed.

'No,' he said sharply. 'I will come with you—to the road at least. Then we shall see.'

Rafael shrugged imperceptibly as they hurried on again, stones grating underfoot, the priest's lace-edged alb rustling and flapping. He consoled himself with the thought that as soon as they turned into the street Father Robredo would quickly be reminded that there were many others who had run away. 'Anyhow,' he muttered under his breath, 'let us hope so.' The woman had disappeared now and he was glad of it. The accusation implicit in their doddering figures had seemed entirely directed towards him. But with them out of sight he already felt less embarrassed, and he increased his pace, anxious to ease his conscience further by letting the priest see how everyone else had behaved.

They came to the point where the path narrowed between the pale blue walls of the houses. A dog scampered unexpectedly across the gap from right to left; the sound of voices began to filter round the end of the buildings. And then, a moment later, they quit the stony gravel of the path and the metalled surface of the road rang sharply as they halted at the corner.

The curving street buzzed with the excited talk of perhaps thirty people who stood in small, widely-separated groups. Everyone seemed to be speaking at once and other voices joined in the cross-talk from doorways and windows. Children were busy collecting oranges that had scattered in all directions from a great pile near the petrol-station. The panic of a few minutes earlier was gone; its place taken by the initial reaction of relief which showed itself in the slightly unnatural pitch of the men's voices and an occasional staccato burst of nervous laughter.

Father Robredo gazed thankfully from group to group, at the splendid solidity of the balconied, colour-washed houses; at the children gathering the scattered oranges. He had scarcely dared to hope that it would be like this and he crossed himself slowly in gratitude for what he saw.

'Thanks be to God,' he said, and his tongue slurred over the words as he tried to swallow back the emotion that suddenly constricted his throat.

He and the grey-haired old man stood together for perhaps a minute. Nobody appeared to notice them. Some of the whitewashed surface plaster had come away from high up on the wall of the post office, exposing a flower-like scar of dried mud; the lantern above the door of the nearest café had lost most of its glass, which now lay glinting around the worn concrete step. But in the fifty or so yards immediately to either side of them they could see no other signs of damage. A chattering trio of girls separated from one of the groups and ran, hand in hand, to another; the bright glare of sunlight on the houses facing towards the east was patterned by the indigo right-angled shadows projected by those opposite; oranges lay in the road and gutters like golden balls; pigeons fluttered overhead. The narrow street had something of a pre-fiesta atmosphere, and the priest felt his body trembling as the pent-up tension left him.

'I will go back now,' he said, turning to the sacristan. 'While I am away, walk down to the square and see how everything is. I shall not be long.'

It still seemed incredible that the village had suffered so lightly, and he would not be wholly convinced until he had visited every part of it. But from what he had already seen he believed he could delay further exploration for five or ten minutes. If the damage had been more serious elsewhere he felt sure they would have heard of it by now : bad news spread fast.

Rafael nodded. As he did so he noticed the civil guard coming down the street from the square and he cupped his hands to his mouth.

'Hey, *guardia!* What is it like further on ?'

A few heads turned in their direction. The pot-bellied civil guard hitched the slung rifle higher on to his shoulder and bawled back, 'Much the same as here, old one.' He wanted to add that Rafael had wetted his trousers for nothing, but he thought better of it because Father

Robredo was there. 'I am going to telephone before Castellón and Alcalá fill the place with fire-engines and soldiers.' He felt suddenly important: it was not often that people listened to what he had to say, and he addressed himself to the whole street. 'Alquena knows how to look after itself if the earth shivers once in a while. Is that not so, my friends?'

Father Robredo hurried up the slope towards the church, the sun strong on his eyes, the glare pricked through with the sparkle of flints embedded in the red-brown path. He moved with his alb clutched up almost to his knees, his trousered legs working like connecting rods.

Poor Rafael, he thought; he is most concerned for having run when the shock came. Yet he should not be. It is easy to be carried away when everyone else has lost his nerve. Had I been at the door I would almost certainly have run too—I am sure of it. But cannot tell him that. The best I can do is to say nothing and hope he will soon forget. He is a good old man, and I was very proud of him when I saw him returning.

Some of the priest's earlier anxiety revived as he neared the church door, pushing Rafael from his mind. Since that awful, apparently endless time when he clung to the shaking sacristy wall it seemed that he had done nothing but move from point to point, his relief on turning one corner immediately overcome by fears of what he might find at the next. And now, as he reached the coolness of the doorway, he was momentarily afraid lest he had been mistaken in believing that the church had escaped damage.

He could not see much at first. After the glare of the sun the shadowed interior was like an opaque green wall. But, as he blinked the glare away, the church gradually took on a third dimension; its outlines assumed their familiar shape and colour. The dust had almost settled and was only visible now in five parallel shafts of sunlight sloping in from blurred-edged windows. His eyes roved round the church. A brass vase of yellow and pink flowers on one of the side altars had toppled over. He quickly made his way between two rows of straw-seated chairs to right it, then dabbed at the soaked patch on the embroidered altar-cloth with his handkerchief. An open prayer-book was on the floor; close by lay a black lace square. He picked them up and walked back to the centre aisle. Nearer the chancel someone had left a hat behind and the priest tucked it under his arm.

I shall leave them on the chair by the door, he thought; then the owners can collect them without having to ask me for them. In the circumstances they might not like doing that, and I do not want these things permanently on my hands.

The painted wooden statues of the Virgin and of Saint John, the patron, stood untouched.... Nothing seemed amiss with the smooth white vault of the roof.... In the chancel the sanctuary lamp winked its deep wine-coloured red, and, as he glanced at it, he recalled that steadying it had been his first rational act after the shock. Those frantic moments already had something of the quality of a dream, and when he found himself staring at the round yellow flames of the altar candles he remembered that Ernesto had been part of it. Until then he had completely forgotten about the boy, whose duty it was to extinguish the candles after the Mass.

'Ernesto,' he called, once more troubled by a flicker of alarm which drove him nervously forward. Though he felt sure the boy must have slipped out by the other way, his apprehension was not checked until he reached the door and saw that the sacristy was empty. Ernesto's cassock and surplice were together in a black and white heap on a window-ledge; the back door was ajar.

He sighed heavily with satisfaction and began to remove his vestments. There was more dust here than in the chancel or the nave and it made him cough, so he pulled the door wide open and stood where the air was clearer.

We have been very lucky, he thought; truly very lucky. I still find it difficult to believe. The most terrible things might have happened. As it is, Alquena appears to have suffered hardly at all, and here in the church nothing is harmed. Certainly there is a great deal of dust, but that is an insignificant matter compared with what there might have been.

Once, a year or so before, at a cinema in Valencia, he had seen in a news-film the result of a hurricane in the West Indies. He had often wondered since why it was that a church should have been smashed to pieces while —almost alongside it—what looked like a dance hall remained practically intact. It seemed that God did not always spare what was His; that a church was not necessarily inviolable against the forces of nature. He did not profess to understand these things, but now, as he remembered the scene, his relief and gratitude were suddenly intensified and he dropped on his knees, overwhelmed with humility....

Five minutes later Father Robredo left the sacristy in his cassock, snuffed out the candles on the altar and made his way along the aisle to the west door. It was not yet half-past seven, but already the heat shimmered on the red roofs of the village. Outside the porch he turned, shielding his face with his shallow-crowned hat, and glanced perfunctorily at the elaborate, ochre-coloured façade of the church where the weathered image of Saint John stood in a niche above the twisted black columns flanking the door. All was well. He looked higher, at the squat, ornate tower topped by a decorated arch in which the bell was hung. And then, with his eyes screwed against the light, he saw something that stiffened his body and made him cry out in horrified dismay.

The heavy bell had come away from its mounting. All that prevented it from falling on to the roof was the wooden headstock, jammed diagonally across the sky-blue aperture.

Honorato Montes was in the cobbled yard of his father's house when the shock hit Valandorra. He was pumping air into the rear tyre of his bicycle. When that was done, and he had eaten, he intended to ride over to Alquena to see Maria. It was his free day—otherwise he would have cycled in the opposite direction, to the canning factory further up the coast where he worked as a clerk in the offices.

When he thought about the earthquake afterwards he could recall no preliminary roar; no queer sensation of time having stopped. The first he knew was that the bicycle began to rattle furiously against the wall and the cobbles pulsated under his knees as if a succession of heavy electric charges were being passed just below ground level. Whitewash fragments splintered and shivered off the house; a tile crashed into the yard beside him. There was no sound from inside the house and its absence increased his feeling of isolation. He knelt stiff-backed, in an attitude of prayer that was as unintentional as, lately, it was unaccustomed, acutely conscious of what was happening yet more astonished than frightened. He saw the dirt bounce between the cobbles; heard the bell on the handle-bar ring in futile anger as it vibrated against the wall; was even aware of a startled bird climbing steeply away from the roof. Then, with the same abruptness with which it had begun, it was all over. . . .

He clambered to his feet—suddenly concerned for his family—and burst into the small kitchen where his father and mother and two sisters sat rigidly round the table in numbed silence.

Were they all right? Yes, his father said with as much dignity as he could muster, they were all right. A saucepan rocked slowly on the floor. Not hurt? No, his father said. A cardboard calendar had fallen from the wall. In the name of all the saints, his mother wanted to know in a shrill voice, what had happened? An earthquake, Honorato answered, a little unsteadily; an earthquake. His father nodded vigorously. His young sisters started to cry. His mother crossed herself twice in a tremendous flurry of agitation.

'God forgive us,' she whispered.

Her husband jumped up from his chair and made for the door. 'Where are you going?' she asked nervously.

'Out,' he jerked back. 'To see what damage has been done.'

Honorato followed him. 'A tile came off the roof.... It fell within a few feet of me.' He kicked at it with his shoe. 'Nothing else is damaged.'

His father was not impressed. 'If that is all, then we are fortunate.'

They had something of the appearance of landsmen finding their shore-legs after an unfamiliar hour at sea. They were much the same build, of medium height, slim-waisted and broad-shouldered, though it was obvious from their clothes which of them was the office-worker and which the agricultural labourer. Both were good-looking, but Honorato was the less swarthy, and —as was generally the case—certainly the less agitated. His father trotted anxiously from end to end of the small yard, examining the house from every possible angle.

'The only thing broken is a tile,' Honorato said again.

His father did not answer for a moment. He was still unnerved by what had happened, but he would have given a lot to have spotted something his son had missed. Honorato was always right. He knew too much; had an answer for everything. Since he went to the cannery offices four years ago he had mixed with people who had infected him with all manner of modern ideas. As head of the household it was embarrassing to have his son speak with assurance about things he did not understand himself; distressing to have so many of his lifelong beliefs laughed at by a lad less than half his age—and before his wife and daughters, too. 'I will look inside the house,' he said testily, and hurried across to the door.

As it opened Honorato heard his mother and sisters gabbling through a Hail Mary in a shaky, high-pitched monotone; before it closed he was out of the yard and in the narrow, high-walled street that led down to the village square. In the few seconds that they had been together he had found himself irked by his father's apparent inability to consider anything except his own property.

Surely, he thought hotly; surely he can see that the house is practically untouched—and he is aware that my mother and the girls are not hurt. And yet, until he has examined everything a dozen times, Valandorra will not exist. I know it. The whole place can be in ruins for all he cares. . . .

The fact that Valandorra was not in ruins did not curb his irritation, but curiosity had driven it from his mind by the time he reached the little square. The street along which he had run was scarcely more than an alley between the peeling, colour-washed backs of houses and he met no-one on the way down; saw not so much as a dislodged tile. In the square, too, there was no immediate evidence of damage, but there was a good deal of confused shouting and hurried, apparently aimless, movement. On the far side an old man was chasing a loose donkey through a squawking crowd of indignant chickens. Nearer, in the centre of the ring of tub-planted palms, a huge brown dog careered wildly round the marble water fountain.

'Honorato,' someone called. 'How is it up your way?'

He turned on his heels to find his friend José. 'Well.' He answered with studied calmness. 'A few shaken nerves, but no bad damage that I saw.' José's shabby grey suit was powdered with dust and Honorato was momentarily perturbed, forgetting that he worked in the bakery. 'Are you all right?'

'Yes.' José stuttered excitedly. 'Yes. This is only flour. I was on my way home when it happened. *Jesucristo!* But I thought the building were coming on to my head!' He fumbled for cigarettes. 'It must have been a big shock somewhere. I wonder how things are in Alquena.'

Alquena! It was as if an ulcer had burst in Honorato's stomach. Only by making a great effort did he check himself from swinging round without another word and sprinting up to the house for his bicycle. Alquena meant Maria. He loved Maria and, as he refused José's proffered cigarette, he reviled himself silently for having forgotten about her at such a time. But he was too proud to let his companion know of the anxiety that was spreading through him, and he answered as casually as he could.

'Much the same, I expect. I shall be going there soon.'

'They are certain to have felt the shock. Perhaps worse than here.'

Honorato began to back away. 'It is possible.'

28

The brown dog had stopped circling the fountain and was sniffing suspiciously at the water; the old man and the donkey had disappeared into a side street. A woman with a bright red scarf fluttering from her shoulders ran diagonally across the square, sobbing nervously.

'Women!' José scoffed. 'They run and cry at the least thing.' As he cupped his hands to light his cigarette he hoped that Honorato would not see they were trembling. He was eighteen, three years younger than Honorato, and it was a good feeling to stand talking with him while practically everyone else was scurrying from one place to another. 'I was over there—by the bus halt—when the shock came. *Jesucristo!* You should have seen the commotion. Truly, you would have thought it was the end of the world.'

Honorato continued to edge away, but José followed him, describing with voice and hands exactly what an earthquake was like. In his excitement he did not realize that he was not being listened to; that his friend was oblivious to everything except the desire to get started on the road to Alquena, and it was both a surprise and a disappointment to have his story interrupted.

'I must go back to the house now,' Honorato said curtly, unable to master his impatience any longer. 'We have tiles off the roof and my father will need help.'

He left José standing and walked with a deliberate show of unconcern until he had turned the corner into the alley. Then he put his head down and ran hard, the sound of his feet ringing sharply between the houses. He had an unpleasant feeling that José had followed him to the corner and was watching him, but he no longer cared. His thoughts were centred on Maria and what might have happened in Alquena.

When he arrived at the yard his father was placing a

ladder against the side of the house. 'Help me with this,' he demanded without looking round.

Honorato squatted quickly beside the bicycle and began to unscrew the pump. It maddened him that his father should be doing the very thing that had served as an excuse to escape from José. 'Another time,' he answered, gasping for breath. 'Not now.'

'I shall not require help another time,' his father snapped. 'Come and hold the ladder.'

'No.' He clipped the pump angrily into position under the crossbar. 'I am going to Alquena.'

'First you will hold this ladder. I command you.'

'No!'

'Do as I say,' his father shouted, mahogany-faced. 'I shall not ask you again.'

'That you will not,' Honorato shouted back, 'for I shall not be here.' He lifted the bicycle away from the wall and mounted. 'I am going to Alquena to see if Maria is all right. There are more important things to worry about at this moment than your stupid tile. Do you think the earthquake shook our house and ours alone?'

He bumped over the cobbles into the alley. It was a long time since he had been so completely swamped with rage and, as he free-wheeled down the slope to the square, it drowned his concern for Maria's safety. In his fury he found himself wishing that Valandorra had suffered more extensively, so that his father would be shamed by what he saw when he eventually went into the village. He glanced left and right as he reached the square, almost hoping to see damage that had previously gone unnoticed. Yet, though for a moment he felt cheated when he saw none, the tide of his anger ebbed a little before the instinctive logic which told him that destruction here might well be matched in Alquena.

And with that thought growing in his mind he began to worry again about Maria, the bitterness against his father's indifference accentuating the fears he felt for her.

He flicked at his bell as he pedalled round the long-shadowed square, more crowded now than when he had last seen it. Groups of people were gathering under the trees, outside the shops and cafés, in the roadway. The old blind Moor sat in his usual place by the door of the tavern, waving his thin arms and shouting plaintive abuse at the world in general. José was still there, chuckling nervously with a couple of girls. Pigeons and chickens pecked at some grain scattered from the panniers of the donkey that had broken loose and was now being led back by its angry, sweating owner.

Honorato swerved and braked hard and pedalled round two sides of the square, seeing these things yet not seeing them. A girl called his name, but he did not turn his head. He searched only for signs of damage, and his anxiety was not lessened by the apparent absence of anything more serious than broken glass and plaster. 'It must have been a big shock somewhere,' José had said, and now the phrase had come alive in his brain. Valandorra was no longer a yardstick by which he might judge what he would probably find on the other side of the ridge that separated the two villages.

He swung out of the square, riding fast along the narrow, coloured street that pointed to the green and brown glare of the fields. A dozen people blocked the road opposite the last house but one, and he rattled his bell, speeding through the gap they reluctantly made for him. As he flashed by he saw that the front wall of the building was split by a jagged crack from top to bottom and the balcony railings had fallen to the ground.

He rode then as he had never ridden before, rolling from side to side as he stood on the pedals, crunching in and out of the pot-holes. The road climbed steadily, winding across the long slope of the ridge. His wheels ploughed rim-deep in the reddish dust and he grunted as he strained against its drag and the pull of the ascent.

When I get to the top, he fretted, I should be able to see. Not much, it is true, but enough to tell whether they have had it worse than Valandorra. Another kilometre and I should be able to see. . . .

To his right the hills were a vague brown shadow in the morning haze; on the other side the sun was edging a grey-ribbed strip of cloud away from the blur of the horizon. Sweat ran from his face, soaking the open collar of his shirt, trickling greasily across his chest and shoulders. By the time he had gone half-way to the top he felt that his lungs were on fire and his navy-blue jacket seemed to have stuck to his back. What José had said circled around in his brain with every turn of the wheels, and he groaned suddenly, biting his lip, as the thought struck him that if he had not been so obsessed with the idea of cycling to Alquena he could have telephoned for news before leaving the square. Then, lifting his head, he saw to his relief that in two or three minutes more he would cross the spine of the ridge. The gradient was less severe now; the strain on his thigh-muscles less cruel. He had cycled this road a thousand times, but never had it seemed so long or steep; never had he been so desperately anxious to see the red roofs of Alquena and to start on the snaking, two-kilometre descent.

A few hundred metres from the crest a rickety, snub-nosed truck was drawn in to the side of the road. The dishevelled driver, his breeches and orange shirt blotched with grease, heaved himself from under the front axle when Honorato shouted.

'*Hola!* How is it in Alquena?'

The man brushed a tangle of black hair away from his eyes. 'Alquena?'

'Yes.' Honorato braked and toppled sideways until his shoe touched the ground. 'Are things bad there?'

'Bad?' the man repeated stupidly.

'Yes. Yes. You must have come through after the shock.'

'Shock? What shock?'

Madre de Dios! 'The earthquake.'

The driver's lips curled. 'You are not by any chance trying to make a fool of me—' he began, but Honorato cut him short incredulously.

'Do you mean you felt nothing?'

'Of course I felt something—why else should I stop where I have? My steering went loose suddenly. . . . It was a miracle I did not lose control.' Hairy hands zigzagged dramatically. 'I was all over the road. . . . A miracle, I tell you.'

Honorato kicked the pedals round. He was wasting time. 'And I tell you there has been an earthquake,' he said, impatient to be off. 'Valandorra was rocked by it.'

The man's eyes widened. 'An earthquake,' he muttered doubtfully, sampling the word, remembering the feel of the lorry shuddering and the wheel going loose, then locking, then going loose again in his hands. '*Caramba!* It could have been. . . .'

Honorato did not wait. He stood on the pedals, clear of the saddle, the bicycle swaying between his thighs as he laboured to pick up speed.

'Hey!' the man called after him, his voice suddenly sharp with alarm. 'What about Tortosa? Did they have it there?'

'How can I tell?' Honorato retorted roughly over his shoulder. 'I do not even know what has happened on the other side of this hill.'

Idiot! he thought. But for him I should have reached the top by now.

The road spurned the short cut, curving in a leisurely sweep below the smooth outline of the ridge. The blood thumped heavily in his ears; the sweat prickled his body. He heard the truck grumbling away in low gear but he did not look round. All his attention was focused on the point where the ledge of the road levelled off and disappeared in a sharp right-handed turn. . . .

He braked when he reached the corner, blinking to clear the dust-caked sweat from his eyes. Alquena lay like a scatter of tiny coloured bricks amid the rolling green of the fruit-orchards and market-gardens. He stood there, noisily sucking air into his lungs, staring at the village which seemed to bounce with each thundering heart-beat, endeavouring to pick out Maria's house from the others. But it was impossible—and equally impossible to be comforted by what he saw. Doubt still filled his mind. There might be a dozen broken houses down there for all he could tell: any one of that jumble of tiny bricks might be split from top to bottom, as the house in Valandorra had been. Only the church was clearly distinguishable, its roof glittering like a fragment of glass in the sunlight. Undamaged? Yes, he decided cautiously, it seemed to be . . . though he was much too far away to be sure.

It occurred to him then that Maria would almost certainly have been at Mass at the time of the shock. He stared more intently as the thought came to him, a delayed sense of relief welling up inside him. With his eyes fixed on the church he began to free-wheel down the winding, poplar-lined road. The air slid like silk over the clamminess of his face and neck; the red dust sprayed out from under the wheels; the spokes whirred. In his anxiety for Maria it did not seem strange that he should now be staring at the church with a mounting feeling of hope. For the moment he had forgotten that during the last six months or so he had come to look upon it as symbolic of something that might separate him irrevocably from the girl he loved.

FATHER ROBREDO passed Maria on the path as he ran in search of Rafael. She greeted him as he went by but, in his dismay, he could manage nothing better than a curt nod. A close examination of the bell had only confirmed his fears : the least disturbance would send it crashing through the roof. And now he ran to find Rafael, spurred on by the seriousness of his discovery and the knowledge that he was utterly incapable of dealing with the situation by himself. He was not a practical man and all his life he had regretted his almost childish incompetence at times of crisis. But never so much as now.

He clattered noisily into the street and made for the square, responding automatically to the voices that spoke to him, unaware of the eyes following him curiously as he hurried by. Twenty minutes had passed since the shock and the people who saw him were puzzled by this belated show of concern.

Surely, they said amongst themselves, surely the *padre* has not taken all this time to realize what happened? Or is it that he has learned of something still unknown to us? . . . No, that cannot be, they said. We have seen what damage there is—or have been told of it. . . . Glass and plaster; a café window broken; old Señora Cuesta with a cut forehead; a tile or two off the roofs. Beyond that there is nothing—except the dust in the houses. Why then does the *padre* hurry as if he had seen a ghost? . . .

Father Robredo heard none of all this. His thoughts were congealed around the mental picture of the bell's headstock wedged precariously across the arch of the open belfry and the necessity of finding Rafael without delay. It needed very little imagination to visualize the havoc that would be caused if the bell were to fall. And fall it might—at any moment. The possibility appalled him, but he could not even guess at what should be done and the lack of any sort of idea accentuated his agitation. More and more, as he hastened frantically along, he put his trust in Rafael. . . . Rafael would know what to do. Rafael *had* to know. . . .

He found the old man in the square, squatting on his haunches in front of two grubby, giggling children. Rafael straightened up when he saw Father Robredo, the smile fading from his wrinkled face. He did not need to be told that something was wrong: one glance at the priest's distraught expression was enough.

'What is it, father?'

'The bell,' Father Robredo began breathlessly. 'The bell is loose—'

'Loose?' Rafael queried, frowning.

'Yes.' In his haste he could not find the right words. His hands came into play. 'It is on a slant in the arch. The wood . . . the yoke . . . the piece across the top of the bell. It is loose. Jammed.'

'Loose?' Rafael repeated. 'Jammed?'

The priest nodded, gulping in air. 'Across the arch.'

'How can it be loose if it is jammed?' the sacristan asked, a little bewildered.

'It is as I say—jammed. At any second it might crash through the roof.'

Rafael scratched the side of his squat nose. If the bell were jammed . . .

'At any second,' the priest insisted, his voice wobbling with anxiety.

37

There was a slight pause. 'It will perhaps be best if I go and look,' Rafael suggested, long experience having taught him that Father Robredo would only confuse him further the more he tried to explain.

'Yes, at once. There is not a moment to lose. The wind might move it or it might slip on its own.' The old man seemed in no hurry. 'I tell you, Rafael, this is urgent, most urgent. When you see the bell you will understand. We shall have to get it down as soon as we can.'

Rafael's slowness rather than an appreciation of what must be done prompted this last remark, and it surprised the priest that he should have mentioned anything so essentially practical. It surprised the sacristan, too, though not for the same reason. Until then he had fancied Father Robredo was exaggerating some minor damage to the bell arch. To a man who was no good with his hands even hanging a picture-frame was a major operation, and Rafael had come to learn that the priest invariably magnified the difficulties of almost any task confronting him. But this mention of getting the bell down—that was drastic talk, even for the *padre*. . . .

'Is it so serious?'

'I have told you. The slightest breath of wind might set it free.'

The old man still hesitated. 'It is not customary to have much wind in August,' he stalled.

'Neither is it customary to have an earthquake.' There was a note of exasperation in the priest's voice now. 'Look, Rafael, go back to the church and see what I have seen. Go up to the platform as I did. . . .'

'The bell weighs at least two hundred kilos. To get it down will require proper tackle. Only one man in Alquena could do it, and that is Señor Hoyas, the builder. Even so he would find such a task very difficult.'

Father Robredo jerked his head. 'I shall speak to him immediately.'

'You will not come with me?'

'No, I will find Señor Hoyas and we will join you at the west door. Now, hurry! And, while you are waiting, judge for yourself what must be done.'

Maria knelt in the cool whiteness of the church, her eyes closed, elbows resting on the chair-back in front of her. She was alone, though she was not aware of it. The whole village might have been present for all she knew. At times when she prayed she seemed completely insulated from the world, and this was such a time. She did not feel the hardness of the stone floor or hear the faint rubbing of her rosary-beads against the chair. If the church had been crowded—the silence broken by coughs and whispers and the scrape of shoes—it would have been no different. This was one of the rare occasions when, without effort, her prayers pierced the invisible sounding-board that so often seemed to keep her pleas and promises earthbound, transforming their echoes into nothing more worth while than wishes and earnest resolutions.

She prayed now out of immense gratitude that Alquena had been spared all save the most minor damage. She offered up thanks that her mother, who was ill, had escaped injury; that their house was untouched; that nobody in the village had suffered. And she prayed that the same good fortune had befallen others elsewhere, particularly Honorato and his family in Valandorra.

Let it be that Honorato is safe, her lips said. Let it be, I beseech Thee, that no harm has come to him or to those in his house. He is a good boy, and may he soon find his

39

way back to the Church. It is not that he has turned against it—rather it is that in recent months he has begun to question what he once believed. Some of the young men in the cannery office are responsible, her thoughts explained—in case the facts were not known They have confused him with their ideas. Let it be that —in addition to his safety—Honorato will not lose his faith. . . .

For a moment she stopped praying and opened her eyes. If that happens then I will lose him, she thought. No matter what we feel for each other I will lose him. Such a thing would drag us apart. . . .

It was the first time she had allowed herself to admit what for weeks she had known to be true. Hurriedly she tried to force the thought away, shutting her eyes again and flooding her mind with a stream of Hail Marys. But it was no use. All the while, as she endeavoured to recapture the spirit of her earlier prayers, the possibility of breaking with Honorato distracted her. Gradually she forgot why she had come to the church; forgot there had been an earthquake. She cupped her chin in her hands and gazed unhappily at the altar, her thoughts a compound of conflicting emotions, completely unaware that—at that very moment—Honorato was tip-toeing along the aisle towards her.

He had paused in the doorway before entering the church, strangely moved by the sight of her upright figure, the long-drawn tension of the ride from Valandorra disintegrating suddenly under the sharply-rising pain of relief. Now, partially blinded by the apparent darkness after the glare outside, he came to where she knelt and, reaching forward, touched her lightly on the shoulder.

'Maria,' he whispered.

'Honorato!' Her brown eyes widened with surprised delight as she turned her head. 'What are you doing here?'

He grinned. 'I allow you one guess.'

Maria pushed herself off her knees as he sat quickly beside her. 'You felt the shock?'

'Yes.'

'Badly?'

Honorato shrugged. 'Some would say so. For my part I can imagine worse things to cry over—'

He likes to boast, she thought. 'No-one was hurt?'

'Plenty in their minds. Physically, no-one that I know of, though you would not have believed it to see some of them. How has it been with you? And your mother?'

'Well.' Her eyes caressed him. 'I was in her room, straightening her bed-covers, when it happened and it—'

'You were not at Mass?'

She shook her head. 'Not this morning.' There was a slight pause; then, 'How did you know I would be here now?'

'Where else should I find you?' he laughed, teasing her, but instantly regretting the remark when he saw the slight answering frown. 'Has there been damage in Alquena?'

'A little, but nothing serious.' Again there was a pause. 'It was good of you to come, Honorato.'

'I always come on my free day. You know that.'

'I know,' she said. 'But usually not so early in the morning.'

'I was concerned for you.'

It cost him something to say that, she thought. He does not find it easy to admit such things. I can see by the sweat on his face and neck that he rode hard to get here, and the look in his eyes tells more than any words. But, nevertheless, it was worth a great deal to hear him say it. . . .

She smiled at him. 'Well, now your worries are over.'

'Yes.' He smiled back. Truly, he thought, she is very beautiful. I do not believe I have realized before how beautiful she is or how much I love her. It has taken an earthquake to make me understand. . . .

They sat together for a few minutes, talking in whispers, recounting their impressions of the shock. Honorato did not refer to the quarrel with his father, nor did he again mention the anxiety for her that had consumed him as he cycled from Valandorra. But he told her of meeting José in the square and of the truck-driver on the road. It was easy to be amused now, and Maria laughed quietly as, with exaggerated gestures and expressions, he described the man's insistence that his steering had failed.

His hands zigzagged. '"I was all over the road. . . . It was a miracle I did not go over the side." You should have seen him, Maria—'

She raised a finger to her lips. 'Not so loud, Honorato.'

He nodded, then glanced round impetuously, suddenly impatient to get outside. 'Are you ready to go?'

'In a little while.'

She pulled the dark blue scarf further over her smooth black hair and slid gently to her knees. Honorato continued to sit, nursing his impatience, staring abstractedly towards the chancel where a band of sunlight leaned above the altar like a dusty strip of rainbow.

'Honorato.'

'Yes.'

Maria had turned and was holding out a hand. 'Give thanks with me before we leave.'

He did not answer for a moment. His mouth tightened.

'Please.'

It would have been easy to kneel with her without question. Yet stubbornly—almost against his will—he asked. 'Thanks for what?'

'For Alquena and Valandorra, and what might have been.' Her lips quivered; there was an edge to her voice. 'You know very well.'

Their eyes held each other. 'If you wish it,' he said at length.

With bad grace he knelt beside her, covering his face with his hands. It was only a pretence and he made no attempt to pray. He was angry that she should have asked him and angry, too, that he should have quibbled at her request.

If only, he thought indignantly, if only she would let me make up my own mind. The more she pushes me the more I try not to be pushed, and when things are like that we are no good for each other. Everything starts to go wrong. . . .

Rafael had no head for heights and did not relish the prospect of climbing to the inspection-platform. But as soon as he came near to the church he knew it could not be avoided. Father Robredo was correct. The bell was most certainly askew in the arch: yet, without going up to the platform, he could not tell how precariously it was balanced. Obviously, one end of the headstock had jumped from its mounting, but Rafael found it difficult to understand what had prevented the other end from slipping free and the whole thing—bell and headstock together—falling from the arch.

I must go up, he told himself regretfully; there is no

alternative. Then he shrugged and muttered, '*Lo que ha de ser, será*,' which is to say, 'What shall be, shall be.'

In the north-west corner of the church an iron stair-case spiralled to a trap-door opening out on to the roof. From there, immediately behind the false west façade, a steel ladder stretched across the tiles to the base of the squat tower. Father Robredo often expressed the view that although the architect had probably loved God dearly it had not made him any better at his job, and Rafael heartily endorsed the opinion as he clambered bow-legged towards the top of the ladder.

As an architect, he thought, this man—whoever he was—would have made a good fisherman.

The ascent became vertical when the ladder ended. Twelve evenly-spaced rungs led up the back of the tower to the inspection-platform. Rafael climbed slowly —left hand, left leg, right hand, right leg—making sure of his grip and testing the feel of his rope-soled sandals on each rung before proceeding further, not looking down but staring at the pitted stonework immediately in front of him.

After what seemed a long time his head drew level with the floor of the arch. No detailed examination was necessary. A deep, bowl-shaped patch of masonry, centred around the loosened gun-metal mounting, had crumbled away and, for about sixty centimetres, the short steel pivot on the headstock had scoured a raw, shallowing rut across the side of the arch.

Rafael heaved himself cautiously on to the flat top of the tower behind the arch. He dared not risk standing up so he stayed on all-fours among the bird-droppings, try-ing to concentrate on the bell, trying to pretend that he was not over twenty metres above the ground. The priest had not exaggerated. As far as the old man could see the only reason the bell was still there was because the other pivot was stuck fast in its mounting. The headstock sloped at a forty-degree angle and the end that had come loose merely rested against the wall.

It is astonishing, truly astonishing it has not fallen, he thought. All the strain is on one pivot and that must have very nearly come out of its socket. Otherwise, at that angle, the stock would not touch the other wall as it does.

For the first time since Father Robredo spoke to him in the square Rafael was alarmed. His inherent dislike of climbing to the inspection-platform had made him temporarily unappreciative of the real danger. But now, crouching within arm's length of the arch, he was suddenly and disturbingly aware that—as the priest had said—the bell might break loose at any minute . . . wind or no wind. It was unreasonable to expect that the heavy, yoke-like headstock to which the bell was fixed could be held indefinitely by one steel pivot. The combined weight would either draw the pivot completely from its mounting or, without warning, snap it off like a twig. And—whichever happened—the result would be the same.

A gull appeared from nowhere, planing in with stiff, wide wings, and settled on the centre of the stock.

'*Reina de los angeles!*' Rafael said aloud, wincing. 'This is no place for me.'

He shuffled backwards on his knees, moving with extreme care, then lowered himself gingerly until his feet found the uppermost rung. The gull eyed him with beady disdain. The rungs on the tower and the steel ladder across the roof were warm to the touch as the old man descended. If it had seemed a long way up, it seemed twice as long now, and never was he so relieved

45

to reach the staircase inside the trap-door. Vertigo was bad enough, but the thought of the bell breaking loose and taking him with it had pursued him at every step. He paused to mop his face with a rag of a handkerchief before going heavily down the staircase to the floor of the church.

Undoubtedly the bell will have to be brought down, he thought. And soon. But—thanks be—it is not my job. Señor Hoyas will undertake it. I will help all I can—but I shall do it from the ground.

In his haste to get to the roof the old man had not noticed Maria and Honorato, and he was surprised to see them now as he crossed from the staircase to the door. For a second or two he blinked at them doubtfully. It particularly surprised him to see Honorato, who—it was said—had not been at Mass in Valandorra for the last couple of months. But his curiosity was quickly stifled when he realized they were unwittingly endangering themselves by kneeling so near to the back of the church. If the bell crashed it would be thereabouts that it would fall. . . .

He walked over to them and touched Honorato on the arm. 'You must move from here,' he whispered with gruff urgency.

The boy and girl turned their heads, but it was Maria who spoke. 'Why, Rafael?'

'The bell is loose.' He pointed vaguely upwards. 'The earthquake has damaged the arch and there is danger of it falling.'

'The arch?' asked Honorato, clambering from his knees.

'No, the bell. It would be best if you moved either to the front, near the chancel, or came outside.'

'We will come out,' Honorato said at once.

46

They followed the sacristan into the harsh brilliance of the sunlight, turning when they were a few paces beyond the door and backing away, shielding their eyes with their hands.

'Here,' Rafael said. 'You can see better from here.'

The gull was still perched on the stock. A creamy twist of high cloud glided smoothly across the aperture, making the arch and the whole façade of the church seem as if they were toppling slowly forwards.

'What exactly has happened?'

'One of the pivots—that on the right as we look—has broken from its mounting. At each end of the headstock there is a short iron stump which fits into a socket in the arch—'

Maria was not concerned with the details. 'Do you truly believe the bell will fall?'

'I am afraid so.'

'You cannot see much from down here,' Honorato said. 'How can you tell—'

'I have been up to the platform. There can be little doubt of it.'

'Meanwhile you wait to see if you are proved right or wrong?'

Rafael shook his head. 'Father Robredo has gone to fetch Señor Hoyas. It is a matter for an expert. Believe it or not, that bell weighs all of two hundred kilos.'

And with that bird on the stock, he thought anxiously, it weighs about a kilo more.

Señor Hoyas was on the point of driving out to the mill when the priest found him at the far end of the village. He was a burly, middle-aged, blue-chinned individual, generally believed to have more money than anyone in Alquena. If this were true it did not mean a great deal but, at least, he owned a ramshackle car and employed half-a-dozen men. Whenever a builder was needed the people of Alquena and the neighbouring villages invariably sent for Señor Hoyas. They had done so for over twenty years. Not because he was particularly good at his trade, but because there was no-one else—unless they called in somebody or other from one of the towns, and that was always a good deal more expensive.

Despite twenty years of monopoly Señor Hoyas still retained his smartness as a man of business. He knew unerringly what was profitable and what was not, and this morning the job at the flour-mill was going to be profitable. Very profitable. The flour company had money enough to pay the fancy prices of the larger builders in the towns and it was only because it was an emergency that he had been sent for. It was a wonderful opportunity. His men had already gone over there in the truck. The odds and ends of damage in Alquena and elsewhere—and his first reaction had been that they were disappointingly small—could wait until later. . . .

With his finger he dislodged a grape pip from between two of his back teeth, then opened the car door. As he clambered into the bucket-seat, squeezing his belly under the wheel, he heard somebody call his name.

'Señor Hoyas!'

'Yes?' He turned his head impatiently to find Father Robredo lolloping frantically along the street towards him.

'Señor Hoyas!' the priest called again, fearing that the car might yet be driven away. The builder had a cast in one eye and might have been looking anywhere.

'I hear you, father.' What can he want? Señor Hoyas

48

thought peevishly. I do not wish to be delayed—today of all days. 'What is it?'

Father Robredo did not stop running until he reached the car. 'Something terrible has happened at the church,' he began, and once again, as he struggled for breath, he was unable to find the right words to explain himself accurately. The builder shot a number of professional-sounding questions at him and he answered them as best he could, but all the while he was conscious of the precious minutes that were being wasted. Talk, talk, talk.... Rafael had been the same. Why not start for the church at once and talk on the way?

'It is of great urgency, I assure you. I would appreciate it if you would come back with me now.'

Señor Hoyas frowned. 'There has also been damage at the mill, father. I am told that one of the departments is completely out of action, and—'

'Two men would be enough, I am certain.'

'All my men have already gone, father.' He glanced at his watch, partly to show his impatience, partly because he felt uncomfortable meeting the priest's gaze. 'The truck will be at the mill by now.'

'Then,' Father Robredo persisted, 'I must ask you to assist us personally. Rafael is very capable, but we need your help and advice. Believe me, I would not ask if it were not so serious.'

Señor Hoyas wound the watch-spring tight. If it had been anyone else he would have been bluntly frank; told him to wait until later in the day. But this was a most delicate matter. In a few weeks now Father Robredo would be marrying his eldest daughter, and he wanted no unpleasantness. *Madre de Dios!* If only he had driven off a minute earlier....

49

'It is very difficult, father. Unless I go to the mill I cannot decide exactly what is to be done.' He shrugged, spreading his hands, and glanced briefly at the priest. 'My men are only labourers, you understand. Without me they would be uncertain how to tackle the job.'

'Rafael and I are not even labourers,' Father Robredo answered sternly, his flat chest heaving. 'Without you we are lost. And this is a church, Señor Hoyas, not a flour-mill.'

The builder shifted awkwardly, pushing his grease-rimmed hat off his forehead. He glanced up again, but the priest imagined that he was looking past him, down the street. 'Tell me once more how the bell is placed,' he said, as patiently as possible.

Father Robredo was not deceived by this belated show of interest, sensing that—no matter what he might say—Señor Hoyas had already made up his mind to go to the mill. And, as he briefly repeated what he had seen from the inspection-platform, the old helplessness began to flutter through him again. Finding Rafael had quietened it once; the first glimpse of the builder's car had stilled it a second time. But now it returned, setting his brain spinning.

Señor Hoyas was nodding before the priest had finished speaking. 'From your description I do not believe there is any real cause for alarm. The bell is obviously jammed—otherwise it would have fallen at the time of the shock.'

'Could you not look at it?' Father Robredo pleaded, disconcerted by the other's squint.

'There is no need, father. No need at all. I understand the position perfectly.' He arched his thick eyebrows, as if hurt that his judgment was in question. 'If I had any doubt I would do so—as you know. But I am completely satisfied—from what you say—that the bell will hold safely until I can put my men on to it.'

'When will that be?'

'This afternoon.... Tomorrow. I cannot tell until I have been to the mill.'

'Tomorrow!'

The priest was appalled. He almost choked with dismay. For a fraction of a second Señor Hoyas worried lest his anxiety to get moving had made him over-emphatic about the bell's safety. He knew from experience that Father Robredo was inclined to exaggerate matters. Yet if he had committed himself too strongly to an opinion—and something *did* happen—there would be serious repercussions....

'I have a suggestion, father,' he said, choosing his words with care. 'Use what you like from my yard. Take anything you wish. Scaffolding, ropes—' he waved a hand, '—it is all there. Get started on what you want to do and, as soon as I and some of my men are free, we will finish it for you.'

The priest stared at him without expression. 'Rafael says the bell weighs more than two hundred kilos—' he began in a flat voice.

Señor Hoyas hardened his heart. The minutes were slipping by. 'In the circumstances I can suggest nothing else. An entire department at the mill is idle. And so, until I get there, are my men. If I delay now I am delaying my return to assist you.' That was a good point, he thought; I should have made it sooner. He reached for the self-starter. 'I assure you, father, what I am doing is best for all concerned. I will be back as rapidly as I can—you may be certain of that. Perhaps in a few hours. Meanwhile, everything in my yard is at your disposal.'

Father Robredo scarcely heard him. The engine chugged noisily; spluttered into life. Señor Hoyas pulled his hat down over his eyes and hoped the smile he gave looked sufficiently apologetic.

'It is much regretted, father. If only you had found me a quarter of an hour earlier. . . .'

A reddish-grey cloud of dust spewed round the priest as the car lurched away. He made no attempt to evade it, but stood there with his head slightly bowed, more astonished and aggrieved at the builder's refusal—and the manner of it—than immediately distressed by its seriousness. For a moment he felt nothing except a hot, bubbling sense of hostility towards the man. Then, as the dust cleared, his indignation subsided also, giving way before a renewed rush of dejection and hopelessness. His thoughts were chaotic. All his trust had been centred on Señor Hoyas. 'To get the bell down requires proper tackle,' the sacristan had said. 'Only one man in Alquena could do it. Even so, he would find such a task very difficult. . . .'

He turned slowly and began walking towards the square, feeling suddenly tired; utterly dispirited. What can we do? he asked himself miserably. There is only Rafael and me—an old man and an incompetent one. How can we possibly get the bell down, even if we take everything there is in the builder's yard? Such an operation requires skill and experience, and we have neither. What *can* we do? . . . The more he asked himself the further he seemed from finding an answer.

The street was almost empty now. Along the west side the upper portions of the colour-washed houses— some balconied, all with their window-shutters thrown wide—implacably reflected the sun's glare. The men of the village had gone to their work—to the flour-mill and the orchards, to the nearby railway-line where a number worked as gangers; a few to the fishing-boats that went out from neighbouring Murinda; others to the market-gardens. Until sundown—with few exceptions —the population of Alquena would consist of women and children, dogs and chickens.

They cannot help, Father Robredo thought despairingly. But a couple of the remaining men might do so. The *guardia civil*, for instance: and Raimundo, at the petrol-station. . . . He took heart as the idea came to him. . . . It is early yet for the taverns, so perhaps Manuel will be prepared to assist. He is a likely one. And Juanito —only the other day he was telling me that business was very slow. . . .

He quickened his pace, the need for immediate action reasserting itself simultaneously with the revival of hope. First, he decided, he would find Manuel. . . .

Rafael waited with Maria and Honorato as Father Robredo came up the path to the church. He came slowly, like a man twice his age. The nervous energy which had driven him from place to place during the last hour had burned itself out, leaving nothing to combat the bewildered despair that now gripped him. Five times since Señor Hoyas left him his appeal for help had been rejected; five times, with a sinking heart, he had listened to excuses—all manner of excuses. Now— with no-one else to whom he could turn—the spark of hope was finally extinguished, and he kept his eyes fixed on the glinting brown path rising in front of him, not daring to look at the bell again until he had the comfort of the sacristan's company.

Rafael was puzzled. He brushed past the boy and girl and started towards the priest. 'Where is Señor Hoyas?' he called.

Father Robredo shook his head and flapped his arms wearily, as if it were too much effort to speak.

'Is he coming, father?'

Another shake of the head. 'No.'

'No?' Rafael was astounded. 'Why not?'

'He has gone to the mill. His men too.'

'*All* of them?'

'All of them,' the priest said.

They were together now, the old man moving sideways at the priest's elbow as he asked his questions.

'What has happened at the mill that is so important?'

Did it really matter? 'One of the departments is out of action,' Father Robredo said mechanically. 'Señor Hoyas assured me—'

'Señor Hoyas!' Rafael growled indignantly. 'Señor Hoyas is a fat, rich hypocrite—'

'Rafael! You have no right—'

'What I say is true. He has a squint, but there is also a squint in his heart. Did you explain about the bell?'

'Of course.'

'And still he would not come?'

'Have I not told you?' Father Robredo retorted sharply, unable to restrain his exasperation. 'Am I not here on my own?'

They walked a few yards in awkward silence. Then the priest said, 'He will come as soon as he can. Meanwhile we are at liberty to borrow what we like from his yard.'

Rafael grunted. 'That is generous of him. A beggar can write a cheque for a million *pesetas*, but he will not be able to buy a meal with it. We need more than the equipment. ... We need help. Strong arms, experience....'

'I have asked as I came through the village.'

'Yes?'

'They are busy.' A shrug of the shoulders. He wanted to be charitable. 'You know how it is.'

'What about Raimundo? Or Manuel? ...'

'Raimundo, Manuel, Juanito, Alberto, the *guardia*—I have asked them all.'

Rafael blinked unbelievingly at his companion, then lifted bleary eyes to the sky. 'Witness this ingratitude,' he muttered angrily through clenched teeth, and Father Robredo was too depressed to reproach him. The sacristan struggled briefly with the temptation to run to the square in the hope of persuading one or two of the able-bodied men to return with him. But the thought had no sooner entered his head than he realized the futility of it. If the priest had failed what chance had he of succeeding? '*La buena vida hace olvida al padre y a la madre*,' he said in a low voice. 'Good fortune forgets father and mother.' And with that he dismissed them contemptuously from his mind. We are on our own now, he told himself. This business is ours alone....

He stared at the bell as they came to a halt near the door. The angle of the headstock was like a challenge, but the longer he looked the more he was infected by the dismay and feeling of puny impotence that had driven all spirit out of the priest. Yet, instinctively, he sought for a practical solution to the problem. And because he knew that the responsibility of deciding on a course of action was now squarely on his shoulders he found strength to suppress his consternation.

Nobody spoke for a moment and it was Maria, uncertain of what had happened, who eventually broke the silence.

'Is there anything I can do, father?'

Father Robredo seemed to come out of a dream. 'Eh?'

'It is a man's job, Maria,' Rafael answered, thinking out loud. 'Three or four men's job. We have to get the bell down before it decides to come down by itself. This I have explained to you. But now there is a complication; a major complication. Señor Hoyas and his men are a dozen kilometres away and everyone in the village is busy. That leaves the *padre* and me. Normally, for two of us even to try to move the bell would be madness. We really need two others ... at the very least one. But as no-one is available we have no choice—and little time. Somehow we must do what is necessary. The problem is—how?'

He spoke in a rough, matter-of-fact voice, but she sensed his concern. She saw, too, the strained expression on the priest's upturned face, blotched with sweat-caked patches of white dust so that he had something of the appearance of a clown, and she turned impulsively to Honorato.

'Will you help them, Honorato?' she whispered.

'I?' Honorato smirked defensively. 'You ask the strangest things.'

'Will you?'

He glared at her. 'This is not my village,' he began. 'There are—'

'If you love me you will do it.'

'You know that I love you.'

'Then you will help. Please.'

Do not push me, he thought. 'Why do the people of Alquena not help with their own bell?'

56

She stamped her foot. 'You heard what Rafael said. They are busy.'

'Busy!' He tossed his head scornfully. 'Selfish. Lazy. Either of those—but not busy. Do not tell me that everyone is ...'

He left the rest unsaid. As he faced her, the colour mounting in his cheeks, he suddenly remembered how —only an hour before—his father had stood with the ladder in their yard in Valandorra and ordered him to help fix the tile. He remembered, too, how he had fumed at his father's indifference to what had happened elsewhere, and now, as if in defiance of that indifference, his mood softened.

'If you love me you will do it, Honorato,' Maria said again.

He glanced at his feet, twisting the toe of a shoe in the dust. I love you, he thought. How much, I realized only today. And I will do as you ask. But let me take my time so that I do not feel I have been forced into it.

She waited, watching him, as if reading his mind, answering the smile that came slowly to his lips and puckered his eyes.

'I love you,' he said at length. 'And for that reason I will help with the bell.'

Hand in hand they turned back to the others, but Father Robredo and Rafael had not missed a word. The old sacristan's frown had crumbled away and the clown-faced priest was stepping emotionally towards them with outstretched arms.

IT WAS now a quarter to nine and life in Alquena had reverted to its normal languid tempo. The shadows were shortening, intensifying their printed patterns. Already the pale blueness of the sky was discoloured by the gathering heat; the thin pearly haze of an hour ago had evaporated. In the village, chickens high-stepped gawkily about the dusty main street; children scrabbled in pools of shade beneath the tattered palms in the square. A few women came and went; paused to gossip. Inside the flaking, bright-fronted houses others were cleaning rooms, tackling the small repairs that could not wait until their men came home. Now and then a chain rattled, a wheel squeaked, as water was drawn from one of the garden wells. Somewhere a gramophone was playing, its jazzy imported music brittle and incongruous on the still air.

Most people had heard about the bell. Curiosity had driven a handful—all of them women—part of the way up the church path for a brief look. The rest accepted what they were told, nodding with satisfaction at the news that the priest and Rafael and Maria's Honorato were at work on it—the knowing ones raising their eyebrows at the mention of Honorato. But few gave the matter more than a passing thought. It could not be of great seriousness, otherwise the work would have been entrusted to Señor Hoyas—and had he not been seen to drive away? 'Herradura que chacotea clavo le falta,' someone said with a shrug. 'The horseshoe which clatters wants a nail.' Without an understanding of what was involved it was as simple as that. Meanwhile they all had their own jobs to do. Earthquake or no earthquake, the day had but twenty-four hours.

Only those who had been spoken to by Father Robredo felt an occasional jab of conscience. Yet each of them managed to convey the impression that the priest's predicament was entirely forgotten The civil guard sat alone in a fly-blown café, noisily sucking at a hollow tooth, wondering if his promptness in reporting the shock might help towards the promotion he had been hoping for over the past ten years. Raimundo, the petrol-station proprietor, lolled against the rusting frame of a derelict car, waiting without enthusiasm to serve, from his solitary pump, the early-morning Valencia bus. Manuel and Juanito, and Alberto—who ran a fruit and vegetable stall in the square—self-righteously busied themselves with all manner of odds and ends that would otherwise have gone unattended. It was not that any of them disliked the priest, or were antagonistic towards the Church. Each would have sworn, hand on heart, that this was not so. Did they not go to Mass? Receive the Sacraments? Give alms? Most certainly they did. But this business of the bell—that was beyond the normal run of things; something for the enthusiast. . . .

Maria had returned to her mother's house. There was nothing she could usefully do at the church and her mother needed her. Besides, lowering the bell was going to take time and, anxious though she was to see the task successfully accomplished, she was not sure that she could stand the strain of waiting. It had pained her to watch Father Robredo's concern, to see his almost pathetic trust in Rafael and Honorato, to hear his suggestions dismissed with impatient or preoccupied brusqueness. And she had only to listen to the others to know that they were far from confident of the outcome; that the priest's complete reliance on them was the product of despair.

'It is madness,' Rafael said pessimistically, shortly before she left. 'But, unfortunately, a necessary madness—and we cannot wait for the full moon to assist us in it.'

Once Maria had gone Honorato began to have misgivings about having offered his services. It will be an embarrassment, he thought, if the news reaches the factory that I have helped with this bell. And it surely will. Some of those I work with will joke about it. I can take care of them—but, to a few, it is not a joking matter. The more serious will not understand my reasons. They will point out that personal ties should never affect one's course of action. To them, what I am doing is a betrayal.... He frowned slightly, pursing his lips.... Because they are my friends and because I have recently shown an interest in their way of thinking they are impatient for me to align myself with them completely. But I will not be rushed. Nor am I at all sure they are right. There is much good in the theory of what they believe, yet—from what I have been told—the theory does not necessarily work in practice. Perhaps I expect too much of it—just as, perhaps, I also expected too much of the Church.... I cannot say. It is a problem that has begun to make life very complicated—first with Maria; now, almost certainly, with some of my friends. I am increasingly pulled two ways and often I do not know what I believe myself. And now this bell has complicated the position further....

I must not let the others see that I am unhappy about climbing to the inspection-platform, Rafael thought. It would not be to my credit if they knew. For a sacristan to have such a failing is like a sailor not being able to stomach the sea. And once already this morning I have behaved in a way that is best forgotten. It is an act of God that this bell has been broken and it is my duty to see that it is safely brought down. Father Robredo is relying on Honorato and me to do it, though from my heart I wish it were otherwise. But, since it is not, I must accept what God sends and do what is required of me....

This old man is made of pure gold, Father Robredo thought. He has never liked going up to the platform and, for that reason, he has not always attended to the maintenance as regularly as he should. He believes I do not know, but I read him like a book and—because I see him as he is—I admire him all the more. He will do this thing because of his sense of duty. And Honorato here—he is working with us because of his love for Maria. It is not the best reason, but perhaps it is the next best. In any case, I am grateful to him; immensely grateful. Together we shall save the church from being damaged. We *must* save it. I am very useless and I know that I get in the others' way, but, provided they tell me what to do, I have a constructive part to play. Merciful Father, look favourably on our efforts to lower this bell....

By nine-fifteen they had made two trips to the builder's yard. The yield was disappointing, but their choice had been limited. Ten timber scaffold-poles, a long coiled length of heavy rope, several shorter lengths and a single snatch block lay on the ground near the church door. Rafael and Honorato had shed their jackets; Father Robredo his cassock. The priest had knotted a white handkerchief round his head and, in his patched shirt and black trousers, he had lost his clownish look and now had something of the appearance of an emaciated pirate.

'Tell me again what you have finally planned, Rafael,' he said.

The sacristan dragged the back of a wrist across his chin. 'To begin with we must get the poles up to the platform, father. Then we will put four on either side of the top of the arch, two over the roof and two under in each case, and lash them together close to the stone-work. That will hold them in a horizontal position, parallel to one another. Do you follow?' The priest nodded, his eyes on the bell, trying to visualize the procedure. 'When that is done we will secure two more of the poles—at right-angles across the others—a short way out from the front of the church. To them we will fix the pulley-block so that it hangs underneath.' Rafael paused. The plan was sound enough—though crude—but words and actions were very different things. 'It will not be easy, father. We must work with great care in case we dislodge the bell before we are ready.'

'And then?'

'Then we knock the other end of the headstock away.'

'After first tying the rope to the bell?'

Honorato smirked, but Rafael said patiently, 'Naturally, father.'

The priest nodded again, but he was still uncertain if he understood correctly. This sort of thing always confused him. 'After that we lower the bell by hand?'

'That is so. It will have swung out from the arch and will be hanging beneath the poles.'

62

'And all three of us will be on the inspection-platform?'

'Yes. I have explained that this is necessary because we did not find sufficient rope of suitable quality to permit us to lower from the ground.'

Father Robredo nodded again. Then he suddenly pointed to the poles, and groaned. 'We have overlooked something.'

'What?'

'We will never get those up the circular staircase.'

Rafael and Honorato exchanged glances. 'There is no need,' Honorato said, a little roughly. 'We will haul them straight up from where they are now. Only the rope needs to be carried.'

'Ah.' The priest washed his thin hands with invisible water. 'I see; I see.' For about the third time that morning his sallow face found the suspicion of a smile. 'Well ... Are we ready?'

'Yes,' they said. Honorato flicked a curling tassel of black, oiled hair out of his eyes. Rafael half turned away and crossed himself.

'Then,' Father Robredo said, his attempted cheerfulness no more convincing than his smile, 'let us make a start.'

HONORATO stood inside the front of the arch, on the edge
of the drop, and hauled up the poles one by one. Twenty
minutes earlier he had climbed to the inspection-platform and wriggled under the slanting headstock, squeezing with infinite care between the bell and the right
wall of the arch, and had thrown the rope down to
Rafael. Now all but two of the poles were on the platform. As each was drawn up he passed it beneath the
headstock until the priest could reach forward and help
slide it back. They were heavy, slightly tapering poles
about six metres long. At first Rafael had roped them in
the middle, but the tapered end then swung uppermost
and, when he had them level with the arch, Honorato
had difficulty in getting enough length over the edge to
balance them before dragging them further in and passing them through to the priest. Now they were roped
nearer the thicker end and came up almost horizontal
so that he found it easier to manoeuvre them into position. But it was still tremendously difficult. He had very
little room. The bell was larger than he had imagined,
restricting his movements, and he was scared lest he
should so much as brush against it. Its rim was barely
more than a backward pace behind him and—all the
time—he also was conscious of his nearness to the edge.
The height itself did not worry him, but occasionally
his shoes slipped on the crusted spatter of bird-droppings
and once, when a pole was half-way up, he almost
tripped over the gathering coil of rope at his feet.

'Two more,' Rafael shouted as the rope snaked down

again. 'Have you space for them now or shall we wait until later?'

Honorato twisted cautiously round and cocked an eyebrow at the priest crouching on the other side of the bell. 'Rafael asks if we have space for the remaining two.'

'I think so.' The poles were stacked in the gap beneath the headstock along the right wall of the arch, their blunt ends poking out into space beyond the rear limit of the platform. 'There is still room on the left of the bell. I have put nothing there.'

'You forget that I have to come back,' Honorato said. He was about to ask if Father Robredo thought he was a bird, but the priest's chastened expression killed his intended sarcasm. 'Let us have them up now,' he called to Rafael, his voice metallic and hollow-sounding in the tunnel-like arch. 'It is best to get this part finished. We can find a place for them somewhere.'

The old man grunted and began roping one of the poles about a third of its length from the thicker end. Honorato leaned sideways, one shoulder against the stonework, watching the stunted figure of the sacristan, feeling the rope twitch as if, deep down, a fish nibbled at a baited hook.

It is a slow business, he thought. I have no wish to be here all day. Sooner or later people will walk up from the village to watch us, and I do not want that. I want to finish by noon at least. I came to see Maria, not to waste my time on this bell....

He craned his neck forward. 'Señor Hoyas is out of date,' he said, the arch amplifying his voice. 'Wooden poles are things of the past. In Barcelona and Valencia and Madrid they use tube steel for scaffolding.'

Rafael grunted again.

'It is light and much stronger than wood. If we had it we could do this job twice as quickly.'

Rafael said nothing.

'The whole of Alquena is out of date,' Honorato said, irritated by the lack of response. 'It is behind the times in everything.'

Rafael straightened up and waved an arm. 'Ready,' he called.

Honorato paused before bracing himself to take the strain. 'Have you heard what I said?'

'Every word.' The sacristan's face squeezed into a grin. 'Now be good enough to lift this out-of-date pole. Unless, that is, you would prefer to take the bell to Valencia and lower it there with modern equipment.'

Honorato heard Father Robredo chuckle quietly—a nervous safety-valve of a chuckle. The sound angered him, but he checked the retort that sprang to his lips and started to lift the rope, snatching at it roughly as if it were the pole that was the cause of his indignation. He could feel it bounce and swing on the rope as he hauled it up, hand over hand, and twice it scuffed against the wall of the church.

'Careful!' Rafael shouted the second time. 'That was Saint John.'

Can a saint not defend himself? 'So?'

He hauled away, the rope looping on the floor, salty trickles of dammed-up sweat seeping through his eyebrows. He stood with his legs set wide, body bent slightly backwards, keeping his smarting eyes fixed on the tiny black spires of poplars that marked the course of the road beyond the village. Then, as the pole jerked into sight, he shuffled crab-wise to his left and went down on one knee, extending his arms as far as he could in front of him so that the thicker end of the pole could swing in, clear of the right wall of the arch. It took a long time for the end to come round and his arms shook under the weight. None of the other poles had seemed so heavy.... His shoulder-muscles were jumping; a swelling vein branded his forehead. The pole circled slowly: the end scraped over the edge. As it swung gradually towards him he lifted his arms higher and twisted the upper part of his body until he almost faced the opposite wall of the arch.

'Steady.' Rafael's voice was anxious; curiously distant. 'Steady now.'

Honorato bit hard on his lower lip and dropped his arms a little. The end grated on the blotched cement. Less than a quarter of the pole was inside the arch, but he could not hope to bring it in further in this fashion. Nor could he hold it much longer. The rope cut deep into his hands; his arms seemed to burn with the strain. He sucked down a chestful of air, steadied himself for a second, then grabbed at the end of the pole with his right hand, taking the whole weight momentarily on the other. But he lacked the strength, and the pole, pivoted on the edge, whipped its blunt end upwards as the rest of it dropped. He took it in the stomach, gasping as it hit him, and, with both hands gripping it now, leaned heavily across it to force it down. Something like a sigh came from Father Robredo on the other side of the bell. Honorato paused, blinking to clear his eyes, then began to rock and drag the pole further under the arch, steering the end towards the gap beneath the headstock.

'All right?' Rafael called from below.

'All right,' the priest assured him. He was on his knees, his thin arms thrust through the gap in readiness

67

to help slide the pole to the rear. 'Fine work, Honorato. That was a difficult one.'

Honorato was silent. His irritation had not been entirely dispelled by the struggle. It still niggled at his mind—just as the sweat pricked maddeningly across his back and his fingers throbbed as his blood filled out the whitened imprint of the rope. He heaved at the pole again, ramming the end hard into Father Robredo's outstretched hands, and now that most of its length was safely on the floor of the arch, he started to loosen the rope.

I am doing this because of Maria, he told himself. Not for the *padre* or the old man below. Frankly, I do not care one way or the other what happens to the bell. It is they who are concerned about it, not I. Yet without me they would not be able to lower it and, in the circumstances, they should be more careful what they say. If there is anything in this world that infuriates me it is the small-mindedness they showed just now. What is so wrong about wanting to keep pace with the times? ... He jerked the rope free. His mind would not settle until he had pin-pointed the cause of his irritation.... It is Maria's fault that I am here. For her I will do anything —I know that now—and I must not complain, because I agreed to help. But why did it have to be the church? ...

He left the pole for Father Robredo to deal with and edged forward, casting the rope down. The end whacked on the ground at Rafael's feet, raising a puff of reddish dust.

'Let me have it,' he said flatly, and Rafael stooped over his dwarf-like shadow to deal with the remaining pole.

When this pole is safely up there I must follow it, the old man was thinking. Having watched Honorato at work I fancy the prospect even less than I did. The lad has done wonders. Let us hope that I manage half as well and do not give way to my stupid giddiness. They need me on the platform if we are to succeed.... .

From the tower the sea was visible now. It spread out beyond the ragged extremities of land like a smooth expanse of frosted blue glass. Nearer the soft blur of the horizon it was a darker colour, pock-marked with ruffles of wind, and dotted with a handful of fishing boats. The narrow coastal strip bumped and crumpled rapidly into an indeterminate shapelessness of greens and rusty browns. Out of this jumble a succession of well-defined spurs, like knobbly, splayed fingers, climbed inland and merged into the solidity of the pine-clad hills behind Alquena. In the brassy glare of mid-morning the eye could pick out individual trees far up on the hills, see the specks of black and red and white that were men and women at work in the orchards and vineyards. There was a sharp-focused clarity to everything except the village, where the coloured roofs shimmered violently as if they were about to disintegrate and melt under the heat.

It was approaching ten o'clock and Rafael and Honorato were alone on the tower. The platform was dangerously small for the three of them to be there together and, with that as an excuse, Father Robredo had been sent on a succession of errands. The truth was that, until the time came for the bell to be lowered, he was a passenger. He would be needed then, but meanwhile —more often than not—he got in the way. He had gone now to the builder's yard. More rope was required—

thin-gauge rope for tying the poles together—and, as if sensing the others' opinion of him, he had volunteered to fetch it.

Honorato lay across the convex top of the arch. A stumpy decorated pillar, surmounted by a small cross, rose from each corner. From front to rear the arch was almost two metres deep and Honorato sprawled over its curving roof, his legs in a V. The stonework burned through his shirt; dark crescents of sweat formed beneath his armpits. Four poles were already across the top, two at either side, where they rested against the corner pillars. The job now was to lash them, in pairs, to other pairs that would be run through the underside of the arch and held by Rafael against the ceiling.

The old man stood only when it was necessary; otherwise he either crouched on his haunches or remained on one knee. When he got to his feet the small rectangular platform seemed to shrink, and if he looked below for any length of time the ground began to slide, first to one side, then the other. When he moved, heaving the poles up to Honorato, he did so with deliberate short-sightedness, endeavouring to eliminate from his vision the shifting background to the arch. All the time, somewhere deep in his stomach, there was the fluttering sensation of nausea.

He was standing now, his back against the right wall of the arch, straining to hold a pole lengthways against the ceiling while Honorato squirmed about on the roof, roping the out-jutting ends to those of the poles above. As he stood there, his bow-legged knees slightly bent, he alternated between trying to forget where he was and calculating how much longer he would have to remain on the tower.

A sound like a pistol-shot made him open his eyes and

instinctively flatten himself against the wall. He was in time to see a burst of stone splinters explode from the wall around the mounting close to his right. The head-stock seemed to quiver. A ghastly watery feeling of emptiness flooded through him. His nerves flexed taut, then loosened, and he made a noise like a man gulping for air after being long submerged.

'What was that?' Honorato's voice was no more than curious.

'The bell.' He stared at it as if transfixed. 'The bell moved.'

'*Cristo!*' A scraping of shoes on the roof and Honorato's head appeared, upside down. 'Much?'

'No. But it moved and that is enough. Some of the stonework came away.'

Honorato studied the angle of the headstock. It looked much the same as before; at the nearest point the rim of the bell was about forty centimetres from the floor. But he did not doubt Rafael. He had heard the crack and could see the chips of stone. The sight of the old man, still holding the pole against the ceiling, his arms raised as if in surrender, stirred Honorato from his in-difference.

'We will change places if you wish.'

Rafael shook his head, scattering beads of sweat. 'No, Let us go on as we are.'

'After a while, then? Yours is the heavier work.'

'No.' The bell had frightened him, but the thought of lying on the top if the arch frightened him even more. 'As we are. But hurry. I cannot hold this pole all day.'

'Right.' Honorato disappeared. A minute later he sang out, 'Ready. You can let go now.'

Rafael moved thankfully away from the arch and squatted in the centre of the inspection-platform. There was no time to be wasted, but he had to rest. It was essential for him to wait a moment or two before starting on another pole. His head throbbed and, even when he shut his eyes, he was unable to escape the feeling of giddiness.

How much longer will that mounting hold the headstock? he wondered. It will take us an hour or more to fix these poles. And if the bell breaks loose before we are ready it will surely take me with it. I was badly scared just then, and the lad knows it, yet I would rather he knew of that than of this ridiculous dizziness. There is no dignity in such a complaint. . . .

Five minutes or so before Father Robredo returned the pot-bellied civil guard wandered half-way along the path to the church. He was not the first to come and stare from a discreet distance, but his arrival angered Rafael.

'Looking for work, *guardia*?' he shouted.

The guard offered a gap-toothed grin. 'No. Just looking, old one.'

'You have courage to come—or did you know the *padre* was not here?'

'I am not afraid of the *padre*.'

'Indeed you are not.' If he had been anywhere else Rafael would have spat. 'You deny his request even to his face.'

The guard lifted his shoulders. 'I am on duty. How could I be expected to help with the bell?'

'Duty! Forgive me if I laugh. What do you do from morning to night except sit on your backside or wander about scrounging a drink or a smoke? Answer me that. And when, in all the years you have been here, has anything happened in Alquena that required your attention?'

'I am on duty,' the guard repeated, fingering his rifle. 'It is a matter of principle.'

'Principle!' Rafael snorted. 'You do not know the meaning of the word. Raimundo and Manuel and the others are the same—and Señor Hoyas, too. Is this not your church? Your bell?—'

'The sun has touched your head, old one.'

Honorato twisted round on the roof of the arch. 'But not mine, *guardia*. Rafael is right. Now leave us before Father Robredo returns? Or are you anxious to show us that you can still look him in the eye?' His lips curled. 'But do not forget to be at Mass on Sunday. That also is a duty, is it not?'

The guard swivelled indignantly on his heels and began to move away. Their taunts followed his bulky retreating figure.

'The *padre* will be coming soon. Hurry, *guardia*!' Rafael bawled.

'Lip-service fraud!' Honorato added.

When he had gone they looked at each other. First Rafael, then Honorato, started to chuckle. And Rafael, temporarily unmindful of his whereabouts, unexpectedly found himself drawn closer to the young man who shared his laughter. Truly, he thought, we are brothers in this business of the bell. When we began I should never have believed it. He was surly, and very sharp with Father Robredo. I would have protested but did not want to antagonize him. But now, I have learned, we are brothers, and I feel that we will succeed in lowering this bell together. Our only enemies are time and our own clumsiness.

The priest had not yet returned, but they scarcely noticed his absence. Fixing and manoeuvring the poles demanded all their attention. They worked methodic-ally, with as much speed as safety permitted, Rafael forever glancing at the angle of the headstock. Hono-rato straining his ears for a second crunching report that would mean it had shifted again.

A gull once came in from seaward and, after making a sudden upward sweep, planed unsuspectingly into the arch. Rafael almost dropped the pole he was holding in his anxiety to scare it away and stood, momentarily aghast, as the startled bird beat frantically against the bell before making its escape. Later, as he bent to lift a pole up to Honorato, the end of it struck the ornamental wrought-iron lever on the headstock from which the pulling-chain ran down into the church through a raised funnel in the floor of the arch. It was a glancing blow and the stock did not so much as shake, but again he experienced the involuntary tightening of his stomach muscles and the quickening thump of blood in his ears.

'I hit it then, but it did not move,' he said, relief and astonishment at such good fortune combining to make his voice tremble. 'You heard?'

'I heard. I am still waiting for my heart to return to where it belongs.' Honorato craned over the edge of the roof and looked down. The back of Rafael's neck was lined and fissured like perished brown rubber. 'Can you manage?'

'Yes. But I do not mind saying that I am glad there are only two more.'

He made a long, low whistling sound as he exhaled. The green and dun-coloured hoop of foothills framed by the arch began to rock gently from side to side. He wanted to squat down quickly, to shut his eyes and touch the firmness of the platform with his hands, but

Honorato was reaching over to rope the pole and, for a moment, he could not let it go.

'What is it that is written on the front of the bell, Rafael?'

Black specks circled in a pinky-grey light. The old man felt the weight lifted from his hands and he sank unsteadily on to one knee, covering his face with his hands. That was bad, he thought; that time I felt it badly....

'It is in Latin,' Honorato was saying.

'What is?'

'The writing on the bell. It is raised on the metal and it reads "Laudo Deum Verum Plebem Voco." The "Plebem Voco" is underneath the rest. I can read it from here. It is all in capitals.'

Rafael shook his head. 'I do not know.' He was a little steadier now, but he talked because he was anxious that the boy should not see his sickness. 'You tell me. You are the scholar.'

'But it is your bell. You pull it: for as long as I can remember you have pulled it.'

'I have done it longer than you can remember, but I still do not know.' He did not like to admit that he had never crawled to the front of the arch; that he was surprised to hear of anything being written on the bell. 'You tell me,' he repeated.

Honorato did not disguise his astonishment. 'You are joking.'

Not at this height, Rafael thought. 'Truly, I do not know.' He tried to dismiss the subject. 'Are you ready for the next pole?'

Honorato nodded and hung his arms down in readiness. The sweat-circles around his shoulders steamed at the fiery touch of the stonework.

Has he no curiosity at all? he wondered. I do not understand how a man in his position can go all these years without finding out what the Latin meant. It is not as if the information is difficult to come by—Father Robredo would tell him.... Tiny white wedges of dust-caked saliva filled the corners of his lips.... It is strange how so many people are without curiosity. Even those who *do* enquire about something usually accept what they are told, as if it were sinful to question it. Yet where is the harm in wanting to learn; in trying to sift the truth from all one sees and hears? ...

'The Latin means nothing to you?' he persisted.

Irked by what he considered unreasonable insistence, Rafael's tone roughened suddenly into near-anger. 'What does it matter what is written on the bell? Would it ring better if I knew? Would it sound more musical on the ear? Would such knowledge prevent it from falling?' His eyes glinted. 'If it worries you, ask the *padre*. For my part I am content to remain in ignorance.'

Honorato was about to fling back an answer but, for some reason, he hesitated . . . let the reply go begging. For a moment he glared at the old man. Then, dropping his eyes, he began lashing the poles furiously together.

As he drew near the church Father Robredo called his apologies for having been away so long. He apologized again as soon as his handkerchief-capped head was level with the inspection-platform.

'There is not a great deal of suitable rope left in the yard. It took time to make a selection. These lengths are the best I could find.' Hopefully he brandished a handful of looped strands. 'I thought they would do.'

'They will do,' Honorato said brusquely from the roof of the arch.

76

'I was delayed by one or two of the women, otherwise I would have been back sooner. They told me that the mayor has driven through. It seems the earthquake did not cover a wide area and very little damage has been done. The mayor was making a quick tour of inspection.'

'Very quick,' Rafael commented dryly. 'If he travels at such speed he will see no damage at all.'

'I also met Maria,' the priest went on, clambering on to the platform. 'She will bring us food in a short while.' He paused, hands on hips, breathing heavily, and stared at the out-jutting poles. 'You have made good progress.'

'It is as well that we have,' Rafael said. 'The bell moved just now. It is still as much a question of time as it was at the beginning.'

Father Robredo frowned anxiously. 'How much longer?'

Rafael shrugged. 'Perhaps an hour. If fortune is with us, by noon at the latest. Then the worst of the danger will be over and we can knock the bell free.'

'Fortune will be with us if we are worthy of it,' the priest said, but he spoke to encourage himself as much as the others.

He had become accustomed to the crazy slant of the headstock, but his concern had not lessened. Even to his inexpert eye it was obvious that the heavy, inexorable strain of the bell's weight could not be taken indefinitely on the one pivot. He watched Rafael lift one of the poles and hold it against the ceiling of the arch. The old man stood with his eyes closed, the tendons in his neck like taut strings under the flabby, weather-beaten skin, his arms trembling more and more noticeably as the seconds passed.

'Let me hold it, Rafael,' he said, stepping forward, but the old man, without opening his eyes, shook his head.

Father Robredo backed away reluctantly. I am not much use, he told himself, for an instant succumbing to self-pity. I should be doing more than I am. Apart from lending my weight to the rope I shall have contributed very little to lowering the bell. . . . He sighed audibly. . . . Yet, perhaps it is as well for these two to handle this part of the business. Speed is obviously essential and they seem to know what they are doing. It only needs a breeze to spring up and the bell will surely fall. A breath of wind would do it—or another earth tremor. . . .

Until that moment he had not considered the chances of there being another shock and, because he had stumbled unwittingly on the possibility, he was suddenly alarmed. All at once the danger to which they and the church were exposed was greatly magnified; the need for urgency more pressing than ever. In his agitation it now seemed that Rafael and Honorato were taking an incredible time to fix the pole. He was on the point of blurting out his fears, but the ever-present feeling of personal incompetence tussled with the jittery nervousness that was taking hold of him and he said nothing.

'Tell me,' Honorato said, not stopping what he was doing. 'What does the Latin inscription on the bell mean?'

We would have warning of a breeze, the priest was thinking; but of a second shock, none. It might happen at any time. Yet how can I urge them to work faster if I cannot myself set an example? If only I could *do* something.

Rafael grunted. 'Honorato never wearies in his quest for knowledge.'

'I do not wish to live in ignorance.'

78

'Then the Lord pity you. Knowledge by itself does not bring happiness.'

'Let me know what does, then.'

'I am up here to lower a bell, not to explain my philosophy.' The ground was beginning to slide again. The old man went down on one knee. 'Ask Father Robredo.'

'It was to him I spoke when you interrupted.'

Father Robredo, wiping a dribble of sweat from his nose, heard himself say, 'The Latin means "I praise the true God; I call the people."'

'There.' Rafael spoke with the air of an exasperated parent. 'Now are you satisfied?'

'I praise the true God; I call the people.' Honorato considered it as he bound the last of the out-jutting poles together close to the front of the arch. Then he said, 'It is a good phrase, though the last part is scarcely accurate.'

'How can you say that?' Rafael asked wearily.

Honorato shrugged. 'I do not remember being elbowed out of the way by the people of Alquena this morning. I saw no great rush for this job.'

The sacristan turned almost despairingly to the priest. 'Honorato defeats me with words, father. Tell him he is wrong.'

Father Robredo dragged his eyes away from the brown and olive-green backcloth of hills rising behind the heat-shimmering village and endeavoured to collect his thoughts. He had not really heard the others talking. His mind was fretting with barely-suppressed anxiety and he had been gazing at the surrounding countryside as if, somewhere, he expected to discover a sign that would confirm or deny his fears.

'What is it that Honorato has said?' he asked a little abruptly, astonished and indignant that the old man and the boy should wrangle at such a critical time.

Honorato twisted round, a curling lock of hair dangling almost to the level of his mouth. 'I merely commented on the Latin, father.' The "father" came grudgingly. 'I said that if the bell claims to call the people its claim is false—at least, it is on this occasion.'

'To call and to have a call answered are two very different things,' the priest said automatically.

Rafael nodded enthusiastic agreement.

'Besides,' Father Robredo added, his thin fingers fighting jerkily with each other, 'you overlook the fact that today it has called you.'

The bell has *not* called me, Honorato insisted to himself—not in the way *he* means. I am doing this for Maria. Now that I have gone so far with it I am anxious to get it down safely. That is because, sometimes, I feel sorry for the *padre*, who is so helpless, and also because I have come to like the old one. It is easy to see that he hates being up here, yet he does not complain. I admire him for that and I will give him all the help I can. But, when it is done, let there be no nonsense from either of them about why I did it—or from anyone at the factory, either. Today's work is for Maria. . . .

The *padre* is clever when it comes to words, Rafael thought. He soon quietened the boy then—and not before time. *Dios en cielo!* what a place to choose to discuss such things. I have enough on my mind as it is, and I pray to God that we can get the bell down by noon for I do not fancy I can stand much more of it on this platform. If it were not that they need me I should go down now, but Honorato cannot manage alone and that is what my quitting would amount to. He is a fine lad, this boy, despite all his talk. And it is true what the *padre* said of him just then. The suggestion annoys him at the moment—I know that well; but he is annoyed more because of what he imagines some of his mad-hat friends will say than because he is ashamed of what he is doing. The shame is for them and their like over in the village there. . . .

I was not really thinking when I spoke to Honorato, Father Robredo reflected, yet what I said had the ring of truth in it. All morning I have tried to understand what purpose God had in dislodging this bell. At one time I began to wonder if, like us, the elements have been given complete freedom by Him to behave as they please; if what is termed an "Act of God" is, in fact, no such thing. But now I begin to see the rightness of the old belief that nothing is done by Him without a purpose. Good will come of today's work, of that I am sure. What form it will take I cannot imagine, but something tells me that it will be so. . . . He tugged the damp, corner-knotted handkerchief more firmly on to his close-cropped head. . . . The thing to do is to accept what comes and try to profit from it. I see that now and, in my position, I should have seen it earlier. I must not let my nerves get the better of me again. If another shock comes, it comes—and there will be a reason. That is all there is to it. . . .

IT WAS eleven o'clock when Maria walked up the path with a basket of food and wine for the three of them. She moved gracefully, her dark, centre-parted hair shining like enamel, metal-tipped sandal laces catching the sun as her feet stepped out of the small accompanying pool of her own shadow. Honorato paused for a moment to watch her coming, admiring the ease with which she carried herself, noting again how, even in a plain, workaday blouse and skirt, she had the knack of looking neater and more beautiful than anyone he knew.

'*Hola!*' she called as she drew near the church. 'How is is going?'

'Well,' he answered. 'An hour and all will be done.'

She stared at the arch anxiously, shielding her eyes. 'When do you begin to lower the bell?'

'As soon as we have a couple of poles across these others.' She could not have seen from where she was, but he spread his first and middle fingers as he spoke and laid the fore-finger of his left hand at right-angles across them. 'We fix them next, with the block underneath.'

She nodded, then raised the basket on a straight arm. 'Shall I bring this up?'

'No, Maria,' the priest said. 'Stay there. I will come down for it.'

'Accept my thanks,' Rafael said, clearing his throat. 'How is your mother?'

'Better, thank you, Rafael. In a little while she should be about once more.'

'Good.'

'Accept all our thanks, Maria,' the priest said. 'And do not wait. Place the basket by the door. I will come for it shortly.'

'As you wish, father.' She addressed herself to Honorato. 'I shall see you this afternoon?'

He showed his teeth in a smile. 'Who else?' he said, and she smiled back at him briefly before turning away.

Twice she glanced over her shoulder before reaching the street. When she was almost there Rafael shouted, 'Tell them what we think of them in Alquena,' but she did not catch what he said and merely waved acknowledgement.

They appear to have done very well, she thought. They are not as they were at the beginning when they were discussing how the bell was to be brought down— I was afraid to watch them, they were so undecided and pessimistic. But they seem more confident now. I would like to stay, but there is work to do and, besides, I might distract Honorato. It will perhaps be best if I keep away for a while—I can see how they are progressing from my bedroom window, and I can return later, when the job is almost done. . . . Her fingers toyed with the small gold crucifix suspended from her neck. . . . I am so proud of Honorato. I have loved him for a long while and wish to do so all my life, but to see him up there, with the *padre* and Rafael, is something I shall never forget—come what may—because I know how much I asked of him today.

'We have no time to eat now,' Rafael said, when Maria had gone. 'I shall not be happy until the poles are across and the bell is roped, ready for lowering.'

'I could do with a drink,' Honorato said. 'But I have no stomach for food.'

'In any case, I will fetch the basket,' Father Robredo said, eager to put his hand to something practical.

'There is no room for it up here, father. Bring the bottle, by all means, but leave the basket below. Neither Honorato nor I want food. If you wish to eat, do so—but not on the platform.'

It was unusual for Rafael to speak so forcibly to the priest, but the constant strain of fighting away each spasm of dizziness was beginning to tell. He had been on the tower for over an hour, and since that ghastly, nerve-jangling moment when the headstock shifted a little he had been half-expecting it to move again.

Truly, he thought as Father Robredo clumped dutifully across the roof-ladder, this bell makes me sweat. The very look of it makes me sweat—and not only from my skin. I feel as if all my insides are screwed up into a ball, wringing the strength out of me. Thank God it will soon be done. . . .

'I will take the first of the poles now,' Honorato was saying.

'Good.' The old man pushed himself off his haunches and cautiously dragged one of the remaining poles from beneath the headstock. 'They will need to lie across the others at least a metre clear of the front of the arch. More if possible. Can you manage that?'

Honorato nodded. As he reached over to grab the pole which the sacristan pointed unsteadily up to him, he said, as if to himself, 'Señor Hoyas takes his time.'

'Ah.' Rafael's tongue explored his dry lips. 'I do not think we shall see that gentleman until much later in the day. His heart is made of *peseta*-metal and there is no

84

magnet to draw him here. I spit at the way he has behaved.'

'I would like him to come now.' The pole scraped
over the roof of the arch. 'It would give me much pleasure to tell him that his services are not required.'

'In the manner of telling him I believe I would excel
you,' the old man said with great seriousness. 'It is perhaps not right to admit this with a church beneath me,
but I can think of nothing better than having him come
now and for the bell to land on his thick skull.'

Honorato gave him a sidelong glance. 'After all this
trouble I would not care to see the bell damaged,' he
said, and, despite his giddiness, Rafael found himself
chuckling.

I like this boy, he thought. There have been moments
when I have despaired of him—but the longer I am with
him the more I know where his heart is.

Honorato wriggled over the convex roof, pushing the
pole before him as if he were swimming behind a log.
He lifted each end of the pole clear of the stumpy pillars
at the corners of the arch and rolled it along the parallel,
forward-pointing rails of those already lashed in position
in twin banks of four. The pole was slightly warped; it
did not move easily, and the thicker end tended to roll
further forward than the other. When it was about a
metre from the front of the arch he could only reach it
with the tips of his fingers, so he placed a length of thin-
gauge rope in his mouth and, lying flat, began to squirm
out along the narrow, right-hand group of poles, gripping them with his knees and elbows, until the cross-
placed pole was at a sufficient distance from the arch.
Then, with infinite care, he began to use the rope, shifting
his position so that his arms could work from underneath.

It made Rafael feel sick to look at him. '*Tiene nervios de hierro*,' he muttered, covering his face. 'He has nerves of iron.'

Honorato had been well aware of the risk, but when the moment came he had purposely not hesitated, sensing that the longer he delayed the more difficult it would be. And now that he was there he was too intent on keeping his balance to be alarmed by the consequences of a slip. He lay on the poles, gripping tight with his knees, the upper part of his body quivering as he flexed it upwards from the region of his diaphragm in an endeavour to give his arms greater freedom. Out of the corner of his eye he saw a mongrel bitch, tongue lolling, empty teats swinging, lope across the church path. Beyond the village an insulator on a telegraph-post gleamed like a mirror in the sun. In the far distance a smudgy spiral of reddish dust rising from between the breasts of small hills heralded the approach of the late-morning bus from Vinaroz. He noticed these things with the same curiously heightened, yet disinterested, perception that had been his at the time of the shock, but they were no more than an out-of-focus background to the poles and his hands at work with the rope. Nothing distracted him from what he was doing. Sweat needled his scalp; smarted in chafed patches on his forearms. He worked clumsily, in short, muscle-trembling bursts, holding his breath and raising his body a little while his fingers frantically tugged and twisted and looped the rope over and under and round the overlapping poles in figures of eight. Then, when at last it was done, he edged cautiously backwards until, with his chest heaving, he was once again kneeling on the roof of the arch, wiping the palms of his hands on his thighs. And Rafael, crouched on the inspection-platform beside the priest clasping the wine bottle, could only shake his head admiringly and say, *'Hombre; hombre.* Rather you than me.'

Father Robredo held out the bottle. 'A drink, Honorato?'

'No.'

'There is plenty.'

'Later. First I will finish this.'

The sooner the better, he thought. When the block is in position and there is no necessity for me to perform any more of these monkey-tricks—then I will drink. . . . Somewhere in his mind was the hope that Maria would see him stretching precariously into space. . . . *Madre de Dios!* I will drink—the remainder of the bottle, most likely. . . .

He selected a length of rope and went immediately out on the left-hand group of poles. The old man and the priest waited helplessly on the platform, anxiously watching every move he made. The minutes dragged, the silence broken only by Honorato's grunts, the chunky scrape of wood on wood and the creak of the poles under his weight. Once a black-shawled woman waddled up the path and Father Robredo, realizing at the last moment that she had not come to stare, shouted at her not to enter the church until the bell was down. 'Come back later,' he called after her retreating figure. 'In an hour or so. There will be no danger then.' But the renewed sight of Honorato quickly made him add, to himself, 'Merciful Father, grant that this will be so.'

By half-past eleven the two poles were securely lashed across the others and the block, already threaded, was suspended beneath them by a dozen twists of stout steel wire. A few minutes more and the bell could be lowered. Rafael sent the priest into the church to unhook the bell-rope from the length of chain which ran through the roof from the lever on the stock.

'You will need to use the steps, father,' he warned as Father Robredo disappeared over the edge of the platform. 'They are near the door.' He had misgivings about entrusting the job to the priest, but he knew that if he left the tower to do it himself he would find it almost impossible to return. The sickness was very bad now; the fluttering in his stomach like birds' wings. 'And do not jerk the chain, I pray you.'

Honorato slid gently from the roof of the arch and began worrying at his thumb with his teeth.

'You are hungry?'

'A splinter.' He plucked at his sopping shirt with the other hand, then picked up the bottle. 'But thirsty—yes. I could drink until the sun goes down.'

'You have done well,' the old man said, resting on one knee. 'Magnificently. Without you we would have managed little. Watching you on the poles made me realize how much we took on when we started this business— how much we are in your debt.'

Honorato tilted the bottle, rinsing the thin red wine round his mouth before swallowing, then grinned. 'I thrive on flattery, old one.'

'I do not flatter.' Rafael shook his head, partly to emphasize his words and partly because the ground was sliding again, this way—then that, and he wanted to steady it. 'Maria will be proud of you.'

Honorato shrugged.

'She is a fine girl,' Rafael went on. 'And today you have won her.'

'You think so?'

The chain rattled slightly in its casing and they stared at it, suddenly tense, the sacristan's lips parted, Honorato frozen in the act of wiping his glistening face. After a little while, still with his eyes on the chain and head-stock, Rafael said:

'Take some advice from an old man. Do not lose her now that she is yours. There is no finer girl in Alquena and you will live to regret it if you allow your heart to be muddled by the confusion that is in your head.'

'We have our differences, if that is what you mean.'

'Who has not?' Rafael scratched his nose. For some reason it seemed important to go on, if only because talking took his mind off his sickness. 'Father Robredo could explain better—I lack the words. But this I *can* say. When the confusion in your head has cleared you will realize that Maria has the key to true happiness and contentment. And that, surely, is what you seek.'

Honorato drank again from the bottle. 'I seek the truth,' he said, a little pompously but with sincerity. 'Whatever it is.'

'Truth!' Rafael stifled a cough, his cheeks ballooning eyes watering. '*Hombre*, we find that for sure the day we die—all of us. The moment we are conceived we are on our way to the discovery of it, but there are no short cuts. You cannot solve the mystery merely by puzzling your brains. You must have faith.' He tapped his head, then his breast. 'You do not find the answer there, but here . . . here. If it were otherwise an old simpleton like me would have no chance of Heaven.'

Directly the priest returned Rafael drew the chain gingerly from its casing. Then the three of them, work-ing to the old man's instructions, looped the lowering rope around the headstock on either side of its junction with the bell. They put it round twice—Father Robredo wanted to bring it round again, to be certain, but Rafael insisted that twice was enough—and the block-wheel screeched angrily each time they moved a little more rope through it. All the while, as they crouched in a semi-circle—tense, uneasy, their movements clumsy through excessive caution—they feared that the bell would be disturbed and break free. But it hung there at the same crazy angle that had taunted them all day, and even when the priest struck it hard with his knuckles as he slid the rope under the stock it held steady. And when eventually they stood back they stared silently at their handiwork for a moment as if unable to believe that at last the job was done, the danger almost over.

It was Rafael who spoke first, his sense of exultation tempered by anxiety to set his feet on firm ground as soon as possible. 'A final task, Honorato.' The boy responded wearily, suddenly tired now that the tension had gone. 'Help me to get this end of the rope round the arch. The arch must take the strain when we kick the stock away, for the bell will drop as it swings out under the poles and the three of us could not hold it then. Come. . . . It will soon be done.'

They uncoiled the rope and Honorato took the end with him under the slanting headstock and flipped it round the outside of the arch for Rafael to catch at the second attempt and pass through to him again for securing. He knotted it half-a-dozen times, pulling it taut against the stonework, and heaped the rest of the rope in a compact pile. Then he slithered carefully under the headstock to rejoin the others.

'Now,' Rafael said gravely, licking his lips. 'Now is the moment we have worked for. You, father, must knock the bell away.'

'I?'

'Yes,' they both said.

'Very well.' The priest moved to the side of the arch and steadied himself.

'Kick it hard, father. Then stand clear, for after it swings out it will swing back again.'

Rafael and Honorato edged away a little. Father Robredo raised his right leg and kicked cautiously at the centre of the headstock with the sole of his shoe. The stock vibrated but did not move.

'Harder,' Rafael commanded. 'And more to the right.'

The priest kicked again, hard this time, grunting as he let fly. The stock quivered; dust erupted from around the mounting.

Honorato laughed. 'It is as firm as a rock,' he began. 'And to think that all morning—'

Father Robredo kicked once more, crashing his shoe against the timber. There was a tremendous splintering report as the pivot broke from the mounting. For a fraction of a second, before it began to swing outwards, the bell seemed to be poised in the centre of the arch as if it were floating on air. And it was then—while the three of them shielded their eyes against flying chips of stone and plaster—that the second earth tremor hit Alquena, shaking the tower under their feet.

THERE was no warning. Honorato felt the floor of the platform lurch and, instinctively, he threw himself flat. For a moment he supposed that the bell, as it went clanging out under the groaning framework of poles, was shaking the tower. The possibility of another shock had not crossed his mind: the bell held his startled attention. He watched it reach the limit of its outward swing, jerking ponderously on the rope, and begin to come back. The tower shuddered again. The empty wine bottle crashed on to the roof below. Not taking his eyes off the bell, not daring to look away, he flattened himself more rigidly against the platform. Then, abruptly, the strange, mesmeric spell was broken by a cry that made his neck-hair bristle.

Screwing his head to the left, he saw Rafael topple from the side of the platform, his arms flailing, his rope-soled sandals beating a desperate, last-second tattoo on the edge. For one awful, seemingly-endless moment Honorato stared incredulously as Rafael fell backwards into space. The sacristan hit the slanting roof and bounced off like a sack, struck the gutter, then disappeared. One of his sandals flip-flopped slowly across the moss-covered tiles.

'Rafael!' Honorato screamed.

As he twisted his body the bell came skimming back over the floor a second time, yawning past where he lay. The priest had risen to his knees, gaping at the spot where Rafael had disappeared. The rim of the bell caught him somewhere below his right armpit and, with a hollow-sounding grunt, he collapsed in a heap, his legs hanging over the rear of the platform. Honorato lunged sideways in an attempt to slew the priest round, but Father Robredo struggled from his grasp and, scrambling to the edge, almost threw himself over on to the rungs.

He went down in a nightmarish frenzy—rungs, roof-ladder, circular staircase—negotiating them all without caution, oblivious to the pain that was swelling inside his chest. Half-blinded by the interior darkness, he ran to the door, dazzled again by the sunlight as he burst into the open.

Rafael was lying just beyond the corner of the church, close to the side wall. He lay on his back, legs neatly together, arms outstretched, as if he had been crucified on the brick-red ground. Father Robredo dropped awkwardly to his knees beside him. The old man's face was the colour of potter's clay and dust-filmed ribbons of blood curved from both nostrils across his cheeks. But his eyes moved, the pupils contracting as they focused, and, as the priest leaned forward, the lids seemed to narrow in an attempt at a smile.

'How is it, old one?' he asked gently.

A syrupy gurgle came from deep in Rafael's throat.

'Is it your back?'

Another gurgle. The bell was still crashing out uneven hammer-strokes above them.

He is dying, the priest thought helplessly. There is blood in his mouth and his back must be broken.... He raised his head and looked wildly about him. Somebody was running up the path towards the church and, in the distance, he believed he heard shouting. He was dazed and confused by the suddenness with which everything had happened and even the proof of Rafael on the ground in front of him did not give a sense of reality to what he saw.... There is no time, he decided—conscious of his responsibility—no time for anything but this. . . .

He reached over and took hold of Rafael's right hand and squeezed. 'Do you feel that, old one? If you feel it, press my fingers.'

I feel it, the fingers said.

'Rafael,' he said quietly, fighting to control the emotion that was shaking his voice. 'Are you truly sorry for the sins you have committed during your life?'

Again the weak answering pressure on his hand. Father Robredo swallowed hard, trying to unravel the chaos of his thoughts, desperately anxious that his memory should not fail him now.

'*Clementissime Deus, Pater misericordiarum et Deus totius consolationis....*'

Rafael did not understand the Latin, though he was aware of its significance. But there was no pain and he could not believe that he was dying. Death and pain were inseparably linked in his mind. Not only was there no pain but, except in his hands and feet, there was no feeling of any kind. Almost the whole of his body was numb; cold and numb. He kept his eyes fixed on the priest, endeavouring to concentrate on what he was saying but, for some reason, he found himself thinking about the afternoon Mejiás had been killed in the bullring at Coruña. That had been a long time ago; a lifetime ago, or so it seemed, and he was not sure now whether it was Mejiás—or even Coruña for that matter. It was difficult to be sure about anything, but the scene was vividly clear and he remembered it as if it were yesterday. Of all the bullfights he had seen that was the one he remembered best of all—though why he should recall it now he could not imagine Truly, life was very strange....

'...*ut ejus anima in hora exitus sui te judicem propitiatum inveniat....*'

Rafael stared contentedly at the priest, listening to the meaningless flow of words. Father Robredo gradually began to move backwards and forwards and his voice became muffled, as if a door had been shut between them. The old man wanted to ask him to come nearer, but when he tried to speak he only made a gargling noise through the blood that gushed into his mouth. Then, all at once, the priest was swinging backwards and forwards as if he were on a piece of elastic, backwards and forwards, faster and faster, and Rafael could not hear his voice at all. For a moment, as the silence closed in on him, the numbness seemed to leave his body and a great surging wave of pain burst through him. It came with a violent rush from somewhere near the small of his back yet, before it exploded in his head, he had time to know what it meant.... But Father Robredo went on speaking for almost a minute before he realized that the sacristan was dead.

The tremor shook the people from their houses, scattering them into the square and the narrow streets. Maria was standing at her bedroom window when it came, watching the three men on the tower. In the moment of clutching at the bed-rail to steady herself she saw the small doll-like figure topple from the platform. Fingers to her mouth, horror driving all thought of personal danger from her mind, she ran from the room. At the bottom of the stairs the floor twitched again. She staggered slightly as she reached the kitchen and her mother, suddenly roused from an invalid's sleep by the noise and the movement of her rocking chair, met her with a querulous, 'What is it, Maria? What is it?'

Vaguely Maria heard herself reply, but what she said she never knew. She was across to the doorway, clattering through the bead-curtain and running along the street towards the church, dodging wildly past others who ran hither and thither or stood as if petrified outside their houses.

One of them fell, her thoughts pounded. . . . One of them fell. . . .

C-clang! the bell stuttered, its note throbbing on the air. C-clang!

Who was it? . . . Which one was it? . . .

Someone bumped into her shoulder, turning her completely round. She ran on, gangly-legged; half-stumbled over a small child, then ran on again. The icy spasm of horror was still cold and hard in the pit of her stomach, like a cramp, but part of it was thawing away and flooding her now with the dread of discovery.

Which one, dear God, which one? It is my fault. . . . I should never have asked Honorato to do it. . . .

C-clang! More people running and shouting. C-clang!

She was at the end of the path now and could see the bell. And someone lying on the platform. She stopped abruptly, breasts heaving, hands shakily shielding her eyes. Her vision was blurred and she could not make out who it was, but her fears increased because only one person was there. Desperately she broke into a trot. As the church rose out of the ground she saw the head and shoulders of the priest in the strip of shadow along the side wall and from his attitude she knew that he was kneeling beside someone. Thirty metres away she stopped again. The strength seemed to have gone from her legs and she could not trust herself to move any nearer without knowing.

'Who is it, father?' The angle was too sharp for a view of the platform.

The priest stared at her but did not answer. It was as if she were not there.

'Who is it?' She shouted the question, her voice breaking hysterically.

His lips moved, but the words seemed to take a long time to reach her. 'The old one,' he said at length in a flat, far-away manner. 'Rafael.... And he is dead.'

Her eyes lifted to the platform. Honorato was peering over the edge and she stared unbelievingly at the silhouette of his head and shoulders. Tears blinded her eyes. Relief and sorrow went shuddering through her, racking her frame, and suddenly she ran forward and fell to her knees beside the broken body of the sacristan.

Honorato had not seen her come. The first he knew of her being there was the distraught sound of her voice as she shouted at the priest. Until then he had remained flattened on the platform, dazed by the monstrous, skull-splitting crash of the bell, unable to bring himself to move, as a man experiencing his first shelling, seeing his first casualties, is often unable to move. Rafael had fallen, the priest had gone.... Only minutes ago, but time was distorted by the shaking and the din and the impact of horror.... Rafael had fallen, scraping moss from the tiles where he hit the roof; Father Robredo had gone, green-faced and frantic. It was like the climax to a sudden nightmare. As he had lain there—his head in the crook of his arm, the bell swinging past him with a swish of air and the crash of metal, the platform lurching, the poles jerking and straining—the recurring sequence that began with Rafael's terrified cry rapidly lost its dream-like quality and became an ugly, accepted truth. By the time Maria's shouted question startled him into twisting over to peer down at her he knew that it really *had* happened; that somewhere near to the wall of the church the sacristan was lying smashed on the ground. And Maria's tears as she suddenly blundered out of sight below the projection of the roof told him just as surely that the old man was dead.

He rose stiffly and started to descend the tower, the iron rungs burning his hands. The bell was swinging more gently now, the clapper missing its strike as often as not. He went down slowly, bracing himself against the sight he knew would greet him, yet still with a part of his mind fighting stubbornly against believing it. One minute Rafael had been there, the danger practically over, the three of them on the verge of triumph; and the next . . .

'*Dios!*' he breathed. 'How did it happen?'

The dust in the church gave him his answer, and he checked momentarily on the staircase, astonished that he had not hit upon it earlier. He crossed to the door and hurried outside, his heart-beat quickening illogically as the cause of the disaster dawned upon him, reviving the memorized impact of the shock; his thoughts a compound of the immediate past and the immediate future, horror and grief intermingled as he rounded the corner of the church.

Father Robredo was still kneeling by the body. The only sound came from Maria—a long, shuddering sob. She swayed to her feet on seeing Honorato, her lower lip quivering, the tears dribbling like grease into the corners of her mouth.

'He is dead, *chico*,' the priest said, in the same far-away manner as before, almost without conviction. 'Dead.'

Honorato nodded, but said nothing. He did not like to look at Rafael. All the lines seemed to have gone from the old man's face and its expression was strangely peaceful, but he did not let his eyes dwell on it for long. He had seen the dead before, but never like this. Never with a sandal torn off and weeds crushed and bent under the body and the flies eager for the blood before the sun dried it up. And, most of all, never within a few minutes of working with someone, someone he had grown to respect and have an affection for....

Suddenly he found the silence intolerable. 'There was another shock,' he said, as if he alone knew, as if—somehow—there were comfort to be had from the explanation. 'It was the shock that did it—not the bell.'

Neither of them answered. The silence swelled again, tightening its hold on them all. For what seemed a long time they remained grouped around the body, each of them lost in a private wilderness of emotions, too near the event to be able to disentangle one from another. Then, at last, the spell was broken by Father Robredo flicking a hand at a fly in a weary gesture of disgust.

'We must take him inside,' he muttered woodenly. His deep-set eyes were expressionless, the dark hollows almost blue-black against the pallor of his cheeks. 'Into the sacristy.'

He pulled the grimy corner-knotted handkerchief from his head and placed it gently over Rafael's face. As he bent forward, wriggling thin arms under the sacristan's thighs and shoulders, he groaned suddenly, catching his breath as a rough-edged pain stabbed

99

brutally through his chest. A rash of sweat broke cold on his forehead.

'*Aí,*' he grimaced. He paused, then tried again, but this time the pain was worse and he withdrew his arms, pressing both hands uncertainly to his ribs. '*Aí. . . .*'

Honorato was on one knee, facing him across the body of the old man. 'What is it, father?'

'Here.' The priest winced, hands side by side below his armpit. 'There is a great pain here. . . .' His voice trailed away. He sank back on his haunches, continuing to prod and press. After a while he added plaintively, nodding at Rafael, 'I cannot lift him.'

'The bell caught you,' Honorato said. With death at arm's length he was incapable of sympathy.

'*Aí. . . .* The bell.' Father Robredo winced again as he breathed in. 'Can you manage to take him? We cannot leave him here.'

Honorato nodded. If I must, he thought, I must. He took the sacristan in his arms, hating the limp, sagging feel of the body when he lifted it. As he began to walk towards the door the lingering sensation of unreality was suddenly at an end. It was as if he had needed this physical contact with the dead to clear the last traces of disbelief completely from his mind. His thoughts found room for anger—a prickling sense of hostility against everyone who, however unwittingly, had contributed to the tragedy. It centred principally around Señor Hoyas, but it reached out to engulf all those whose selfishness had angered the old man that morning. It took in the civil guard and the others in the village on whom, in their absence, the sacristan had vented his contempt—Manuel and Alberto and Juanito and the rest. It went further—lumping together in the accusation those of his own friends at the factory who would say that by helping with the bell he had violated a principle, given way to the pressure of personal ties. . . . To hell with their principles!

The body was warm under the clammy chill of its sweat-soaked shirt. He glanced briefly at the handkerchief-covered face, reacting from anger to sudden tenderness. Rafael, he thought; old one. You know all the answers now. . . .

He crossed the chancel, rigid-legged under the weight. A candle had fallen from the altar. A mist of dust still hung on the air. Father Robredo slipped ahead of him and pushed the sacristy door open. Inside, in the dim light, Honorato turned questioningly, 'Where, father?'

With his left hand the priest swept some vestments from a low, flat-topped chest-of-drawers. The other arm dangled by his side. 'Here,' he said. 'On here.'

Honorato laid the old man down and Father Robredo bundled a cassock into a ball to make a pillow. Backing irresolutely towards the door Honorato was moved to compassion by the sight of the priest, who, immunized though he was against a show of emotion by long familiarity with death, was now, all too surely, losing the struggle to control himself. The tears that brimmed his eyes did not spring from the pain that was consuming him, yet Honorato, bruised and distressed by his own grief, could find nothing—word or gesture—that offered comfort.

'I . . . I think I will go now, father,' he began. 'Unless—'

The priest shook his head. 'There is nothing, *chico*,' he whispered brokenly, looking the other way.

'I will try to finish the bell. . . .'

'Yes.' This time he nodded, but he did not realize what

he was saying. 'Yes; do that.' His shoulders were beginning to shake. 'Do that, *chico*.'

Honorato's gaze moved to Rafael, then back to Father Robredo. He had spoken unthinkingly, fumbling for words because he had found himself unable to turn on his heel and leave the sacristy in silence. Until that moment he had given no thought to what must be done with the bell, but now—as if the suggestion had been made by someone else and he had agreed with it—he recognized the necessity of returning to the platform at once. All day the bell had been a challenge and, suddenly, the challenge was renewed, unexpectedly intensified by the memory of Rafael's body in his arms and the incongruous look of him on the chest-of-drawers and the bitterness of the priest's silent tears.

I will get it down yet, he thought defiantly, his anger rekindling, searching unreasoningly for something to engulf. I will get it down if it is the last thing I do. He strode impetuously into the chancel, hesitated for a moment, then returned to the sacristy door.

'Go to the doctor, father,' he said, gently but with authority. 'You have probably broken a rib.'

There was no answer. He walked swiftly through the empty church, his shoes making a crisp clatter on the tiled floor, already obsessed with the thought of what had to be done, calculating how he could tackle the bell on his own. He was making for the staircase when he saw Maria standing disconsolately outside the west door, and he stopped abruptly.

'Maria.'

'Yes, Honorato.' Her eyes were red-rimmed.

'Go down to the village and see if you can find the doctor.'

'He is not there,' she said. 'He was called to a confinement in Murinda an hour ago. I saw him drive away.'

'Then leave word at his house that the *padre* has been hurt. And at where the *padre* lives.' He jerked a thumb over his shoulder. 'He is with Rafael now, but the doctor should see him soon for he is in much pain.'

She was very pale, her fingers intertwining ceaselessly. 'Are you staying here?'

'I am going on with the bell,' he said.

'You are *what*?'

'Going on with the bell.' He went to the edge of the porch and looked upwards. 'And do not stand where you are—you are right under it. Come in here.'

She did not move. 'Honorato, are you mad? How can you—'

'Come in here!' he commanded.

She remained where she was, more appalled by his intention than defiant, and he walked out angrily and dragged her by the arm into the porch. She twisted from his grip and glared at him.

'What is this nonsense?'

'It is not nonsense. The bell must be brought—'

'By you alone?' She tossed her head; the tears were coming again. 'Is Rafael's death not enough for you? And what has happened to the *padre*? ... The bell is secure now, and—'.

'Secure!' he retorted. 'Another shock and the whole lot will come down, perhaps the arch as well.' He was unprepared for opposition and could not see that she was frightened for his safety. 'The job is still unfinished. If the bell were to fall now it would damage the front of the church—'

'You cannot do it,' she cut in, her voice rising distractedly. 'You must not!'

'I can and I will.' He turned away furiously. 'And do not order me about!'

'Honorato,' she cried in desperation, following him. 'If you go up to the bell I will never speak to you again....'

'So?'

'... Never!'

He wheeled on her. 'Do you think that will stop me? The old one dead and the *padre* injured and you offer that as a threat? ... Hah!'

He started up the staircase. 'Honorato,' Maria began again, pleading now. He did not listen. He thumped to the top of the spiralling stairs and heaved himself through the trap-door to the roof. The sun hit him and he flinched instinctively, as if from a blow. For a moment or two he imagined that Maria was still following, but when he was half-way up the rungs behind the tower he knew that he was mistaken.

As he clambered on to the platform the arch looked larger now that the bell had gone, and it amplified the scrape of his shoes against the stone. He knew exactly what he was going to do, though he was far from sure whether it would work. The rope slanted down from the block, a fuzzy-edged scar against the sky, and was secured round the left-hand wall of the arch. He believed that by using the corners of the wall as a brake he would be able to control the bell's descent when he freed the rope and took the strain. At any other time he would have hesitated; paused to reflect on the rashness of the task he had set himself. But the accumulated confusion of shock and grief and anger impelled him irresistibly forward. Only when he looked at the greenish, dropping-streaked bell hanging motionless under the curving poles did he feel a brief stomach-squirm of fear.

'Be kind to me, bell,' he said aloud. 'I am on my own now.'

Almost without knowing it he crossed himself. Then he began to struggle with the rope to set it free.

HE HAD fastened the rope against the forward end of the arch with half-a-dozen loose knots, but the weight of the bell had drawn them tight. Now, as he dug his fingers into the last of them to prise it apart, he could feel the rope begin to slide, moving almost imperceptibly across itself through the knot like a snake uncoiling, the fibres not gripping sufficiently to check the insistent drag.

'*Dios!*' he grunted, glancing accusingly at the bell. 'You are big and strong enough to have been in a cathedral.'

He leaned on the rope, close to the wall, facing along the spine of the roof. The bell was behind him, a metre or so clear of the façade of the church. His left hand gripped the rope a short way back from where it looped round the rear end of the arch wall and his body inclined at an angle of about thirty degrees. Working with his right hand, it took him fully a minute to loosen the final knot and, all the time, the strain on his other arm gradually increased.

Now! he thought.

He was prepared for the snatching pull that he knew must come when the knot was freed, but he had not expected it to be so violent. The rope suddenly came alive, wrenching him viciously into an upright position, snapping his teeth together. Dust squirted from the friction-point on the inside corner of the wall; behind him the block-wheel screeched. He threw his body backwards, stamping his heels hard against the concrete in an effort to get a better foothold. He heard the clapper jiggle, then strike the bell lightly, and the faint, low-pitched reverberation seemed to rattle round the inside of his skull as he fought desperately to stop himself from being dragged through the arch.

It took all his strength to gain control. Gradually, by leaning further back and pressing his shoulder against the wall, he checked the movement of the rope and held it steady.

'Cathedral bell!' he gasped, almost admiringly.

He could hold it, but—*Cristo!*—he realized now what he had undertaken. The strain was so great that he would be unable to spare one hand, even for the briefest period, to knot the rope again. He could hold it—for a while, at least—but there would be no escape from the unrelenting pull until the bell touched the ground, and that might not be for an hour or more.

I am hooked, he thought, momentarily scared. *Aí*; well and truly hooked....

He lay back on the rope, breathing deeply. He knew that if he once let it run he would not have the strength to check it again. Somehow he would have to keep control over it, braking the rope on the corner of the arch, paying it out a few centimetres at a time. But he was reluctant to make a start, dreading a repetition of what had just happened.

The walls of the arch obscured the view to either side. He shut his eyes, trying to picture how high he was above the ground. Fifteen metres? ... Twenty? ... He glanced at the tawny, grease-speckled rope looped at his feet, gauging its length, then at the spine of the roof stretching out beneath him from the base of the tower. Neither gave him encouragement and he groaned at the thought of the time it would take to get the bell down.

An hour? He snorted. Always an optimist! More likely three....

The struggle had shaken the anger out of him. As he leaned on the rope, blinking the sweat from his eyes, he glimpsed the naked, moss-bared patch where Rafael had hit the roof. He looked away immediately, but the memory of what had happened scampered through his mind again, distracting him, and the rope jerked suddenly forward. He snatched at it, stopping it from taking command.

Careful! he reproved himself. Keep your mind on what you are doing. There will be time enough later on to think of other things....

His first attempts at paying out the rope were not a success. Each time the bell threatened to gain the mastery. He found it impossible to judge how much to relax the strain so as to start a controlled movement. When he began to ease his counter-pull the rope would not stir; a split-second later it would leap savagely away without warning, almost jerking his arms from their sockets. After ten minutes he knew that he would have to find some other way. Already his thighs ached intolerably and his shoulder-muscles were twitching in protest—yet, as far as he could estimate, the bell had dropped no more than a metre. When he screwed his head round he could still see it, the rim only a little below the level of the floor of the arch.

'Rafael,' he muttered anxiously. 'I wish you were here. You would know what to do.'

Then he thought—Why not try widening the angle at which the rope comes round the corner of the wall? That might be the answer....

He shifted cautiously away from the wall, deliberately flat-footed, leaning well back with his knees bent.

Ugly worm-like veins bulged and throbbed in his neck; the empty arch magnified the sound of his laboured breathing. When he was half-way across to the other wall he felt the rope start to move. With the next step the movement became more insistent, and he retreated clumsily to his right. The movement ceased immediately.

Ah, he thought, relieved by the discovery. So that is the way. At least I can control it if I do it like that. The only question is—how long can I stand this tug-of-war? I feel tired already, but the thing on the other end will never get tired. Not unless gravity ceases....

He shuffled sideways, uncertain as to how far he had gone the last time before the rope moved. When it began to slide again he let it run a few centimetres, then braked it in the same way by clumping heavily back to the wall. He began to calculate how many times he would have to repeat the manoeuvre. Six or eight times for every metre ... fifteen to twenty metres ... *Dios!* It might be anything between a hundred and a hundred and fifty times.

He groaned. I wish I had not worked it out. The old one said he preferred to remain in ignorance. Now I see what he meant.

The rope was gradually cutting a shallow groove in the corner of the arch, deepening a slight horizontal gap between two ochre-coloured blocks of stone, but it was taking punishment itself. The dust that puffed from the friction-point was as much frayed fibres as it was powdered stone, and he worried lest any part of the rope that had yet to grate over it should already have been damaged. Hasty glances at the length still coiled on the floor were inadequate to reassure him, and he began to wish that he had shown more interest at the time they made the selection of equipment at the builder's yard.

He worked back and forth three or four times more. Now and then the block-wheel squeaked, and once a sharp cracking sound came from the poles, making him swing hard on the rope, craning his neck fearfully to see what had happened. But everything seemed in order and his concern gave way to satisfaction when he realized that the bell was at last out of sight.

It must have dropped another metre at least, he thought.

He had no idea how long he had been there. The interior of the arch was still in shadow, so the sun could not have moved very far. He had become obsessed with the struggle. The wrenching shock of the bell's initial pull had stunned his emotions. So long as it was in relation to what he was doing he was able to think about Rafael with curious detachment, and though the memory of Father Robredo's distress and Maria's tearful threat was not far below the surface it seemed imprisoned by the throbbing muscle-ache that was spreading through him.

Another five minutes must have passed. He was lying on the rope, close to the wall, grunting and sweating, his hands sore and cramped, when the pale fat face of the civil guard appeared in front of him at the end of the inspection-platform. Honorato was so surprised that he slackened his hold on the rope, and immediately—almost as if it had been waiting for him to relax—it ran, scorching the palms and fingers of his hands, then snatching him forwards as he got a grip on it, scraping his knuckles agonizingly along the wall. The rough stone bit deep into his flesh and he cried out, almost vomiting from the ripping burst of pain. To save his hands would mean losing control over the bell, so he let them grate bloodily across the wall, stamping his feet, jerking his body backwards, until at last he had the rope steady.

For a moment, as the raw pain burned to a white heat, he thought he would faint. Gasping for air, he stared blankly at the blurred face of the alarmed civil guard, waiting for it to emerge from the dusky-greyness that seemed to have enveloped everything. Behind him the poles were creaking ominously; the bell clanging to a tipsy rhythm.

'What in God's name do you want?' Honorato heard himself ask.

'I have come to help,' the face reported without enthusiasm.

The boy's anger stirred. '*What* did you say?'

'I have come to help,' the guard repeated uncertainly, already regretting that he had yielded to Maria's pleas. 'Rafael is dead and I thought—'

'*Madre de Dios!* You have the audacity to tell *me* that!' His hands seemed to be stiffening with the pain, but the feeling of nausea had passed. He paused, eyeing the unshaven face in front of him with contempt. 'So— now you come to help?'

The civil guard nodded. When he started up the staircase he had neck-slung his rifle, and now the muzzle was pushing his cap over his nose, giving him a jaunty appearance that was as false as it was ludicrous.

'I spit at your offer,' Honorato said bitterly. 'Now go away.'

The man flushed indignantly. 'Careful of your words, youngster,' he said. 'Do not forget who you are speaking to.'

'Forget!' Honorato strained against the rope, his rage mounting. 'That I shall never do. Are you not the same fat-bellied slug who had his chance to help earlier in the day? Was it not you whose duty kept him from helping a couple of hours ago?' He snorted. 'My memory is not that short. And nor would Rafael's be, if he were here ... which he would be if you and your yellow-livered, lip-service friends had given the *padre* your aid at the start—'

'I am warning you—' the other began half-heartedly.

'Warn away! But make one move to get on to the platform and you will have my shoe in your face.'

There was a long silence. They glowered at each other. 'You will kill yourself, you young fool,' the man growled, trying to straighten his cap.

'What is that to you? Since when have you been concerned for anyone's skin except your own?' He was shaking with anger. 'Now go. Get out of my sight. Go back to your precious duty and see what you can scrounge. There is nothing up here worth having except a kick in the teeth....'

'You are mad,' the guard spluttered, secretly relieved to be going. 'Crazy. I did not come here to be insulted, so I shall leave you to it.' His head disappeared, then bobbed up again. 'And if you think you can lower the bell alone you are crazier than I imagined.'

'Go away!' Honorato shouted.

He listened to the man making his cumbersome descent. His mouth was dry and sour. The backs of his hands were a mushy scarlet and there were glistening seals of blood among the bird-droppings on the floor. The pain jangled the nerves in his arms as far as the elbows and, in his weariness, he yielded momentarily to despair as the pull on the rope reminded him of the single-handed struggle to which he was committed and the help he had so scornfully rejected.

Then, consoling himself, he said aloud, 'I did right to send that fraud away. Rafael would have done the same.' He lifted his eyes to the roof of the arch. I did it because of you, old one, he thought. You were worth ten of him while you were here—and, but for the likes of him, you would be now....

Fifteen minutes after the second tremor the excitement in Alquena had died down. No-one was hurt; the damage was negligible. But the villagers were not again deceived into supposing that what had happened was a non-recurring, twenty-second wonder. There had been two shocks, so why not a third? Another might come at any time and they were reluctant to leave the comparative safety of the square and the narrow, sun-drenched streets. From end to end of the village groups of people stood or sat in the broiling heat. Some of the older ones had brought chairs out from the houses. A black goat strutted stiffly around the square; a cat took objection to some chickens near the post office and sent them scattering. Conversation, animated at first by alarm and nervous reaction, ebbed and flowed into gradual stagnation.

It was then that Maria brought the news of Rafael's death. She spoke only to a few, but word buzzed rapidly from mouth to mouth.

'Rafael has been killed....'

'Who?...'

'Rafael. The old one; he fell from the belfry. The *padre* has been injured, too. The Montes boy from Valandorra is trying to get the bell down on his own....'

A handful of people immediately hurried to the end of the path, paused to stare at the sight of the bell slung beneath the poles, then began to move towards the church. The majority remained where they were, incredulous, but the silence was ruptured by the outbreak of a hundred voices.

'I heard the bell ring when the shock came, but I never thought . . .'

'Rafael! *Malo; muy malo.* He was a good fellow. . . .'

'Fell, you say? . . . What was he doing up there? . . .'

'Yes, yes. The padre did ask me, but I knew it was a foolish thing to do. I told him so. He should have waited for Señor Hoyas. . . .'

'Maria is very frightened about Honorato. Listen! There goes the bell now. . . .'

It was some while after the civil guard had gone before Honorato realized that people were watching him from below. He could hear, not see them, for even if he turned his head he could only glimpse the shimmering roofs of the village and the irregular shell-bursts of trees dotting the crest of the dun-coloured ridge in the distance. For the most part those who watched were silent, but now and then an isolated voice filtered through the blood-pumping din in his ears, telling him that they were there.

The sun had shifted now and burned hot on his back, drying the sweat as soon as his shirt sopped it up. He had lost count of the number of times he had clumped into the centre of the arch; forgotten how often he had felt the rope start on its gritty run through the deepening groove in the stonework. He was desperately tired, more tired than he had ever been in his life, the whole of his body racked by the unremitting strain.

If only *you* would get tired, bell, he thought.

From the angle at which the sun slanted into the arch he supposed it must be about two o'clock. At a guess he put the amount of rope looped at his feet at between six and seven metres, but he was past calculating how much longer it would be before the bell touched the ground. Sometimes he almost believed the moment would never come. Once, for a fraction of a second, the rope went slack, seeming reluctant to slide through the groove, but it jumped taut a moment later, spraying dust and fibre, and the wrenching jerk on his arms killed his hopes before they had a chance to stir.

He had not eaten since the previous evening; except for a couple of mouthfuls of wine nothing had passed his lips. Every minute dragged a little more strength out of him. A hollow numbness spread upwards from his stomach into his chest and he began to feel increasingly light-headed.

'Now I know how you must have felt, old one,' he muttered once, after a head-roaring surge of dizziness. 'I hope to God it gets no worse.'

In front of him, to the west, a majestic cream and pewter-coloured lather of cloud had pushed above the furthest ridge. Nearer, where the road shied away from the parched bed of a stream, a local eddy of wind suddenly raised a column of dust.

We were afraid of a breeze earlier, he thought, watching the dust fan out and disappear. We were afraid in case it shifted the bell. But now I could do with it: I could do with anything that would help to cool this furnace on my back—if only for a moment.

Sagging-kneed, he clumped across the arch again, leaning on the rope, the palms of his hands blistered to rawness. The block-wheel squeaked; the poles protested. The bell-clapper jiggled faintly, but failed to strike. Simultaneously there was a murmur from below: shoes crunched on the path. He peered over his shoulder, but the closest point that he could see was the rubbish-dump on the waste ground a hundred metres away. Two or three minutes later he heard the crash of gears as a car drove off down the village street. He linked the two sounds in his mind, wondering dully what they meant, and a moment's consideration told him that it was most probably Father Robredo on his way to hospital with the doctor.

Some forty people were waiting in a ragged semicircle around the church porch. Every few minutes others joined them, coming up the path singly or in twos and threes to stand and stare. Maria had been one of the first to arrive. As soon as she had called at the houses of the priest and doctor she had hurried home to her mother, moving her rocking-chair into their small yard, then run anxiously back to the church.

That was an hour and a half ago, and she had returned in time to meet the disgruntled civil guard on his way to the street.

'I thought you were going up to him,' she had said, frantically grabbing at his arm.

'I did,' he had retorted, spitting. 'And I advise no-one else to try. He is like a wild animal.... I am sorry, Maria, but I have done all I can.'

She would have climbed up herself, but others dissuaded her. Fearfully, living every second of the struggle, she had watched the bell lurch gradually earthwards. The only time she had taken her eyes from it or the partly-obscured figure framed in the arch was when Father Robredo left the church. Grey-faced and bent, he had paused, glanced upwards as if about to call to Honorato, then shaken his head wearily and gone with the doctor. Otherwise nothing had distracted her. The intensity of her concentration was such that she was only vaguely aware of the crowd gathering silently on either side of where she stood.

A little after three. Honorato knew he could not hold the bell much longer. He had scarcely the strength to keep the rope from running even when he had it braked on the corner. There was a noise like distant thunder in his ears and everything had gone a strange greenish-grey.

Twice more he let the rope slide, working as if in a dream, and each time it nearly took him off his legs. The numbness which had started somewhere deep inside him had enveloped his whole body. He moved drunkenly, swaying on the rope, sucking down great draughts of air. His thoughts flitted feverishly from point to point, lighting at random on one or other of the day's events, then moving on with the restless uncertainty of a moth.

Rafael falling.... Señor Hoyas.... Father Robredo's tears in the sacristy....

There was no end to the succession of impressions but he was too spent to be moved by what he remembered.

The early-morning ride from Valandorra after the shock.... Snatches of his conversation with Rafael.... The *guardia civil*.... The truck-driver on the road.... Rafael falling....

Thoughts came and went. His limbs functioned automatically, but the fretful wandering of his mind roused no emotions in him now.

Quarrelling with his father over a dislodged tile.... *Aí*, it had been a day of quarrels; beginning with that one, culminating with Maria—and a confusion of doubt and pain and grief sandwiched in between. . . .

He stirred himself to make another effort. 'Give me strength to finish this,' he panted, bracing himself against the wall. '*San Juan*, help me now so that I do not fail. I began on this bell because of Maria . . . because I love her and she wanted me to do it. I went on with it for the same reason, but because of Rafael and the *padre*, too. . . . But Rafael is dead and the *padre* is hurt and I am doing it now against Maria's will. . . . I am too tired to understand anything any more, but if there is a reason for all that has happened today, help me to finish what the three of us began'.

SEÑOR HOYAS glanced at his watch as he rattled over the pot-holes into Alquena. He was not in the best of moods. It had been a wasted day—a profitless day. At the flour-mill the second tremor had added to the damage caused by the first and the management had decided to call in a larger firm. He had argued, threatened, abused—but in vain. They were adamant. It was an emergency, they had said; the mill must be in full work within twenty-four hours. That had been the understanding when they had originally sent for him, but since he and his men were obviously incapable of finishing the work in time. . . .

'Thieving swine,' he grunted, and turned his attention to the village, hopeful that a dozen or so immediate repair jobs awaited him as compensation. First impressions were not encouraging: Alquena looked as solid and indestructible as when he had left it in the morning. He drove slowly past his own house, relieved to see that all was well, then cruised noisily towards the square. It was some moments before he was struck by the fact that the village seemed completely deserted. He was puzzled. True, it was late enough in the day for the *siesta*, but that did not clear the main street; people did not abandon doorway chairs like this or ignore the returning shadows.

Jesucristo! he thought, racking his brains for an explanation. What can have happened?

The square was empty; the stalls unattended. Dogs slept in the shade of the palms and a listless donkey was tethered against a wall. Except for them there was no sign of life. He was perturbed now rather than merely curious, and he accelerated into the continuation of the main street.

Someone must be about, he thought.

Then, near the end of the church path, he spotted the grey-green uniform of the civil guard. Directly the guard heard the car he started to walk in its direction, and there was something about the manner of his approach that filled the builder with apprehension.

He braked to a standstill and leaned sideways round the dust-fogged windscreen. 'In the name of all that is holy, what is going on here? Where is everybody?'

The civil guard jerked his head. 'Up there.'

The church? Why should everyone be up there—at this time of the afternoon? ... His forehead wrinkled. ... What could be—*Madre de Dios!* The bell! That was it. He had completely forgotten about the bell. ...

He started to get out of the car in a hurry. Thank God he was not too late! It would have looked bad if he had arrived when it was all over. 'How are they managing?' he asked, as casually as he could.

'They?'

'Father Robredo and old Rafael. ...'

'*Hombre*,' the guard cut in. 'Where have you been all day? Rafael is dead and the priest has gone to hospital—'

Señor Hoyas squinted at him incredulously. 'Dead. ... Rafael dead?'

'That is what I said. He fell from the tower when the second tremor came. The *padre* was injured at the same time. They had just got the bell secured—' he shrugged '—when it happened.'

There was a long silence. Eventually, as if in answer to a question, Señor Hoyas said defensively, 'They should never have started on it without waiting for me.'

The guard spat. He found a curious satisfaction in the builder's shocked discomfiture. 'The bell would have gone through the roof if they had waited. Besides,' he went on, 'the story is that you told them to go ahead with what they could find in your yard.'

Señor Hoyas swallowed. He was still dazed by the news. 'Who are working on it now?'

'Just one. Honorato Montes. He has been on it from the beginning.' His eyes twinkled coldly. 'If I were you I would get up there and lend him a hand.'

'Yes.' The builder nodded. Rafael dead; the priest in hospital. . . . God above! What a position to find oneself in! Yet perhaps there was still time to retrieve his reputation. 'Yes. I will do that.'

The civil guard accompanied him to the end of the path. Señor Hoyas let out a grunt of dismay when he saw the crowd. He hesitated for a moment, then began to walk forward alone.

'I had better warn you,' the guard said. 'The boy is like a wounded tiger.' Then, leaning on his rifle and lifting his eyes to the arch, he reluctantly added the thought: But you cannot help admiring him.

Señor Hoyas did not hear. He strode up the path, aware that heads were already turning in his direction. The bell was two or three metres from the ground, a little above the top of the door, swinging ponderously on the rope. It clanged faintly as if to announce his arrival. More heads turned; his name was whispered. The path seemed to stretch endlessly in front of him.

Aí, he thought, thrusting out his chin, the whole village must be here. . . .

He pretended to ignore the crowd and stared upwards at the framework of poles. As he neared the church people edged aside, leaving a gap for him to pass. He walked through the narrow lane, tight-lipped, sweating, still clinging to the hope that they would welcome his arrival. But he could sense their hostility : the silence was like an accusation. At the door he wheeled round, sweeping his hat from his head, throwing his arms wide.

'I came as soon as I could,' he began. 'I . . .'

His voice trailed away. No-one answered. The silence was the most frightening thing he had ever known. He could not face them and he turned swiftly, escaping into the darkness of the church. He went up the staircase at great speed, moving with surprising agility for a man of his build; made his way across the roof-ladder—still moving as if pursued—then began to climb the hot rungs of the tower.

Honorato heard him coming. Through a greenish blur he saw the builder's head and shoulders rise above the edge of the platform. He lay back on the rope, trembling with exhaustion, trying to bring them into focus.

'You,' he said weakly.

Señor Hoyas nodded agitatedly. His lame eye was fixed on the other side of the arch. 'I have only this minute returned.'

'Save your excuses. You may need them for others, but they foul my ears.' He could see him clearly now, the sweaty blue chin glazed like pottery.

'I have come to help.'

'Yes. And so you shall. We waited all day for you.' The builder started to clamber on to the platform, but Honorato checked him. 'The *guardia* has been up, but I sent him away. But I take you. You know why?'

'No.'

The builder was blurring out of focus again. Everything was swimming. His head was full of thunder. 'Because . . .' His voice was kilometres away. 'Because . . .' He felt the rope slip on the corner and start to run. He tried to hold it, throwing himself backwards, but now it had taken hold and it scorched viciously through his raw hands. The blockwheel whined madly, but he did not hear it. He slumped in a heap on the floor of the arch and the remaining loops of rope whipped up and out into space over the builder's head. From below there came a brittle, metallic thud as the bell hit the ground and a sharp, echoing cry from the crowd.

When he opened his eyes Señor Hoyas was bending over him.

'What happened?'

'You lost control and the bell went' He saw the look on the boy's face. 'It is all right. It only fell a couple of metres.'

'Eeee. . . .' Honorato sat up slowly. Muscles were jumping involuntarily in his legs and across his shoulders. He felt sick and empty, yet strangely elated. The buzz of voices from below sounded like a swarm of bees. The effort of getting to his feet seemed beyond him, but, after a while, he pushed himself up and staggered to the edge of the platform, waving the builder away.

He never remembered how he got down. Afterwards he could only recall the moment when he came out of the church door into the sunlight.

'Olé!' someone shouted; others took it up. There was a swelling burst of applause. He blinked uncertainly at the semi-circle of faces, swaying as he halted. And then, suddenly, he saw Maria break from the crowd and come running towards him with her arms outstretched.

'Honorato!' She threw his arms round him, then stood back and gazed at him, moist-eyed, repeating his name.

'Now you will *have* to marry her, *chico*,' a woman shouted and laughter came like a wave breaking.

Maria looked at his mushy hands and grazed forearms. 'Come home with me, Honorato,' she was saying gently. 'Your hands need seeing to.'

He nodded. I will do anything, he thought. Anything she wants. The bell was standing the right way up, its rim burrowed into the cracked ground, and it suddenly seemed incredibly small and insignificant. He was bewildered by the noise and winced when people clapped him on the back as he walked unsteadily with Maria through the dispersing crowd.

'Honorato!'

He stopped in astonishment at the sight of his father.

'What are you doing here?' he heard himself ask.

His father was smiling. 'News travels. I heard about it over two hours ago, and as soon as I could I got a lift in a truck coming this way.'

'I did not see you,' Maria said.

'Nor I you.' He chuckled. 'Each of us only had eyes for one person, eh?'

Three or four people were grouped round the bell, bending close to it, painstakingly reading the inscription. 'Laudo Deum Verum; Plebem Voco,' one of them pronounced slowly, finger-tracing the letters. 'What, my friends, do you suppose that means?'

His father laid an arm on Honorato's shoulder. '*Chico*,' he said earnestly. 'I am proud of you—more proud than I can find words for. . . . I tell you truly that what has happened here will not be forgotten for many a day—either in Alquena or Valandorra or for miles around. Of that you may be sure.'

Then the three of them—Honorato in the centre, Maria and his father on each side—went arm-in-arm down the path together.

Extract from the Anglo-Iberian Tourist Agency's guide-book for this year:

Alquena and Valandorra, their quiet peace undisturbed through the centuries, are typical of the many charming unspoilt villages along this stretch of Mediterranean coast. Both are small: Alquena—the larger of the two—has a population of some 350 persons.

Its 200-year-old church—*San Juan*—though not unattractive architecturally (Baroque), has no particular noteworthy history. A mile south-west of the village, however, there are some well-preserved Roman fortifications which the visitor will find well worth inspection. . . .

TIME IS AN AMBUSH

To Peter Probyn

"Take what you want," said God. "Take it, and pay for it."

Spanish proverb

CHAPTER ONE

Iᴛ had rained again during the night, as if from habit, but the morning was fine enough. Air and water were fused in the haze along the horizon; sea and sky two shades of the same soft blue. Once or twice during the past ten days the freak weather seemed to have spent itself. There had been other mornings of deceptive promise; brief, burning after-noons. Then the rain had come again, falling vertically from sullen, slow-moving clouds for hours on end. Even now there were a few dark strings of it showing against the blur where the sea and sky began, but the scarred peaks of the sierras behind the town were sharply defined and, without being weather-wise, I guessed that the worst was over.

For the time being the long crescent beach which curled towards Bandaques had lost its silver-white glitter. It was as drab as soaked coconut-matting, and for a hundred yards or so from the shore, beyond the line where the heavier waves started their final run, the sea was turning the colour of rust. Given an hour's sun the sand would bleach dry, but it would be days before the water cleared; weeks maybe. This was only the beginning. A vast mass of muck and rubble, borne on yesterday's flood from the shattered Lareo Dam, had smashed into the sea five miles to the south, and now the currents were at work, bringing the livid brown stain up past the promontory where the great tower of the Church of the Incarnation stood like a lighthouse, spreading it along the fringes of the beach far beyond the Villa Miramar. Already there were trails of debris lifting like dead fish on the crumbling waves and, inevitably, I wondered where Scheele's body was; and whether Ilsa had gone to her hotel window yet and seen what was happening. Only yesterday

9

afternoon she had said : "It's the first thing I do, Ty. I can see your house from there," though neither vanity nor hope could make me believe that would be her reason now.

It was warm on the terrace. For five months I had worked under the striped awning which slanted away from the wall facing the sea : a thousand words a day, five days a week. Weekends apart there had been no break in the routine until the morning Ilsa called to me from the beach—since when I hadn't written a single word. The typewriter cover was still on, and when I took it off and read the few lines on the page coiled in the machine they seemed stilted and unimportant; concerned people I'd almost forgotten. Recent events had made them remote and unreal and I recalled what Scheele had replied when Ilsa told him what I did : "I would have thought otherwise, Mister Tyler. I would have said you were a man who was interested in fact. Not make-believe. Real flesh and blood : real life and death. . . . I am, Mister Tyler. There's no substitute for it."

It was still early; barely eight-thirty. Old Catalina, who cooked and cleaned and laundered, never came before eleven. I went into the kitchen and got the percolator started over a low gas, then ran a bath. As usual the taps, though boldly branded "Cataract", hissed and spat dementedly to no great effect, but I had long since perfected a schedule and was shaved by the time the bath was ready; dressing as the coffee came on the boil. Twenty-five minutes after leaving the terrace I was outside again, lighting my first cigarette, allowing the coffee to cool a little before sipping it.

Bandaques vibrated minutely in the returning heat, white and saffron and brown. For the most part it stood on slightly higher ground than the villa. On the promontory the buildings seemed to be all piled up on themselves, but as they scattered inland and along the coast they achieved a fairly uniform plane. There was a quarter of a mile of empty, dune-topped beach between the villa and the squalid outskirts of the town and it was still deserted except for the lonely figure of a civil guard. Every morning he trudged along the sand to a control-point three miles to the north, then retraced his steps into Bandaques. Another guard traipsed back and forth in the afternoon : yet another during the night. As an anti-smuggling patrol it was next to useless because I could almost set my watch by their bored comings and goings.

I checked the time now : nine o'clock exactly. The guard was a couple of hundred yards away, moving leisurely, looking curiously at the salt-laden waves. In the distance somebody opened a window in the Hotel España and the glass winked in the sun, catching my eyes. The España was Ilsa's hotel, a modern building with the shape and whiteness of a block of salt. It was half-way along the promontory, perched at the edge of a low, rocky bluff, and when sunlight was complemented by rain-washed air it was almost possible from the terrace to pick out the name emblazoned in gilt across the building's front, so close did it seem. Her room was on the third floor, the windows immediately above and to either side of the S, and I strained forward in an attempt to pin-point them, wondering again whether she was gazing out and seeing the after-effects of yesterday's disaster.

I had promised to call on her at ten-thirty. My parting words were : "I'll come earlier if you like. At any time. I'm here to help, Ilsa. Tell me what you want." To which she'd answered : "I want to sleep, Ty. Just to sleep. . . ."

High and invisible, an aircraft was gently tearing the pale blue cloth of the sky. I drained the last of the coffee and stood up, an emptiness in me as I thought of her, a yearning that seemed to radiate outwards from some tiny and untraceable point within me. I lit another cigarette and started down the steps towards the crimson and purple flower-beds in the paved garden. Quite by chance I lifted my head for a moment, glancing along the beach. The civil guard was roughly where I had last seen him, except that he was now knee-deep in water, bent like a reaper as he struggled to get a grip on something close to his feet. I stopped to watch, imagining him to be after driftwood or some such prize. A discoloured wave crunched in, practically knocking him off balance, and whatever it was he groped for was apparently sucked away from him on the backwash. He waded after it for a couple of paces, then turned about and staggered clear of the water, looking my way. Even then I hadn't really grasped what was happening. It was only when I saw him start urgently towards the villa that a slight chill went through me and I guessed what he must have found. And by that time I was running myself.

We stumbled towards one another, sinking through the sand's drying crust. I called : "Is it Scheele?" but the guard came on without answering, hampered by heavy boots and a slung rifle. When we were about twenty yards apart I called again : "Is it Scheele? The German?"—without realizing that he wouldn't know who Scheele was.

"A body . . . in the water, señor." He was badly out of condition. "A man."

Stupidly, I said : "Is he dead?"

"Yes, señor." Halting, he sucked in air. "Dead. Very dead."

He started to explain about the backwash, but I cut him short. "Come on."

There was a froth of scum left by the tongues of failing waves, beyond which the sand was dark and soggy; shelving. A marbled rush of water whooshed in as we got there, breaking about our ankles.

"Where?"

The guard paused, uncertain for a moment, then pointed, and I saw something lift like a sack in the foaming shallows. Without speaking we waded towards it, growing less agile as the force of the waves increased and the backwash tugged at our legs. Twice we were almost within reach of the body, but each time it was snatched away. What looked like a jacket was twisted round the head and reddish water boiled furiously over the submerged trunk and rag-doll arms and legs.

Another wave crashed down. I managed to grasp an arm as the body floated level with me and tried not to think how slimy it was; how alive it seemed. Blobs of spray stung my face. Half-kneeling, I yelled at the guard to get a grip on the other arm before the backwash set up its counter-pull. If he had had any sense he would have left his rifle behind. Now it slipped from his shoulder on its sling, knocking off his black patent-leather hat.

"Leave it," I bawled.

He lunged forward and made contact, nearly fell, then straightened up. The water sang as it slid back off the beach and what hung between us jerked like a puppet. We were no more than a dozen paces from dry land yet it took minutes to get there and all the time I was thinking : I'll have to look at him soon.

We dragged the body clear of the scum line. Without buoyancy it had become limp and heavy. I rolled it on to its back, then pulled the jacket away from the head. It was Scheele, all right, though the shock I felt was not because of recognition. From the first I hadn't expected it to be anyone else. But to bend close and see what had happened to him tightened my scalp and sent a flutter of nausea through me. Fear was frozen into the facial muscles. The thick lips were peeled back over the teeth; the blue eyes wider than I had ever seen them. Bright green weed was matted into his smarmed-down side hair and a single ribbon of it came from one clogged nostril. It was years since I had been involved with death, the first time in my life with drowning, and the ice-blue pallor of the skin sickened me. Even the freckles on the high bird's-egg dome of his head seemed to have dissolved.

I heard the guard grunt and say : "Blood." It was a relief to look away and I frowned up at him questioningly. "On the stomach, señor."

It was oozing thinly through the shirt : a fly had found it already. There was more coming from both knees which

13

gleamed rawly through ripped trouser-legs. For some reason I hadn't expected a corpse to bleed.

"Rocks, probably," I heard myself say. "Rocks—and all the battering he must have had before he even reached the sea. His temple's grazed, too." I stood up, noticing that one of Scheele's shoes had gone. "I'm going over to the house to get a blanket. Then perhaps you'll help me carry him."

The guard nodded. As I turned he asked: "Who was he, señor?" Before I could answer he went on: "Was he the man who was at Gondra?" and I said: "Yes. That's who he was."

I poured myself a brandy as soon as I got inside. When I came back the guard was standing in the water vainly looking for his hat. Scheele's dreadful fish-slab eyes seemed to stare at me as I spread the blanket out. I called to the guard and together we lifted him and covered him over.

"You take the legs," I said.

We had some difficulty getting him through the beach-gate into the garden : otherwise we managed without much trouble. But it was a slow business, for he was heavy, and I never once stopped thinking about Ilsa and how I should break the news. When we reached the living-room I was undecided where to lay the body. The guard suggested the window-seat, but because the blanket was sodden through I chose the floor. An odd gurgling sound came from Scheele as we put him down. It was unnerving, and the guard stepped back quickly.

I hadn't really observed him before. He was young, thick-set, with a peasant's face. I gave him a brandy and took another myself. My hands were shaking. He emptied his glass in two gulps, then said: "I must telephone Captain Romero."

I lied to him. "Mine is out of order."

"Ayee." He clucked his tongue ruefully. "I will have to walk it then. . . . Do you know the dead man's name?"

"Scheele. Erich Scheele."

He nodded. "The captain will ask." He seemed disconcerted by the loss of his hat; or perhaps it was inexperience. "On the other hand," he thought aloud, "I should remain with the body."

"I won't move it."

He hesitated. "And your name is— ?"

"Stephen Tyler."

He repeated an approximation of it. "Thank you, señor." He stepped out on to the terrace, then came back, troubled by an afterthought. "You were acquainted with him?"

"Yes," I said.

"Then you have sadness." He glanced round the room as though he felt he ought to memorize a few details. "*Adios, señor.*"

"*Adios.*"

This time he went for good, jog-trotting along the beach. A more practical man would have used the road, but I had no intention of shouting after him to suggest it. Ilsa had to be the first to know : not some official. And I wanted to tell her myself.

My watch showed nine twenty-six. I went to the telephone and asked the operator to put me through to the Hotel España. Moments later they were connecting me with her room.

"Ilsa?"

There was no life in her voice and she sounded a long way off; her slight accent more marked.

"Can I come and see you now? I know I said half-past ten but I'd like to come right away. Are you up?"

"I am dressing."

"I could be there in five minutes."

She seemed to sense something. "What is it, Ty?"

"Can I come?" I insisted.

There was a short pause before she replied. "All right, then."

"Where will you be? Downstairs?"

"Here. . . . The number is forty-two."

A pool of water was spreading over the tiles around

Scheele's blanketed figure. As I shut the big windows which opened on to the terrace I could see the guard lumbering along the beach towards Bandaques. Then I walked quickly through the house and out to the convertible, glad of the air.

The Lareo Dam had broken at about four o'clock the previous afternoon. Some people in Bandaques were saying they had heard it go. It was possible, I suppose, though I didn't really think it likely because the dam was every bit of ten miles from the town, and barricaded off from it by a knobbly spur of hills. Others, with the wisdom of hindsight, were saying they had been expecting it to go for a long time. Already there was talk of a scandal over the maintenance contracts and there may well have been some truth in this.

It was a concrete dam : not large—three hundred feet or so wide—though large enough to carry a narrow road along the top of its high, curving wall. I had driven across it several times, usually of necessity, and had never thought it the safest place to be. Where the water poured over the swelling face of the dam from the spillway crest the concrete was patched and broken; and on the other side, when the level of the reservoir was low, the exposed area of sun-dried encrustation could be seen to be scribbled over with cracks. I once pointed them out to a man I met there, an official of some kind, who assured me with a shrug that they were only superficial. "If *you* were over forty years old, señor, and had had *your* face in water for a long time, wouldn't you show it just a little?"

I had smiled then, acknowledging my ignorance, but now, as I accelerated away from the villa, his words struck me as horribly applicable to Scheele. Yet it wasn't so much what immersion had done as the stark terror of his expression that haunted me : I imagined it must have formed in the very instant that he saw the huge, house-high torrent crashing down the empty valley towards him. And death must have come very quickly, fixing it long before the thundering head of water pistoned him into the sea below Bandaques.

For some time after it happened neither Ilsa nor I were aware that the dam had given way. It was only when we arrived back at the hotel and found the entrance lobby buzzing with talk that we heard the first garbled accounts. It would have been almost six-thirty by then, and another hour had elapsed before Scheele's continuing absence began to niggle as possibly significant. We had sat in the American Bar and waited, expecting him to push through the glass doors at any minute; privately willing him to do so. *Where* had he said he was going? I couldn't remember and Ilsa had reminded me : "Gondra."

Gondra. That was it. Gondra. . . .

A little later, provoked by Ilsa's increasing anxiety, I had asked the bar-tender where the place was. He was busy breaking ice and didn't glance up. "Gondra is about two kilometres down the valley from the dam, señor."

Ilsa's Spanish was limited, but she had caught the gist of it—helped, maybe, by the look on my face. "Where, Ty? Did he say near the dam?" And I, stunned, had been unable to soften the blow : "Below it."

Even then there had been hope. Scheele might not have been there at the vital time; could have been forced to make a wide detour to reach Bandaques. She had clung to every straw. And then, just on eight o'clock, Ilsa was paged. I had gone with her to the telephone, knowing that she would probably find herself in difficulties. Sure enough she very soon parted with the receiver, and it was to me that Captain Romero had introduced himself; explained that he was making inquiries about the owner of a cream-coloured Mercedes. They had found it near Gondra, overturned, embedded in red slush : and empty. . . .

Much later, after I had eventually left Ilsa at the hotel and stopped off at Romero's office, he had given me the broader picture. Apart from some sardine boats swamped on the south beach and a missing herd of goats there was thought to be no other damage or loss of life. X million cubic feet of water had broken out and disfigured an already barren valley; crushed an already ruined village where no one lived or went. People were saying it was a miracle—as much a miracle as the dam was a scandal. But I was too tired and shaken, both then and on the final run home in the rain, to care about things like that; or to cope with all the questions that had besieged my mind.

She responded quickly to my ring. The door opened immediately and I could tell, as I fumbled for words, that she knew why I was there. Almost before I entered the room she said : "They've found Erich, haven't they?"

"Yes."

"Where?"

"On the north beach."

Her eyes moved to my legs and I suddenly realized that my trousers were wet from the knees down; caked with sand.

"You found him," she said almost accusingly. "It was you."

It wasn't a moment for splitting hairs. "Yes, Ilsa."

I told her about it as best I could. After a while she began to cry, quietly but without restraint. I gave her a handkerchief, damp from the sea. She sat on the edge of the bed and her grief swept me with a sort of despair.

Restlessly, I moved to the window. I had to go on talking. "The guard wanted to phone Romero but I told him mine wasn't working. He decided to foot it. I suppose he'll have reported by now; there's no sign of him."

The long beach was shading from brown to yellow as it dried. The villa seemed closer than it really was and its pink, crenellated walls had the appearance of something made from icing sugar : it needed a conscious effort of the mind to accept that Scheele was lying there. Despite the remembered look and feel of him, despite the high view of the sea's tell-

18

tale discoloration, an element of incredulity still had a foot-hold in my thoughts.

I turned away. Ilsa's eyes looked bruised, enormous in the smallness of her pale, oval face.

"Did you manage to sleep?"

She shrugged dismissively. I felt shut out and the silence became unbearable.

"I ought to go down to Romero myself. He'll want to know—"

She broke in : "How near the house was Erich?"

"A hundred yards or so."

For the first time in minutes she looked at me. "What . . . what's he like, Ty?"

I should have known she would ask. There should have been a ready-made phrase on the tip of my tongue. Instead of which all I could say was : "All right."

Her eyes hadn't left mine. "All right," she repeated slowly. "*All right*. . . . Oh, Ty—"

Her voice broke and she cried again. This time I went to her, held her, saying : "I'm sorry, Ilsa. God, I'm sorry." And though she clung to me I felt in my heart that anyone would have done in my place; another stranger like myself.

The telephone rang and she started. I released her and she walked round the bed. From where I was I could hear a man's voice and I guessed it to be Romero's. After a short while she began shaking her head. "*Momento, por favor. Señor Tyler. Señor Tyler. Si . . . Momento.*" With a gesture of defeat she pushed the receiver in my direction. "Please."

I took it from her : "Captain Romero? This is Stephen Tyler."

My being there obviously surprised him. He began : "One of my patrol guards has just come in from the north beach—"

"I know. I was about to get in touch with you."

"He tells me the body is that of Señor Scheele."

"That's correct."

"Where is it now?"

19

I thought it a stupid question and told him so. "At the house, of course."

"Alone?"

I closed my eyes. "Yes."

"You should not have left it, señor. Not unattended."

I heard another voice in the background and presumed the guard was saying something by way of self-justification.

"Look," I said. "I'm coming to see you. We both are. Can't all this wait until then?"

"How long will you be?"

"Ten, fifteen minutes."

"Make it less," he said with unexpected sharpness. "This is an urgent matter."

As the receiver went down, Ilsa asked : "What does he want?"

"To see us."

"When?"

"Now."

There was more than weariness in her sigh.

"It's inevitable, Ilsa," I said gently. "He's got a job to do," but I might have been talking to a statue. Once again I was filled with a sterile despondency. "Are you ready?"

She collected sun-glasses from the dressing-table and I followed her out to the lift. Nothing was said during the whining descent. As we crossed the lobby together the plump manager gave Ilsa an immaculate bow of sympathy and I was reminded of his words when bidding me good night eleven hours or so earlier—"A terrible tragedy, señor. I feel it almost personally. He was a most popular visitor here. Believe me, everyone is deeply shocked."

I screwed my eyes against the forecourt's dazzle. The heat was beginning to bounce off the tarmac and our shadows were as black as Indian ink. I glanced at Ilsa as I settled beside her in the car. Her lower lip was quivering but I could find nothing to say. We swung out from behind a pair of creaking manure-carts and headed along the prom-ontory. The news-stands were doing a brisk trade in the morning editions and there were scores of people looking down at the sea over the pavement balustrade. I drove on—right past the fish market, left past the crumbling amphitheatre—and the nearer we got to the main square the more narrow and congested and noisy the streets became.

The Civil Guard building was a depressing, three-storeyed affair of grey cement and barred windows. As we reached it Ilsa broke our long silence. "What made him go there?" she said, in a sudden release of bewilderment. "What did he want to go to Gondra for?" It was a complaint rather than a question. Either way there was no answer and probably never would be. I waited a few seconds, then touched her arm. "Let's get this over."

The guard on the door eyed Ilsa with slovenly appreciation. Inside were peeling walls and a smell of must. There was a wooden barrier some yards beyond the entrance and the duty sergeant took his time in allowing us through the pass-gate. When he did so we were led along an echoing corridor by a uniformed clerk who looked as though he'd slept in his clothes since their day of issue.

Captain Romero's office was at the very end of the corridor. It was a big room, larger by daylight than I had believed it to be when I was last there. A fan with only one surviving blade churned uselessly over the main desk, behind which, on a green wall, was a framed and flattering four-colour print of the Generalissimo. There were a few filing cabinets, a board full of keys, a smaller desk with a typewriter on it and a wooden bench set under the windows. The guard from the beach was sitting on the bench, still sweating from his exertions.

Romero rose to his feet as the clerk ushered us in. He was on the tall side, wide-shouldered, with a bullfighter's hips and neat, long-fingered hands. In contrast to the guard he was incredibly smart—the grey-green uniform newly pressed; his shoes shining like anthracite.

"Permit me again to offer my condolences, señora," he

began gravely. "Perhaps there is some slight consolation in the fact that Señor Scheele's body has been found."

Ilsa nodded automatically and I didn't bother to translate. I envied Romero his formula. I said: "I suppose you'll want to go to the house?"

"In a minute or two. First I should like to have your version of what happened on the north beach this morning."

He was too officious for my liking. It had been the same last night, but I was beyond being irritated then. Now my nerves were on edge and his manner grated. I gestured towards the guard: "My version's the same as his. It's bound to be."

"Naturally. But I should like to hear it."

I snapped in English: "What bloody nonsense!" I gave it to him though. About six sentences were sufficient and I noticed that the clerk was taking them down. I finished. "The facts aren't in dispute, surely? They're simple enough."

Romero shrugged. "It is merely for the record."

"Should I add what I had for breakfast? Which hand I shave with?"

His sallow face flushed. "I had thought better of you, Señor Tyler." He took his tricorn hat from the end of the desk. "All that remains now is for the señora to identify the dead man."

"Is that necessary?"

"Absolutely necessary."

"Despite my having done so?" I was thinking of Scheele's bared teeth and wide, terror-struck eyes; of the green weed trailing from one sand-blocked nostril. "Can't you spare her that? He's not very pretty."

"I don't lay the procedure down, señor. My duty is to see that it isn't ignored." He could be brusque when he chose. "Shall we go?"

We went with him to the street. The sergeant on the gate dragged his heels together as we passed. Romero's

official car was waiting at the kerb. With bad grace I said :
"There's room in the back of mine if you like."

He accepted the offer; squeezed his long legs in behind
us. A blue-chinned corporal accompanied him. When we
were clear of the worst of the traffic I spoke to Ilsa. "He
expects you to make a formal identification. If you don't
want to I'm sure I can talk him out of it." She stared
straight ahead without answering : I was an intruder still.
"What d'you say, Ilsa? . . . You can refuse if you wish."

I shot her a sidelong glance. She was biting her lips in an
effort to master emotion. After a few moments she muttered
something I didn't quite catch. I leaned a little closer and it
seemed to antagonize her because she turned her head with
a fierceness that shamed me.

"I *want* to see him. . . . I want to see him anyhow."

The town petered out amid patches of vegetation and
leprous-looking rubble. The road ploughed a straight black
furrow along the top of the dunes. To our right the waves
appeared to be growing more and more sluggish as their
colour deepened. Now and again I glimpsed Romero's face
in the rear-view mirror—his brown eyes narrowed against
the rushing air; fingers stroking his pencil-line moustache.
It was only a matter of minutes to the villa. I turned the car
into the gravel drive and we gritted to a standstill by the
porch.

I led the way inside, then allowed Romero to go ahead.
"Straight through." He entered the living-room. The sound
of his shoes on the tiles stopped after a few paces. I heard
his knee crack as he bent down. Ilsa shivered violently as
we stood in the white, square hall and I could feel the
goose-flesh on her upper arm.

"Would you come in, please?" Romero said quietly.

He was squatting by the body. The water had spread all
over the place. Romero held one corner of the blanket in his
fingers.

"A little closer if you would."

I continued to grip Ilsa's arm. It was like nearing a place of execution. Romero lifted the blanket.

"Do you recognize him, señora?"

She gave a small, choked cry. Time seemed to run to a stop. Scheele's terror had me mesmerized and all I could think was : That's long enough. *Long enough* —

"Yes?" Romero prompted expectantly, a vein branding his forehead as he looked up. "You know him?"

And Ilsa said : "He is my husband."

CHAPTER TWO

I

PRIDE and desire shrivel in the presence of death. But even then, behind the façade, they are at the mercy of a chance word, a secret glance, a casual gesture. One cannot hide from oneself for long. When Ilsa said "He is my husband" a part of me immediately countered: Was. *Was.* . . . The guard on the beach had got the tense right: "Was he the man who was at Gondra?" And so had I: "Yes. That's who he was."

Was. *Was* my husband.

Romero let the blanket drop: stood up. He looked at me meaningly and I took his cue, muttering: "Let's go on to the terrace . . . Ilsa?"

She was quite calm. Her face was like a mask and, when Romero opened the doors, she moved with me willingly. Under the awning was an upholstered cane seat where I sometimes threw myself when the writing went badly and I led her to it in preference to the hard chair by the typewriter. When I came back with a glass of brandy she was still bolt upright, sitting with the unnatural rigidity of someone about to be photographed.

"It would have been all over for him in a second, Ilsa. Try and hang on to that."

Her eyes closed behind the dark lenses and she nodded.

"Drink the brandy," I said.

"Can I have a cigarette?"

She had to steady it with her fingers before I could light it for her. "Thanks, Ty," she said huskily.

"Will you be all right for a minute or two? I want to speak to the captain."

She nodded again, but that was all. I went back into the room with Romero and we kept our voices down.

"What happens now? D'you remove the body?"

"Yes."

"There'll be an inquest?"

"A formality only."

"Will she have to attend?"

"No."

"When will it be?"

"Tomorrow." The slight lift of his shoulders indicated that this was only an opinion. Then he said : "She has taken it well," and you would have thought he believed that only the Spanish knew how to combine dignity with suffering. "Very well indeed."

Reflected sunlight shimmered on the ceiling. The rich scent of flowers and drying earth filled the room.

"My housekeeper will be here in about forty minutes," I said. "I'd rather she didn't arrive and find things the way they are now. How soon— ?"

"The mortuary wagon is standing by in the town. If you would be good enough to drive me back to headquarters I can authorize its departure. Alternatively, I can start my corporal walking." He produced a wintry smile. "For the moment I'm in your hands."

"Why not telephone?"

"But yours is out of order."

"That's what I told your patrol guard."

"I see." He gave me a lengthy, quizzical look. "Well, that is the solution then."

I left him while he put in the call and returned to the terrace. Ilsa didn't seem to have moved : the cigarette had burned almost to her fingers. I took it from her and threw it away.

"We'll go back to the hotel when you're ready," I said. Then, carefully : "There's nothing more you can do here."

"Thank you."

"Is that what you want?—to go back there?"

26

"I suppose so."

"Another brandy?"

She shook her head.

"Romero's using the phone. As soon as he's ready we'll go."

He came through the door as I finished speaking. "Five minutes," he said cryptically. "Will that suit you?"

"Yes."

"I intend leaving my corporal here. Outside the house, naturally."

"Very well."

It was necessary to pass through the living-room to reach the car. Romero was not without feeling, for I noticed he had positioned a chair so that Scheele was partly obscured. But he needn't have bothered : I doubt if Ilsa glanced towards the humped blanket. She seemed to have shed her agony on the terrace. Outwardly she was taut and strained-looking, but she was more in control of herself than at any time that morning, and the part of my mind which had reacted against her use of the present tense had its say again. Even then, as the living-room door clicked behind me, I was able to think : She'll resign herself. A little while and Scheele will diminish. . . .

The blue-chinned corporal was getting his instructions as Ilsa and I left the porch. Romero's manner worsened in the presence of his men : perhaps he felt a need to demonstrate his authority, but I didn't know him well enough to judge.

I drove slowly, disturbed by conflicting emotions. None of us spoke. The air pushed warm and gritty against our faces; toyed with Ilsa's straight fair hair. The high sierras were undergoing their first change of colour. They'd been blue two hours ago; now they were shading through mauve to brown. They made a fierce yet melancholy backcloth to the town.

The mortuary wagon passed us when we were about half-way to Bandaques. It was a closed truck, painted fawn, with nothing that I could see to distinguish it. Only the pressure of

Romero's fingers against my shoulder told me what it was.

I dropped him outside his office. Ilsa's lack of Spanish was sometimes a blessing. I was able to say : "Will you want her any more?"

"I think not."

"If you should, I'd like to be present. Today, tomorrow—whenever it might be."

He gave me the same quizzical look as before. "I will try and remember, señor." Then, heels together, he saluted Ilsa. "Thank you for your co-operation, señora. You have been most helpful— and most brave. *Adios*."

I drove round the square and returned to the hotel. It seemed a long time since Ilsa and I had been alone together. As we mounted the steps, I said : "What are you going to do?" It was no more than twenty to eleven. The day had somehow lost its shape. "You ought to eat. You haven't had anything yet."

"I couldn't."

"Coffee, then?"

We went into the American Bar and ordered. It was quite empty. We sat at a table in the corner under the mounted head of a bull which had killed four men in the Bandaques ring one September afternoon. A chromium plaque recorded their names and the date. There was no escape from the reality and permanence of death. The waiter who brought the coffee was grave and deferential : even his tired black tie had the stamp of mourning. When he had gone I lit a cigarette for Ilsa, then my own. Once more I was defeated by the futility of words and our exchanges were as brief as the tongue-tied silences were long. It was here, barely a week ago, that I had first met Scheele; here, last evening, that we had waited for him to return from Gondra. And now, though a fawn truck was jolting him towards the mortuary, his presence still lingered. I could hear his deep, mirthless laugh; remember his crushing handshake, the sensual lips, the glazed look in his eyes when he drank too much. . . . It is ridiculous to be jealous of the dead, but the depth of Ilsa's grief was making it possible; and although I could tell myself that time would loosen his hold on her I already begrudged the waiting. Only yesterday I had said: "I love you, Ilsa." After living blindly and intently for a long while a door had opened on another world with fierce and heady suddenness, and I wasn't able to slam it to as Ilsa had done.

In a fresh effort to break the silence, I repeated what Romero had told me about the inquest. I wanted her to need my help; to find me indispensable in the face of the various formalities inevitably awaiting her. Bandaques was a small town and did not, as far as I knew, offer much in the way of consular services.

"Have you thought beyond tomorrow?"

She moved her head slowly from side to side.

"You've got to be practical, Ilsa."

"You be practical. You be practical for me." She ground her cigarette in the bowl. "But don't let's talk about it now. Please, not now."

Chastened, I said: "I'm sorry."

She made a small, fluttering gesture of conciliation. Even so, her manner was detached and she didn't look at me. "I'm sorry, too, Ty. You've been very kind. Don't think I don't appreciate it. . . . But everything's happened so quickly that I haven't really grasped it yet. I keep telling myself it's all some sort of dream."

"I know. I know."

"In the car just now I was thinking: I'll wake up soon. It can't be true. It *can't* be . . . I really thought that. It was the same in the house when I saw Erich." She shuddered a sigh. "And again just now when you were speaking about tomorrow."

"I should have had more sense."

"Tomorrow can wait."

I said cautiously: "What about today, though? There's an awful lot of it left. How can I help, Ilsa?"

There was no reply. She had withdrawn from me again; gone into the dream. "If there's anything—"

"I'm going up to my room."

"Shall I come back later? In the afternoon, say?"

"This evening if you like." She tempered the qualification : perhaps she sensed that it wounded. "Make it this evening, Ty."

"And there's nothing I can do meanwhile?"

"Nothing," she said wearily. "Nothing, thank you."

Minutes later I drove back to the Villa Miramar. It was well past eleven and for once Catalina had already gone to work on the living-room. The water was all mopped up, the chairs re-arranged, the used glasses removed to the kitchen, and for a moment I shared Ilsa's recurring sense of fantasy.

"Was anyone here when you arrived, Catalina?"

"No one, señor." Her face was as dark and lined as a bat's. If she wondered about the water she passed no comment on it. "Were you expecting to find somebody?"

"No," I said. "Not really."

I walked out on to the terrace and gazed at the white cube of the Hotel España. The strings of rain along the horizon had vanished and the sun blazed on the rust-red waves curling in towards the beach. This was where it had begun— less than a week ago. And I thought : God forbid that it ends here, too.

2

By eleven o'clock on that particular Thursday I had written a couple of hundred words or so; no more, certainly. They never come easily. Two days' torrential rain had temporarily driven me from the terrace, but the morning's fitful sunshine encouraged me to re-emerge. I preferred to work in the open and have the slow heave of the sea as an accompaniment to my thoughts. People who exist only in an author's imagination become no less real in his mind than those with whom he lives his natural life. While he is involved with them they imprint themselves over his vision and at times, while he strives to see them more clearly, his stare is oblivious of the existence of anyone other than them.

Vaguely I heard a voice call: "Señor, Señor," but not until the third or fourth time did it really penetrate my consciousness. She told me afterwards that I looked at her for so long without showing any reaction that she thought I must be blind. *"Señor!"*

She was near the beach-gate, head and bare shoulders showing above the wall. I got up, a little startled. An arm appeared and she pointed towards the house. *"Por favor?"*

I gave her the benefit of the doubt and replied in Spanish. "By all means. Come on in."

Clearly, she hadn't understood. The dumbshow began again. *"Sí?"* she appealed. *"Sí?"*

"Sí?," I grinned, not playing fair now. "That's what I said. *Sí. Sí.*"

I remember, as she came through the gate, both my surprise and the thrill of pure pleasure that the sight of her gave me. She was wearing the briefest of bikinis and the tiny white triangles accentuated the deep tan of her body. She shut the gate carefully, then started up the steps between the flower-beds. She was slim, as small-breasted as a ballerina, and her hair was plastered about her head from swimming. In one hand she carried a schnorkel mask; flippers in the other.

"Buenos días," I said, cheating still. "What's the trouble?"

The majority of good-looking women have an animal awareness of their physical attractiveness: this one had not. Her embarrassment was entirely due to her inability to communicate. Punctuated by sighs of exasperation she broke into another gesturing bout of mime. It was delightful to watch, but ungallant to let her go on.

"D'you happen to speak English?"

31

Her eyes widened with relief. "Yes, I do." Then she laughed. "Oh, thank heavens for that. I was making such a fool of myself."

"Far from it. But we weren't getting very far."

Beads of water sparkled on her skin. She had an almost boyish face, well-boned and symmetrical, with a generous mouth and wonderfully soft brown eyes. I imagined her to be in her late twenties—thirty, maybe; and guessed that her hair would dry out very fair.

I said : "It's a wonder the civil guard didn't pinch you."

"Pinch?" She frowned, and her literal interpretation went hand in hand with the slight accent. German? Swiss? Dutch, perhaps?

"Arrest you. Every Spaniard's a Moor at heart. He expects his women to be covered up."

"I know. I saw the notices." She had no inhibitions about my gaze; looked down at herself. "Perhaps that is why he took my clothes."

"The guard?"

"It must have been him. It's so ridiculous."

"Where were you at the time? In the water?"

She nodded, lifting the flippers and mask. "The only person in sight when I came out was the guard. I shouted at him but he was too far away and didn't hear."

"He couldn't have seen you either—while you were swimming, I mean. That's the only explanation."

"Then all I can say is he didn't look very hard." She was more amused than angry. "Why else would some shoes and a blouse and slacks be on the sand?"

Her shadow lay between us, fading as a cloud dragged over the sun. After all the rain there was a latent chill in the air.

"You'll get cold," I said. "Won't you come in?"

"I don't want to bother you. I was going to ask if your wife could lend me something to wear. When I saw the house—"

"I'm not married."

"Oh," she said. "Well—you, then. I can't go back to the hotel like this, can I?"

"Hardly," I smiled.

Had she been ten years or so younger I might have teased her in avuncular fashion : but I was too conscious of her body and the artless sophistication with which her eyes held mine. As she dropped her gear into a chair I noticed that the inside of one of her thighs was bruised and that she was wearing a wedding ring—discoveries which touched me with an absurd and fleeting envy.

I said : "Will you have a sherry while I look for something?"

"Thank you." She sat down, crossing her legs, pulling back a wet twist of hair. Completely at ease, she glanced round. "This is a lovely room."

"It's a lovely house altogether, but unfortunately I only rent it." I handed her the sherry. "If you busy yourself with that I'll see what I've got. Jeans and shirt?"

Alone in the bedroom I looked for them with fussy and unaccustomed eagerness. They didn't take much finding and, on my return, I displayed them like a draper. "What d'you think?"

"They're splendid."

"I don't know about that. We aren't exactly the same build, but they ought to do the trick." I placed them over the arm of her chair. Sunlight flooded the terrace again, shafting through the open windows, but her damp shoulders were mottled with cold. "There are clean towels in the bathroom if you want to dry off. Then I'll run you back in the car."

She protested, but I could tell she was grateful.

"And while we're about it we'll retrieve your things from the Civil Guard."

"You really shouldn't. I've caused you enough trouble as it is."

"It's no trouble."

33

She finished the sherry and stood up, absently brushing grains of sand from her stomach. More sand jarred from her ankles as she crossed the tiles. In the doorway she paused. "You know—when I called from the wall just now I was sure I was in for a dreadful time."

"How d'you mean?"

"I expected you to be an indignant Spaniard—all hands, eyes and moustache." She grinned extravagantly; struck an attitude. "With my vocabulary it could have been disastrous."

We both laughed. She was the most unexpected person.

"Are you English?" she asked.

"Yes."

"I thought so."

Presently, from the bedroom, she called: "What do you do?"

It was somehow flattering to be still in her thoughts. "I write."

"Write?"

"That's it."

"Books? For newspapers?"

"Novels and screen plays."

"It sounds most exciting."

"Far from it. It's a hermit's life."

I moved to the door and leaned against the jamb. Her voice shook a little and I supposed that she was rubbing herself down.

"And you live here always?"

"Oh no."

"Where, then?"

"All over the place. I've been here five months. In a month's time my lease is up and I go home."

"With a finished book?"

"I hope so."

There was silence for a while. I left the door and wandered out on to the terrace. Pewter-grey clouds were massing overhead. A small wind stirred, bringing with it the alien

smell of a foreign land, reviving an old, inexpressible yearning.

"All those questions. You will think me very rude." She
was behind me, clutching the top of the jeans into herself.

"Not at all." I watched her amused mock-pirouette. "A
bit baggy here and there, but otherwise—"

"Baggy?"

A schoolday pun came to mind. "Toulon et Toulouse."

She frowned, baffled. "All right, though?"

"All right," I smiled. "Will you have another sherry?"

"Thank you, but I really shouldn't. I ought to go back.
My husband will be wondering where I've got to."

"What's he been doing?"

"Sight-seeing. Wandering round the town. . . . He is more
enthusiastic even than an American."

"There's not much to see in Bandaques."

"You don't know my husband. Every brick, every
stone—" She shrugged expressively, then gathered up the
mask and flippers. "Did you really mean what you said
about driving me back?"

"Of course." I stood aside to let her precede me into the
hall. "Where are you staying?"

"At the España. We came the day before yesterday and it
has rained ever since."

"The weather's gone haywire lately."

"Haywire?"

"Unpredictable—like my housekeeper. She should have
been here at eleven."

"What is it now?"

"A quarter to twelve."

As I joined her in the car she asked : "Is she Spanish?"

"Who?"

"The woman who looks after you."

I nodded. "She is also very old and very ugly."

"I don't believe it."

"It's true," I said. "Regrettable, but true."

One ensnares the future in the gaiety of sudden escape

from loneliness; unwittingly lays stepping stones towards some distant and unforeseen pain. At one time, if you had asked me where and how it all started, I would have answered: "When she called to me from the beach." Chronologically that was so. But every second offers a new beginning and now—much later—asked the same question, I would tell you that it was on the road into Bandaques, in the brief moment of banter when our eyes met and she chuckled: "You must be a very single-minded man." Something moved in me then and I sensed that she was aware of it—as surely as if her fingers had been on my wrist and felt my pulse quicken.

The grey-faced sergeant on duty at the headquarters of the Civil Guard was profusely apologetic; only too glad to part with the missing clothes. I imagine he'd already suspected that the patrol guard had been stupidly zealous and was relieved to have the evidence off the premises. The clothes were loosely tied with string. He wanted the owner to sign for them but when I explained that she wasn't adequately dressed to leave the car he accepted my signature instead.

I held the bundle aloft delightedly as I came out, then tossed it on to the back seat. "You were quick," she said.

"I gave them a piece of your mind."

I began honking my way through the noon-day traffic. When we were passing the amphitheatre she said: "Will you dine with us one evening? It would be ridiculous not to meet again."

"Indeed it would. I want my jeans and shirt back."

She caught my mood. "Then you will?"

"I should love to."

"Tonight, perhaps?"

"Tonight would be fine."

"I'd like you to meet my husband. He'll want to thank you, too."

"There's no need for thanks. Really there isn't. I've enjoyed every moment of this morning."

36

"Would seven o'clock suit you?"

"Perfectly." I was braking outside the hotel. "Here?"

"Yes. In the American Bar."

She extracted a pair of canvas sandals from the bundle of clothes and put them on before getting out of the car. I held the door for her.

"D'you know something? I don't even know your name."

"Ilsa Scheele," she said, holding everything precariously into her waist.

"Mine's Stephen Tyler."

She laughed infectiously. "I can't stop, Mister Tyler. And if I tried to shake hands I am sure those jeans of yours would fall down.... Until seven, then?"

"Until seven. Good-bye."

I watched her hurry awkwardly up the steps. She didn't look back, but I drove home whistling.

Before seven o'clock came round I had opportunity enough to wonder what Scheele would be like. But he fitted none of my preconceived notions. To begin with I hadn't pictured so big and powerful a man. He was all of fifteen stone, though there was nothing flabby about him: his grip was as crushing as a vice. Heavy brows, pale blue eyes, hairy wrists, brown freckled hands, bald head—all these I noticed in the space of Ilsa's introduction. But what surprised me most was his age: as near as makes no difference he must have been fifty.

Weeks earlier, elsewhere, I overheard two waiters commenting upon a marked disparity in age between husband and wife. The younger one said: "I don't care to think of them together. It distresses me." When asked by his colleague why, if that were so, he continued to punish himself, he replied: "I can't help it. The state of my mind is the despair of a succession of priests." I had smirked with amusement at the time, but now, as I drew up a chair be-

37

side Ilsa, I experienced a pang of the same sort of sensual dismay.

Scheele was saying : "You did my wife a great service this morning. It could have been awkward for her if you hadn't come to her rescue."

His English was as good as hers but the accent was thicker; unmistakably German.

"It was my pleasure. I was under the impression that ladies in distress went out with the silent pictures. I'm grateful to your wife for disillusioning me."

I smiled at her. She was startlingly attractive. Her dark green dress was simply styled and her hair was short and fringed : except for the artificial redness of her lips, she wore no make-up. She looked very slight beside him; disturbingly fragile.

"Mister Tyler—" she began.

"My friends call me Ty." I was quick, too quick, perhaps. "Ty?"

"That and no more."

"Ty is a writer, Erich. I told you, didn't I ?"

Scheele nodded, big fingers wrapped around a sweating glass of Scotch. He delivered his dictum about the relative merits of reality and make-believe, then added : "I imagine you know Spain well?"

"Not particularly."

"You have been here before?"

"Once—but not to Bandaques. I was near Malaga for a time some years ago." I accepted a cigarette from the proffered packet of Chesterfield. "Is this your first visit?"

"Yes," Scheele said. "We came by car."

"What made you pick on Bandaques?"

He shrugged. "I have business to attend to in Barcelona and thought this would be a suitable place for a few days' relaxation."

Ilsa explained : "Erich is a sales executive."

Scheele shifted his elbows on the table. "Typewriters." He mentioned a trade-name. "We're from Hamburg,

38

Mister Tyler. One can have too much of cities. We wanted somewhere quiet—off the beaten track."

"Bandaques is certainly that."

Ilsa said : "The Tourist Office told us there is a fiesta on Sunday."

"That's so. It's the Feast of the *Virgen de la Tarde*. The Moors were driven from the town early in the twelfth century and legend has it that victory was due to the Virgin's miraculous intervention. I'm told they parade through the streets at dusk in her honour—generally cut loose with fireworks and so on."

"It sounds wonderful," Ilsa said with enthusiasm.

"Will you be here for it?"

Scheele answered. "We're staying about a week."

"If our belongings last that long." Ilsa smiled ruefully. "You'll begin to think we attract trouble, Mister Tyler—"

"Ty."

"I'm sorry. . . . Ty." She leaned forward and I could see the shallow trough between her white, firm breasts. "This morning a guard took my clothes. This afternoon Erich had some things stolen from our bedroom."

"No !"

"I'm afraid so."

"That's bad," I said. "Were they valuable?"

Scheele said : "A watch, a cigarette lighter and a ring."

"While you were out?"

"No. That is what"—he searched for a word—"annoys me so much. Ilsa was sleeping : I was having a shower. It was after lunch—siesta time. I left them on a table between the two windows. When I finished my shower and came back into the bedroom they were missing."

"Have you reported it?"

"Naturally—to the manager and to the Civil Guard." His voice was suddenly charged with disdain. "But what can you expect? They are useless and inefficient and nothing will be done."

"That's a bit hard," I protested.

"I do not think so."

Ilsa sided with me. "At least give them a chance, Erich."

I said : "Generally they're the most honest of people. . . . Isn't it possible there's been some mistake?—that you've mislaid these things?"

"Mistake? No." Scheele was adamant. "They were stolen."

"But how? Was your door ajar?"

"Ajar?"

"Open."

"It was not. And the veranda is separate from the others— you know, private. And the room is on the third floor." He drained his whisky; signalled for another. "Someone let themselves in with a key. There is no other explanation. But the manager defends his staff and the Civil Guard shake their lousy heads."

The theft dominated the conversation for some while. Ilsa endeavoured to make light of it, but Scheele's manner hardened the longer the matter was under discussion. I liked him less and lesss. He was a quick and heavy drinker and by the time we went in to dinner his mood had become one of contemptuous complaint concerning all things Spanish. Ilsa eventually said something to him in German, and without understanding what it was I knew that she had delivered a reproof. He lapsed into a period of silence, but there was a continuing tension between them which seemed somehow to falsify Ilsa's attitude towards me. I began to have the feeling that she was using me; that her laughter was a shade too easily found, her interest in whatever I chanced to say a fraction too intense.

My conceit suffered. For a while I thought bitterly : Why fool yourself? You're a Boy Scout being patted on the back for having done the day's good deed—that's all. That's the only reason you're here. After tonight she'll have gone out of your life along with Herr Bloody Scheele and his surly manners and great enveloping hands. . . . Yet not long afterwards, when I danced with her at the Bar Sinbad and

Scheele was too fuddled, his bulk almost lost in the tobacco-smoke, for her to need to be anything but herself, I found that I was driven to say : "Am I going to see you again?"

"I hope so," she murmured. We were crushed together on the crowded floor and my lips were inches from hers. "I hope so, Ty"—and it was sufficient to relieve and excite my mind. We rejoined Scheele. For an hour or more we listened to the jazzy flamencos; watched the orgiastic expressions of the girl dancers. And all through the intricate rhythms struck by hands and guitars I was filled with a glow of anticipation that stemmed from the mood and isolation of our morning meeting at the Villa Miramar.

Scheele's speech had become slurred; his eyes slightly glazed. The theft had apparently ceased to concern him and he grew affably maudlin. Once he said meaninglessly : "They remember saints and visions because it doesn't hurt their pride. Otherwise they forget." And another time, leaning close, he muttered confidentially in his own tongue. I paid no heed : he could have said what he liked for all I cared so long as the whisky sapped his strength and arrogance. I was smugly content to suffer his arm round my shoulder and listen to his rambling, humourless anecdotes.

It was pouring rain when I took them back to the España. We had made our farewells and I was about to drive away when Ilsa emerged from the artificial brightness of the foyer. For half a moment I thought she might be going to ask : Where? When? But instead she thrust the borrowed jeans and shirt into my hands.

"Souvenir," she said gaily. That was all—but it satisfied; implied a secret shared.

3

Only last Thursday, less than a week ago. . . .

The long afternoon dragged by. I picked at the meal Catalina had prepared; drank the best part of a bottle of wine. As usual she left soon after two o'clock. Had I not been going out that evening she would have returned at about five : as it was she had finished for the day.

I found the silent house unendurably lonely; the dull sound of the sea a constant mnemonic. For a while I either paced up and down like a caged animal or lay restlessly on the bed. The wine may have blunted my nerves a little but it had also plunged me into the blackest melancholy. Around four, on an impulse, I tried to telephone my agent in London in order that he should know that the novel was lousy and would be late. But there was a three-hour delay, so I cancelled the call. Later I wandered into the garden, plucking at the feathery tendrils of the pepper trees, mooching without admiration or delight between the scarlet flowers of the castor-oil plants and purple cascades of bougainvillea. Later still I took my shadow on to the dunes above the beach and, with my knees under my chin, watched the dung-beetles endlessly making tracks in the hot sand between the scattered clumps of marram-grass.

There was no purpose in anything I did except to kill time. It would have been about five-fifteen that I re-entered the house with the intention of having a bath. Hardly had I started it running than, above the hiss and belch of the taps, I heard a car crunch into the gravel drive. I went to the door immediately, only to have the sudden and unreasoning hope snatched away the moment I stepped on to the porch.

It was Romero. Disappointment must have filled my voice. "What on earth d'you want?"

"A talk with you, señor."

"Social or official?"

"Official."

"I'm going out in half an hour."

"Half an hour may be sufficient."

"It'll have to be."

He took my rudeness very coolly. "May I come in then?"

"If you insist."

He left his hat in the hall. There was a red weal round

his forehead where the rim fitted. I turned the bath taps off before joining him in the living-room.

"What exactly's on your mind?"

"Señor Scheele," he said.

"I guessed that much."

"Guessed? Guessed what, señor?"

"That you hadn't come to talk about the weather."

He was moving around the room as if it were a shop—fingering a table, examining a lampshade—and I wished he would remain still.

"In a way you could say that it is about the weather."

I didn't understand.

"All the rain these last few days—the consequent strain on the Lareo Dam—the drowning of Señor Scheele." He seemed to think a picture needed straightening. "They are all stages in the same tragedy."

I still didn't understand. "Why's it suddenly necessary for you to speak in riddles? If you've anything important to say, then for God's sake say it. . . . But hurry, please. I have to be in town by six."

He came to a halt by the terrace door, developing an apparent interest in something out at sea. "Would it surprise you to know that Señor Scheele was not—as everyone has supposed—drowned?"

I snorted. "It would astonish me."

"In that case I should like to see your astonishment." He turned with theatrical effect. "The fact is that Señor Scheele was shot."

CHAPTER THREE

I

THERE was utter silence in the room. Outside, a seagull's cry pricked the soft thunder of a spent wave.

"*Shot?*"

Romero nodded.

"That's ridiculous."

"I'm afraid not." He was watching me, fingering his small, boomerang-shaped moustache. "A dead man cannot talk, Señor Tyler, but his body speaks for him."

I moved my hands in total disbelief. "But he was drowned. . . . Drowned."

"No."

"There must be some mistake."

"A wound doesn't lie, señor. And there is a wound in his stomach."

My thoughts were going all ways at once. The seagull mewed once more and the thin thread was like a cry of pain. "I . . . I don't believe it."

Romero moved from the door. "I'm sure it is difficult, but you will find that you have no choice."

I stared back at him.

He said : "Don't you remember the blood?"—he touched his abdomen—"the blood here?"

"Yes, but—"

"It came from a bullet wound. He wasn't drowned. He was dead before the dam broke."

"How d'you know that?"

"Because there is no water in his lungs. As I said, señor, a body tells the truth to anyone interested enough to look for it."

I ran a hand over my face; sat on the arm of a chair. Some

44

seconds elapsed. "I'm sorry. . . . It takes a bit of getting used to."

"That is only to be expected." His eyes hadn't left me.

"Have you been to the hotel?"

"Not yet. I only saw the autopsy report an hour ago."

Shock blunts the ability to reason. Automatically, I said: "Why've you come to me?—first?"

"Because you were a friend of the dead man. . . . Because it is easier—since you speak Spanish—for me to talk with you than with his wife."

"He was hardly a friend," I objected. "An acquaintance."

"But you knew him."

"Only superficially." I quit the chair. "Anyhow, I don't see how I can help."

"That remains to be seen. Accidental drowning is one thing. But a shooting is a very different—"

"For God's sake!" I flared. "I'm not at school."

I brushed past him and stepped on to the terrace, angered by his pedantry, distracted by a dawning acceptance of the facts. The sight of the white cube of the Hotel España filled me with dismay. Telling Ilsa was going to be like saying that Scheele had died twice within twenty-four hours.

Romero joined me. "I'm sorry," I said again. "But the longer you remain with me the more you will have to endure my imperfections."

He shrugged. "You have been under a good deal of strain. I like to think, though, that you are going to be co-operative."

"In what way?"

"By answering my questions."

"I've got some myself."

"Such as?"

I turned my back on the sea and faced him. "Have you any idea who could have done it?"

"That is what I have to find out, señor."

"Or why?"

45

"No."

"There must have been a reason. People don't get shot without there being a reason." It had all come too fast for me. I was floundering. "Was he robbed?"

"No."

"How can you be sure?"

"There were notes worth over nine thousand pesetas in a wallet in his hip-pocket."

"He was robbed once before," I persisted.

"But not killed. This time he was killed but not robbed." I started to speak, but he went on: "Nine thousand pesetas is a considerable sum of money in a country like mine. Men work for a year for less. If robbery had been intended it would not have been ignored."

There was another silence as his logic sank in. Bewilderment made me restless. I walked back into the living-room and Romero followed me, as close as a shadow.

I said: "He was a stranger here. A tourist. Why should anyone want to shoot him?"

"With your help, Señor Tyler, I hope to come nearer to answering that."

"I've already told you—I barely knew him."

"You knew him better than anyone in Bandaques except his wife."

I felt his gaze boring into me again. I met it without caution. "Look," I said, breaking the pattern of the conversation, "I want her to hear about this from me. She's had a terrible twenty-four hours as it is. I'd rather tell her myself."

Romero touched his moustache as if to check that it was still there. "Is that where you were going at six o'clock?—to the hotel?"

"Yes."

"I think it would be wiser if you were to telephone to say that you will be late."

The sun-burst clock on the wall showed almost twenty to the hour. "What's going to delay me?"

"I am, Señor Tyler."

46

For the first time his tone bore a hint of menace and I re-acted with some heat. "All I can tell you about Scheele will take five minutes. . . . Less."

"That may be. But there are other questions I need to ask." He permitted himself half a smile. "Up to now, prac-tically all the questioning has come from you."

"What other questions?"

"About yourself. . . . About Señora Scheele."

"It sounds," I said acidly, "as if you have every intention of wasting as much time as you possibly can."

"When you are looking for something in the dark, señor, you grope. That's what I am doing—groping."

"I can think of other words for it."

He looked at me with disapproval, then subsided into one of two leather armchairs which faced each other across a low wrought-iron table. It was the act of a man embattled with authority. He extracted a cigarette from a metal case that came from his breast pocket, lit it with a match and blew a thin stream of smoke which deflected off the mosaic surface of the table and spread.

Against my will I conceded temporary defeat. I said: "How long's this going to take?"

He lifted his shoulders in the lazy, infuriating manner I was coming to know so well. "It depends."

"On what?"

"On you, señor."

"For God's sake—can't you give me some idea?"

He shook his head. "I'm sorry."

I wheeled away from him indignantly. The telephone was in a recess surrounded by bookshelves. As I reached it Romero said: "I would rather you did not mention what you know about Señor Scheele for the moment."

"You needn't worry." I was curt. "And don't spoon-feed me."

I could see the hotel through a window as I waited for Ilsa to be found. They tried her room first, then—getting no answer—arranged to page her. I suppose I had to wait a couple of minutes, but it seemed longer. The day was beginning to burn itself out behind the darkening sierras and a few pale lights were already showing in the hotel and elsewhere along the promontory. I practically forgot Romero's presence as the seconds passed. I was more conscious of a crude and burning resentment that the door which Ilsa seemed to have shut between us was now—through a twist of fate—going to be equipped with bolts and bars. Dismay was burrowing through me again, swamping my irritation, and with a sudden stab of hatred for Scheele I remember thinking quite without shame: Why couldn't you just have been drowned? Wasn't that enough? . . .

"*Momento, señor*," a woman said. Then Ilsa was on the line. "Ty?"

"I'm going to be a bit late, I'm afraid. I'm awfully sorry."

There was a momentary pause. "It doesn't matter."

"I can't say how long I'll be"—I glanced at Romero in appeal but he ignored me. To blazes with you, I thought—"but I shouldn't be later than seven."

"Seven?" She echoed it flatly.

"Yes. I'll explain when I see you." I asked her where I should find her; again apologized. "I wouldn't have had this happen for the world."

"It doesn't matter," she repeated, and her voice carried a hint of indifference which fed my longing with another dose of the same dull, jealous hurt that had been growing ever since we knew for sure that Scheele was dead.

I stared at the hotel for a second or two after ringing off, battered by a confusion of thought. Then I crossed to the centre of the room and sat in the chair opposite Romero. He stopped examining his long fingers and looked at me critically.

"Well?" His lips curled.

I lit a cigarette. "What d'you want to know?"

"Everything you can tell me."

"Starting where exactly?"

"At the beginning."

"Shouldn't someone take it down?" There was no one else on whom to vent my mood and I had a strong desire to taunt him. "For the record? Or did your sergeant plant a microphone this morning?"

"Not this time," he said evenly.

"What sort of beginning d'you want? Mine? Where I was born? Who my parents were? Theirs? . . . In which case we'll be here all night."

Romero uncrossed his legs; leaned towards me. I caught a faint whiff of garlic. "Let's not play games, Señor Tyler: you know very well what I'm after. I'm groping in the dark, remember? Very well, then. I'm simply asking for a day-by-day account of your association with Señor Scheele. Surely that isn't too much to expect of you?" He settled back in the chair, tapping the leather arm with a thumb. "A day-by-day account of your association with Señor Scheele . . . and his wife."

His timing and inflection succeeded in squeezing a maximum of meaning into the apparent afterthought. I felt my face colour, but I was too tormented within myself to realize that his mind was already working towards what was, after all, an elementary conclusion.

2

I told him about the morning Ilsa had her clothes taken from the beach by the patrol guard; about the three of us dining together at the hotel and finishing up at the Bar Sinbad. I gave him the bare bones of it, without frills, deliberately abbreviating the account so as to emphasize my point that he was wasting his own time as well as mine. Somewhere a murderer was going begging.

Romero had a chess-player's concentration; a croupier's coldness. But he was more dogged than astute and was labouring beneath the icy exterior. I became aware of this almost immediately I had launched into my side of the story because he queried my statement about the guard having

49

taken Ilsa's clothes. It was a completely unimportant detail, but since the incident had never been reported to him he spent precious time cross-questioning me before he seemed satisfied that I was telling the truth. Had my eyes not been on the clock I might have made more of it, but as it was I had no patience with him.

Eventually I protested : "What in the hell has it got to do with Scheele, anyhow?"

"I like to be methodical, Señor Tyler."

"Then all I can say is God help the drunk or the petty thief who finds himself in one of your cells. He's there for life."

He didn't rise to it. Very deliberately he drew on his cigarette. "This happened on Thursday, you say?"

"That's right. Last Thursday. A week ago tomorrow."

He nodded. "And then?"

"And then, what?"

"What happened after that?—after you drove Señor Scheele and his wife back to their hotel?"

"On Friday, d'you mean?"

"Friday, Saturday, Sunday . . ." He flipped the days along with a motion of his hands. "You have scarcely started, señor."

The rain bucketed down until just before dawn on the Friday, and the sun didn't break through until after the nine o'clock guard had passed by. I was on the terrace by then, drinking black coffee and trying to will myself to start the day's work. I got as far as taking the cover off the typewriter, but that was the nearest I came to picking up the threads and immersing myself in an imagined situation. The sunshine wasn't going to last and I kept looking along the beach in the hope that Ilsa would appear before the rain set in again.

Despite the length of the beach the most popular stretch was below the promontory where there were umbrellas and fixed bamboo shades for hire and the odd gaseoza stall did business. Urban people talk wistfully of wanting to escape the crowd but they find the reality of isolation hard to bear, even for a short while. Only a comparatively few ever seemed to find their way along the dunes towards the villa— the more dedicated sun-worshippers, the lovers, an occasional family, the very shy.

And Ilsa. . . .

I was somehow sure that she would come down for a swim, but almost an hour went to waste before I saw her. There was scarcely anyone about: even where they usually concentrated only a handful of diminutive figures was visible and I picked her out when she was still some distance off.

She was wearing a light-coloured sun-dress and was near enough to the water for me to guess that she was letting it ebb and flow around her ankles as she sauntered away from the town. I left the terrace with the alacrity of an autograph-hunter whose vigil had not been in vain and hurried through the beach-gate on to the shore, suddenly elated, striding eagerly over the dark, pock-marked sand. I waved once, but she didn't respond. Instead, deliberately perhaps, she stopped walking and turned seawards, shielding her eyes with a raised hand.

I had come quite close before she acknowledged me. She called a greeting, but her words were lost in the sucking hiss of the backwash. She was carrying her sandals and the hem of her dress was wet.

I grinned, and called back: "I thought you were saluting someone."

She splashed nearer. "Is that what it looked like? I was watching the gulls. They fly so close to the waves sometimes."

"They're hungry. You take risks when you're hungry. . . . Aren't you swimming today?"

"I couldn't believe the sun would last long enough. "

"You weren't far wrong." I frowned quickly at the sky. "The rains in Spain fall mainly on Bandaques: meanwhile, perverse world that it is, there's probably a heat-wave in Hamburg."

She smiled, tossing her hair. "And in London? . . . Is it London?"

"Outside London," I said. "A place called Richmond. If I know anything it'll be raining there too."

We had started walking, slowly, without any destination. A pair of sand-martins sprinted away from us like clock-work toys : a scalloped tongue of water creamed in.

"You sound depressed."

"Englishmen invariably sound depressed when the weather's under discussion. But I'm not, believe me. Not now, anyway—though I would have been if I hadn't seen you." We moved on a little. "That's gospel truth," I said clumsily.

"Gospel?"

"Genuine. Honest . . . I wanted to see you very much."

I was in momentary dread of her reply. Loneliness and life by proxy are dangerous training-grounds when desire suddenly excites the will : one can delude oneself, presume too much. If she had chosen to disarm me there and then I suppose I could have reverted to the role of Boy Scout without more than a mild bruising. But as it was she said nothing and her silence served as another stepping-stone towards wherever it was the next few days were heading.

Soft, invisible spray found our faces. We strolled with a sort of aimless intent. Presently she said : "Shouldn't you be working?"

"My publisher would think so. In any case, he certainly wouldn't approve of what I'm doing now."

"Relaxing?" She gave the word a delicious upward curl.

"Meeting a young woman without her husband's know-ledge."

She pouted in a way that conveyed any number of things. "Erich isn't interested in swimming or the sea. This morning he wanted to go to a museum."

"At the cork factory?"

52

"I think it was there. Anyway," she said, "he wasn't able to go because there is something wrong with the car. He is busy with that instead."

Without warning, a flurry of rain spattered the sand. The world seemed to shrink as the sun vanished behind a bruised, shifting fist of cloud. Instinctively, I gripped Ilsa's arm. "We'd better run for it."

It was seventy or eighty yards to the villa. By the time we reached the protection of the awning on the terrace the rain was slanting down in cords. We laughed together, a little out of breath, slapping our clothes.

"Is this where you write?"

I nodded. "And breed ulcers."

"It is difficult for you?"

"Sometimes it's difficult. At others it's just pure hell." I put the cover over the typewriter. "How about a sherry? — or is it too early?"

"Thank you."

I went inside and filled two glasses. When I returned she raised hers. "What do they say here?"

"*Salud . . . Salud y pesetas.*"

"*Salud y pesetas.*" She savoured it, head cocked. "I can understand that. My Spanish must be improving."

She was enormously appealing when she smiled. Her proximity disturbed the senses. Physically, I knew all but her ultimate secrets : vividly remembered from the previous day the soft, tanned skin beneath the light blue linen dress and the lithe feel of her body when we danced. I was thirty-eight years old but my mind had the gauche uncertainty of twenty years earlier. I wanted to say : "You're very beautiful. I've never met anyone like you before." But the impulse died under the pressure of the reality of who she was, of Scheele's existence, and with a degree of calculation that surprised me, I thought : Wait.

I said instead : "Any news of your husband's stolen things?"

"Not yet." She drank, meeting my gaze. "I'm sorry about last night. He behaved very badly."

"He had reason to be annoyed." I was trying to be generous. "What with that and your car giving trouble he'll begin to hate this country."

"I think he does already."

Without surprise, I said : "Why?"

She hesitated fractionally before dismissing the question with a shrug. "Maybe it's the weather. . . . Can you wonder? Just look at that rain."

It was drumming on the roof; flooding the terrace. The sea and the town were hidden from us. It was just past ten o'clock : Catalina wouldn't come until about eleven. For an hour or more—or until the rain lifted—we were totally isolated. All my inclinations were to snap the taut bonds of restraint : but I could not. Perhaps pride was at the root of it, but I waited to be sure—more sure than I was. She had given no sign of how her own mind was working; accepted our solitude with the same tantalizing unconcern with which she had brought her near-nakedness into the house. True, at the Bar Sinbad, when I'd asked her if I would see her again, she'd replied that she hoped so. And on the beach just now her silence had seemed to imply approval of what I'd said. But I could have misconstrued both the answer and the lack of one : misread what was no more than cautious tact. On the other hand I kept telling myself : She's here, isn't she? Why else should she have come to the beach and walked this way? . . .

I showed her round the house. She was genuinely entranced by it. Twenty minutes or so passed and I let every opportunity go. We returned to the terrace and smoked another cigarette; drank another sherry. The rain was easing off and the sea showed with the vague mistiness of a Chinese water-colour but I doubted if we would see the sun again that day. I used the rain as an excuse to delay suggesting driving her back to the hotel, but in the end Catalina's arrival made the decision for me.

Ilsa grimaced. "I suppose I'd better go. . . . Thank you for showing me your lovely house."

"I've enjoyed it." Catalina was clattering about in the kitchen. Now that our seclusion was at an end I was angry with myself. Ruefulness made me take the plunge. "Will you come again tomorrow?"

"Tomorrow?"

For a moment my heart sank : she sounded almost startled.

"Tomorrow morning."

I could hardly bear her frank scrutiny. It seemed to go on and on. Then, with an unexpectedness that constricted my throat, she said : "It might still be raining."

"And if it isn't?"

"I should like to."

All at once my lips had found hers : clumsily, painfully. For a few seconds she yielded. A swift, wordless passion possessed us, compounded out of frustration and longing and uncertainty. Then, gently, she pushed me away.

We left the house like conspirators laden with surreptitious guilt. From the kitchen Catalina sang out *"Buenos dias, señor"* and I answered her with unnatural casualness. My thoughts were aflame with excitement and wonder. On the drive into Bandaques I reached for Ilsa's hand; received an answering pressure. But neither of us spoke. Already I was wishing the hours away that were about to divide us; becoming enviously distressed by thoughts of Scheele.

The cream Mercedes was parked some way along the street from the hotel as I drew up. If Ilsa hadn't been observant enough to notice it I daresay we might have sat together for a while and tried to find words with which to recapture and prolong the fierce moment of mutual discovery, then parted. As it was she pointed the car out. "He hasn't made it go." The disappointment in her voice echoed another relationship of which I had never been part. She clucked her tongue. Now he will be furious again."

The bonnet was open. Ostrich-like, a couple of men in

stained overalls peered at the engine : Scheele was there too, protected by an umbrella which bore the hotel's name.

"Shall I drive up?"

Ilsa nodded.

I went into low gear and crawled forward until we were alongside.

"What's the trouble?"

Scheele's glance took in the pair of us without surprise or suspicion. He was too resentful to be anything else.

"These men are fools," he announced. "Fools. They've been here over an hour and done nothing. They're monkeys, not mechanics." Ilsa and he shared a tart exchange in German : then he reverted to me. "If they can't do something tell them to find someone who can. I'm tired of making signs."

I might have been a servant. I opened my door and squeezed out into the drizzle. Scheele pushed the two men roughly aside to give me room. His bulk dwarfed the pair of them.

"We think it's the pump," the older one said in answer to my question.

"Can't you fix it?"

"Not here. The car will have to be taken in."

"For how long?"

"Perhaps a day." He was a mild little fellow, but he conveyed the impression that his patience had about run out. "We have tried to explain to the gentleman, but he does not understand. Again and again we have tried. It has been very difficult."

He had my sympathy. When I told Scheele he retorted : "Time means nothing to these people. A day could mean a week. They're unreliable." He wore his contempt like a uniform.

"Not if you keep after them." I broke off to speak to the mechanic again. "He can't swear to it but he's pretty sure it will be ready by tomorrow."

Ilsa said something and Scheele nodded.

I made a spur of the moment offer. "I'll take you to the museum, if that's what's bothering you."

Scheele grunted. "I'm thinking about Monday. I have to visit Barcelona."

The news lodged in my mind like a spark. "Monday's a long way off. How about this afternoon?"

"The museum?"

"Your wife told me you wanted to go. It's five or six miles. I'll willingly help you out."

Without noticeable enthusiasm, he said : "That's kind of you."

"Perhaps you'll both come?" I was as off-hand as possible.

"I don't know about my wife, but I would certainly appreciate it."

Ilsa was silent.

"About three?"

"Thank you."

He had mellowed a shade. At his request I instructed the mechanic to have the Mercedes towed away : stressed the urgency. Scheele invited me into the hotel for a drink, but I declined on the grounds of having work to do. It seemed best to go : I was too close to the moment in the villa to be able to trust myself. A glance could have betrayed us.

"Three o'clock, then?"

I drove off, leaving Ilsa on the steps with him under the umbrella. Her farewell was warily casual. I was torn between hoping that she would come to the museum with him and hoping that she would stay away. As it happened she chose not to come and I think she was wise, though when— just after three—I saw Scheele coming out of the hotel alone I experienced a dull stab of disappointment that was akin to physical pain.

The museum was within the precincts of the cork factory. Years ago, during excavations for an extension to the plant, an early-Christian burial ground had been unearthed together with numerous Roman antiquities. The company had erected a grandiose sandstone building which had be-

57

come one of the main tourist attractions of the district, but
– probably due to the rain – Scheele and I had the place to
ourselves. A wizened old man in a moth-eaten beret showed
us round. For an hour or more our footsteps echoed off the
high ceiling as we moved about between funeral urns and
sarcophagi and broken statues and numerous show-cases of
pottery and verdigris-coated trinkets. I had seen them all before, but I was more uneasy than bored. My dislike for
Scheele had entered another dimension—more intense,
more subtle. I was learning that one can pity the cuckold
and hate the deceit in the same breath as wanting to weaken
his position, undermine his right.

Mostly he was silent while the guide chattered and I in-
terpreted. He nodded from time to time; occasionally asked
a question. Disparagement, I felt, was never far below the
surface. It was nearly five before we left. The rain hadn't let
up. I took him back to the hotel, accepted his thanks, once
more refused a drink, then went on to the Bar Sinbad. As
usual the waiter Joaquin was anxious to experiment with his
English, but before long I returned to the villa and tried to
kill the evening hours with a bottle of Fundador; willed
the rain to stop before morning.

My version of this to Romero was severely curtailed;
somewhat adapted. In point of fact all I said was: "Quite
by chance I met Mrs. Scheele on the beach during the morning. It started to rain and we sheltered here—in the house—
for a short while. She told me her husband's car had broken
down, and when I drove her back into Bandaques I offered
to take him to the museum at the cork factory in the afternoon. He was keen to go there. I picked him up after lunch
and dropped him back at the hotel around five o'clock. I
didn't see either of them again that day."

Romero listened intently, chin on hands. "Not at all?"

"Not at all."

"When did you see them next?"

"On Sunday."

"Not on the Saturday?"

"On Sunday." Spite made me add: "Shall I speak a little slower?" His jaw muscles bulged under the sallow skin: otherwise his self-control was complete.

Saturday had been the worst of days, the rain heavier and more continuous than ever, and I had known from early on that there wasn't the slightest possibility of Ilsa venturing on to the beach. All the morning I had mooched about the house, unable to work or read or concentrate in any way, until frustration forced me into Bandaques. For more than an hour I had sat on a high stool at one end of the American Bar in the Hotel España, watching people come and go while I toyed with an air-mail edition of the previous day's *Daily Telegraph*. But neither she nor Scheele had put in an appearance. The bar-tender had had no knowledge of their whereabouts and I had curbed an impulse to have them paged: to inquire after Scheele's car was too flimsy a pretext, and it wasn't the weather for offering them the use of mine. For the same reason, when I returned in dejection to the villa, I had resisted a recurring temptation to phone. But I couldn't stay indoors for long: I felt imprisoned. Two or three times more before the day was done I had lingered over unwanted drinks in the hotel or at the Bar Sinbad. Once I had even cruised slowly about the desolate, rain-beaten streets in the vain hope of glimpsing them in a café or outside one of the shops that catered for tourists. But all to no avail. By nine o'clock I had become sullen and defeated as the day itself and had gone early to bed, filled with an aching intensity of longing for Ilsa that was in no way assuaged by the thought that on the Monday Scheele was going to Barcelona. Monday, on Saturday night, had seemed an unbearable distance away—as far-removed as our last brief, disturbing contact. . . .

Romero flicked cigarette-ash from his black pistol-holder. He was as fastidious as a woman. "On Sunday, then," he prompted.

I dragged my thoughts back to where he wanted them. "We went to the bullfight together."

"By chance?"

"No. I called at their hotel and invited them."

"In the morning?"

"Yes," I said without patience. "In the morning."

I was watching the time. It seemed increasingly to me that this was a quite pointless questioning. Mostly, antagonized by Romero's manner, I was inclined to forget the supposed purpose of my recital. Now and again, in a renewed moment of near-disbelief, my mind fastened on to the fact that Scheele had been shot, murdered; and that before long Ilsa would have to learn of it too. At such moments Romero's questions struck me as all the more outrageously futile.

I went on: "The rain stopped at about half-past ten. I went to the España some time after eleven. The Scheeles were in the bar and asked me to join them."

(Nothing about the manner of our meeting, the disciplined thrill I experienced when I saw her, the way her eyes belied her careful greeting. . . . Nothing about my saying casually: "What did you do with yourselves yesterday?" and the blunt, twisting pang that came when Scheele answered with a mirthless chuckle: "We spent it where days like that were made for—in bed.")

"He was complaining about his car not being ready. I drove him to the garage where he found that he was mistaken. We rejoined Mrs. Scheele at the hotel and it was then that I suggested going to the corrida."

Romero's dead stare relaxed momentarily. "You wasted your time. There are no bulls or men any more. . . . I take it you stayed until the end?—saw the final farce?"

"Yes," I said. "It was a bad bill, I agree."

(Nothing about my not caring whether the fights were good or bad. . . . Nothing about Scheele's almost mesmerized concentration, his grunted appreciation when a bull twice tumbled the scraggy, caparisoned horses, or the way in which sweat beaded his heavy neck and his lips tightened when, barely ten yards from where we sat, death waited on the tip of a poised sword. . . . And nothing about the delicious agony of sitting thigh-by-thigh with Ilsa, bending close in order to explain what was happening—close enough sometimes for her hair to touch my cheek—and never once being able to speak one word of what trembled in my mind. . . . These things were not Romero's concern.)

"And afterwards?" The question-mark was hung out like a baited hook.

"I reserved seats for the three of us for the evening's procession. They were in the tier on the east side of the Plaza Mayor." With malice, I said : "Under the plane tree with the Coca-Cola advertisement. I forget the exact numbers."

Romero produced another cigarette : it was a smuggled brand. "You saw the disturbance, then?"

I nodded. "We had a grandstand view."

The procession in honour of the *Virgen de la Tarde* had begun at nine o'clock. All day long frantic preparations had been under way from one end of the route to the other—tens of thousands of lights draped from tree to tree; garish, fragile-looking arches erected; tiers of seats scaffolded together at special vantage points and hundreds of benches placed end to end along the narrow pavement edges. A stranger passing through might well have thought that the frenzied activity was due to some impulsive overnight decision to honour the Virgin's favours on that particular day. Around eleven, when I had driven hopefully to the España, all was chaos. Every street looked as if the inhabitants had been in the process of fleeing the town in the face of an invader instead of arranging to celebrate the very opposite. Seven hours later, when we left the bullring, it had seemed impossible that the zigzag route could possibly be in readiness by the advertised time. Even at a quarter to nine, when we were struggling to our seats in the tier, a score of harassed men had still been hammering the outer shell into place.

And yet, astonishingly, the procession had started on the stroke of the hour. A horn blast from the far end of the square had brought silence slithering over the crowd like a dying leaf-rustle. For a short space of time Bandaques seemed to hold its breath. Then had sounded the muffled tap of a single drum and the head of the column emerged from the shadowy street which leads into the square from the precincts of the Church of the Incarnation. Behind the solitary drummer, at a slow march, had followed detachments of the armed services, followed in turn by a group of civic dignitaries. Then the priests had taken over, double files of swaying black and white figures, some chanting, some silent. Close in their rear had come a huge figure of the crucified Christ, borne aloft by many hands and surrounded by incense bearers, after which the first of the lay brotherhoods had made their way by in their coloured robes. Each member held a lighted taper and together they had presented a medieval spectacle, solemn and mysterious and awe-inspiring. The various brotherhoods were separated either by a phalanx of the Civil Guard or by another lone drummer or by emblazoned banners carried by youths dressed like pages. Eventually the huge sculptured Virgin, the miraculous one, had come into view. Mounted on an ornate platform which rested on the shoulders of numerous straining men she had lurched past our tier, complete with a gleaming halo of electric light bulbs, and all around us people had fallen to their knees and blessed themselves.

At a suitably discreet distance she had been followed in turn by penitents, hooded, masked, cloaked, some barefooted, others with their arms thrown painfully wide, some in chains, a few bearing heavy loads. Behind them again had come more brotherhoods, more detachments of soldiers, more dignitaries, more priests, and—finally—bringing up the rear, a bishop busily distributing his blessing to the accompaniment of restrained music from a brass band.

It had made an impressive hour and a quarter; impressive enough to ease the tension of the charade that, since morning, Scheele's proximity had forced upon Ilsa and me. His presence had fostered my natural distaste for him, and it was a relief to be distracted. Ilsa and I scarcely spoke, though a glance can convey more than a spate of words. The parade had had a magnetic quality and the only time our attentions were seriously diverted was immediately after the Virgin had jolted past. Suddenly there was a shout; a scuffle. A man—it happened too quickly for any of us to be sure whether he was participant or onlooker—had dodged through the moving columns, pursued by a couple of Civil Guards who lined the route. For half a minute or so there had been pandemonium as hunters and hunted thrashed their way through the watching crowds. There was a tumult of boos and laughter, gradually drowned by indignant hisses. The chase eventually passed from our field of vision, but after silence had settled over us again I well recall Scheele leaning forward and—across Ilsa—saying to me with heavy humour : "I wonder if that's the fellow who broke into our room?"

The memory made me ask : "Did you catch him?" I leaned back and clicked on a light.

Romero shook his head. "No one has ever caught Zavella." Perhaps my surprise at the name showed itself. "You know of him, of course?"

"No." It was best to lie, if only to prevent more wasted minutes. Already we'd been an hour together.

"I thought everyone in these parts knew of Luis Zavella."

"You must complete my education some time."

There was an arid pause, during which, once again, the incredible thought came to me that, while we talked, Scheele's body was stiffening in a refrigerated cabinet in the mortuary with a bullet-wound in the stomach.

Romero lightly tested the proof of his moustache. "On

Sunday, then, Señor Tyler, you were with the Scheeles for most of the day?"

"I've just told you that."

"And on the Monday were you also with them for most of the day?"

"No," I said. "Scheele went to Barcelona on Monday."

"Alone?"

"I believe so. It was a business trip. His business—not mine," I added pointedly.

"What did *you* do?"

"I don't see how that's relevant—no matter how much you say you're groping."

"No?"

"No, I don't."

Again the measured shrug. "At what time did he return from Barcelona?"

"About eight, I believe."

"You saw him?"

"We met at the Bar Sinbad." I anticipated his follow-up. "Quite by chance."

"Together with his wife?"

(Somewhere deep in my mind the correction insisted: Widow.) "She was there, yes."

"How had she spent the day?—during her husband's absence."

I shifted in my seat; felt a slow flush colour my face again. "That's not relevant either."

"You don't know?"

"Good God," I snapped. "What *is* this?"

"Just another question, señor."

"Well, I don't answer that sort of question."

Smoke wandered from Romero's mouth across his narrowed eyes. Unblinking, they never budged from mine. I suppose I should have realized by then what was coming but I was still blind to it.

"I won't press you," Romero said. "I hoped, though, that you would co-operate as much as possible."

64

"I have. But once you become unreasonable I shut up like a clam. And the line you're taking *is* unreasonable. More— it's damned impertinent." I smashed out my cigarette in the tray; glanced at the clock. "There's nothing more I can usefully tell you. I didn't see Scheele again after we met at the Bar Sinbad on Monday night—not alive, that is."

"No?"

"No," I said angrily. "D'you want it in writing or something?" I stood up, intending the move as a gesture of dismissal. "Now, if you'll excuse me—"

Romero stayed where he was. "There is one more thing, Señor Tyler."

"What?"

"Yesterday . . . Tuesday." He waited.

"Yes?"

"Where were you?"

"Where was *I*?"

"What were you doing? Who were you with? Where did you go? . . . In other words, señor, I should like you to account for your own movements between dawn and the time I spoke to you on the telephone at the Hotel España to report that a Mercedes saloon had been found wrecked below Gondra."

I was dumbfounded

"And on this occasion," Romero said, his voice gritty with revived menace, "it would be better if you chose to reply."

Eventually, when the initial turmoil of amazement subsided, I think I said : "Have you gone absolutely mad?"

He didn't react.

"Are you implying that you suspect I had something to do with Scheele's death?"

"I am asking you to account for your movements at the material time, that is all."

"It amounts to the same thing." I snorted indignantly;

laughed. "If it weren't so absurd I should enjoy this. My God! And to think that for the last hour or so—"

"Where were you yesterday, Señor Tyler?"

With deliberation I took a cigarette from the box on the table in front of him and lit it; tossed the match down. "I suggest you find out. And then I suggest that you come back here and apologize."

His eyes flashed. "I will apologize to no one about this matter. Least of all to you, señor."

"Perhaps you'll resign instead." I blew smoke. "What you're suggesting is too ridiculous for words."

"It is for you to prove it so."

"You haven't got me in a cellar with lights on my face yet."

"That can be arranged, if necessary. This is a small town, señor, and what happens here is my affair."

He glared at me. In the long pause that followed I heard the dull sound of the surf again. It was nearly dark outside : a bat flitted past the window.

"Tell me this," I said, rashly now, and with scorn. "Why should *I* kill Scheele? There are perhaps two thousand people in and around Bandaques. Why, with your second-hand omniscience, d'you pick on me?"

"I have picked on no one. I have merely asked you a particular question."

"Why?"

He took his time. "You yourself said earlier that people don't usually get shot without there being a reason."

"Agreed."

"Very well, then . . . . There may be two thousand people in and around Bandaques, Señor Tyler, but I suggest that you are the only one who is personally interested in the dead man's wife."

CHAPTER FOUR

I

My voice, when it came, had no edge to it; only a sort of weary exasperation. "You should have been a priest, capitán."

"I considered it once." Now that he was more in control of himself and had regained the initiative Romero allowed himself another of his rare half smiles. "The Church is in error, señor. Priests should marry, then they would have a closer understanding of the world."

"Yours, to say the least, strikes me as warped and naïve."

He rode it smoothly. "You are entitled to your views. My sole interest is in where you were at certain times : what you did. If my request is as preposterous as you make out, you have a very simple remedy."

I turned abruptly away from him and poured myself a brandy.

"Answer me," Romero said to my back. "Have you got a gun?"

"No."

"Have you ever had one?"

"When I was about six. It fired a bit of cork on the end of a piece of string. I killed my parents with it almost daily."

He was icy. "A real gun."

"During the war. They took it away afterwards." I faced him again. "Really, this has gone beyond a joke. You come here, ostensibly in search of information about the way in which Scheele spent his time in Bandaques, and when I've told you all I know you virtually charge me with his murder." I used my hands. "Where was I yesterday? Have I ever had a gun? . . . It's fantastic. Utterly fantastic."

"Is it?" He rose, instinctively flicking ash from his tunic.

67

"I would say that your refusal to answer a straightforward question more than excuses my having asked it."

Nonsensical though his suspicions were I supposed that it would be claimed that they were not without some justification. But the greater part of Monday and Tuesday was my preserve—Ilsa's too—and, because of her, I had no intention of sharing it with a third party.

I said: "I can only repeat that the last occasion I saw Scheele was on Monday night at the Bar Sinbad."

"What," he branched off, "did you think of him?"

"Did I like him, d'you mean?"

Romero nodded. "Exactly."

"No, I didn't."

With what he thought was cunning, he said: "Yet you were frequently in his company."

I countered: "There are many people I don't like, but they're still alive."

I was beginning to feel that there had never been a time when he wasn't either subjecting me to his scrutiny or moving about the room like a customer in a furniture store. He had started doing this again now and I said: "That ceramic isn't mine. I'm responsible for breakages here."

He put it down. "Why didn't you like him, señor?"

"For many reasons."

"And which of these reasons carried most weight with you?"

I said hotly: "You're banging your head against a wall. How many more times have I got to tell you that I had nothing—absolutely nothing—to do with Scheele's death?" It was coming up to seven o'clock, I noticed, and I fretted. "Why don't you leave me alone and do some of your groping elsewhere? You've allowed whoever did it enough start as it is."

"Where do you suggest I begin?"

"That's for you to decide. But I can assure you that you aren't being very clever at the moment." His silence provoked me into presenting an ultimatum. "Either show me

68

better cause for wasting my evening—or go. I'll waive the apology."

Resentment sharpened his tone. "Very well, Señor Tyler. . . . In the first place there is your interest—undenied by you—in Señora Scheele."

"That's not a crime."

"I carry a notebook; not a breviary." His smugness made me wince. "Secondly, there is your admitted dislike of the dead man. Thirdly, there is your reluctance to tell me how you spent the greater part of Monday, and your repeated refusal to account for your movements yesterday." He was working along his fingers. "Fourthly, I am taking into account a combination of minor facts—insignificant in themselves, perhaps, but of some consequence when considered in relation to everything else."

"Such as?"

He drew a long breath. "Your always being in Señora Scheele's company at critical times—last night, for instance; and again this morning. And your request to be present whenever she might be wanted in the future."

"Good God," I protested. "And you think that's suspicious? One day you'll suspect your own shadow."

He shrugged.

"Haven't you ever wanted to help someone? . . . Besides, as you very well know, she doesn't speak Spanish."

His index finger was already touching the thumb of his opposite hand. I had grown tired of fencing with him. "Really," I said. "You'll have to do better than that. What other crass nonsense have you got lined up?"

"Fifthly, señor," he said, with the air of a man throwing an ace, "I have had it reported to me that, on Monday night, you and the dead man fought each other in the Bar Sinbad."

"It was hardly a fight."

"Everything is relative."

"He hit me and I hit him back—it was no more than that."

"What did you fight about?"

"He was drunk," I said.

"You hit him because he was drunk?"

"He hit me."

"Why?"

"We argued."

"What about?"

It was a minute after seven. "Look," I said, "I'm sick to death of this. You'll damn well have to wait for an answer."

I went to the telephone and got through to the España. "I want to speak to Señora Scheele," I said. "You'll find her in the American Bar." Half a minute later I was saying: "No? . . . Well, will you please see she's told that Señor Tyler has just called and that he will be with her in a quarter of an hour?"

I snapped on some more lights, disturbed by not having made contact with her, wondering where she was.

Romero said: "You are a very impetuous man, señor."

"So?" My hands shook as I lit another cigarette. "Under your comic microscope I suppose that always gets distorted into something significant?"

He let it pass. "You were on the point of explaining why you and the dead man had an argument."

"It wasn't about anything in particular. He was just in a filthy, carping mood. He usually was, anyhow."

"Why?"

"Maybe he was allergic to typewriters."

Romero frowned.

I explained. "His business was with typewriters—that's the reason he went to Barcelona. Perhaps he thought selling the things was beneath his dignity, perhaps the weather had got on his nerves, perhaps he was still brooding over being robbed—I don't know. I'm not a mind-reader. All I *do* know is that he was particularly unpleasant that night."

Romero smiled slightly with his mouth. "And because of typewriters and the weather and so on you are telling me he hit you?"

70

I shook my head. "It was because of something I said. I told him the past was a bucket of ashes."

"A bucket of ashes?" It was a disappointingly clumsy phrase in Spanish.

"Words to that effect. Old bones if you like. He kept talking about the war. He'd drunk too much and was growing tiresome and objectionable, so I tried to shut him up. My remark seemed to enrage him. That's all there was to it."

"I am expected to believe this?"

"I don't see why not. It happens to be the truth."

Romero switched a table-lamp on and off. He might have been on the point of saying: "I'll take this one. How much is it?" Instead, thoughtfully, he said: "Why didn't you mention this fight before?"

"Because it isn't of any consequence."

"No? . . . What else haven't you told me, Señor Tyler?"

"Nothing that has any bearing on what happened to Scheele."

"You still refuse to discuss what you did with the rest of Monday, and on Tuesday?"

"That's right."

He suddenly gave me his undivided attention. "I am entitled to an answer and intend to get one."

"Not from me," I said.

"I have the authority to insist." He was entrenched in his quietest, most confident mood. "For instance, I have the authority—here and now—to ask you to surrender your passport."

"You can take it with pleasure. I'm only going as far as Bandaques."

"Then may I have it?"

He held out a hand. I wasn't sure whether he was bluffing, but I didn't much care. By that time I would have parted with almost anything to be rid of him.

"Of course," I said, and my willingness to relinquish it seemed to disarm him a little. "You're beginning to panic, capitán."

I opened the desk and took the passport from its pigeon-hole. I also took out a pen and a sheet of paper and asked him for a receipt. I thought he might refuse, but he accepted the pen readily enough and wrote in a slanting scrawl: *Taken into custody this day one British passport No. 422196 property of Stephen Robert Tyler*. He added the date and, finally, with a spectacular flourish, signed his name: *Tomás Romero*.

Hoping in some way to discomfit him, I said: "Is there nothing else you want, or is the inquisition over?"

"Nothing now, señor."

"Your hat, perhaps?"

He still had another card to play and was therefore armoured against my tongue. "Before I go I would like to make your position quite clear. Let me just say that I have taken your passport more as a precaution than for any other reason—though it is also a pleasure for me to teach you a small lesson."

I suffered in silence.

"And a final thing—"

"Yes?"

"I shall be seeing Señora Scheele in the morning. You can break the news to her about her husband if you wish—I leave that to you. But do not imagine that tomorrow I will automatically accept her word when it confirms your own." He was very sure of himself now. "When I was younger and more vulnerable I might have done so, but nowadays, I assure you, I can smell collusion before it even comes through the door."

With difficulty I continued to be silent. I followed him into the hall; watched him ram on his preposterous hat.

Turning blandly on the step, he said: "And remember this, señor. To spare Señora Scheele embarrassment at a difficult time it will do you no good to telephone my office in a short while to state that on Tuesday you and she were in bed together. That may be the oldest alibi in the world—perhaps the most pleasant—but, unhappily, it is also one of the

72

least impressive. Unless, that is, you happened to be in bed together in, say, the middle of the Plaza Mayor."

The starlight slowly dissolved him. I slammed the door and went back into the living-room. I suppose I had invited his parting shots, but that made them no easier to bear. As I poured myself another brandy I heard his car hiccoughing away over the gravel and my mind pursued him with a moment's abuse. All at once the quick bright glitter of my affair with Ilsa had been tarnished in a way that neither Scheele alive nor Scheele dead had succeeded in doing; ridiculed, somehow tainted. Romero's reasoning was crude and his methods amateurish, but there was a perspective to his thinking which contaminated.

The house was suddenly very quiet. I opened the windows on to the terrace in order to empty the room of tobacco-smoke and the sound of the laden sea beat in, slow and heavy. If it had not been for my anger I would probably have driven off to the España immediately Romero was clear. As it was I delayed for a couple of minutes. It was only ten past seven and I finished the brandy, then crossed to the telephone, wanting more than anything at that moment to talk with Ilsa so that I could arrive at the hotel freed from selfish anxieties as to her need of me. The indifference in her voice when we had last spoken lingered uneasily in my mind, and what I had to tell her now was shocking enough, brutally perplexing enough, to make her shrink even further into herself. I had come to accept that this was inevitable, but I still held to the hope that, given time, she could be drawn out again. Scheele would diminish—I hadn't ceased to believe that.

The smear of Romero's touch was already fading as I waited for the operator to put me through. The receptionist recognized me. "Señor Tyler?"

"Yes."

"I'm afraid we weren't able to get your message to Señora Scheele."

"Oh?" My heart sank a little. "Why was that?"

"She had gone to her room with the request that she did not wish to be disturbed. I wasn't aware of it when you called. I had only just come on duty."

"I see." Seconds passed. Then : "Can you connect me with her now?"

"I am afraid not, señor. The request is still in force." Brightly she added : "Perhaps if you tried again in the morning?"

I put the handset back on the rest, hurt and humiliated. Ilsa's desire for isolation seemed aimed at me personally, and her manner of excluding me was even more wounding than her wish to do so. She could have called me, I thought bitterly. At least she could have let me know. . . .

I walked through the room, nursing my dismay, and went out on to the terrace; stood under the vast white stars. A breath of air was moving furtively off the water and the faint smell of disaster came with it. I was trembling. In my imagination I heard Scheele's thick accents : "Real flesh and blood; real life and death. There's no substitute, Mister Tyler." And this time, aloud, I said to myself : "Why did you have to die at all? It was easier when you were alive."

2

When Ilsa arrived on the beach on Monday Scheele had already left for Barcelona. The previous night, as the fireworks which rounded off the procession split and streaked the sky, Scheele had grumbled : "How long's this likely to last? I'll need some sleep if I'm going to be any use in Barcelona tomorrow." Several times that day I had hovered on the brink of asking him whether the trip was still scheduled, but always I had hesitated for just too long and missed the suitable cues. His own silence about the visit—broken only when the fireworks were nearly at an end—had fed me with doubt and anxiety. Then, I had desperately wanted to hear it mentioned : have it confirmed. But on the Monday neither

Ilsa nor I were once to refer to it—almost as if we believed we could thus deceive ourselves about his existence.

It was a brilliant morning. The sea was a flat calm and the sun had the sky to itself. Ilsa came at about ten, by which time I was already on the beach. When we saw one another we both started to run, and I remember that I laughed as I ran, splashing over the wet dark sand along the water's edge, filled with a crescendo of exhilaration that was like a burst of song. That she should be running too was somehow wonderful in itself, communicating her eagerness in a way that no words could have done.

When we were still a little apart she lost one of her sandals and stumbled; bent to retrieve it. She was hopping on one foot as I reached her, gaily trying to keep her balance while she struggled to get the sandal back on. Grasping her arm I was reminded of how slim she was, how fragile; but desire was muted with the sheer joy of again being with her. Breathless, she thanked me. "We've got a lovely day," she said, and her choice of phrase echoed everything I felt. The whole span of daylight was ours: while it lasted we were free, without restriction, alone.

"What d'you want to do?"

"I don't mind. You say." Her eyes shone.

"We could swim."

"I've no costume."

"Not underneath?" She was wearing tight, cream-coloured denim slacks and a short chequer-board shirt.

"I didn't think of it."

"A drive, then? We could take the car somewhere."

She nodded approval. "But not to anywhere in particular. Don't let's make any plans, Ty. Not today. Let it just happen."

Like a child I cupped my hands to the empty beach. "Any more for the mystery tour? Mystery tour starting in five minutes."

"What's a mystery tour?" she chuckled.

"They run them at home. Coach parties. Two-hour mystery tour, three bob. No one's supposed to know where he's going."

"Not even the driver?"

"He's blindfolded."

We linked hands, laughing, and walked up the slope towards the villa. It is impossible to measure happiness. But if one could draw a graph of it, record with certainty its endless rise and fall, that morning would stand out like a peak. I don't think that, for one moment, I consciously saw myself as a usurper. For too long I had accustomed myself to loneliness and was ill-fitted to cope with the sudden fire of the past few days: release from both was an intoxicant which destroyed the emptiness and jealousies of reality. For me, that morning, happiness was laughter and frivolous nonsense and the beauty of the day itself—all shared; and the knowledge that she had run to share them.

I drove north, away from Bandaques, and the wind streamed Ilsa's hair. Here and there, far out, the smooth cobalt sea was wrinkled a shade or two darker: a twist of smoke balanced on the taut line of the horizon. To our left the sierras were in their blurred, violet mood. Only when we came closer could we see through the deception—the harshness of the upper heights and the bare bones of exposed grey rock.

I sang:

> *Por de bajo del puento*
> *No pasa nadie,*
> *Tan solo el polvo*
> *Que lleva el aire . . .*

Ilsa smiled. "Again." Instead, I spoke a translation:

> *Under the bridge*
> *Nobody goes,*
> *Only the dust*
> *That the wind blows . . .*

76

"I picked it up listening to Catalina—trills and all. Come on, you try it."

We took it line by line, half a dozen times, until she was tune and word perfect. I only knew one other verse and she mastered that as we corkscrewed through the pines away from the metalled coast-road. We were climbing. The sea vanished and we began to feel the great strength of the enveloping hills; our own isolation. Once the trees ended we entered a diseased and inhospitable landscape of grass-tufted and precipitous slopes. We stopped singing, concentrating on pitted road and savage views.

Soon she said : "Somewhere nicer please, Mister Driver."

"Isn't this nice?"

"It's like the wrong side of the moon."

"I'm blindfolded, remember."

It was hard work at the wheel. The road twisted between the deformed breasts of hills, followed a ridge, then began a switchback descent into a valley. Scrawny goats littered the hillsides. A truck laden with timber ground up to meet us, lurched past, spewing dust and diesel fumes. Two men as ragged as scarecrows : an overburdened mule led by a boy. Otherwise our solitude continued. Miles away, along the narrow brown floor of the valley, villages nestled at the foot of blue, barren mountains like heaps of dumped stone. Nearer, smears of yellow broom merged into the tree-line. We plunged down through pines and chestnuts; found a surfaced road and were led between oleanders and tamarisks beside a swollen, khaki-coloured stream. Sugar cane grew here, and there were walled patches of reddish earth in which olive and almond trees stood in orderly rows. The first crumbling village came and went, then another spiked with poplars, its rotting edges somehow redeemed by clematis and splashes of crimson bougainvillea.

"Nice enough now?"

"Oh yes," Ilsa said. "It's beautiful. Sad and beautiful."

She sat very straight beside me, lips parted a little, occasionally turning her head when something or other particu-

77

larly caught her eye. We said little, though even in the silences we seemed to be learning about each other. There would be a time for questions, for explanations, for exchanging an account of ourselves, but it had no place in the mood of that morning. We drove on, cruising slowly along the deep trench of the valley, singing again sometimes, laughing often, immersed in a happiness that seemed indestructible.

By noon we were nosing out of the valley, climbing once more. Somewhere near the crest a turn of the road exposed a small, tight village beside a spouting waterfall. But for the waterfall we might have passed through : instead we left the car and explored on foot. On a rocky platform below a squat, ochreous church we found a reed-covered shack where wine was sold. Benches and trestle tables were set outside and we sat there, watching the falling water fan out and whiten as it crashed on to black, glistening rock below. Some ragged children gathered to stare at us, fascinated, it seemed, by Ilsa's blonde hair. We drank a thin sherry from an un-branded bottle; chewed sweet, husky almonds. The bow-legged proprietor clattered in and out of the bead-curtains which covered the door, grinning, commenting on life and the weather, proudly producing his wife for our inspection. The place was too good to leave. The couple needed only the minimum of encouragement to provide us with a meal, and it was excellent—an omelette followed by red mullet, washed down with an amber-coloured wine. *"Bueno,"* we nodded time and again, to their obvious gratification. *"Bueno. Muy bueno."* The only thing to fail us was the sun. The first clouds pushed above the jagged skyline when we were half-way through the meal and by the time we were sipping our brandy they were thick and ugly. Continents of shadow began to blotch the hills.

"More rain, señor." The proprietor turned down the corners of his mouth. "There is no end to it. Soon we will need an Ark."

"We'll have to go," I said to Ilsa.

"I suppose so." She drained her glass reluctantly. "What a pity."

We paid and left. *"Adios,"* the man and his wife called after us. *"Sano y salvo."*

We waved back, turning in our tracks. "What's *sano y salvo*?" Ilsa asked.

"Safe and sound. . . . *Adios. Gracias.*"

Heavy drops hit us before we reached the car. The sun had vanished already and the air was going grey.

"It was wonderful there," Ilsa said. "So simple; so unexpected." She leaned her head against my shoulder as I went through the gears. "Is the driver still blindfolded?"

"Not any more."

"Mystery tour over?"

"Yes."

"Where are we going now?"

I kissed her lightly on the forehead and desire pushed through me. "Home," I said.

We were quieter on the return run. The rain had so reduced visibility that driving demanded all my attention. I was glad when we found a metalled surface; gladder still when I eventually discovered our whereabouts. Once, peering past the wipers as I slowed at a junction, an arrowed sign thrust itself at me : BARCELONA—and I remember with what swift success my mind disposed of the intrusion. Bandaques was then only a dozen or so miles away and they didn't take us long. By a quarter to three we were through the town and heading along the dunes to the Villa Miramar.

"Even in the rain it looks lovely," Ilsa said.

I smiled. "You're easy to please today."

"I'm happy, Ty—that's why. Very, very happy."

At the house we ducked from car to porch. I followed Ilsa inside and turned on the living-room radio : a local station was pumping out soft, innocuous music.

"Catalina's deserted us. Drinks are on the table if you'd

like one. I won't be a minute: I'm going to put the car away."

When I came back she was standing under the awning on the terrace, turning the pages of my manuscript.

"Did you write this?"

"What?"

"This." She pointed, and I read: *We are swords that spirits fight with. We never see the hands that brandish us.*

"No," I said. "That's too good to be mine; I just jotted it down. But it's a sort of theme to what I'm doing."

"It's not true, Ty."

"What isn't?"

"What it says,"

"No?"

"No," she said.

Her sidelong gaze was strangely disturbing. For a fleeting duration I was aware only of its gravity; puzzled by the change in her. Then I realized that she was nervous; consumed with a burning uncertainty. It had destroyed the softness of her eyes and quivered on her lips. The sound of the rain and the music seemed to swell: desire moved urgently in me again like something that had lain in wait for too long. I heard myself say: "Does it matter? Let's argue about it some other—" and suddenly I was lost in the sensation of her mouth and body against mine. She had come to me as much as I to her and this time there was no gentle pushing away; no forced curbing of passion. Her hands, her lips, her tongue were as eager as mine. Under the drumming awning and in the bedroom we gave up our secrets, and both times, when it was too quickly over, she was generous with understanding. In between, and afterwards, spinning her soft hair in my hands, our limbs slack, brushing our kisses gently, her small, boyish face bore an expression of shyness which somehow convinced me that this had never happened to her before; that I was the first stranger.

"Why me?" I asked her. "Why me, Ilsa?"

She closed her eyes, burrowed her face into my shoulder,

but she didn't answer, and the moment of wonder passed away. I was too content, too drugged, to attempt to retain it.

Later, propped on one elbow, marvelling once more at the smoothness of her slender brown and white body, knowing that I would want her again as soon as she had gone, I said : "Try and see me tomorrow."

"Perhaps," she said.

"Please." I kissed the small blue vein in her neck. "You must."

"If I can," she said.

It was the nearest we came to admitting openly that what had gone before was stolen, like the day itself. Even when time forced us to dress it was Catalina's name which intruded, not Scheele's. She was due at five o'clock and we left the house a few minutes before the hour. Everything glistened but it had stopped raining; when, I had no idea. I drove Ilsa back to the hotel, slowly, dragging out what little was left of our solitude. And there we parted, at the foot of the steps, under the watchful eye of the doorman. There was no sign of the cream Mercedes but the pavements were busy with people, the street noisy with the blare of horns, the belch of exhausts. It was no place to linger. Only in our minds could we still cling to each other.

"Good-bye, Ilsa."

A look, a nod. "Dear Ty." Then she was gone and the doorman was telling me it was safe to pull out.

"*Buenas tardes, señor. . . . Gracias.*"

The last person I wanted—or expected—to see that evening was Scheele. But, more than ever, the house seemed a desolate place, and after bearing with it for as long as I could I went into Bandaques. It was nearer ten than nine when I got there. I had nothing in mind—only a need to destroy loneliness. The restaurants and pavement cafés were packed and the cinema by the amphitheatre was sucking in it last-house audience. I took a brandy at one of the seedy cafés near the bullring and watched with envy the couples who saunt-

ered past or sat nearby. Even if they weren't going to bed together they could at least parade themselves in public. I let a
shoe-black kneel at my feet and produce a shine that would
have rivalled Romero's; refused offers of American cigarettes
and a bargain-price watch. A blind lottery-ticket seller
moaned his way through the tables and because his milk-
white stare moved me to pity I bought from him. He said
automatically : "You will be lucky, señor. This time you will
be lucky." And I thought : Will I? Will I? What do you
know about luck?

I left and went elsewhere; walked the streets, stared into
shop windows, was cannoned into by people with destinations. Joaquin greeted me at the Bar Sinbad, fussed over me,
eager to practise his English. He had an El Greco face; long,
grey, fine-boned.

"You know Browning, señor? Robert Browning?"

"Some, yes."

"A gentleman was drinking here now from England. Ten
minutes ago. He says Robert Browning is very beautiful."

"I wouldn't recommend him, Joaquin."

"No?"

"Not for you."

"He is not beautiful?"

"Difficult."

"And Lord Byron? This gentleman also tells me—"

"Try Wordsworth," I said.

He was signalled to another table : departed shaking his
head. Two women came in; hesitated by the empty chairs.
One said to me : "With your permission?" and I nodded.
"It's all yours. I'm about to go."

I sank my brandy and stood up; started towards the exit.
Then a thick voice separated itself from all the others and I
heard my name called.

It was Scheele. I stopped in my tracks, knowing how the
guilty feel when challenged.

"Mister Tyler !"

He was slightly drunk; I could tell as much before I

discovered where he was sitting. For half a moment I thought with relief that he was alone : then I saw that Ilsa was with him. I waved a perfunctory greeting, hoping to escape, to be spared facing them together, but he lurched to his feet and pushed heavily past a waiter.

"Come and join us, Mister Tyler."

"Thanks, but I was just leaving."

I started on some rigmarole about an appointment, but he brushed it aside. His huge grip closed on my arm.

"You're always refusing me. I'll begin to think you don't like me or something." He swayed; laughed. "Ten minutes won't matter whoever she is."

Short of wrenching myself away I had no choice. People stared as he led me in Ilsa's direction. I could hardly bear to look at her and her tense, desperately improvised smile somehow increased the agony.

She managed to say : "Good evening, Ty."

"Your husband seems to have arrested me."

"He was running away somewhere," Scheele boomed, slurring the words. He called for another chair. "What do you drink?"

"Fundador." Then, lamely : "But I really mustn't stay."

"Nonsense." He ordered imperiously. I was wary as I sat down, unable to fathom his mood, loathing every second.

"I've been to Barcelona, Mister Tyler."

"Oh yes?"

"You told Ty last night you were going," Ilsa put in and I wondered if it were wise. I caught her gaze. She frowned and shook her head, both minutely, as much as to say : "It's all right."

"You've been there, I suppose?" Scheele steam-rollered on.

"Several times."

"It's a lousy, stinking place."

I shrugged, not prepared to be drawn : I was used to his adjectives.

"A lousy, stinking place full of lousy, stinking people."

"It sounds as if you've had a bad day."

"A bad day is correct." He advanced his elbows towards me; brought his face closer. The pale, thick-lidded eyes were blood-shot. "I've been dealing with little men. Little men without memories. You don't know what it's like, Mister Tyler. You work alone. You don't have to humiliate yourself."

Ilsa said : "Erich."

"Some people don't mind humiliating themselves. You've seen them : so have I." He rinsed whisky round his mouth; swallowed. "I am not that kind—least of all here."

"Erich," she repeated.

A guitar twanged in the background : a hoarse, sad voice, like the cry from a minaret, lifted above the hubbub :

> *Cada vez considero*
> *Que me tengo que more ...*

Scheele ignored her; leaned near enough for me to see the small hairs which sprouted on his nose. "Memories are important, Mister Tyler. They last longer than friends." The words came slip-shod; tongue-heavy. "Don't you agree?"

For want of something better, I said : "You can't live in the past."

He laughed silently; lifted his glass. Whisky spilled from it, staining the cloth. A waiter came and mopped up. Scheele focused on him blearily. *"Sprechen Sie deutsch?"*

"No, señor. No deutsch."

I made an attempt to leave, but Scheele restrained me. "Fundador," he said to the waiter. "Another Fundador for the Englishman."

Ilsa said : "You mustn't force Ty to stay if he doesn't want to."

We exchanged glances uneasily, like prisoners in the same dock. But Scheele's hand still rested on my arm and I wanted to extricate myself quietly; without a scene. I was contemptuous of him but I wasn't gloating. In this mood he provoked an aversion that somehow destroyed any feelings of triumph or pity—even of jealousy. But it was bad to be there all the same, a cheating thing, and I despised myself.

He continued : "Were you ever a soldier, Mister Tyler?"

"Of necessity."

"You know something about it then."

"About what?"

"Obedience. Discipline. Authority." He made a mess of each word.

"In a small way."

"Authority. . . . Respect," he added.

"I didn't exactly run the war."

Inadvertently my fingers touched Ilsa's as I knocked ash from my cigarette and I knew I couldn't stand the pretence much longer.

"But you were a soldier?"

"Yes."

"I was also a soldier, Mister Tyler. We have common ground, eh?—something we share."

Ilsa rose abruptly, gathered up her bag, and excused herself. Her face was very pale in the smoky light as she turned away. I thought : God, why did I ever come in here?

Scheele dragged at my sleeve with the insistence of a dog. "Something in common," he slurred.

"It was a long while ago."

"But you can remember it. It's not forgotten."

"Some things are never forgotten." I was free to match him now; release my animosity. "A week after I was married my wife was killed by one of your bombs."

His glazed eyes narrowed. "That's bad," he said. "Bad." He paused for a moment, but the obsession festering in his mind swiftly repossessed him, obliterating any drunken trace of sympathy. He was looking through me, as if I weren't there. "Respect," he said. "Respect is important. . . . We had it once."

"We?" I hated him.

He didn't seem to hear. "*Todo o nada*. . . . All or nothing. Is that right, Mister Tyler? All or nothing?"

"I don't understand you."

"*Nada. Nada. Nada.*" He thumped the table. "For them it was *nada*. Nothing."

I said quickly : "I must go."

"Stay and talk," he pleaded. There was applause as the singer finished his song.

"Some other time."

"We were only just getting started." He tried to summon a waiter but I restrained him. "We've a lot in common."

"You flatter yourself."

It went home; pierced his stupor. He pushed back his chair and hauled himself to his feet.

I went on : "The past's a bucket of ashes. A pile of rubble. Incinerator dust. You ought to know. You made it, you and the rest of your—"

I wasn't expecting the blow. It caught me on the left side of the head, just above the ear. I was more suprised than hurt. I staggered, then countered instinctively, hitting him solidly in the chest. Somewhere close a girl cried out. Scheele grunted and slumped back into his chair, almost tilting it over. His mouth fell open and he blinked up at me in dazed amazement. I saw Joaquin and another white-coated waiter converging on us but I was moving before they reached our table. I walked past Scheele, shouldered between a couple of men who'd jack-in-the-boxed to their feet, and stormed out into the street.

For a while I walked anywhere; anywhere to get clear. My head buzzed, seemed ballooned to twice its size, and I muttered to myself as I pushed through the thinning crowds. I had a vague, short-lived feeling of satisfaction. But, soon, my anger turned against myself and I fretted lest I had ruined the chance of another meeting with Ilsa. The thought nagged at me on the way home, kept me awake until the small hours, disturbed what sleep I could find—more, even, than the pain of knowing that she was with him in the Hotel España.

But next day she came and I apologized, relief making me repetitive. We finished :

"It should never have happened. My tongue gets the better of me at times."

"I thought you were very patient."

"I never expected you'd be in the Bar Sinbad, but it was stupid of me to go there anyhow. Stupid and thoughtless."

"Don't let's talk about it any more."

"All right. But I'm desperately sorry."

Whatever self-deception we had managed to achieve on the Monday was no longer possible. Now we openly acknowledged Scheele; met despite him. "Where's he gone?" I asked, and Ilsa said : "Somewhere called Gondra."

In anticipation of her coming I had given Catalina the day off, but it was almost noon before the clouds which massed overnight had discharged their load and moved away; a quarter of an hour later before my anxiety ended and I saw Ilsa on the beach. She was very quiet to begin with, needing time, it seemed to adjust herself to a more blatant conspiracy. But her gaiety gradually broke through and we found laughter again : if hers was a trifle strained, a little less frequent, I wasn't aware of it. We prepared a cold lunch together, danced on the terrace to the radio, lay naked on the bed— and for me the only difference in the two days was that Scheele was inescapable. Even when I made love to her it was as if I believed I was hurting him. Triumph, jealousy— I knew them then. Even when I told her : "I love you, Ilsa. I love you," his shadow fell across us, for I remembered with dismay that in a matter of days they would be going home.

Late in the afternoon, limp from it all, I was to say : "Don't go with him, Ilsa. Stay here with me."

She traced the line of my lips with a finger.

"Will you?"

She was silent for a long while, studying my face with grave intensity. "You mustn't push me, Ty," she said at last, and at the time it seemed answer enough.

We left the house at about six and drove to the hotel. I wouldn't have stayed but for the crowd in the lobby and the news of the Lareo Dam. Looking back it is easy to be mistaken about what one really felt at some particular juncture. Every hour that passes adds to its distortion. But I honestly believe that, as we waited, I knew subconsciously that I would never see Scheele alive again.

3

Lights glittered along the promontory; winked meaningless signals. I heard a bat squeak on the wing; watched a star plunge to its death. Time had passed since dismay propelled me on to the terrace. The bitter hurt had lost its bite; the smart had gone and I was beginning to think about tomorrow.

Tomorrow morning I would tell Ilsa about Scheele, choosing my words, anticipating her distress. Romero could imagine what he liked; she at least would know how wide of the mark he was. Perhaps I could build on that. Tomorrow I would say: "Ilsa, I don't know how to tell you this, but I'd rather you heard it from me than from Romero. . . ." And before long, inevitably, disbelief would frame the selfsame questions which had earlier sprung from me:

"Who would want to shoot him?" And: "Why?"

CHAPTER FIVE

I WENT early to the España. A few dead goats, washed up overnight, littered the beach; inshore, the sea bed had the consistency of a red-brown stew. Several men were scrounging about near the water's edge, though God knows what they hoped to find.

Ilsa was in the section of the dining-room set aside, at that hour, for breakfast. Because it was early I had somehow expected having to wait for her to come down from her room and was unprepared to find myself immediately directed to her table. That Scheele had been murdered had become, for me, an accepted fact, and all at once it seemed fantastic that she was still in ignorance of it. As I crossed to her corner I felt unsure of myself; in need of more time to rehearse what she must be told.

She looked up. "I wondered if you would come."

"May I join you?"

"Of course." She offered the sad trace of a smile, but whatever hope flickered in me was offset by the deadness of her tone.

She said : "I'm sorry about last night. I just felt I had to go to bed. All the people in the bar, talking, laughing—I couldn't bear it. . . . Did they tell you?"

"When I rang they did." The sense of pique hadn't quite gone. "I could have been here by seven-fifteen."

"There wouldn't have been any point, Ty"—which, with a momentary renewal of bitterness, I took to mean : "I didn't want you anyway."

A waiter arrived and I ordered coffee. A man with a crab-red face at the next table read something aloud from the

Daily Express while the woman with him stared morosely at her finger-nails.

"Romero delayed me."

"Romero?"

"He called at the house and kept me for well over an hour. Otherwise—"

"I've had a message from him."

She let me see it. To my surprise it was in English, and I could only imagine that he'd put it together with the aid of a dictionary : typed it himself, too, probably. I read :

> *Please to present yourself at my office by 10.30 hours of this Thursday morning for particular questions in concern of your husband great tragedy.*

His flamboyant signature had driven the pen-nib through the flimsy green paper.

"Will you go with me?"

"You know I will." I was balanced between hope and dread, desperately anxious to win back a little ground before she was lost to me again in the welter of shocked confusion that was coming to her. "I'll do anything—always. I've told you a dozen times."

She nodded her thanks, but abstractedly, as if I'd done no more than light her cigarette. The professional observer in me heard the man at the next table chuckle and say : "Osbert Lancaster's damned good today"; caught the woman's flat : "Oh, yes?"

"What do you imagine Romero wants me for?" Ilsa's eyes were without lustre, as if she had undergone a fever.

I hesitated.

"What did he come to see you about last night?"

"Erich," I said. It was strange to find myself using Scheele's first name : I had never done it before. The woman complained as she returned the *Express* to her companion : "I don't think it's funny at all." I pushed my cup aside. "Ilsa, there's something you've got to know. ..." And suddenly I was telling her, badly, the thought-out way of doing it forgotten in the face of her incredulous stare and barely audible interjections. I reached out and placed a hand on hers; identified myself with her bewilderment. When it came to it I was surprised by how little I knew. Shot not drowned, dead before the dam broke; no water in lungs, wallet intact. ... That was about all : a few sentences covered everything. But half an hour later I was still trying to guide Ilsa towards belief in what had happened. The man and woman near us left; other tables filled and emptied. Our coffee remained untasted and grew cold. And Ilsa kept saying things like : "It doesn't make sense. ... We'd only been here a few days and hardly knew anyone. ... I don't understand : I just don't understand. ... It must have been an accident—some sort of accident. There's no other explanation. ..."

The previous day seemed to have drained her of emotion. Only once did tears briefly fill her eyes. I watched her earnestly, selfishly. The door between us remained shut fast, as I had feared it would. For all her bewilderment she was remarkably self-possessed. I felt that her defencelessness was going—not because I was present, but because she was involved in another world where she didn't really need me at all. I was the Boy Scout again—someone who could translate when she met Romero; run errands, offer advice, a wall against which she could throw her questions in the hope of a worthwhile answer bouncing back. Vanity urged me to argue : "He's dead, Ilsa. Whether he was shot or drowned doesn't matter. He only died once : you must only grieve once." But I was afraid, lest a chance phrase should violate her memory of him. Instead, seeking in some other way to earn myself merit, I said : "Romero thinks I did it."

Her forehead puckered as she quoted me : " 'Did it'? . . . What do you mean?"

"He thinks I had something to do with Erich's death."

"You can't be serious."

"*He* is. He's gone so far as to impound my passport."

"Im-pound?"

"Taken possession of it."

"But why?"

"He's got his reasons. What happened in the Bar Sinbad on Monday night is one. Mainly, though, it's because I refused to tell him where I was on Tuesday."

"Why should he even ask?" she began, but the sentence never went beyond half way. Her tired eyes widened a fraction. In the long pause that followed I watched the shape of Romero's logic slowly dawn in her mind; her cheeks colour.

"Oh, Ty," she said at length. "I'm sorry"—and I remember how appalled, how laden with personal guilt she made it sound, as if it were the cause more than the effect that she regretted.

"Romero's a fool," I said. "He'll come to his senses in time. Meanwhile he's like a dog worrying the only bone in sight. Don't concern yourself on my account." I laid my hand on hers again, but there was no response. "And don't tell him anything you don't want to. What he expects from me is an alibi, independent witnesses—the usual thing. That's the irony of it."

"What are you going to do?"

I shrugged, "At least *you* know it wasn't me."

"I will tell him so."

"He won't believe you, Ilsa. Not in his present mood."

We were quiet for a while and I could tell that her attentions were elsewhere—wandering in the maze where my news had brought her. I had trodden the same paths throughout the night and could almost trace the circling course of her thoughts.

"What time is it?" she asked suddenly.

"Ten-ten. The car's outside : there's no hurry."

But she was restless and wanted to go. In the car, she said : "Is that all Romero is doing?—just checking on you?"

"Last night it was. He's obsessed by the fact that I had a motive."

Without warning her self-control left her : her hands went to her face and she cried. "Oh God," she sobbed. "What's happened? What's happened suddenly?"

I wanted to bite off my tongue. "Ilsa," I said. "Ilsa."

I doubt if she heard me or felt my touch, but every shudder of her shoulders seemed to carry along my arm and reverberate in my heart. By the time we reached Romero's office she had recovered, but her eyes were raw. We had six or seven minutes to spare and we waited in silence while she fiddled nervously with mirror and handkerchief. Silence was best : I had run out of words.

Eventually, when she'd put her dark glasses back on, I said : "Ready now?" and she nodded.

The smell of must greeted us. In the sunless light by the barrier I spoke to the duty-sergeant. He nodded curtly; opened the pass-gate. I was about to follow Ilsa through but he raised his hand.

"Not you, señor."

"Why not?"

"I have been instructed."

"The lady doesn't speak Spanish," I protested. "Someone needs to be with her."

"Captain Romero has made the necessary arrangements."

"I should like to see him, please."

"He is unobtainable at present."

"Not here, d'you mean?"

"Here, but unobtainable."

I could have struck him for the relish with which he delivered it. "It's no good, Ilsa. Romero wants you on your own. He's got someone with him who'll translate." I pressed against the barrier. "I'll wait for you. I'll wait in the Bar Sinbad."

"All right."

The sergeant said : "Come with me, please," and started along the cooridor.

"Ilsa."

She glanced back wearily, yet with a willingness that implied a continuing need of me. "Yes?"

"Try not to be hurt by anything Romero says. We'll get to the truth one day, even if we have to do it ourselves."

For a moment I thought she was going to speak. But in the end all she did was nod, gravely, as if filled with a sudden resolve. I watched her follow the sergeant to Romero's door and go in. Then I turned from the barrier and walked, blinking, into the sunlight, feeling like a deserter.

The Bar Sinbad was diagonally across the square : I drove round and parked the car under a dusty plane tree. Joaquin greeted me almost as soon as I'd sat at one of the outside tables.

"Good morning, Mister Tyler. How are you today?" I wasn't in the mood to give an English lesson and didn't answer. He said : "The book goes bad?"

"It's not the book."

"No?"

I could just see the entrance to the Civil Guard headquarters between the trees. "Bring me a coffee, will you, Joaquin?"

"With milk?"

"Black."

He found a reason to dust the cloth with his napkin. "I have read Wordsworth." (He pronounced it "reed".)

"Good for you."

He must have thought I doubted him, for he declaimed :

> *"A primrose by a river's brim*
> *A yellow primrose was to him,*
> *And it was nothing more—*

That is beautiful, Mister Tyler. Very much beautiful."

"I'm glad you like it." I thought : Romero can't keep her long. Half an hour at most, surely. . . .

"What is a primrose?"

"A flower."

"In Spanish."

"Primrose? . . . I'm sorry, Joaquin, but I don't honestly know."

94

"Even so it is beautiful," Joaquin insisted loyally.

"Yes." She ought to be out by eleven, I thought.

"Coffee with milk?"

"Without," I said. "*Negro.*"

He went away. Pigeons pecked in the gutters. A coach-load of tourists went by, heading for The White Caves. A nun left the street and came to my table, collecting for the poor. She was young, her face unlined, her smile of thanks innocently generous, and I envied her with sudden intensity because she would never know another person's body; would never be shared.

"Black coffee, Mister Tyler—and a Fundador."

"I only asked for coffee."

"The Fundador is with the compliments of Joaquin. You look like coffee is not enough."

It pleased him that I should take it. "*Salud.*"

He said: "The señora is with Captain Romero?"

"How d'you know that?" I was more sharp than I realized.

He bent his knees a little until his head was level with mine; nodded through the planes. "I see you both come in the car. Both go in. Only you come out." He spread his hands disarmingly. "There is no magic, Mister Tyler. Only what I see."

I looked at my watch and was dismayed to find that it wasn't even ten-forty.

"It was bad about Señor Scheele," Joaquin said. The tables he served were empty: there was no one to take him away. "Very, very tragical."

I couldn't be bothered to correct him. I had forgotten that I hadn't been to the Bar Sinbad since the Monday night and was vaguely discomfited to realize that the last Joaquin had seen of me was elbowing my way out of the place after punching Scheele in the chest.

"There is much talk now about the Lareo Dam." He depressed the corners of his lips. "A scandal, maybe."

"So I've heard."

Waiters have a natural capacity for concealment. I often wondered, when we talked together, how much knowledge Joaquin held back. As always, his long El Greco face was no guide.

"It is a terrible thing for the señora. For him to be there on that day!" He clucked his tongue. "On that very day. Ayee —that is bad."

"Mister Scheele was a great sight-seer." The dark doorway across the square remained empty. I remembered Ilsa's words: "Every brick, every stone. . . ."

"What is there to see at Gondra? It was a forgotten place before the waters came—not even on the maps." Joaquin raised his hands chest-high; started moving them forward towards a point of collision. "How is it called in English, Mister Tyler, when this happens?" My frown made him continue: he moved his hands once more. "I do not mean accident. I mean English for: What makes accident?"

"Chance. . . . Fate."

He selected "Chance"; sampled it out loud.

Chance was an animal which killed when it was hungry; I remembered the phrase from somewhere.

"Kismet, if you like." I thought: The Moor in you should know that.

I glanced through the plane trees; looked at my watch. Ten forty-six. Time was playing its malicious tricks again.

Joaquin cleared his throat, came nearer. "The señora," he began. "You think she would like the ring back?"

"What ring?"

"Señor Scheele's ring."

I stiffened slightly. For the first time in days I felt a tremor of excitement. But I didn't look up.

"It was stolen," I said guardedly.

"I believe."

"There were other things stolen, too. A watch and a lighter."

He queried. "Lighter?"

"*Un mechero*. Talk in Spanish," I said.

"I know only of the ring."

"What became of the other things?"

"I think they were sold."

"To whom?"

"That I don't know." He flipped at a fly. "It is regretted."

"Who sold them?"

"A friend of mine."

"And this same friend has the ring?"

"I am told."

Just when I least wanted it to happen he was summoned to a nearby table. I waited impatiently, trying to recall what Scheele had told me on the night of the theft. He'd suspected the hotel staff, and I wondered whether Joaquin's friend was another waiter. A car drew up outside the Civil Guard building and a man got out; disappeared through the door. The guard on duty rested his rifle between his legs and leaned against the wall: his hat was designed for the purpose.

Ilsa had been there twenty minutes now. . . .

Joaquin returned; bribed me with another brandy. "You think the señora will be interested?"

"I expect it will depend on the price."

"There is no price."

"Either your friend's a sentimentalist or he doesn't know gold when he sees it."

"I can't answer for him. But I know he will return it if it would please the señora."

"You're taking a big risk," I said. "Captain Romero would be very interested. I could report you."

"You'd never do that, señor." His features crinkled sympathetically. "Besides, you are in sufficient trouble as it is."

I raised an eyebrow; paused. "This mysterious friend of yours, Joaquin. You can trust me."

"I've never doubted it."

"Do I know him?"

"From about three months ago."

It was easier to ask than to rack my brains. "Who is he, then?"

Joaquin lowered his voice. "Luis Zavella, señor. You remember him?"

Yesterday, to Romero, I had denied knowledge of Zavella, but only to save time. There had been no ulterior motive.

Yes, I remembered him : we had met at the Villa Miramar, though it wasn't an orthodox encounter. The novel had entered one of its periodic bad patches. Late one evening, after a particularly abortive day, I walked the beach for an hour or more, hoping that—as so oftens happens—the difficulties would somehow resolve themselves if I gave them their head. It was a warm, cloudless night with a waxing moon which cast shadows as strong and clear-cut as many a spring day's in England. Bandaques pulsed brightly : to the left of the promontory, far out, a liner moved—as compact and remote as the Pleiades.

Around nine, I started back towards the house. No lights were on and its moon-washed walls gave it an unreal, two-dimensional quality. I approached through the beach-gate, crossed the garden and mounted the steps to the terrace. There was no sound except for the rhythmic wash of the sea : everything was rigidly still, duplicated in patterns of blue shade. But when I was only a few yards from the door an unidentified noise made me pause. I waited, head cocked, wondering if it would be repeated. Seconds later it was and I realized that someone had coughed inside the house. It was a man's cough, dry and rasping, and as far as I could judge it came from the living-room.

I was wearing sandals and had therefore moved quietly, but I was quieter still as I edged to the wall beside the door. There was a tightness in my chest and the moonlight seemed to bounce with the thump of my heart. I dared not attempt to peer inside lest whoever was there saw my silhouette : in any case the awning was down and the room was in shadow. Just out of reach, close to the typewriter, was a cigarette-lighter designed in imitation of a seventeenth-century flint-lock pistol. Alarmed though I was I couldn't repress a sense of the melodramatic as I crouched down and made a long arm for it. Upright again, flat against the wall, I tensed myself for the only practical course open to me. For a long moment I delayed, rehearsing in my mind exactly what I was going to do : then, sucking in a deep breath, I yanked the door open and flicked on every light in the room.

The man bending over my desk reacted as if he had received an electric shock. He swung round violently, hands jerking wide, and a half-shout, half-grunt came from him. With a prickle of relief I saw that he was unarmed. He remained absolutely motionless, a scarecrow figure, pressed back against the desk as though he'd been impaled.

"What are you doing here?"

My voice shook. I had little confidence in the thing in my hand. I saw his eyes fasten on to it, move rapidly in search of ways of escape, then return to the level of my right hip.

"Who are you? What d'you want?"

Life seemed to re-enter his limbs. His arms fell slackly to his sides and he straightened up, his whole bearing one of sudden resignation.

"Who are you?" I repeated.

"Someone who shouldn't be here."

It was a disconcerting reply, all the more so because it was accompanied by a rueful smile. He was younger than I'd at first thought—about thirty; handsome in a lean, haggard sort of way. Unshaven, hollowed cheeks made him seem older—that, and a hunted look which even the smile didn't succeed in eradicating.

I told him to stand over against the wall and was almost surprised when he obeyed. He moved on the balls of his feet, as easily as a cat.

"What's your name?"

"Does it matter?"

It didn't in the least, but I saw no sense in agreeing with him. "I want to know."

"Luis Zavella."

"Turn your pockets out on the floor."

"It would be a waste of time." He spoke with a natural bravado which was somehow inoffensive.

"Turn them out," I said.

He did so. He wore no jacket; only a blue shirt and corduroy trousers. They yielded little—a few single peseta notes, three chestnuts, a rag of cloth, a small knife with a broken blade, matches, some loose cigarettes. There was nothing belonging to me or to the house. He coughed twice before he was through, a bone-dry cough that arched his back.

"Is that all?"

"I am afraid so." He smiled again, with a sad frankness. "You returned too early, señor. Otherwise I would have made a better showing."

"I've no doubt."

With a shrug of defeat, he said : "I would rather you kept the pesetas than let Captain Romero have them. The cigarettes, too."

"He knows you of old, I suppose."

"By sight only. Not to shake hands with exactly."

He seemed harmless enough; even likeable. I was beginning to feel a little foolish pointing the cigarette-lighter at him. He coughed again. It was an ugly sound and I told him to go to the alcove and pour himself a brandy. He gazed at me doubtfully, eyes watering from the spasm.

"Go on," I said. "There's no trick." Then, impulsively : "This thing isn't a gun, anyhow."

I laid it on the table. He rubbed his slightly hooked nose in astonishment : laughed uneasily. "You are tempting me, señor."

"I shouldn't try anything if I were you."

"On the contrary—if you were me you would."

"Have the brandy first." Mystified, he hesitated. "Go on," I repeated. "And get one for me while you're about it.

Don't worry—I've no intention of phoning the Civil Guard."

Relief eased his features in a way that was disturbing to watch. "What, then?" He was suspicious even of mercy.

"I'd like to talk."

"I am not much of a talker."

"A few questions, that's all."

"What about?"

"You."

"Then I can go?" He was still slightly incredulous.

"Yes."

As if it explained everything, he said: "I am Luis Zavella."

"So you told me. Where d'you live?"

"Here—there." He moved his hands to great effect. "Many places."

"What d'you do?"

"It depends."

"On what?"

"On how hungry I am."

"Are you married?"

"No." The cough shook him again, but he smiled when it left him. "I am nothing, señor. Just a thief. Not worth your while."

"Were you never anything else?"

"A boy. Long ago."

He turned from me, as if hurt by a memory, and went to the alcove; poured the brandies. Close-to, when he handed me mine, I could see that he was ill. There was a sickly pallor beneath the gipsy skin.

"*Salud,*" he said, dark eyes holding my gaze. "And my thanks. You are a strange man."

"Strange?"

"Captain Romero would never forgive you if he could see us now."

"I'll probably never even meet the gentleman."

"Then you are lucky."

Clinically, I said : "Will you, d'you think?"

"One day. If it isn't him it will be someone else. Time is an ambush, señor. It wins in the end."

He couldn't relax for long. I tried to keep him talking, wondering what I would learn. Everything is grist to the mill. But he was as tense as an animal in a pen, even though he knew the locks were off. It seemed a cruelty to keep him. After about ten minutes I gave him some food from the refrigerator and showed him to the door.

By way of insurance, I said : "I'm not a fool, Zavella. And I'm not sorry for you. Don't mistake what's happened tonight for kindness. If you ever want to come here again, ring the bell. Understand?"

"Yes, señor." His face was quite green under the moon as he held out a hand. *"Hasta la vista."*

A moment later he was a shadow amongst shadows, only the diminishing sound of his cough marking his route. And I wandered back inside to write a piece about him in my notebook before his image and choice of words lost their clarity.

"Yes," I said to Joaquin. "I remember Zavella."

"He remembers you. He asked me to speak with you— seeing that you know the señora so well."

I could swallow the insinuation. I had needed to deceive only Scheele, and Scheele was dead. Heads turned when Ilsa and I were together—I noticed them now; but while he lived I had been blinkered by my own intent.

I knocked a cigarette from the packet : Joaquin was the quicker with the match. "It stands to reason she'll want the ring back."

"Then I shall tell Luis."

"And I'll get it from you, is that it?"

"I expect."

"When?" I asked.

"It is impossible to say. Perhaps tomorrow. Perhaps in three or four days."

"When did he first make this offer?"

"Yesterday."

"Not before?"

"No."

"He was in town on Saturday night," I said.

"I know. But he never came to me." Joaquin seemed to feel that some explanation was necessary. "Luis is a cousin of mine. I try to help him when I can. He has had a poor life." He paused reflectively; changed his tack. "I should not like you to think that I approve of what he does, señor. In particular I should not like you to think that I enjoy speaking to you in this fashion about Señor Scheele's ring. Yet Luis isn't a bad person at heart."

The plane trees were shedding tiny showers of yellow pollen. A man prodded some indignant turkeys along the pavement with a stick: children splashed in the marble basin of the central fountain. It was eleven o'clock and there was still no sign of Ilsa.

A newcomer snapped his fingers and Joaquin reacted as if jerked by a string. For a brief spell I gave my mind to Zavella, casting back to our meeting, then to the chase after him through the procession and watching crowds. Strangely, I had never thought of him in connection with the robbery: nor when Romero had mentioned his name did I link it with the memory of Scheele's heavy facetiousness at the time of the disturbance. I found it odd and somewhat ironic that he, of all people, should be the culprit. But what fascinated was his wish to return the ring. Why? Because of his reprieve that night at the Villa Miramar? And why only the ring? Had he sold the other things before word reached him of Scheele's death? Was he, in fact, a sentimentalist, regretful suddenly, anxious to make a gesture of amends?

"Joaquin."

"Yes, Mister Tyler." He was free again.

"Stick to Spanish," I said. "I want to get this absolutely straight."

"*Sí, señor.*"

"What did you mean a short while ago when you said that I was in trouble?"

He hesitated sufficiently to give the slight pause significance. "I hear things."

"From over there?" I nodded towards the Civil Guard building.

"Sometimes."

"Captain Romero?"

"Now you are joking, señor."

"Did you hear what sort of trouble I was supposed to be in?"

"Only that you have been interrogated."

"D'you know why?"

He hedged : "For what reason, do you mean?"

"Yes. I mean precisely that."

It seemed a long time before he answered. "I heard it was because of what happened to Señor Scheele."

Watching him, I said : "He was drowned."

He was cautious to the last. "I was told otherwise, señor."

I didn't have a chance to press him. More tables were filling up and he was called away; kept busy for minutes on end. But I had learned enough to want to learn more. The ring was incidental. Overnight and throughout the morning the question-marks about Scheele had worn thin with use, but all at once I sensed there were hints and rumours to be had if I knew where to look for them.

Twice I tried to catch Joaquin's attention. Busy though he was I had the impression that his blindness was deliberate. At long last, as he hurried within earshot, I baited him by ordering another coffee. But before he could bring it I saw Ilsa emerge from the Civil Guard doorway and my preoccupation was broken. I stood up at once and went to meet her, wondering uneasily to what degree Romero had tainted her grief with regret that she and I had ever met.

CHAPTER SIX

I

I BELIEVE I could have forgiven Romero even the idiocy of his session with Ilsa had I not felt that the very nature of his probing had made him Scheele's ally.

"Has he finished with you?"

"I think so." With a hardness of tone that I was beginning to fear she added : "I hope so."

We walked in silence to the Bar Sinbad. Pigeons scattered, clapping away over the trees. Hardly had we sat down than Joaquin arrived with my coffee. I indicated that it was for Ilsa; ordered another. He was impassively attentive—just another waiter whose world was peopled by strangers, who practised his English and apparently never went to bed.

"Who translated, Ilsa?"

"A man from the Berlitz School." She removed her sunglasses and her eyes confirmed the set of her lips. Confusion, distress, self-reproach—at that moment I read her like a book. I should have known how impossible it is to compete with the dead.

"Was it all about me?" ("Us," I nearly said, but it would have implied no injustice, and injustice was one of the few weapons I thought I had left.)

"Mostly." She accepted a cigarette : shook her head slowly. "I told him again and again that I was with you all that day, but he wouldn't listen. He was like someone hitting a nail into a wall—on and on. It was all so stupid." She clenched her free hand so that the knuckles whitened. "Stupid and cruel."

I said gently : "I warned you, Ilsa."

"He's even had your woman in—"

"Catalina?"

She nodded. "He thinks you gave her a free day on Tuesday for some other reason." She faltered near the end, but finished the sentence. You weren't always ashamed, I thought. But I said : "He's crazy."

"First it was about the trouble here on Monday night; then about Tuesday—where you were, what you did." She couldn't keep the cigarette still. "He isn't interested in Erich. Not really. He is only interested in trying to prove something about you. Erich doesn't matter."

She was bitter, and such was my mood that the complaint seemed not to be levelled against Romero. It wasn't : "Why won't he believe us? Why does he bother himself with you?"—but : "Why did you ever come to blows with Erich? Why did we spend that day as we did?" The true depths of another's grief are impossible to plumb. But I was despairing enough—and therefore sensitive enough—to suspect that it was me she resented. Without me Romero had no power to hurt—and the dead are blameless anyhow; to be murdered is the ultimate injustice. Even so, I said : "I'll give him another twenty-four hours. If he hasn't retracted by then I'm going to my Consulate in Barcelona."

She wasn't really listening. Momentarily exasperated, I thought : You can't live with a ghost. You can't sleep with it, eat with it, talk with it. You betrayed his body when it was yours : why pine for it now?

Joaquin brought the second coffee, slipped the bill-ticket under the saucer with the air of someone leaving a message. I picked it up, turned it over, and the newly-enlisted conspirator in me was put out to find that it bore nothing except the price. Zavella's offer to return the ring hadn't left the surface of my mind, but I had decided to say nothing about it to Ilsa. In her present state the mere mention of it would only have anchored her to Scheele all the more : in any case I wanted to clear the ground of all possibility of disappointment by first having the ring in my possession. Achievement weighs heavier in the scales than any promise.

We talked spasmodically. Soon we were treading old

ground, bogged down amongst the question-marks. It was getting us nowhere and I said as much. For a moment I thought I had hurt her again; added quickly: "You must know I'm right, Ilsa. At least Romero's got a wall to hit his nail into: we haven't got either."

She lifted her chin defiantly.

"It was an accident," I went on. "It *must* have been. A friend of mine—at home, this was—once got some pellets shot into his legs when he was out walking. He could easily have been killed. Mistakes like that *do* happen; dreadful mistakes. . . . Either that, or Erich put up a fight when someone tried to rob him. Whoever it was might have panicked and cleared off—or even been caught by the dam-burst himself. For all we can tell he was killed, too."

Only a couple of hours earlier these had been her own be-wildered guesses, but they no longer seemed to satisfy her. They didn't entirely satisfy me either, but I reiterated them now for the same reason that I withheld my information about the ring. I had no remorse; nothing to avenge. But it was conceivable that I might discover something pertinent if I kept my eyes and ears open. Might: I put it no stronger than that. . . . One becomes more calculating the harder one fights; more dishonest.

"It's not knowing that's so terrible," she said. "Not being sure."

"Perhaps we'll never know. It's a possibility you've got to face."

"I couldn't bear to think that."

Close-to, I heard a woman say: "That's Stephen Tyler, there—with the blonde. She's the one whose husband—" The voice stopped abruptly when I turned my head. Blue-rinsed hair, spectacles decked with diamante, thin, dissatisfied lips—she hadn't the courage to brazen out the hatred of my look. She dropped her eyes and her face coloured. Mean-while her companion was still asking: "Where, Gloria? *Who* did you say? . . ."

I wasn't sure whether Ilsa had also heard; desperately hoped she hadn't. But I wasn't mistaken. There was no end to Scheele's allies. Almost immediately, she said, "Let's go, Ty."

"Of course." Then, as we were getting into the car: "What d'you want to do?"

"I just don't want to be in a cage, that's all."

I avoided the coast-road past the villa, the area of the dam, the hills where we had found the waterfall. For once I was scrupulously fair. Sometimes, on the sharper bends, the centrifugal tug pulled us together, dragged us joylessly apart, and I ached for her as much as if she had teased me. The road was white and dusty. To either side, above terraced shelves of red earth, above mottled patches of chestnut and fir, the hills stood bare and crumpled against the sky. An occasional village broke the lower patterns of almond and olive and the bright strips of young green wheat laid between rows of citrus trees. But I was impervious to beauty. Scheele was present in the car as surely as if he rode with us in reality and I knew, without Ilsa having to tell me, that her mind was filled with the dull, wordless images of the past.

It was a week almost to the hour since we had first met and it frightened me to think how small was my claim on her when measured in time and personal knowledge. In the happiness of Monday and Tuesday I had told myself that we would come to learn about each other later, gradually, when it suited us. Passion is self-sufficient. The botanist destroys the flower he dissects : instinctively, I suppose, one shrinks from delving too deeply or too soon. One needs days, weeks—years, even : and Scheele had cut ours short almost as soon as they'd begun. Without effort I could describe the texture of her hair and the feel of her soft, brushing mouth; recall the exact timbre of her laugh, the strength of her small-boned wrists, the intricate whorl of her navel. Dry sherry, paella, filter-cigarettes, black coffee without sugar—I could have made a list of some of her preferences. From

Hamburg, about thirty, eight years married, fond of swimming, reasonably read, little travelled. . . . After that the enormous blank spaces began. Love is a privileged condition and not an ability to compile a catalogue: yet, jealously, I knew that Scheele would have been able to fill in every gap. Four thousand days against my seven. . . .

She rubbed salt into the wound by starting to speak more freely of him. I suppose she was trying to re-shape the old questions; make sense where none existed. But it was hard to take. Once she said: "Erich didn't find friends easily. But he didn't have an enemy in the world—not that kind of enemy." And, later: "He was excited when the Barcelona business came up. He'd never been to Spain. For weeks he had been talking about it and looking at his maps." Each utterance was like the disjointed revelations of a person with fever whose thoughts now and again flow over into words. Why tell me, I thought, unless you deliberately mean to hurt? Do you despise yourself so? Another time she said: "You met him when he was at his worst. We didn't always get along, but he was never in the mood he was here. He seemed to hate everything about Spain when we arrived— why, I don't know. He wouldn't say." And, finally: "He wasn't always a salesman. Most of his life he was a soldier. I didn't know him then, of course, but I don't think he found it easy to be out of uniform."

What did I care what he was?

I turned for Bandaques at a T-junction. Until then it hadn't dawned on me that we were being followed, but the blue Simca which had quivered in the rear-view mirror for the past quarter of an hour was beginning to make itself a little too obvious. Romero's persistent nonsense angered me and I swore at him under my breath: Haven't you anything better to do? Can't you forget Scheele either?

It was almost one o'clock before the saffron tower of the Church of the Incarnation came into view. When I mentioned food Ilsa protested that she wasn't hungry, but I insisted on her having something. We went to one of the fish restaurants near the amphitheatre where we had not been seen together before. The Simca cruised past while I was trying to park. There were two Civil Guards in it and I sounded my horn at them. Ilsa ate sparingly, immersed in thought. Impossible though it was I longed for one flash of her former self; one renewal of recognition of me. The nearest she came to it was when, as the meal was ending, she said : "You've been a tremendous help, Ty. I don't know what I would have done without you." And somehow it pained me more than if she had remained silent : even if she had looked at me, touched my arm, the acknowledgement wouldn't have seemed so dutifully sterile.

"Tell me what you've decided about the funeral, Ilsa." I was reduced to offering good deeds. "I'll help all I can."

"I will have to see a priest."

"Are you going to have Erich buried here?"

She nodded.

"What about informing your Consul? That may be necessary. In any case he'll be able to advise you."

"I'll ask the priest." Her voice was stone cold. "He will know what I should do."

Without thinking, I said : "But he'll be a Catholic. There isn't—"

"Erich was a Catholic."

"I see." How little I knew : how much of a stranger I was. "Is that what you are, Ilsa?"

"Yes."

I said lamely : "I won't be much help to you there, I'm afraid."

"Perhaps you would take me."

"To the church?"

"Yes."

"Of course. When d'you want to go?"

"As soon as you are ready."

I paid the bill and we left. Whether we were followed again I didn't know—or care. We could have walked, comfortably, but I took the car and sounded my way along a succession of sunless, slot-like streets. Strings of laundry hung across the narrow carriageways : canned music blared from balconied windows. Two days earlier we would have joked about it, pretended that we were part of some triumphant procession, waved at the faces peering down at us. But now we said nothing; looked straight ahead. Scheele was with us still, insisting on being remembered, excluding me with the sheer weight of all the days that I had never shared; labelled in a way that she, and not I, could understand.

The Church of the Incarnation stood on the very edge of the promonotory, fronted by a spacious semi-circle of sprinkled lawns. Concrete paths converged on the tiled area in front of the huge west door. Ilsa paused for a moment as we left the car and stared up at the sombre Baroque façade : clouds moved behind the tower so that it seemed to be about to fall. She borrowed a handkerchief and covered her head before we went in. The intense gloom of Spanish churches invariably takes me by surprise. A sepulchral quiet wrapped itself around us : fully half a minute elapsed before either of us could see properly. Shafts of light, stale with incense, leaned in through lofty windows. The interior slowly took shape : small, furtive sounds began to emerge—the soft slap of sandalled feet, a low murmuring, the abacus click of beads. We were not alone. A galaxy of candles burned before the gaudy figure of the Virgen de la Tarde, each flame as firm as a bud in the lifeless air. Her feet were worn by the touch of the superstitious and a man with the face of a Moor knelt in front of her like a slave. Except that his lips moved he might have been taken for another statue, and I remember thinking : You didn't drive them out after all.

The high altar was draped in green; backed by an ornate, carved reredos. Some women were cleaning the floor by the altar rails, above which was suspended an enormous twisted effigy of the crucified Christ. A group of tourists clustered round a guide near one of the side altars; his bored, machine-gun monotone reached us like a prayer. In the afternoon they would go to The White Caves; to the Bar Sinbad in the evening. They would have "done" Bandaques by tomorrow and be writing their postcards elsewhere.

Ilsa and I moved down the aisle towards the sanctuary. A priest rounded a pillar by a battery of curtained confessional boxes and I stopped him.

"Can you spare me a moment?"

"Certainly." His chin was as loose-jowled as a turkey's; his eyes weary with sad amazement at the world's indifference. "What is it?"

"This lady's husband was killed the other day and she wants to arrange about his funeral."

He peered. "I see." Death was a commonplace. "She is not Spanish?"

"No."

My manner was obviously alien to him. "Are you a Catholic, señor?"

"The lady is. Her husband was, too. He was killed when the Lareo Dam broke the other day."

"The German?" He read the papers, then; wasn't entombed as one might have supposed.

"That's right. I've come with her because she doesn't—"

"I speak a little German."

He took Ilsa aside; engaged her in question and answer. With my handkerchief knotted under her chin her face was like a child's—trusting and obedient. I was disconcerted by the suddenness with which I had been made an onlooker. An old woman genuflected in front of the altar; blessed herself. Another kissed a candle as if it were a lucky charm and lit it from one of many others that honoured a grotesque saint. A notice on the first of the confessionals announced that the priest whose cubicle it was spoke French and German. There were more notices on some of the other boxes: Polish, I saw: Italian, English. Only if one came from some unlikely extremity could one apparently escape the net.

Interrupting, I said to Ilsa: "Is there anything you'd like me to do?"

"No, thank you, Ty."

"How long will you be?"

"It is difficult to say."

"Shall I wait?"

"You'd better not. I may be some time."

"Where shall I meet you, then? At the España? About six?"

"Yes," she nodded. "Make it at the España."

The priest gestured towards a side door and she went away with him, as close as a prisoner. Everything and everyone was pulling on Scheele's end of the rope. I waited a while, staring about me at the esoteric trappings of faith that could help to bring about my defeat. One mocks, I suppose, out of envy. At any rate, I looked up at the effigy on the cross which presided over the great vault where I stood and, with spite, thought : You, too.

2

It was glaringly bright outside. A beggar came, pleading with a toothless gargoyle grin as I paused when the sun hit me. I bought him off and made for the car before others followed suit. One of the tourists, a Cockney with an open-necked shirt who looked like a boxer, was saying indignantly to a woman : "I warned you, didn't I? It was that Vim rouge with your dinner. It's not like beer, you know."

I hadn't counted on having the afternoon to myself. For a while I thought of returning to the Bar Sinbad and taking up with Joaquin where I had left off. But something he had said earlier in the day gave me another idea : I would go to Gondra. A remembered phrase is sometimes like a key to a code. At the time it may do no more than arouse a mild curiosity, but on reflection one realizes that, without it, one might have continued to puzzle in vain. Joaquin had said : "What is there at Gondra? It was a forgotten place even before the waters came—not even on the maps."

Not even on the maps. . . .

Sitting in the car, I checked : as far as mine was concerned he was right. All along I had assumed that sheer chance had taken Scheele to Gondra. I was still ready to think so—until I recalled that he had told Ilsa he was going there; had named it in advance. . . . All right, then : he knew it existed. Was that so mysterious? He could have heard of it : his map could have been older than mine. There were several possible explanations and there was no point in wondering which was the most likely. But no harm would come of my following in his tracks. I had three hours to kill. Before long I would probably be able to say : "Ilsa, I've managed to get hold of Erich's ring." If only I could also say : "I've got an idea how he might have died" perhaps it would help to lay his ghost for ever.

Mildly curious, then, I headed in the direction of the Lareo Dam. I left Bandaques by a deliberately circuitous route, not wanting Romero on my tail if he were still that way inclined. A newspaper illustration on the day after the dam's collapse had shown me roughly where Gondra was—or, rather, where its shell had once been. Almost anywhere except in Spain there would have been coach-parties busily ferrying back and forth : the more orderly the way of life, the more morbid is the fascination in disaster. But the road to the dam was totally deserted. *Lo que sera, sera.* There was suffering enough.

It was said locally that God had made the area to the south and west of the town when He had finished shaping the rest of the earth and was tired. The hills reared up, gaunt and barren, burned dry again after the days'-long deluge. Within ten minutes I had entered another world, savagely desolate and deformed. Scheele would have come this way, staring about him, noting, no doubt, the complete absence of trees, the heat-split sandstone bluffs that towered like fortress walls, the dust-green explosions of cactus. Five minutes later a newly-erected board proclaimed that it was prohibited to continue southwards, but I ignored it and went on. Six or seven miles to my left the sea looked as smooth as a sheet of smoked glass : over the same shoulder Bandaques was like a festering scar, all yellows and whites. The road kept going mad, seeking a way to surmount the next ridge, descend the next slope. Bandaques and the sea presently disappeared and I knew that I was getting near. A little further on, I remembered, was a particularly vicious hairpin, after which there was a level run of about a kilometre before I could expect to see any signs of devastation.

I took the hairpin cautiously, in low gear. I was busy straightening out when a Civil Guard stepped into the road from behind a clump of prickly-pear and signalled at me to stop. The following wave of dust drifted over him as he approached the car. He turned his head sideways, screwing his eyes. As it cleared, I said innocently : "What's wrong?"

"Didn't you see the notice back there?" He cleared his throat.

"No."

Then he spat. "You couldn't have missed it."

"I must have done. Either that or I didn't understand what it said."

"You speak Spanish well enough." He wasn't too sure of himself with a foreigner. "Anyway, you'll have to turn back. The road is closed."

"I don't want to go much further."

"You can't, even if it were permitted. It's impossible. Further on there's a hundred metres of nothing." He squinted at me dubiously. "Where are you from?"

"Bandaques."

"Well, then"—which was another way of saying : "You know what happened, so have some sense."

"I'm not going to the dam at all. I'm trying to get to Gondra."

He whistled with surly amusement. "You're even more optimistic than I thought. Anyhow, the answer is still no."

"I have Captain Romero's approval."

His expression changed. "*You* have?"

"Yes."

"In writing?"

"He said it wasn't necessary." The lies came easily; gave me a degree of malicious pleasure. "I have a personal interest in what happened here. Captain Romero suggested that I came out and saw for myself."

"I see," the guard muttered slowly. He glanced round as if wishing he had a companion with whom to confer. "The captain has given his authority?" He wanted to hear me say it again.

"I've told you."

He paused, then took the plunge. "Very well." I felt a little sorry for him. His hands came into play. "Gondra is about two kilometres downstream of the broken dam. There's a side road leading off a couple of hundred metres from where we are now. The junction is a bit overgrown, but you'll hardly miss it. But I doubt if the road exists any more once it drops over into the valley. It's like a pig's trough down there. You won't be able to use your car."

"I'll take it to the junction." I flattered him. "Is that all right?"

"Certainly, señor." The "señor" was an innovation. He stood back; actually smiled. "But rather you than me."

I drove on. Sprouts of cactus flanked the badly-metalled surface. I couldn't remember having seen the fork whenever I had been this way before, but it was easily enough found now that I was looking for it. Presumably Gondra had once been served by a proper road, but all that was left was a double-wheel track with a central hump. I followed it just long enough to get the car out of sight from the highway, then started to walk. The heat bounced off the rocks with implacable intensity and there was a silence that always seems to accompany fierce sunlight. For a time the area of the dam remained hidden from me and only the ragged upper levels of the opposite wall of the valley were visible. But gradually, as the track pointed downwards, the trough began to open up and I had my first glimpses of what the waters had done. My imagination had led me to expect a more dramatic revelation. True, the narrow valley floor was scoured redder than blood; weirdly strewn with boulders and pock-marked with sodden craters. But from high up it was an almost peaceful scene which somehow failed to communicate the sense of vast and fearful violence. Nature has a way of belittling itself; its cataclysms often need some man-made yardstick to give them understandable proportions. And it was only when I saw what remained of the Lareo Dam that I grasped more fully what must have happened when the waters suddenly took over.

Virtually nothing remained of the dam's lofty curve. A huge V, jagged yet curiously symmetrical, had been driven through the massively thick concrete as contemptuously as if it were an egg-shell. The bottom-most point of the V continued to leak a reddish dye on to mounds of smashed masonry. At the top, left and right, I could see the midget silhouettes of men loosely grouped on the out-jutting sections of road : there was a mobile crane up there, too, its arm like a twig against the sky. One thing dwarfed another, giving perspective to the immensity of the forces that had found liberation.

The track continued its gentle descent, slavishly following the contours, and the trench broadened a little. The sickly odour of drying mud began to hang like a vapour on the quivering air. Looking across the valley I could see that a livid stain had been deposited along the rocky slopes—an uneven veneer which in places still glistened. Here and there huge chunks of sandstone had been ripped away, leaving caves like gaping eye-sockets. Sometimes the line of discoloration rose fiercely upwards like a wave, ten or fifteen feet higher than elsewhere : sometimes there were freakish piles of detritus trapped by an outcrop.

Without warning the track disappeared and I found myself shoe-deep in slime. Almost immediately I passed a thrush impaled on a broken cactus spike, and because I imagined it to have been caught in flight by a leaping tongue of water I could picture the terrifying speed at which the flood-head must have thundered seawards. The mud deepened. Twice I slipped; twice nearly quit and returned to the car. But always, at the back of my mind, was the question : What possessed Scheele to come here? Even when the track had been negotiable it could have promised little—a ruin, a barren view; no more. What was so special about a place that was empty and forgotten before the valley was so savagely flushed out? When was it left to rot? And why? Every question bred another. Even so, despite my curiosity, when I slipped a third time I would have given up my quest as a bad job and gone home but for the fact that, as I got to my feet, I saw what could only be Gondra about a quarter of a mile away. It was merged into the blood-red landscape of the side of the valley as surely as if it had been camouflaged : what gave it away was the regularity of its broken outline—an unmistakable geometry of shapes and angles.

I squelched nearer. From the first I had supposed that Gondra was some ancient settlement—Roman, perhaps. The Mediterranean coast of Spain is littered with them and occasionally the Spaniard seemed to grow tired of the less noteworthy, abandoning interest in them for a few generations at a stretch. But this place had no great antiquity; had been just another village. Even the mud couldn't obliterate the character and pattern of what remained. The few thick walls that still stood were those which had been end-on to the flood—here part of a house, there an archway; the outline of a narrow street, a small central square; stumps of pillars which indicated the position of a tiny church. Broken buildings evoke a special kind of melancholy. People had lived here—married, wept, died, prayed, gossiped, copulated, danced; won favours from an unwilling soil. How many people?—two or three hundred? There could hardly have been more. Now a lizard ran like a spurt of green flame : flies swarmed on the carcass of a dead rat. Life somehow always goes on. Mud filled every crevice; swelled the base of every upright. Sometimes it was like walking in glue. Now and again I went in up to my ankles, and each sucking step seemed to release its quota of trapped stench. I could have kicked myself for coming : all I had done was to ruin a pair of shoes and foul my clothes. Scheele's Mercedes had been found some distance further on, so it was probable that he had driven this far : yet, for all I knew, he had also felt like kicking himself as he wandered in disappointment through the desolation. And then what had happened? I was no nearer to an answer. If there were any clues in Gondra they were inches deep in slime or, like Scheele, had been swept away. Mine weren't the only footprints : others had been here before me—search parties, soldiers, the Civil Guard; God knows who. I was wasting my time.

After some minutes I couldn't stand the smell any longer. I was in what I imagined had been the square. Two or three shattered sections of wall—none of them more than shoulder-high—still remained. The framework of what might have been a communal well was silted right over so that it looked like a lump of raw material on a potter's wheel. I plodded past it, stumbling on a hidden rock, feeling the warm wet stickiness seeping inside my shoes. One of the bespattered walls was plastered a greenish blue and had something written on it—or at least I thought it was writing. I noticed it quite by accident. Curiosity dies hard : I took a stick and scraped the thin coating of mud away. R, I saw, then RÁ, then RÁN. The black paint had worn pale with age, but was still quite clear. I worked to the left, using the stick with both hands. PASARÁN . . . NO PASARÁN. There was nothing in front of the first N. With some excitement I moved to the right and scraped again. The defiant phrase was repeated—NO PASARÁN, except that the stonework splintered to an end across the last letter. My hands might have been bleeding as I stood back and looked at the faded slogans which had survived sun and wind and rain and flood. There had been no need to uncover the repetition. As soon as the two words were readable I had known approximately how long they had been there and when Gondra had died. No one in Spain had scrawled THEY WILL NOT PASS for more than twenty years.

I scraped lower, nearer the base of the wall, and a second phrase slowly gave itself up. TODO O NADA. . . . ALL OR NOTHING. I felt the sadness of the place as never before. All or nothing. . . . For whoever had lived here it had been nothing.

Nothing. *Nada.* . . .

It was as if a light came on in my mind. *Nada.* . . . All at once I remembered Scheele in the Bar Sinbad on the night before he was to die. "*Nada,*" the whisky had made him say. "For them it was *nada.*" And there and then suspicion was born in me that he had been to Gondra more than once.

3

The Civil Guard on the road grinned when he saw me. "I warned you, señor. Was it worth it?"

"I think so."

I drove towards Bandaques, strangely elated. At the first hotel I came to I stopped and went in. The man at the reception desk glanced at my shoes and trouser-legs with undisguised disapproval.

"D'you understand German?"

He gave a prompt, if unimpressive, sample. "*Ja wohl.*"

"I don't, so I'd appreciate your help. . . . I may have got this wrong. Can you tell me what is the meaning of '*hier haben wir wonnen*'?"

"*Hier haben wir wonnen?*"

"Something like that."

"*Wonnen,*" he muttered. "*Wonnen.* . . Are you certain the last word is '*wonnen*'?"

"I'm not certain about any of it."

"*Wonne?*" he offered. "No, it couldn't be. . ." Then he

120

snapped his fingers. "*Gewonnen.* Could you mean '*hier haben wir gewonnen*'?"

"Possibly. What's that in Spanish?"

"We won here."

It made electrifying sense. "We won here?"

"That's right. But—"

"We won here," I repeated; paused for a moment while it sank in. Then : "I'm very grateful."

He was baffled. "I don't understand, señor—"

"A friend of mine asked me to inquire," I laughed off the explanation. "Don't ask me why. Thank you again."

Memory is rarely flawless or obliging : that afternoon mine was both. Names frequently escape me within minutes of my hearing them, and I have sometimes searched all day for an elusive word. Yet on the slushy trudge out of the valley I recalled "*hier haben wir gewonnen*" without effort and with passable accuracy. Scheele had murmured it the evening we first met, when his anger over the theft had been damped down and his speech had become slurred. "They forget," he'd said. Then, confidentially : "*Hier haben wir gewonnen.*"

"We won here . . ." His unending contempt at last took on meaning. Obedience, authority, respect—"we had it once." On the hateful night after his visit to Barcelona his complaint was : "I've been dealing with little men; men without memories. Some people don't mind humiliating themselves, but I am not that kind—least of all here." To have been the victor and no longer to be acknowledged; to be reduced to bargaining with the vanquished—this was what had galled him. He had returned to find that the one monument which stood amid the ruins of his own subsequent defeat had never even been erected. He was a type-writer salesman, a tourist; nothing more. I could remember a score of remarks he had made which, at the time, were unintelligible. He wasn't an object of study then and I had not bothered with them, but now I understood their significance. One triggered off another. And it wasn't only what he had said. . . . On our visit to the archaeological museum there had been a couple of show-cases which, with true Spanish incongruity, were devoted to local relics of the Civil War—a charred bible, a miscellany of buttons, bullets and badges, a printed proclamation or two, some fragments of shell. It was a trivial collection but Scheele had given it the same keen attention as everything else—keener, even. In particular he had removed his dark glasses to peer at a yellowed card which identified some jagged shrapnel splinters and shaken his head critically as if he had once more found fault with something. Again, at the time, I had not been sufficiently interested. Now, armed with new knowledge, I realized that it must have been the numerals which had attracted him—probable the calibration details—because he couldn't read Spanish.

I drove home and changed. I had done no more than piece a few half-facts together but I believed I was forging a weapon which I could use on Ilsa. I was quite certain that she was ignorant of what I had discovered. Her bewilderment was absolutely genuine. Scheele had been here before but she didn't know it; couldn't explain his mood. "A soldier once, before I knew him." Everything fitted, given the first fluky clue. . . . I wasn't concerned with who had murdered him; that was Romero's business. But if I couldn't lay his ghost perhaps I could expose it.

It was nearly half-past five. I called in at the Bar Sinbad on my way to the España and spoke to Joaquin. He wasn't busy. I led off in his own tongue to forestall a confusing excursion into English.

"What exactly happened at Gondra, Joaquin?"

"The flood, d'you mean?"

"The other time."

He lifted his shoulders. "It was a long while ago."

"About 1938?"

"It is best forgotten."

"Remember for a moment."

"The place was destroyed."

"In the fighting?"

"People do not talk about it any more, Señor Tyler."

"Was it that bad?"

"The whole war was bad."

"Who destroyed Gondra?"

"The same people who destroyed Spain. But what does it matter now? It was done. Nothing will be changed by thinking about it. We have an old saying: Today's dust is foul enough... D'you understand me?"

I nodded. "Tell me something else."

"Of course."

"Were you there?" He would have been about twenty-five then.

"No, thank God. There are very few left who were. The rest—" He let a gesture finish for him.

"The women, too?"

"Everyone, señor. Everyone."

Nobody called him but he walked away; flicked his cloth over some empty tables. I had never seen him moved before. A fish-seller pushed a barrow along the street, blowing a conch shell, and the mournful sound sent the pigeons clapping through the plane trees. Romero emerged from the Civil Guard building and was driven off in his official car. I would get my apology yet—as a bonus. Keep on being blind, I thought. Keep on being stupid.

Joaquin returned. "I am seeing Luis tomorrow about the ring."

'So soon?"

"I will let you have it when you are next here."

"Does he come to you, or is it the other way round?"

"I go to him."

Something urged me to say: "I'd like to accompany you." Zavella's quixotic offer had intrigued me from the first. I suppose it was this that prompted me.

When Joaquin realized I was serious he frowned slightly. "Luis might not want anything like that."

"He's in my debt. It's not much to ask."

He thought for a while, pursing his lips, torn between loyalties. "It would be inconvenient for you, Señor Tyler. Very early in the morning, a long walk, a hard climb. ... It would be better if you got the ring from me here."

"I could pick you up in my car. That would save—"

"No." He was quite sharp. "You would be followed."

"Would be, or have been?"

"Both."

Nothing much escaped him. "I wasn't followed this afternoon," I said.

"They are not always clever. But it would be a risk."

"All right : no car. How, then?"

He sighed. "You are insisting, aren't you, señor?"

"No. Just asking. Between friends."

"Luis will probably never forgive me."

"You make me sound like an enemy."

There was no one near but Joaquin spoke more quietly. "Take the bus which runs to The White Caves—the first bus in the morning from the amphitheatre. It goes at half-past six. Buy a five peseta ride. Go as far as the bridge below the caves."

"And then?"

"I will show you."

"We meet there?" I was an amateur.

"No—I'll be on the bus. But in case we can't sit together it will look better if you know where to get off. I will go on to another stop, then walk back."

"What time will we return to Bandaques?"

"About ten."

"That'll be fine." Already, I felt, he was regretting the arrangement and I thought it best to leave before he changed his mind. "Don't let me down, will you?"

"No, Señor Tyler." As I got up he said : "Why are you so anxious to meet Luis?"

I fobbed him off. "Why does a writer do anything, Joaquin? You ought to know me by now."

The sun was pushing long level rays over the rooftops as I walked into the España. Ilsa was waiting for me in the American Bar.

"Did you get anything arranged?"

"For Saturday," she said. "Saturday morning at eleven."

"Was the priest helpful?"

"He couldn't have been kinder."

We were as polite as if it were a first meeting. She'd received a cable from Scheele's firm offering condolences and assistance : also one from her father.

I paraded my ignorance. "Is he in Hamburg, too?"

"In Munich."

I had made love to her, but others knew the detailed framework of her life : I was on hand, but others were breaking up my monopoly.

She asked : "Where were you this afternoon?"

"Nowhere in particular. I just filled in time."

I had never lied to her before. I longed for her body but to win it I would have to destroy the image in her mind. But not yet; not yet. I wanted the weapon perfected first.

Love, as I knew it that afternoon, had never heard of compassion.

CHAPTER SEVEN

THE INTERIOR of the bus reeked with an accumulation of exhaled garlic. I was one of the first to climb aboard. There were ten minutes to spare and I yawned, shivering slightly, out of touch with so early an hour. I had slept badly; after four scarcely at all. At one time I had come close to changing my mind about wanting to meet Zavella. What did I expect to learn? A quixotic gesture loses its curiosity value when one frets for sleep. But in the hour or so before dawn, when there was clearly no more sleep to be found, I had listened to the turgid pulse of the sea and concentrated my thoughts upon Scheele. What little I had discovered about him had been virtually handed me on a plate: if I wanted more I would have to go looking for it. And I did want more: I wanted a glimpse of whatever it was that had lingered in his memory over so long a period. Joaquin was my only useful contact in Bandaques but I doubted if he could provide me with anything more than background. Scheele had sat unrecognized at his tables; been judged, like any tourist, on the standard of his tipping. He knew a good deal of what went on locally, had his contacts, and presumably fed Zavella with news and gossip from time to time. But somebody who lived by his wits would almost certainly have more sources of information than one. At least, that was what I had convinced myself as the greyness of approaching dawn began to filter into the air. I would go: nothing would be lost by it.

The bus filled slowly. Almost without exception the passengers were men—shabby in faded dungarees and patched corduroy. I guessed most of them to be labourers at the tobacco factory being built to the north-west of the town:

constant exposure to a harsh sun and the resignation that comes of fifty pesetas a day had lined the faces of even the youngest of them. I sat and waited for Joaquin, wondering whether he would acknowledge me or not; then, as time passed, whether he was going to break his promise after all. But a minute before the half hour he clambered in and came to the vacant seat beside me. I had never seen him without white jacket and black tie : he still wore the braided trousers—presumably to facilitate a quick change on his return— but the open-necked shirt and black beret somehow destroyed the El Greco mould of his features. He looked a fraction less pale; less drawn.

In English he said : "That chair is available, señor?"

I indicated assent and he sat down. He had a small brown paper packet with him, tied with string, and might have been a guide on his way to the day's stint at The White Caves. A series of glances round the bus seemed to satisfy him that English gave us complete security.

"Were you followed?"

"Followed? Not that I know of : I walked along the beach. What have you got there?"

"Food."

"You ought to have brought your Wordsworth."

He wasn't in a smiling mood. "I think I will be in trouble about this."

"I'll explain. Don't worry."

He shrugged.

"How long's the ride?"

"Twenty minutes."

The driver and ticket-collector stamped out their cigarettes and left the amphitheatre wall. There was a muttered chorus of greeting from some of the regulars. Doors slammed, the engine fired and we lurched away, the horn blaring as stridently as if the streets had been solid with traffic. Soon we were on the main highway to the northwest; the fringes of the town running squalidly to seed among fig and locust trees. Dawn had come with a bloody froth of cloud. Now the sky was at peace, the colour not yet burned out of it, and one bright abandoned star glittered coolly above the blue mist shrouding the sierras.

Ilsa would still be asleep. The thought of her was as potent and disturbing as ever, but the yearning had lost its simplicity; was undermined with doubts, growing vindictive. Why else was I sitting here with a waiter from the Bar Sinbad? Not because of the ring and whatever merit I had once thought its recovery might earn me. And not in the hope of eventually being able to ease her mind about the manner of Scheele's death. She wasn't alone in having changed: only in desire had I remained constant.

Joaquin and I bought our tickets separately. The collector joked crudely with the pair behind us and a woman across the gangway laughed. The sun flooded warmly in. Every so often the bus stopped to pick someone or other up. Before long there were as many passengers standing as there were sitting and the springs groaned ominously as we rattled over the worst stretches of pot-holes. But at the site of the new factory there was an almost complete exodus and we were left with about half a dozen people for company.

"D'you always come by bus?"

Joaquin said : "It depends where I have to go."

"It varies?"

"Again, please."

"There's more than one place?"

"There are several places. But I never go twice like the last time—you understand?" Presently, he added : "You are doing something not many ever done, Mister Tyler."

It still troubled him, but I found it hard to believe that I was a conspirator : the fact that we had to raise our voices to compete with the rattle and crunch of the bus didn't help.

"Do others go sometimes?"

"I believe."

"Who?"

"Friends."

"What about his family? Don't they ever see him?"

"There is only me."

"No brothers or sisters?"

"He never has these. Me, though—and friends. He has many friends." There was an odd note of pride in his voice.

The road was burrowing into the hills. We stopped at a village. An old man got in carrying a live rabbit: its legs were trussed and he pushed it on to the overhead rack from where it looked down at me with eyes huge with terror. A black dog, all skin and bone, yelped at the bus deliriously as it ground away.

I asked: "How long's he lived like this?"

"Most his life."

"Why? What started it?"

"Ask him, Mister Tyler, not me."

"Did he kill someone?"

"Luis? Never! He has done bad things since, but these are to live. Smuggling, stealing—"

"And he's never been caught?"

"Please?"

"Captured?" I leaned a fraction closer. *"Un preso?"*

"Ah. . . . Once—two years ago. In a village over there"— he pointed vaguely. "But he is free before Captain Romero arrives." As if against his will his mouth shaped a smile. "The captain will never forgive him because already he send a message to his chief and it makes him look a fool."

The rabbit eyed me through the quivering slats of the rack. Nothing lasted—freedom no more than anything else: only death was permanent.

"Has he always been near Bandaques?"

"No. After the war, yes: but later, for a long time, he was somewhere different—where I could not say exactly. Albacete, I think: then Calatayud. Now he is here again for six, seven years. Eight, maybe."

The bus shuddered up a twisting incline. A few thinning scarves of mist hung stubbornly below the slag-tip skyline. I looked at my watch: we had been on the move for over a quarter of an hour. The bridge Joaquin had mentioned wasn't all that far away. A Civil Guard suddenly overtook us on a red and black motor-cycle. Joaquin and I exchanged glances : he was tight-lipped, anxious, even when the motor-cycle had accelerated out of our sight.

He said urgently : "If he is at the bridge do not get out."

I nodded.

"Stay here—in bus." It was a command.

"Very well."

We stopped outside a ruined house and the old man hauled the rabbit off the rack and lowered himself carefully on to the road. A tile set into one of the pillars of the gate bore the legend : GOD PROTECTS. The conductor leaned out and bawled : "Why not take the strings off its legs and race it home?"

I had been watching for the house. The bridge was a couple of steep turns further on, another minute, but it seemed longer before it slid into view. There was no one to be seen and I signalled the conductor that this was where I wanted.

"One for the bridge, Paco," he called to his gaunt companion at the wheel. "One gentleman tired of life."

He was very pleased with himself but nobody else laughed. I squeezed past Joaquin's bony knees and dropped out on to the verge about fifty yards short of the bridge. The driver crashed into gear and the bus trundled off, spewing dust and fumes. As a precaution I left the road as quickly as possible, hauling myself up the high bank; found a place to wait among some thorn bushes. A great tide of quiet flowed in as the sound of the bus diminished; the air was wonderfully clean after the concentration of garlic and rough cigarette-smoke. The bridge spanned a deep gorge. I could see neither from where I sat, but in the other direction a fawn-grey encrustation on the olive and terracotta landscape below marked a distant village. I thought I heard the bus stop and start up again, but my hearing was urban, unattuned. Before long, though, Joaquin's gritty step was unmistakable and I got to my feet; whistled him. He came up the bank with unexpected agility.

I said in Spanish : "So far, so good."

"That guard had me worried." His eyes wandered over the hills behind my back.

"He looked to me as if he'd got something else on his mind."

"You never know." He hadn't relaxed one bit.

"Where do we go from here?"

"Follow me."

He led off up the slope. There was low scrub and loose shale; an occasional stunted tree bent by winds which, that morning, refrained. Everything was quite still and a light dew glistened in the flawless sunshine. Sometimes there was a narrow track, sometimes not. The gorge was visible for a time and when I last saw the bridge it looked like a thin plank laid across a series of toy trestles. We climbed without pause for the best part of half an hour until I was forced to call a halt. Sweating, I stood with hands on hips, sucking in lungfuls of burning air.

"I told you what it would be like," Joaquin said. To my shame he was scarcely out of breath. Zavella's reaction to my coming was very much on his mind and I could almost sense him willing me to decide against going further.

"How much more?"

"About the same again."

I moistened my lips and spat. "I expect I'll survive."

We went on. Mercifully the gradients eased a little and we no longer climbed every step of the way. Once over the first ridge Joaquin followed a more switchback course. For some distance we traversed a long belt of conifers : later we were in the open again, moving over ground ribbed with the exposed ends of tilted rock strata. As far as I could tell we were heading south or south-east but I had no clear sense of direction; matching my pace with Joaquin's had me fully occupied. I said to him once : "How in God's name do you and your cousin keep in touch?" Bandaques had begun to seem impossibly remote and I was reflecting on the apparent ease with which information passed between them. But the only answer I received was a grunt. Perhaps he'd decided I'd learned enough as it was : perhaps I was being deliberately confused about our destination. If that were so I had no right to quibble, but there were moments when the strain brought me near to charging him with choosing the longest and most difficult route.

We came at last to a stony plateau which looked as if it had been bombarded by meteorites. There was a scattering of umbrella pines and a great deal of knee-high scrub.

"Wait here, please," Joaquin said uneasily.

I was glad to agree. He walked away under the trees and I found a boulder to lean against; lit a cigarette. The view towards the narrow coastal plain was magnificent. Bandaques was hidden but the sea provided a taut, cobalt skyline. Ridged and furrowed, the hills fell chaotically away, trapping their own shadows. A stream showed in a dark cleft, the village I had seen earlier, a few isolated farmhouses. To my surprise one or two string-like twists of the road were also visible. Height and broken country combine to deceive, but we were nearer to it than I had imagined. Yet, even if I had wanted to, I doubted whether I could have found my way back to the plateau unaided, or even indicated its approximate whereabouts from below. Intentionally or not, Joaquin had done his work well.

A faint breeze came and went, cool on my sweat. I was alone long enough for the cigarette to burn down to the filter. Then I saw Joaquin moving towards me through the pines. He stopped and indicated that I was to join him. "It's all right," he said as I came up, and I slapped him on the shoulders, glad for his sake, gratitude coming to a belated head.

There were no paths, no hint that we were not the first to walk here. We picked our way through the scrub. The ground was pock-marked with innumerable circular depressions, some small, some large and deep enough to have held a horse and cart. When I caught sight of him Zavella was standing on the lip of one of these, a rifle cradled loosely in his arms. He advanced to meet me, smiling, thrusting out a hand in greeting. The smile I remembered, the slightly hooked nose, the sunken cheeks, the sickly pallor beneath the swarthy skin. But the strength of the sinewy grip I had forgotten; perhaps never noticed the whiteness of his small, even teeth.

"I haven't got a front door, Señor Tyler, and this is no fancy cigarette-lighter. But you're welcome."

"I all but blackmailed Joaquin into this."

"Whatever Joaquin does is all right with me."

"You wouldn't have thought so earlier. He's been like someone waiting for a jury to come back. However, if it's any consolation he's taken me half way round the world since we left the bus."

"He needn't have bothered—not with you."

One end of the depression was roofed over with pine branches which hadn't long been cut. My first glance took in the remains of a fire, a blackened aluminium mug, plucked feathers, a rusty knife, some shreds of broken earthenware, a rolled, coarse blanket. The packet Joaquin had brought with him lay opened on an upturned enamel bowl : some of the bread and meat it contained had already been sampled.

Zavella dropped into the shallow pit. "Come in," he said with self-mockery. Then, to Joaquin : "Are you getting the bus at the half-hour?"

"I must, Luis."

"And you, señor?" Zavella looked at me.

"I'll go with Joaquin."

Joaquin said : "It will be necessary to start back in about thirty minutes."

Zavella reached for meat and bread; filled his mouth. High summer though it was it would have been cold here at night. I looked again at his pitiful collection of belongings; at the gun placed within easy reach. It was hard to think of him as a man with friends. A falling cone dribbled through the branches of a nearby tree: it made an erratic, swishing sound and I saw him start, then relax, before I had even identified it.

About the last thing I expected him to say was: "How is the señora?"

"Well—considering."

He nodded; coughed. I remembered the cough, too, but it sounded less terrible in the open. "She is very beautiful. One of the most beautiful women I have ever seen."

"I didn't know you had."

"Once," he said. He fished into his right-hand trousers' pocket, produced a heavy gold signet-ring and held it up between thumb and bruise-blackened finger-nail. "When I came by this. She was asleep on the bed."

I put out a hand but Zavella's fingers closed; withdrew.

I said: "Nobody could understand how you got in that afternoon."

"Over the roof and down a pipe."

"No key? No help from someone on the hotel staff?"

"What I do I do alone." There was more hardness than swagger.

"Joaquin tells me you sold the other things—the watch and the lighter."

"For very little."

"Yet you're prepared to return the ring?"

"Yes."

"Why, Zavella? That's the main reason I've come—to find out."

Joaquin had sauntered away, leaving us alone. I suppose he was underlining his point that this wasn't really his affair.

"Why?" I asked again.

Zavella tore some bread apart; munched hungrily. He evaded my question by posing his own. "Is the señora aware of the ring?"

"Not yet."

"You wanted to be sure it existed first—am I right?"

"Just about."

His knowing smile stopped as swiftly as it had formed. He produced the ring again, like a conjurer; juggled it from one hand to another. "She will appreciate having it?"

"I imagine so."

"As a keepsake?"

The word disturbed me. "It belonged to her husband."

"She is too young to have been with him long."

"They were married eight years. She's distressed, naturally." I couldn't fathom his cat-and-mouse mood, but I bore with it.

"Why should she grieve at all?"

I frowned.

"Why should she grieve when she has you?"

As easily as I could I said : "Joaquin talks too much."

"You would not be here otherwise."

"Nonsense. I came of my own free will."

"Only because you knew I had this." The ring went back and forth, back and forth.

"True," I conceded.

"And I only let you know of it because of what Joaquin had said."

"Which was?"

"That she had finished with him."

A butterfly chopped past. We stared at each other as intently as if a crucial card had been thrown. Vanity always takes precedence, however fleetingly. The truth was practically under my nose but it was obscured by the thought that Zavella was prompted by some romantic streak : the lonelier a man, the more fanciful his imagination.

"Was that so?" he pressed.

I had two choices—"Yes," or "No" : either was riddled with doubt. "Yes," I said, and the half-lie twisted in me like a knife.

"That is all I wanted to be sure of. . . . Here—catch."

The cough racked him as he tossed the ring at me. It was warm from his touch. I turned it over in my fingers; looked at the square piece of onyx embedded into the gold swelling.

ES was engraved fancifully across the mottled green and black surface. It was Scheele's ring, right enough.

Zavella seemed to read my mind. "There's no mistake, Señor Tyler. It was his. Nobody else's."

I was thinking about Ilsa and was deaf to the concentrated loathing in his voice. "I can see that."

"The 'S'"—he paused for maximum effect—"stands for Schafer."

I glanced up.

"His name was Schafer."

"Scheele," I corrected. "Erich Scheele."

"Schafer," he insisted. "I'm talking about his real name. Twenty years ago it was Schafer."

"Twenty *years* ago?"

He nodded. "When I first knew him."

The moment of revelation often comes more quietly than a novelist would sometimes have his readers believe. For me, that morning, there was no blinding flash; no abrupt, astonished reaction. I don't think I even moved. I remember staring at Zavella, elbows on knees, the ring pressed between my finger-tips, and feeling the back of my neck prickle almost as if I were afraid. *You* killed him. It was you, then. ... In the blink of an eye the puzzle had fitted into shape but I was incapable of grasping that it was finished. The answers were almost all there but acceptance of them took seconds to dawn.

Eventually I heard myself say: "That was at Gondra, wasn't it?"

"Yes, that's where." (I recalled from our other meeting: "A boy once. Long ago.")

He stood up. Joaquin took it as a hint. "Can we leave now?"

Zavella glanced at me : "D'you want to go?"

I shook my head; heard Joaquin remark that though we still had ten minutes or so to spare he didn't want to cut it too fine.

Zavella said: "There's a bus every hour. Why not wait for the next?"

"I'm on duty at ten," Joaquin replied, coming across. "You know that."

"Go on your own then. I'll put Señor Tyler on the way to the road when the time comes."

Joaquin hesitated. "Would that be all right?" he asked me. "I can't risk being late."

"Of course." I would have agreed to anything as long as it meant that I stayed.

"Is something the matter?" he looked at us both anxiously.

"Nothing. Don't always worry so." With a gesture of affection Zavella took him by the arm. "Good-bye and thanks. Get on back to your tables, *amigo mio,* and come and see me again soon. On Monday, if you can."

"Here?"

"Above the caves."

Joaquin nodded. "Good-bye, señor."

"Good-bye."

Zavella and I watched him walk away, noiseless on the pine needles. When he was nearly lost to view, I said: "Does he know?"

"As far as he is concerned it is just a ring and I am just a thief with a troublesome conscience."

"But he knows about Gondra."

"Everybody does. They know about Guernica, too, but only if you were there does it live with you." He straightened himself, hands on hips. "I hope he never learns more. He is ignorant of what it's like to hate and might not understand what I have done."

"Yet you tell me."

"Because you're involved. Because you're entitled to know what manner of man the señora grieves for. He was your enemy, too, remember."

Was? The tense jarred.

A small bird flipped overhead, emphasizing the silence; our isolation.

I said: "When you broke into his room that day at the España—were you aware who occupied it?"

"Not until later. The señora shifted in her sleep just as I reached the dressing-table. What with that and the shower running in the bathroom I decided it was best to be quick. I scooped up the first things I saw and got out. I was clear of Bandaques before I discovered what a haul I'd made." He coughed dryly. "A long time ago I used to pray that something like it would happen, but prayers such as mine were then are never answered—not by God, anyhow. It was chance. I sweat sometimes when I think of it. I could easily have picked another hotel; another veranda. His happened to be the nearest to the pipe."

I studied the ring as I listened. Schafer. Erich Schafer. ... Ilsa Scheele. ...

Zavella continued: "I found out whose room it was. The name didn't confuse me. The ring was as good as a finger-print. On the Saturday I came back into the town. I'd tried the day before but there were too many guards about. But on the Saturday, with the crowds, it was easier. I was sure he would be there, somewhere, watching the procession, but one of the guards spotted me and I had to run for it. On the Sunday I heard about you and the señora and about his visit to Barcelona next morning."

(Joaquin, I thought.)

"I hoped to intercept the Mercedes on the road, but somehow I missed it. Then, on the Tuesday, he went to Gondra —as you know. I wasn't here then. I was in another place, near the dam. That was chance, too. I saw his car when it was still a long way away. It was heading for the dam but something told me he would branch off and go to the village. I went down into the valley and waited in the old square. And, sure enough, he came. They say they always come back. He'd changed, of course—gone bald, got fatter. Elsewhere, he might have passed me by unrecognized. But the ring and the fact that he'd returned to Gondra condemned him. He didn't see me in the square at first. Then I called him by name—'Schafer'. He was walking away from me and stopped as if he were tied to a rope which would suddenly let him go no further. He looked to either side. 'Schafer', I called again and he swung round; saw me and the gun I had. He said something I didn't understand. I called : 'I'm the boy who stood here twenty years ago—remember?' I didn't know whether he'd learned Spanish or not but it was unimportant because I thought I had all the time in the world. Then, as I started towards him, the dam broke—and suddenly there was no time at all. Neither of us grasped what had happened—not immediately. It sounded like an underground explosion—muffled, yet violent. There was deathly quiet for a moment or two afterwards, but soon the earth began to shake and a moan came down the valley, louder every second, growing into a roar. It was like a wind, yet the air was dead. All at once Schafer began to run and I shot him, thinking he was running from me. He went down on to his knees and started to scream. Then I saw the water boiling round the bend above the village and I was sure that I was finished, too. It was as high as a cathedral and coming fast, pouring over itself. I threw the gun away and made for the steep ground. I never thought I'd get clear. In the end I had no more than my own length to spare. When I looked back Schafer had gone—everything had gone. I was sick with terror—physically sick : and yet I felt wonderful." He began to cough again. "Wonderful."

He had spoken in a flat, unemotional monotone, as if he were anxious to unburden himself, and the very simplicity of his phrasing made the scene all the more vivid. Gondra I had seen, and the currents had brought Scheele's horror-struck expression almost to my own door. Only when he concluded did his tone change, and then it was viciously triumphant; the final repetition ugly and frightening.

I studied his strained, cadaverous face. "Would you have shot him anyhow?"

"More than once."

"For what reason?"

Zavella swallowed; stirred the fire's dead embers with a worn boot.

"Tell me," I said. "It's important."

It came again like a spate. "The valley was the main defence line for Bandaques and the road to the north. Once it was lost the town and the road were open. This had been recognized for some time. But things had gone badly and the front had moved at great speed—so much so that Gondra hadn't been properly evacuated when the fight for the valley began. It lasted two days and was bitter. Before the war my father worked with explosives for a construction company—he wasn't in the army because he'd lost three fingers from his right hand. But he fought then. When the situation had become almost hopeless he led a group of milicianos upstream to try and blow the dam. They hadn't a chance in a hundred and those who weren't killed were captured—my father among them. They were taken in front of an officer of the Condor Legion who was in command and asked where they came from. Next day, when the valley was lost, they were marched into the square. About a hundred people were still in the village. They were herded out of cellars and basements—old people mainly, though not all. My mother was one and I was another. We were lined up against a wall with the men from the dam, two deep. I was in the front row with my mother. Through an interpreter the officer ordered me away from the rest and made me stand beside him. He was slim, sandy-haired, and smoked a cigarette. I came up to his waist. He stood with his left hand hooked into his belt and there was a ring on the small finger. I was close enough to see the initials. I thought he was going to make a speech. Everyone lining the wall was very quiet and I suppose they thought so too. Like me, I can't believe they knew they were going to be killed. But they were—every single one. Without any warning, without explanation. The officer suddenly lifted his hand and machine-guns opened fire from two corners of the square." Zavella paused, lifting his chin as if he were suffocating. "It was all over in a minute, then some men started cleaning up with rifles and revolvers. The officer got the interpreter to say to me : 'That's what happens if you resist. Now go and warn them in Bandaques.' Then he walked away. He was still smoking. Later he put his guns on the village and flattened it."

Again, by sparing the details, he allowed my imagination every scope. The lapse of time since these things had happened was no barrier. "Obedience, authority, respect" — Scheele's phrase added its counterpoint to my revulsion.

Zavella said : "The interpreter called him Schafer. And he answered to the name the other day, even if he had changed it to Scheele." He pecked his head towards the ring turning in my fingers. "That was the same, though. That was what led me back to him."

"How old were you?"

"Twelve."

It wouldn't have been fair to tax him, but it was impossible to deny myself a few last questions. "What made him pick you out?"

"I've asked myself a thousand times."

"Were other children there?"

"A few. Babies, mostly. Some of the men tried to break away when the shooting started, but only three or four managed it. They've died since; either that or they've gone somewhere else. In any case I was the only one to hear the officer's name and see the ring close-to. Believe me, Señor Tyler, those initials burned themselves into my brain."

"Did you go to Bandaques?"

"No. I went and hid in a cave. It's hard to remember exactly. I was petrified. Deep down I was hysterical yet I couldn't even cry. A woman found me and took me to her house : fed me. That wasn't the same day—it was the next or the one following : God knows. I think she must have guessed where I was from but she said nothing about it—only fed me and gave me a place to sleep. I believe she was intending to hand me over to some nuns but it didn't come to that because I left the house in the second night and never went back. I just wandered. I was able to cry by then. The fighting had gone north and everything was chaotic. I was too young to realize that it would have been better if I had been killed, too. I don't know where I went. I scrounged when I wasn't taken pity on. For a few days I was with gipsies; later with a family who had a saw-mill. Then, about two weeks after the shooting, I found a live grenade. It was in a ditch where I was collecting berries. The feel of it in my hand somehow thawed the numbness out of me—it's difficult to put it into words. But there and then I seemed to grow up. Tears weren't enough. I waited on a bluff overhanging a road and threw the grenade on the first staff car that passed along north. It missed, but men got out of the car and I was fired at; had to run." The cough bent him over. When it eased, he produced a grim smile. "I've never stopped running since, señor. And it's too late now to hope that I could."

A gold-rimmed cloud was dragging over the sun. The weapon I had sought was forged and ready for use. It was more damaging than anything I had ever visualized and yet it scared me, almost as if I feared that it could also bring about my own destruction.

Zavella said: "Spain was like a slaughterhouse when I wanted to talk about Gondra. Everyone had had his bellyful of death—and there was still more to come. So, after a while, I kept what I knew to myself and learned to live with it. It ate me out like a cancer, though. Even when there was no pain it was always there, gnawing away in secret—five, ten, twenty years afterwards." He lifted his arms away from his body: let them drop. "And now it's all over. A name, a ring, a pipe from a hotel roof—there are miracles to this day."

He led me down from the plateau until I was close enough to the road to be able to continue alone. The last time we parted I had told him that I wasn't sorry for him, but now I was filled with pity. I could neither blame nor judge him. Nothing had gone right for me since Scheele had died and desperation had warped my passion for Ilsa out of recognition. I told myself that Scheele would probably have been killed anyway, bullet or no. Fate is a ruthless redeemer and rarely makes mistakes. Watching Zavella's scarecrow figure ahead of me on the descent I wondered how it would eventually end for him; whether he would find laughter first and know the peace of a woman's body without always straining his senses for the sound of footsteps furtively closing in. Perhaps I wished him these things especially because I had also been deprived of them and inherited a cancerous ache of my own.

As we shook hands, I said : "Maybe we'll meet again."

"I hope so."

"Good luck anyhow. And many years."

"And to you, Señor Tyler."

Twenty minutes later I stopped the bus near the gorge. I saw no guards, no cruising Simca, either while I waited or when I was in the bus. The sun had come out again and the countryside was deceptively tranquil as we left the rough brown folds of the hills and rattled in towards Bandaques. It was just eleven o'clock when I climbed out under the bull-fight posters plastered along the amphitheatre wall and started walking to the España.

CHAPTER EIGHT

I

ILSA wasn't at the hotel and the girl at the reception-desk was no help. I went into the American Bar and drank a Fundador. A man sitting under the mounted head of the bull with the chromium-plated legend was avidly reading the football reports. The bar-tender hadn't seen Ilsa either but he had noticed the juxtaposition of the man and the bull and grinned at me. "Things change," he said, and because the thought of death hadn't lifted from my mind I wanted to tell him how wrong he was.

I had no idea where Ilsa had gone. I was handicapped without the car and, after a short while, took a taxi to the Villa Miramar. The mail had been delivered since I went out and it included a letter from my agent to say that the serial rights of my last novel had been sold to a London newspaper. His note ended: *You lucky mortal. The weather's foul here and it's all I can do not to ask outright for an invitation. Or would I be* de trop *in that icing-sugar villa of yours? Your silence makes me wonder*. There was also a PS in his own hand: *How's the new book coming along?* His letters invariably resulted in elation or disappointment. It was the nature of our association. But now I felt neither pleasure nor gratitude. There was something unreal about the success and his last paragraph was as if he had wilfully pummelled a bruise. I threw the letter down. "Make-believe," Scheele had said, and make-believe was my trade; but I had lost touch with it.

Catalina emerged from the spare bedroom as I passed on my way to the hall.

"*Buenos dias,*" I said. "I won't be eating in, either now or tonight."

She nodded. I would have gone by, but she began tenuously : "Señor—"

"Yes?"

Her date-brown eyes seemed sadly youthful in contrast to the walnut-wrinkled skin. "Captain Romero had me at his office yesterday. I haven't seen you since and I wanted to explain."

"I heard about it. It doesn't matter."

"I had to go. I dared not refuse."

"I understand. And I'm sorry you were sent for. But nothing's wrong."

"He asked many questions." Her concern was almost maternal. She would have been afraid of him : they all were. But she could be bold with me. "Impertinent questions."

"It was all a mistake," I said. "A misunderstanding"— and she clasped her hands with relief. By the time I had gone out to the car and filled the radiator she was singing with her usual contentment.

I drove back into the town. The sea was a shade less red but the beach was filthy and a few more swollen goats had come in, as stiff as bagpipes. At the Bar Sinbad I saw Joaquin moving purposefully between the outside tables, tray held high. He looked more at home there than on the plateau; innocent of secrets. It was strange to think that he knew less than I.

There was no sign of Ilsa and I decided against stopping to ask whether she had been in. I was coming to inflict pain and my mood wasn't pliable enough to indulge in deceiving him about his cousin. Later I must, always; but that I could learn to do.

I returned to the España and waited. Some men, they say, strew rags and dirt about the shrine at which they kneel, blaming the self-same gods for not making it possible for them to offer something finer. If, when Scheele had died, Ilsa's distress had not locked a door in my face I could have borne with it. I would never have been provoked into visiting Gondra or ransacked my brains for clues or questioned Joaquin or gone hopefully on the bus to meet Zavella. Only yesterday—was it yesterday? I had lost track—she had said that she couldn't bear to remain in ignorance of the reason for his death. How I was going to tell her I didn't know—or quite when. The only certainty was that she wouldn't believe me; would demand proof. Zavella was the immediate proof and I didn't want him on my conscience. But I needed to mention no names. "Someone I met" would do. The enormity of the disclosures would prolong her disbelief rather than provoke any desire to accuse. Repugnance and horror automatically generate incredulity and I, who had known Scheele for only a matter of days, still found myself giving way to it whenever I matched the man being buried in the morning against the slim, sandy-haired Condor Legion officer of Zavella's story. How much more, then, would she? There was an eight-year bond in his favour. But eventually—surely?—she would recoil from him; need me as never before. She couldn't blame me for telling her because she had wanted to know. And if there was spite in my motive—a sort of hatred, even—I was no more capable of seeing it than the blind can discern the shifting colours of the day. Desire, yes. Despair, yes. Love, yes. ... These three. Why else should I have armed myself as I had?

I took out the ring and examined it. A plump woman came to the bar and sat precariously on the stool next to mine and I covered the ring over quickly, like someone found out. I moved to a table; opened my fingers again. ES ... Schafer. Erich Schafer. ... What happened to you after Gondra? I thought. When did you become Scheele? There would be answers somewhere; all the proof in the world if need be.

People were continually coming in or leaving, but at last the sharp clack of Ilsa's heels sounded on the patterned tiles of the lobby and I put the ring away. Her step was instantly familiar—part of the trivia about her which my senses had amassed. She was wearing a dark grey costume and its severity emphasized her tanned pallor. As if I had every

right to know, I said: "Where've you been?" One forgets
that a lover has no rights; no responsibilities.

"To the shops."

"I've looked all over for you."

She hitched her skirt and sat down. "I went also to the
agency about my flight."

"Oh?" There was a tightness in me; a sudden withering
contraction. "When for?"

"Sunday," she said. "There is an Air France to Paris and
I can make a connection there." The careful precision with
which she always spoke, the slight lilt of her accent, conveyed an alarming determination.

"Must you?"

"Must I what?"

"Leave so soon?"

"Yes, Ty; I must." Then: "Can I have a cigarette,
please?"

"But that's only two days from now." I was stunned.

"There is a lot to be seen to at home."

"I daresay. But—"

A waiter came, flicking a lighter. It seemed I wasn't even
to be allowed to do that. The world was full of Boy Scouts.
Woodenly, I ordered a dry sherry; watched the flame dance
and the smoke curdle. Half a minute must have passed before either of us spoke again. A pendulum was swinging in
my mind—"Tell her now. ... Don't tell her now." Under
the concealed lighting her face was exquisitely beautiful.
The lips whose watery taste I could still remember, the
smooth forehead that the act of love had beaded with
sweat, the small blue jugular vein on the side nearest me—
I couldn't believe they weren't mine any more. Look at me,
I thought. For God's sake look at me. ... The weapon was
in my pocket. I had only to produce it to find a way through
her indifference: then, like an armour-piercing shell, it
would demolish her obsession. Grief and regret couldn't live
with that I knew. The pendulum swung again and again:
the half minute seemed endless. But what remained of my

vanity wanted her without Scheele's aid : now that I was in her presence I would enlist him only if I must.

I said : "What about us, Ilsa?" I spoke quietly, in dread, leaning forward; but a burst of male laughter from the bar drowned my voice. To my dismay, she misheard. "Lunch? Yes. I was going to ask whether we could have it early. I want to go to the church afterwards. They're taking Erich there at two."

I sat back defeated, filled with venom.

"Will you come?" she asked.

"You won't want me."

"Ty." She said it gravely, dragged-out, as if she were reproving a child. Our eyes met at last and hers were tolerant with understanding. "I'd like you to."

I shrugged. "I'm no Catholic."

"Even so—"

"And I'm not sorry about anything either."

Now it was I who looked away; avoided her gaze. I could wound her worse than this. These were scratches.

"It's just as you wish," she said evenly.

"*You* are, though."

"I don't follow you."

"Sorry. . . . You're sorry about us." My mind pleaded for a denial; unconsciously spelt out ESPAÑA on the ash-tray. Seconds passed.

"Oh, Ty."

I looked at her again. "That's not an answer."

She sighed. "Not now, Ty. Please."

"He's dead, Ilsa."

Her mouth went taut, as if I had struck her. She stubbed her cigarette in the big blue and white tray and stood up. "Forget I ever mentioned the church." She asked the waiter : "Is lunch possible?"

"Yes, señora."

I went with her, surrendering pride with every step. Heads swivelled to watch her pass; the buzz of general conversation faltered. But for me there was only bitterness in the rhythm of her stride. When we reached her table and were alone I said, with bad grace: "I'm sorry," but she didn't answer. For a long time we ate in brittle silence. The manager presented his compliments in person and we spoke to him almost as if we were strangers to one another. As he was about to bow himself away Ilsa asked if he would arrange for a taxi to be at the door at two o'clock.

"Of course, Señora Scheele."

I waited until he had gone. "That was quite unnecessary."

"It is too far to walk."

"You know very well I'll take you."

"I didn't and I don't."

"Well, I will."

"There's no point in your coming. You said so."

"I want to."

"Oh my God," she flared.

I had all but lost her. Without Scheele I could do nothing. Yet I still forbore to use him as my pimp. It may have been that I was too angry with myself; too wretched. Or that I sensed that to produce the ring in rage would have robbed my denunciation of its effectiveness. Whatever the reason I held my tongue and let what I knew continue to poison me.

Later: I had thought it yesterday and now I thought it again. I would tell her later, when she was calmer; when *I* was calmer. ...

We finished our coffee and left. A taxi was drawn up at the bottom of the flight of steps and I paid it off like a spoilt child; opened the door of my own car. Ilsa got in without a word and I drove her to her tryst with the ghost I was going to kill.

2

It was as dark as ever in the church. The wine-red sanctuary-lamp glowed through the permanent twilight; people moved like shadows, anonymous in their humility or

149

on their conducted tour. On the huge suspended cross the nailed figure with the slumped head looked as if He slept. I let Ilsa precede me up the central aisle. Scheele was already there, the draped coffin to one side of the high altar, flanked with yellow tapers. She genuflected and such was my mood that her obeisance seemed almost as though it were directed towards him. I chose a seat two rows behind her; watched her kneel and bless herself. The flames of the thick candles guarding the coffin leaned as if stroked by an invisible hand, fluttered, then swelled and grew tall again. The old turkey-jowled priest came to her row, bending close, whispering secretly : his arrival was so prompt that it gave the impression he had been in wait for her. I should have feared him more, but I didn't believe that a few hours in a bed could result in an eternity of anguish. My hunger was for the body, and the soul was an intangible vapour; a memory in other minds.

The priest flapped away. I looked again at the coffin in its honoured position and wondered at which end Scheele's head was. "Real life and death—there's no substitute, Mister Tyler." He was my ally now, my last and only one—yet traitorously so, because Ilsa was thinking of him too. Her mind was dwelling on him in ignorance of the square at Gondra and the machine-guns hammering through the screams; or of the boy who hid in a cave and remembered the German officer who smoked a cigarette.

I rested my chin on clasped hands, though not to pray. Schafer; Scheele—whoever you were; whichever way they've put you round—it didn't end at Gondra, did it? Where did you go afterwards?—after you and the rest of your lot celebrated with that parade in Berlin? Was it Poland? Norway? France? Greece, perhaps? Russia? You went somewhere. Spain was merely the guinea-pig. You didn't hang your uniform on a peg in 1939—not with all that useful experience. Others like you went on to Warsaw, Lidice, the Ardennes. . . . There were scores of places, each one of them a monstrous sin. Where did *you* go? And what happened that was sufficient to make you change your name? Wasn't Gondra enough for you?

A group of children scurried along the aisle; crowded a candle-lit saint. It didn't move as their rapt expressions seemed to expect.

Hier haben wir gewonnen. ... I thought: You didn't, Scheele – not personally; not in the end. You only imagined you had. If there's anything living left of you anywhere it must see that. By this evening Ilsa will have begun to believe me; started asking herself the same questions about you. And tomorrow she'll cancel her flight home.

The priest returned, surpliced; passed under an arch and went out of my view. I saw Ilsa bend her head lower. What use to Schafer were her prayers when she offered them up for Scheele? If I could have prayed, if I had felt that a plea would achieve something, I would have asked to be allowed to win my own victory, without Scheele's help. But God looked as if He were asleep, anyhow, and I was too twisted with selfishness to believe in any but my own powers. Lust suffereth little and is unkind. I could have reached forward and all but touched Ilsa's straight fair hair with my finger-tips. The desire to do so was still active, but only Scheele could make contact possible.

She pushed herself off her knees. For a moment I assumed that she was leaving and half rose myself. But, instead, she moved crab-wise along the row of cane-seated chairs and disappeared in the direction the priest had taken. Turning, I saw her enter one of the confessionals in the side aisle. A curtain twitched: when she knelt down her shoes and slim calves protruded like a conjuror's assistant's. She couldn't have hurt or soured me more. I put my head in my hands. Is that why you asked me to come? – to humiliate me? – to let me witness it? I couldn't give her the benefit of the doubt that the priest may have urged it on her there and then. I knew of the formula: "Bless me, father, for I have sinned. . . . Four or five times, father: on two separate occasions. ... No, never before...."

It was impossible to stay, listening to the imagined whispers. I got up and banged out of the church; found sunlight. On the worn steps I stood and stared at the flower-sellers that Christ would have ordered away; at the sprinklers vainly at work among the patterns of diseased grass. The whispered repudiation was lodged in my ears and I entered an intensity of despair such as I had never known. The thought formed like an angry fist: All right, then. You've asked for it now.

Ilsa was inside a long time. I waited in the car. Even hatred has periods of calm—and what was this but hatred? I smoked through two cigarettes; willed her to come before reason applied a blunting edge. Jealousy builds the narrowest of bridges between enmity and desire; sometimes fuses the two.

At last she came—shriven, presumably; pure again, washed clean of me. I said coldly: "You needn't have been so obvious about it."

"I'm sorry. But it was not intentional."

"Rubbish." I crashed a gear.

"That's true."

"I'm surprised you should even risk re-contamination."

The word defeated her but I had said enough. "Don't make it worse for me, Ty."

"For you!"

"Yes, for me."

A wobbling Vespa slowed us down. "You loved me once," I said. "Does a set of rules kill all that? They didn't mean much to you while he was alive."

Her voice was low; the restraint fresh from absolution. "Try not to hate me, please."

"I don't understand you. And I haven't got time to be delicate—not if you're walking out on me on Sunday."

"I must do that."

"I don't see why."

The España was in view and I swung the car across the

road through a gap in the traffic. The manœuvre checked her reply. We were gritting into the kerb before she said: "I've already told you why."

"You're free now—rules or no rules. I repeat: I don't understand. What about you and me?"

"It wouldn't work." She shook her head.

"You've hardly tried."

"I could never forget that I was with you when Erich died. Never."

"He's best forgotten."

She wheeled on me, restraint ebbing fast. "You mustn't say a thing like that."

"I'll say it again. He's best forgotten. You don't know what sort of person—"

She was out of the car before I had finished. I caught her up near the top of the steps; gripped her by the arm. She wrenched it away but I regained it. "D'you think I enjoy doing this?"

"Go away."

"No. You come with me."

The reception-desk staff eyed me curiously as I led Ilsa into the American Bar. She didn't want to sit down but I insisted, saying: "I've got something here you ought to see."

"What d'you mean?"

"Your property."

I took out the ring and handed it to her. Surprise softened her expression a little. "But this is Erich's."

"Of course."

"Where on earth did you find it?"

"I didn't. It was given me."

A waiter approached. "Later," I said.

"*Given* to you?"

I nodded, watching her earnestly. Now it was coming.

"Who by?"

"I don't know who he was."

She fingered the ring; brushed the onyx with a thumb. "It was one of the things stolen from our room."

"I know." Were we so estranged?

"When did you get it?"

I should have been less honest. "I heard about it the other day. I actually got my hands on it this morning."

"And you didn't tell me?"

"I have now."

"Do you mean you've known of it all this time and never said a word? That's unfair and unkind."

"I was anxious not to disappoint you." Her gaze accused, hardening my heart. I said bluntly: "Are those Erich's initials?"

She looked from me to the ring; from the ring back to me. "Of course they are."

"Erich Scheele?"

She frowned, mystified. "What are you talking about? It's his ring."

Someone at my elbow said: "Señor Tyler?" I thought it was the waiter again; turned irritably to find a uniformed message-boy, ridiculous in a pill-box hat.

"What is it?"

"Telephone, señor."

"You must be mistaken. I'm not a guest here."

"For Señor Tyler." He blinked and spoke like a parrot.

"Who's asking for me?"

"I don't know, señor."

His timing was a conspiracy. I glanced at Ilsa. The denunciation was on the tip of my tongue—"It may have been his ring but that wasn't his name. He fooled you. His name was Schafer and twenty years ago he destroyed Gondra and everyone in it. Murdered them. That's why he's best forgotten." It would have been a dramatic exit-line; something to return to and bludgeon home. But I faltered and said: "Excuse me, will you."

I followed the boy into the lobby; was shown the booth. The door padded, sealing me in.

"Yes?" The mouthpiece was damp with another's condensed breath. "Tyler here."

"This is Captain Romero."

"Oh?"

Wherever he was he cleared his throat. "I have a favour to ask."

"You've come to the wrong person."

"I'm not asking it for myself."

"Don't tell me you have friends."

"The favour is asked by a friend of yours, señor. At least, he claims that distinction."

"Who?"

Romero let it drop like a stone. "Luis Zavella."

There was absolute quiet in the booth. A rustle of paper reached me along the line. "Zavella?"

"Yes. He wants to speak to you."

It could have been a trick. "Put him on then. I'm listening."

"That is hardly possible. But I know where he is; where you can reach him."

My heart was sinking. I stalled : "So?"

"We've got him bottled up in The White Caves."

Silence again as my thoughts whirled. "And he wants to speak to me?"

"So he says."

The verb implied close contact between them. "For what reason?"

"I am as curious as you, señor. All I can tell you is that he will be dead in half an hour if you don't come."

"And if I do?"

He was cryptic. "Something might be arranged."

"It'll take me the best part of half an hour to get there."

"As long as I know you're coming I will wait."

"I'm coming," I said. "Now."

I took a deep breath and backed grimly out of the booth. Ilsa was still fondling the ring when I reached the table.

"I'm sorry but I've been called away. It's urgent. I'll explain later."

What I did and where I went were of no interest to her any more. Her only question was: "Why did you ask if these were Erich's initials?"

For a long moment I held her puzzled gaze. Now—of all people—it was Zavella who conspired against her knowing: the irony bit deep. But it would have been a crime to squander even a few minutes of his half hour. Why he wanted me I couldn't imagine, unless it were to blame me for having put Romero on his track. Uncertainty elbowed my vendetta with Scheele aside. I stared hard at Ilsa, mentally protesting my innocence.

"We'll talk when I get back."

Seconds afterwards I was going down the hotel steps, two at a time. And of the faces which haunted me on the drive—hers, Zavella's, Scheele's, Romero's, Joaquin's—it was that of the rabbit on the rack of the morning bus which overprinted them all.

CHAPTER NINE

I

THE bus had taken twenty minutes to reach the bridge which spanned the gorge : I did it in twelve, laying a spreading trail of dust over wayside crops, exploding birds out of trees. The road was fairly clear and only once—because of a shepherdless flock of sheep—was I reduced to a crawl. The White Caves were a kilometre or so beyond the bridge but I reckoned that Romero would hear me coming before I even crossed it. The snort-snort of my horn trumpeted off the hills at every snickering corner.

The first of his guards was positioned on the far side of the gorge. Some kind of road-control was apparently in operation because the man made a half-hearted attempt to stop me, jumping clear when he thought better of it. Some distance further on a notice-board read :

THE WHITE CAVES
UNIQUE AND ORIGINAL FORMATIONS
OWN ELECTRICOL PLANT

I had been there before, like any tourist, and didn't need the help of the arrowed direction sign when the road presently split left and right :

400 METRES
THE WHITE CAVES
OPEN EVERY DAY FROM 10 TO 20 HRS

I turned beneath a bulging, lichen-grey cliff. Just past the fork there were two guards standing in the middle of the camber; beyond them, a Perspex-topped coach. Freshly-

157

tanned faces peered through its windows as I slowed. There wasn't enough room to force past at speed. An exasperated young woman was protesting to the guards : "This is a scandal. My organization has a contract with the Caves— every Monday, Wednesday and Friday. What right have you to forbid us to go any further?"

They ignored her; moved over to me. "Señor Tyler?" one asked.

I nodded.

"Captain Romero is at the hut."

I thought I knew where he meant; dropped into gear. Drawing away, I heard the woman complain volubly : "Why should *he* be allowed to go up? I've got thirty-four people here . . ."

The road curled under the craggy wall of rock : at regular intervals white posts marked the brink of the gorge. A tight bend was followed by another. Then the road straightened and pointed towards the entrance of the caves, widening as it did so, to form an oval-shaped area large enough to accommodate a sanded car park, a café and several souvenir stalls. Normally crowded, the car park was empty except for a solitary Seat saloon and about a dozen red and black motorcycles. Every waiter, stall-attendant and guide had disappeared. A score of guards made a rough semi-circle near the dark mouth of the caves, their rifles unslung and variously at the ready. The sight of them chilled whatever hopes I had entertained for Zavella. Was I responsible? The persistent doubt flowed through every bleak and poisoned part of me. I braked near the big Seat and got out; walked over to the wooden ticket-office. There was a side door which opened into a small room lined with shelves stacked with rolls of coloured tickets. Romero was sitting on a table talking into the telephone. He didn't notice me immediately and swung an immaculate leg, delighted with himself.

". . . that's correct. Oh no—quite impossible. . . . Yes. . . . Very good, I'll report back within the hour. . . . What was that?" He listened, then nodded, chuckling. "Thank you very much."

He rang off; smoothed his tunic. Only then did he see me. "You were quick." His moustache accentuated his slightly embarrassed smirk.

"I know the road."

He gave no hint that he was aware of it. With an attempt at blandness, he said : "There is an English proverb, I believe : 'A friend in need is a friend indeed'."

"I didn't come to hear you air your knowledge."

"But you came—and fast."

"I was asked for."

He touched his moustache gingerly, as if it pained him. "You told me the other day that you had never heard of Luis Zavella."

"Maybe I did."

"Yet you were the one person he mentioned when I spoke to him. Would you care to explain?"

"Not to you."

He warded off my contempt with one of his shrugs.

I said : "What d'you mean—'spoke to him'? Isn't he inside the caves?"

"There's a speaking-tube near the turnstiles. The guides use it to make sure that parties of tourists don't tread on each other's heels. It's a control. When a guide with one group gets to a certain point he reports to the turnstiles; then the next one starts off."

A beetle laboured across the floor, advertising life. Some men can be appealed to; bribed. But not Romero.

"When I was in the España you said something might be arranged."

He nodded. "I wondered if you could persuade Zavella to give himself up."

"That won't be why he's asked for me."

"I want you to try."

"Say he won't?"

159

"Then we will go in. But it would be better if there were no shooting."

Through the wire mesh of the ticket aperture I could see the semi-circle of guards waiting in the hot afternoon sun. Misgivings dragged at my heart.

Romero went on: "Zavella has all the advantages in there. Otherwise I wouldn't have called you. To catch a fox one must become a fox—that is a proverb in *my* country."

The feeling of guilt boiled over. "How did you know where he was?"

"A corporal of mine saw him enter."

"Just that?"

"Just that. The corporal was off-duty, with some friends from Madrid." Romero must have noticed my relief. "Was it troubling you, Señor Tyler?"

I looked at him hard. "Yes, it was." Then I said: "What will happen to him if he decides to come out?"

"He'll be tried and sentenced." He paused; crunched the beetle with a gleaming shoe. "Either way he will die."

"For what reason?"

"For murder."

He knew, then. "Whose?"

"Señor Scheele's." He narrowed his eyes a little. "I expected you would show more surprise. It must be a weight off your mind."

"Perhaps I will if you can prove it."

"We have the gun. It was brought in yesterday from Gondra. It is one of two rifles which he stole from the guard-house by the Lareo Dam last year."

"And that's proof?"

"For me, yes. When it's someone like Zavella, yes."

Why I persisted I don't know. Zavella was doomed. Perhaps it was because I felt that the seeds which men like Scheele had planted continued to bear fruit in others like Romero: the pitiless strain still flourished given the conditions. Whatever the reason, I said passionately: "What do you know of Zavella?"

"Enough to finish him. No more is necessary."

I made for the door like someone in need of air. Romero followed; fell into step with me. Success had thickened his skin. The prospect of promotion sounded in the gritty strike of his heels. The line of guards stirred expectantly as we passed through and approached the turnstiles : beyond them the rock-face ahead of us tunnelled sharply in towards the gaping entrance of the caves. The turnstiles clicked round under the pressure of our hips. A sergeant occupied a recess in the left-hand wall near the plugged end of the speaking-tube. It was tacked along the rock like a cable, shoulder-high. Nearby was a lidded power-switch and—on the ground—four wooden boxes.

Romero tapped a foot against one of these. "Tear gas," he explained. "If the worst comes to the worst we must take every precaution. Have you explored the caves ?"

"I've been round."

"Then you will appreciate my responsibility. They're unique. One centimetre of stalactite takes a hundred years to form." He ordered the sergeant to switch on the lights : the tunnel was suddenly bright and inviting, white-washed as far as the eye could see. "Do what you can to make him realize how hopeless it is."

The sergeant eased out of the recess. Romero un-plugged the speaking-tube and blew into it, his sallow cheeks ballooning. He blew twice, waited a moment, then spoke. "Zavella ?" It seemed impossible that his voice was carrying beyond the visible limits of the tunnel. "Zavella ?" He put an ear to the tube, neat eyebrows pinched together as he concentrated. Presently, he was acknowledged. I heard nothing, but he suddenly nodded and transferred his mouth to the cup-like aperture. "I'm sending your friend in now." A pause. "D'you hear me, Zavella ? Your friend, Señor Tyler, is coming in now."

Apparently satisfied, he plugged the tube-end; addressed me. "I will be here should you wish to speak about anything."

"It's unlikely."

"You never know. But remember—if he has some idea of using you to his advantage—as a hostage, say—it will not dissuade me from taking the necessary measures."

"I can look after myself."

"So long as you appreciate the position. . . . Have you a watch?"

"Yes."

"It's just coming up to ten-past four. I'll give you until half-past."

"I'm not being 'given' anything," I said. "Let's get that straight here and now. I'll come out when I choose—and not before."

It is possible that if his sergeant had not been present Romero might have taken it more coolly. As it was he began to bluster : the smooth veneer was surprisingly thin. "You seem to forget who you're talking to. When I say I'll give you until half-past—"

"I forget nothing where you're concerned. Nothing, d'you understand? I'm here because of Zavella; not on behalf of you or a caveful of stalactites. There'll always be another million years."

I left him standing; felt his anger boring into my back as I made for the entrance. I was sweating, ice and fire, though not because of the heat. In four languages a notice by the tunnel's mouth forbade smoking. The English version was written: NO SMOKING ALOUD. A worn cement floor threw the sound of my step on to rough-hewn walls and ceiling, deadening it, making it at once flat yet metallic. Names were occasionally scribbled on the walls; initials, dates. Two I remember to this day—HARRY MILNE 1957 . . . BILL AND RENE, DURHAM, U.S.A. . . .

The air was warm and damp; smelt vaguely urinal. Like flint arrowheads, moths basked in the light around each naked bulb. The tunnel sloped gently downwards. After about forty yards it suddenly opened out into the first of the caverns. One moment I was in a functional whitewashed pipe; the next in a world of utter fantasy. Hidden illuminations silhouetted a multitude of grotesque and astonishing forms. Months before, the guide had paused and said mechanically: "The Entrance Hall, ladies and gentlemen, discovered by accident in 1910. The dominant colour is the result of a concentration of calcium carbonate. The stalactite formations here are characteristic of the entire caves. . . ." But now I walked straight through, following the railed, undulating path, moving cautiously because of the gloom. The speaking-tube was somewhere, but I couldn't see it. Where the cavern narrowed I stopped under a draped curtain of transparent stone.

"Zavella?"

A swift echo: then silence, eerie and total. I moved on through a glistening archway and found myself in the second cave, larger and more lofty than the first. The concealed lighting was bluish-white. Here were The Candle Factory and The Enchanted Garden, The Ruined Castle and The Snowy Mountain. It was a place for innocent wonder, not for dying in. I was coming like a priest, alone and confidential, yet bringing nothing except an awful sense of inadequacy. Why had he asked for me? I was powerless to help: he must have known that. Why then? For what?

"Zavella?" I called softly.

"A-a-a-ah." The echo was followed by a single plop of dripping water, that was all. I had a fleeting, almost deranged belief that I was talking to myself; was completely alone. A freakish stalagmite—Saint Christopher, according to the guide—stood in a natural alcove, cunningly lit from behind. I moved on again, reassured by the existence of the railing; sometimes, when the path dipped, resting a hand on a damp upright. Banded, fluted, tapering, goitred—the spindly pinnacles grew everywhere, reaching up in vertical monotony towards the spiked, petrified roof, sometimes achieving union. The pumice-like stone was as warm and smooth as skin. Each few yards transformed the dioramic vistas; opened up others. I passed into The Hall of Flags.

There was still no answer when I called but I was beginning to sense that Zavella wasn't far away. The lights flickered alarmingly, held on, brightened. I suppose I had been inside for no more than a couple of minutes yet already it seemed many times as long.

"It's me . . . Tyler."

The flat echoes were all squeezed tight together, like a flutter of wings. Zavella was watching me, I knew; making sure, straining his eyes. The feeling of being observed was physical; unnerving. I remained still, the quiet like wadding in my ears. Then I heard him cough, and though I had been waiting for some clue to his whereabouts the hollow bark raised the short hairs on my neck.

"Zavella?" I looked about me, peering left and right, tense. "Where are you?"

And at last he said :

"I'm here, Señor Tyler."

Even then I couldn't distinguish him : he had to move first. To my left was a grotto which held The Chessmen—a packed formation of stalagmites adequately enough shaped and grouped to justify the name. Zavella's silhouette was partly merged into that of an approximation to a horse-headed Knight. The grotto was slightly above the level of the path and his thin, scarecrow body looked somehow larger than life. A cold shiver brushed my nerves before recognition slackened them off. I started towards him, but he checked me; slithered down, clutching his rifle.

I said : "I'd never have seen you."

"Good." He was thinking ahead. Close though we were the light wasn't sufficiently strong for me to notice the play of his features, but his handshake conveyed emotion to an extraordinary degree. "Thank you for coming."

"What brought you in here?—of all places?" It was a lament.

"It's an old route of mine. A short cut."

"*This* is?"

"I've a friend on the gates."

"But it's such an obvious trap."

"Not normally. There's another way out—a fissure which leads far back to the top of the cliff. I've used it for years. I doubt if more than half-a-dozen people knew of it. But today, when I needed it most, it failed me. The rains have blocked it up."

"Tell me what happened."

"Someone recognized me—a guard. I was through the turnstiles when the shouting started, but I wasn't much concerned. A group of people had just finished going round and I had the place to myself. I didn't even run after I was past here—I was that confident. Then I discovered the fissure was blocked. They'd put the lights out by that time."

"And then?"

"I used up every match I had finding my way back to the tube."

"Where's that?"

'Behind you." He pointed. "I couldn't hope to get as far as the tunnel in the dark. The railing isn't continuous and I'd have lost myself. It would have been too late, anyhow : I knew that. I waited here for a while—a long while. Ayee, it seemed like days. Eventually, I blew into the tube and spoke to someone who fetched Romero."

He coughed : once I had imagined it would be the cough that would destroy him.

"They've got your gun," I said. "The one you threw away at Gondra."

He nodded, face profiled. "Romero told me. . . . You're talking to a dead man, señor."

"If you stay here, yes."

"Here—outside ; it'll make no difference."

"If they heard your story they'd take a less serious view."

He scoffed quietly. " 'They' !"

"I'm sure of it."

" 'They' are Romero and others like him, with or without uniform."

"They're not all the same. Your defence at a trial would give you the opportunity—"

"You're speaking about some other country, Señor Tyler. I'd be found in one of Romero's cells with my throat cut before there was any trial. They don't want the past raked over."

Thinking he might have asked me to enlist my advocacy, I said : "I'll tell them."

"They wouldn't listen."

"I'd make them."

"No. Thank you, but no." He shook his head. Clearly he had come to a decision with himself during his wait in the darkness. "I prefer The White Caves." All the bravado had gone. His voice trembled as he controlled his fear. "At least I've got this." The butt of the rifle grated on the path : I presume he had carried it past the turnstiles down a trousers' leg, though at the time I accepted his having it without question.

"You won't have a chance."

"More than they had at Gondra."

I saw his Adam's-apple bounce. A drop of water fell and the tiny splash sounded like a living thing. Above our heads were The Flags of Many Nations. "Notice the colours," the guide had said, "and the way each hanging sheet of stone is folded as if a breeze is blowing." But there was no breeze and never would be. The grave would be like this, for ever and ever.

Zavella said : "I first came in here when I was a boy— with my father. I remember him telling me that I'd never see any change even if I came back in a thousand years. . . . Ayee." The sigh was like a prayer. "How right he was. It seems like that."

The lights flickered again. He took a cigarette from me; eagerly lowered his lean face towards the match as if he thirsted. The flame bobbed as he drew and I had a brief glimpse of his suffering. I could hardly grasp that it was nearly over. As if to try and shake my disbelief I handed him the packet and the box, but even his fumbling acceptance of them seemed part of the unreality.

Yet I said : "Won't you change your mind?"

"No." His profile was dark again, etched against the soft, orange illumination of The Chessmen.

"Then why did you send for me?"

He coughed. "I wanted to ask you about the señora."

"What about her?"

"Does she know?"

"About you?"

"About Schafer."

"Not yet."

The glow of his cigarette brightened; dimmed. "Don't tell her," he said.

"I must."

"No." The echo fluttered. "There's no need."

I said uneasily : "He was her husband."

"But she had finished with him. It was over."

I was silent, nails digging into my palms. The sense of unreality reached out to include Ilsa. Was she still in the American Bar?—still nursing the ring?

Zavella said : "That is so, isn't it?"

Vanity made a final stand. "Yes."

"Never tell her then. That's all I ask."

Water dripped somewhere. I shut my eyes. Don't extract a promise from me. I'll break it as soon as I'm clear of here. Don't make me despise myself more than I do already.

"I was a long time alone in the dark," Zavella continued. "I thought about this more than anything else. It's the only reason I asked Romero to get in touch with you."

"The truth will come out." My voice was low. "You had no other motive."

"Robbery."

"But Scheele wasn't robbed."

"The dam-burst prevented it." He paused. "Romero's satisfied with that. Why tell her something different if you love her?"

You're dead, I thought. I can't pretend that I'm dead, too.

Zavella said : "Hatred is a disease. Why pass it on to her? It could eat her away from the inside just as it's eaten me away. I've had it for twenty years. It disfigures you; cripples you. And in the end it destroys you." The cough shook him gently. "I wish it on nobody."

I shook my head in silent protest.

"She would never forgive you."

The whistle in the end of the tube sounded impatiently. I wrenched out the plug and let it dangle from its chain. A faint bleat came from the aperture.

"She would never forgive you," Zavella repeated.

I stared at him as if he had betrayed me.

"Have you given her the ring?"

"Yes." Then I said hopelessly : "What about *my* hatred? Where's the cure for that?"

Inevitably, he misunderstood. "Why should you hate Schafer? He's neither destroyed nor deceived you. You've won, in fact. Hang on to your victory, Señor Tyler."

The aperture bleated a second time, nudging shame into me. Romero wouldn't delay much longer. Zavella must have been wanting me to say : "If that's your wish I'll honour it." But I was too split in myself to be able to speak.

"Don't tell Joaquin either," he said.

I nodded.

"It would be a burden for him. He could never keep it to himself. He'd clash with Romero and bring much trouble on his head. Let him know you saw me, though."

"Of course."

He dropped his cigarette and the glow hissed on the damp stone. "Good-bye, then." He was abrupt.

I urged desperately : "Walk out with me and stand trial."

Zavella shook his head. He shifted the gun beyond my reach, almost as if he suspected me of selfish intentions.

With a gesture of impotent helplessness, I argued : "They've got tear gas."

"I'll welcome it. It is a lifetime since I cried." He drew himself up, afraid, yet with dignity. As he faced me the light from The Chessmen touched his beard-stubble; softened one sunken cheek. "Good-bye, Señor Tyler."

I could hardly trust myself to look at him. "Good-bye."

"Many years," he wished me and the poignancy of the phrase forced the words emotionally off my tongue : "I won't forget what you've said."

"I know you won't."

I began to grope along the railing. What I was doing didn't seem possible. I felt sick. I heard Zavella moving behind me, presumably coming to select a vantage-point nearer the tunnel, but I didn't look back. The Hall of Flags ended and I passed between the forest of petrified stems of The Enchanted Garden, blind to it, an agony of distress beating a tattoo against my senses. By the time the light of the terrace showed up I could hear Zavella no longer. I saw the speaking-tube snake in from the walls of The Entrance Hall and the path led me back to where time existed; where there was a future and no peace.

The sun poured into my eyes. There seemed to be even more guards than when I went in. I bawled at them, beside myself : "There's only one man in there ! . . . *One man!*" Romero was by the speaking-tube. He came towards me as I walked, closing in from the side with the stiff-legged suspicion of a dog approaching another.

"Is he coming out?"

"No."

A sluggish breeze twirled some torn-up tickets across the sanded clearing. I pushed through the turnstiles, Romero lengthening his stride in an effort to draw level.

"What did he want you for?"

I didn't answer.

"What did he want you for?"

I grimaced against the light. A guard shifted out of my way. Romero was almost at my shoulder.

"Señor Tyler !" He tried to grasp my arm but I shook

him off, making for the car. "Why did he want to talk to you?"

I opened the car door and got in; slammed it after me. The hood was down. I touched the starter and the engine fired.

Romero raged: "I demand an answer, Señor Tyler. What did Zavella want?"

"Go in and ask him," I said in a voice that didn't sound like my own. "He's waiting for you."

2

I stopped at a flaking wayside bar about a mile short of the town and drank three or four quick brandies, standing at the counter. A caged canary above the radio rocked on a metal swing and the woman who served me tried to tempt it with a piece of stale black sausage.

"How much?"

"Twelve pesetas."

A hysterical impulse made me say: "I want the bird as well."

She laughed, gap-toothed. "Paco is not for sale, señor. I'm sorry." Nevertheless she asked: "What would you do with it?"

"Set it free."

"But it would die." She was indignant and muttered resentfully. "What a thing to suggest! It would be killed."

I drove off, the nauseous feeling gaining ground. I promised him nothing, I thought. Nothing. I just said I wouldn't forget. That's not a promise. . . .

It had gone five: they'd be inside the caves. Hurry it up, for God's sake. Finish with it. . . . My mind's eye kept seeing Zavella, not the dark silhouette by The Chessmen but as he was in the Villa Miramar when I confronted him with the ridiculous cigarette-lighter and he said: "Time is an ambush, señor." You're right, poor bastard, I thought. It was for Scheele and it's proved so for you. . . .

170

I passed the España. I couldn't force myself to go in and rejoin Ilsa : not so soon. I went on as far as the Bar Sinbad and parked under the plane trees, crossed the road and sat at one of Joaquin's tables. But another waiter tended me; balding, stooped.

"Where's Joaquin?"

"Off duty, señor. Since lunchtime."

I glanced across the square at the Civil Guard building. So he'd heard; someone had slipped him the news. I was relieved it wouldn't have to be me : the last hour had made me a coward.

"Family trouble, I believe," the waiter remarked. "What can I get you?"

"Bring some Fundador."

Some boys played with a ball by the central fountain and their shrill happiness insulted everything that haunted me. I told myself : Even if I *did* make him a promise I'm not bound by it. He didn't know what he was asking.

The waiter came with a new bottle; peeled the lead foil and drew the cork. "Leave it," I said. He wasn't used to me and I all but had to take it from him.

Zavella would be dead by now. . . . I drank, watching the light fade, unmindful of time. I had been spared Joaquin. I would see his long, pained features soon enough—tomorrow, the day after : I could suffer with him then and perpetuate the lies. A week hence, even. But tomorrow and the day after were all that remained where Ilsa was concerned. Yet I continued to sit and drink; made no effort to return to the España. "She would never forgive you." Was that why? I put my hands over my ears, as if to stop the flow of memory. I was coward enough without Zavella's logic.

Dusk came, thickening fast. Lights were switched on around the square and in the Civil Guard headquarters; above the crowded tables. I thought I saw Romero's car slide in but it had grown too dark for me to be sure. The bottle was a third empty. I was already unforgiven. Only a few hours ago she had said : "I could never forget that I was with you when Erich died." Never forgive, never forget. . . . The weapon I had so assiduously forged was ready too late. "Hang on to your victory, Señor Tyler." What victory? If I honoured any promise it would be because of defeat. . . .

The brandy burned deeper, deadening all but pain. Around me were the ebb and flow of laughter, music, voices. Someone came and sat opposite me; a man, fifty-ish, with a thirty-six hour tan. I didn't reply when he first spoke. Later, he inquired : "Are you feeling all right?" I raised my head. There were two of him, both as soft-edged as a dream. "All right?" he asked and I nodded, gripping my glass.

"You're British, aren't you?"

"How did you guess? I usually insist on a flag on the table."

My tongue apparently couldn't cope with acid because he gave a smug smile, approving his discernment. "I can generally tell. Sort of sixth sense—you know? My missus hasn't got it at all. Yesterday, for instance, she made a most frightful bloomer. . . ."

I thought : Ilsa. Oh God. Ilsa.

Presently I heard : "I say—you ought to go easy with that stuff, you know." His two images came momentarily together : buck teeth, wiry hair, pointed chin. "The vino's so damned cheap in these parts that one forgets one's not used to it. A fellow-director of mine—"

"I'm drinking for a friend." I wasn't able to hold the focus.

"But—"

He stopped short. I stared blearily into the square, alone with my wretched permutations of Ilsa and Scheele, Zavella and Romero and Joaquin, corrupted with the conviction that I had been cheated out of what was mine. Slowly, glass by glass, I was learning that there are other ways of dying.

Dimly, I realized the man was warming to a new topic. "My missus and I come to Spain every year. It's different, you know : I always say Africa begins at the Pyrenees. And we try and get acquainted with the people—the real peasants. No organized tours for us, thank *you*. They're fifty years behind the times here, of course, but they've got something we lack at home. The old virtues—honour, decency, courage, patience, manners. . . . I told my missus only today that it's a result of a combination of the acceptance of the Catholic and the fatalism of the Moor. To suffer is to live, after all. . . . I'll put up with the plumbing and the way they knock their animals around just to—"

My chair screeched as I pushed it back and got up. A glass went over. I lurched away from him. The man complained loudly : "You're a rude sod, I must say !" I blundered through the purple streets and found refuge in another bar, strewn with sawdust and with brass spittoons beside every marble-topped table. It would have been easier to cry but, like Zavella, I seemed to have lost the ability. A flamenco singer chanted nasally, simulating emotion, yet the cheap words had a terrible potency :

> *The roses we plucked*
> *Are all thrown away,*
> *But sharp thorns*
> *Are still in my flesh. . . .*

I'll never know how long I stayed or where else I went. Afterwards, in the Street of Jesus and Mary, a girl with a crimson mouth whispered from a shadowy doorway, but one can lust and still be faithful and I wanted nobody but Ilsa.

A taxi eventually took me home. At least, that's where I found myself next morning, with hope drained out of me and the taste of death in my mouth.

CHAPTER TEN

I

I WAS late at the church: Scheele's Requiem Mass was already in progress when I tiptoed to a seat. Ilsa I saw at once. She was alone in the front row of chairs, not more than three yards from where the black-draped coffin rested on its catafalque at the foot of the sanctuary steps. The old priest was at the altar, gabbling his way through the Mass as if it were some private rite of no concern to the hunched congregation. The number of people present surprised me. Some, no doubt, were routine worshippers, accustomed to be there at eleven o'clock. But others had come for a specific reason. Romero was one of these; the manager of the España another. I noticed the Mayor and his wife, the proprietor of the Bar Sinbad and an official from the Tourist Office. I asked myself leadenly if they had never winced and bristled at Scheele's arrogance; never seen the contempt in which he had held them all? Was I the only one who hated him? And, if that were so, would I have been as blind as the rest of them if he had had no wife and I had never learned his secret? One key had opened many doors, though never the one I wished to enter.

I watched Ilsa from my place at the back. As recently as yesterday I would have been jealous of her proximity to the coffin, but I was too weary to be irrational any more. The priest went about his business—murmuring, gesticulating, genuflecting—offering up the unfathomable mystery on behalf of Scheele. Yes, I suppose I should have feared him more, but I couldn't grapple with what I didn't understand. It was strange to think that he would have been my implacable enemy if Scheele had lived—he and half a mil-

174

lion like him. But Ilsa was free now. The only restraint to which she was subjected came from within herself—and Scheele had planted it there as surely as he had once used Spain as a seed-bed for brutality and wickedness. And for both these things I knew that I would go on loathing him until the end of my days.

I had come a long way since Zavella died. But one can sever a limb and still feel the pain in it; cut out one's tongue and still have to curb the urge to speak. When Ilsa went to the altar-rails and took the bloodless bread I had enough bitterness left to think: What about me? What about Zavella? Or don't the losers count?

The Mass ended. Half a dozen stocky men came forward and lifted the coffin on to their shoulders with professional reverence. This time I could see which end of the box was which. They brought Scheele up the aisle head first and I wondered briefly as he passed whether his facial muscles remained taut with terror.

There were three cars at the door besides the hearse. The mourners sorted themselves from the rest of the congregation. I rode in the first car with Ilsa and a man I had seen in the church but couldn't place. Ilsa introduced us perfunctorily: he was from the German Consulate in Barcelona. We acknowledged one another gravely. Ilsa was dressed in the same dark costume she had worn the previous afternoon, in addition to which her head was covered with a black veil. Except for introducing me to the German she did not speak. She had cried recently; her eyes were puffy. The brandy had left a pump hammering in my head and I would have preferred not to have had to sit on the tip-down seat facing her. It would have been more comfortable beside her, but the German had got there first.

I tried to look everywhere but at her. Occasionally people blessed themselves as we passed them in the streets. There seemed no end to those who would honour Scheele. Alive, I could have exposed him and watched him destroy his place in Ilsa's heart. But now he was sacrosanct. He'd won here after all—each time he'd come : and only I knew it.

It was a ten-minute ride to the cemetery. I had never been there before and not knowing how far we were going somehow made the journey seem longer. Once we were clear of Bandaques the road was unsurfaced and the hearse raised a pall of dust for us to grind through. The windows grew dirty and the German sweated a great deal. We stopped once and I presumed we had arrived, but some of the wreaths had apparently fallen from the hearse and we had to wait until the attendants collected them. The three of us swayed in unison as the car rocked over the inevitable potholes, separately concerned with grief and defeat and—I imagine—the bore of duty. I thought it likely that Romero had already told Ilsa about Zavella. He would have been full of himself last evening; a knight in shining armour. Murdered for gain. . . . The knowledge could account for the air of injustice moulded so clearly into her outward and visible distress, and for that reason alone I feared catching her eye. It takes courage to surrender the truth without hope of reward.

When we next stopped it was at the cemetery—a huge walled rectangle of weather-beaten sandstone on a desolate slope above the town. A brown, blind woman squatted beside the open gates on a rush-plaited chair surrounded by a number of yellow clay pitchers. I suppose she was there to sell water, but—those on the hearse apart—the only flowers I could see were artificial; inside the walls the tombs and rusting crosses under the dark cypresses standing like fixed explosions against the noonday sky were decorated with nothing else.

We filed in behind the coffin—nine of us, together with the priest and a boy assistant. The boy, at least, made no bones about his indifference. But the Mayor and his wife and the rest put on the required faces as they gathered round the boarded pit. Romero's, in particular, was detestable. For the first time in days I looked at Ilsa with something like charity. Across the narrow width of the grave my mind asked her indignantly : Why are they here? Who are they? You're the only one who's suffering. I've come because of you, not because of Scheele-cum-Schafer. But at least I know who he was—and you think you know. . . .

I studied some of the tombstones nearest me. A worn plaque read : RUBIO SALINAS; GONDRA, 12.4.1938. YOUR MOTHER WILL NOT FORGET YOU. . . . FRANCISCO DIAZ; GONDRA, 12.4.1938. . . . ESPERANZA CABRER; GONDRA, 12.4.1938. HONOURED FOR EVER. . . . The false roses and mimosa, brittle and bleached with age, belied the vain promises. The priest had begun to scatter earth on to the lowered coffin : it landed with a hollow sound, as if the varnished box were empty. The wreaths lying on the heaps of stony red soil were fresh and indecently beautiful—lilies and carnations and iris predominated. Only a couple of cards were readable from where I stood. One merely said : FROM ILSA. She had printed it, as a child might. The other was from Romero: WITH DEEP AND LASTING REGRET. The flourish of his signature was as preposterous as the wording.

The priest closed his missal : it was all over. Dust to dust. . . . Ilsa scooped earth into the pit and the others followed suit. I turned away and walked slowly back to the gate. A corroded, three-flapped piece of metal on which a likeness to the Virgin was embossed hung loosely from a nail above a tomb set in the wall. The plaque bore the names of Zavella's father and mother—TOMEO CANALS and MARIA ZAVELLA DE CANALS. There was no pious declaration cut into the stone; merely the place and the date—GONDRA, 12.4.1938.

The irony was complete. And I thought : Good-bye, Schafer. They've all been waiting for you.

We climbed back into the cars after Ilsa had shaken hands with everyone except the German consular official and me. I sat beside her on the return run, tongue-tied, my head still hammering. The German smoked. Like me, he couldn't find anything to say but the regulation mourning-look was beginning to crack a little. I guessed he was wondering about his train. The windows had been cleaned and there was no hearse ahead of us to shower us with dust, but I don't remember anything particular about the sun-gutted countryside. At the España, in the awkward moment or two after we stepped out on to the pavement, she spoke to the German, who looked at his watch and nodded.

"And you, Ty?" Her eyes were leaden.

"I'm sorry. I didn't understand what you said."

"Mister Meinhardt is coming in for a drink. I wondered—"

"Not now, if you don't mind." I'm sure she was glad, though there was no way of telling. "But perhaps you'd dine with me tonight?"

She hesitated momentarily. "Thank you."

"I'll come about seven." I paused. "Is there anything I can do meanwhile?" I said it like something learned by heart.

She shook her head. I gripped the German's sweaty hand, muttered a farewell and left them going up the steps together.

I made my way through the heat to the Bar Sinbad and collected the car, hoping that Joaquin either wasn't on duty or wouldn't see me. There were two things I wanted to do and I drove first to the church. I couldn't find a priest, but a cleaner on her knees in the sanctuary obligingly went and fetched one. He was very young and serious and wore horn-spectacles which somehow gave him the appearance of a comedian's stooge. It was hard to think of him as one who was invested with special powers.

"I want a Mass said." I suppose he was used to people calling him "father".

"At any particular time?" He had a quiet, pleasant voice which he employed slowly and deliberately, as if he were none too sure of my intelligence.

"I doesn't matter in the least. Is there some offering I should make?"

I thought he was weighing me up, about to double the price as they do in the shops when they spot a tourist. But he said: "That is entirely up to you."

I gave him two hundred pesetas: he protested mildly. "It's much too much."

"You could say more than one Mass, perhaps?"

"I could do that, of course." He wrinkled his nose. "What is the name, please?"

"Zavella," I said. "Luis Zavella."

As he wrote it down he remarked: "I seem to know the name."

"It's probably in the morning papers."

"A relative of yours?" His eyesight must have been extra poor.

"An acquaintance."

I started to leave, but he said: "You'll want to know the days; when they can be fitted in."

"I'm not particular."

"But you'll wish to attend, surely?"

"No."

"It is customary."

"Say them when it suits you."

I thanked him and went away, the pigmy gesture made. I have heard it said that only when one is happy can one entirely lose one's identity. But pity can also annihilate selfishness, and hatred can give the illusion of doing so. I walked past the side altars on my way out: the candle-lit gloom gave the same eerie quality to the statuary as in The White Caves. The Saint Christopher, in particular, bore a disturbing resemblance to the stalagmite near the entrance to The Hall of Flags and the sight of it clinched my mood for where I was heading next.

I took the car to the square. A notice outside the main entrance to the Civil Guard building insisted that the space be kept clear, but I parked in front of it and went in. I'd last seen the sergeant who was on duty when Ilsa had called on Romero earlier in the week. He'd stopped me from going beyond the barrier then, and though he tried to do so again I shoved him aside and barged through the pass-gate.

I opened Romero's door without knocking. He was cleaning his finger-nails, lolling back, jacket off, feet resting on the desk. The sergeant lumbered in after me, protesting, apologizing. Curtly, Romero ordered him out of the room. Apart from lifting his head he hadn't moved, but his jaw-muscles knotted, quaking his sallow cheeks.

"This is a surprise, Señor Tyler."

During the Mass and in the cemetery he'd pretended I wasn't there, close though we had sometimes been. Now he had no option, but his mind clearly wasn't on what he imagined was a condescending smile. More than anything he must have begrudged me my secret.

I stopped in front of the desk. "I hope you didn't damage too many stalagmites."

"I'm happy to say not."

"That must have been very gratifying."

"Fortunately it wasn't as difficult as we had feared. He didn't have much ammunition. We switched the lights off until we were through the tunnel, of course. One of my guards was slightly wounded, but that was all."

"Someone must be very proud of you—in addition to yourself."

"I only did my duty, señor."

"That's what Scheele would have claimed."

It was an unguarded retort, but Romero applied his own interpretation and nodded. "What happened yesterday can only be a source of satisfaction to his wife. I took the opportunity of calling on her last night."

"I was certain you would." The broken fan squeaked overhead; endlessly flicked a bar of shadow round the room. "When's his funeral?"

"That is a matter for the Church, not for me."

"You just kill them, is that it?"

"Very rarely." For all his superficial aplomb he was unsure of himself. As if to buttress his uncertainty he said with careful derision: "I keep forgetting Zavella was your friend. In the circumstances, Señora Scheele must find it a most baffling relationship." Encouraged, he added: "However, that won't be why you have come to see me."

"No."

"What do you want then?"

"My passport."

His face clouded. I tossed the receipt he had given me on to the desk. It skidded under the blotter and disappeared, but he didn't attempt to retrieve it. Instead, he made a pretence of studying his finger-nails.

I said impatiently: "You're a bad actor, Romero. I want it now."

"I'm afraid I can't oblige you at the moment."

"No?"

"No."

"Give me one acceptable reason."

"It is locked in a filing-cabinet."

"Then I suggest you open the cabinet up and get it out."

He failed to brazen out my glare. But he said. "My clerk has the keys and today he is off duty." He shrugged unconvincingly. "It is regretted, but there it is. You will have to wait. Come back another time: tomorrow, say."

"*You* carry the keys," I said. "You forget I was here on the night Scheele died and that when your clerk left he handed them to you." A thin, white-metal chain looped from his right hip to right-hand trousers' pocket. "You also forget that you aren't wearing your jacket."

He coloured, but said nothing.

"Quickly, please. I'm in a hurry."

He didn't budge.

"If I don't get it now," I said, "I'll take this whole business right to the top and have you blasted out of that chair for good and all. You had no right to my passport in the first place. I only let you have it that evening because I was sick to death of your pestering. You over-reached yourself then—and you know it. . . . Now, perhaps, you'll be good enough to take your feet off the desk and give those nails of yours a rest."

He swallowed, then stood up, supposedly believing that by taking his time he could retain his poise. I watched him sort out the correct key and open the middle drawer of one of the cabinets. The fan's sole surviving blade squeaked round and round, like a dog after its own tail. Romero started fumbling through the exposed rack of files, too slowly for my liking.

I prompted him icily: "Don't tell me you're inefficient on top of everything else. What you're looking for is dark blue, over-printed with gold. And in case it's slipped your mind the name is Tyler."

He produced it sullenly; thudded the drawer back in. Returning, he threw the passport down on the desk in front of me. It hit one corner of the blotter, spinning it, and the receipt was ejected on to the floor at his feet. I said: "Thank you for nothing," then turned on my heels and strode from his office and down the long corridor to the pass-gate and the bright glare of the main door beyond, trembling under the impact of the smallest and most futile of triumphs.

2

Ilsa said: "Captain Romero came to see me last night. Did you know?"

"Yes."

"You were there, he said—at The White Caves."

I nodded. "He asked me to go."

"He told me it was Zavella who asked."

"So it was. But it was Romero who telephoned. That's why I left you in such a hurry."

"You might have explained."

"There wasn't time, Ilsa. He gave me only half an hour to get there."

"Even so you could have said something. It wouldn't have taken a minute."

"I'm sorry."

"You've changed, Ty."

"That's not true."

She shook her head. "You've changed."

We were in the Siroco, a small restaurant which overlooked the south beach. I had taken Ilsa there so as to be on neutral ground : it had no associations for either of us. The Bar Sinbad would have been impossible, and most of the other places where we might have eaten faced northwards towards the Villa Miramar. It was quite dark and, below us, the sea was already black under the ice-blue stars. The tell-tale stain from Gondra still disfiguring the north beach would have been invisible but our wounds were raw enough without deliberately confronting the long arc of sand where we had walked together and where Scheele had floated in.

"In what way have I changed?"

She was silent, telling herself.

Without hope of being believed, I said : "I promise you I haven't."

"You must have been aware of what a terrible thing Zavella had done."

I replied carefully : "Romero didn't inform me until I arrived."

"Afterwards, I mean. Yet you didn't come back. I waited for you, but you didn't come. I can't understand that."

"I'm sorry."

"Why didn't you, Ty?"

She was more bewildered than vindictive. There was no sharpness in her tone : it matched her appearance—weary to the point of exhaustion. Sleep was what she needed.

"I meant to."

She raised her chin incredulously. "It was the same with Erich's ring. You said nothing about that either until it suited you."

"I wanted to get hold of it first—I told you so yesterday."

"And then you said something about the initials not being his."

"I was only making sure there wasn't some mistake."

"How could there have been?" A memory provoked disdain. "You behaved as if ES stood for someone else—as if more than one person had lost an identical ring."

I thought: Don't tempt me, Ilsa. I'm as tired as you are and can't bear to be hurt any more. And this hurts above all. I love you—that's why I've tied my hands behind my back. So don't molest me too much. Otherwise I'll only start defending myself.

Inshore, ghostly ribs of white moved on the dark sea as though it breathed. Presently, Ilsa said: "What did Zavella want?"

"He hoped I'd deliver a message to a relative of his."

"And will you?" She looked at me as if I were an accessory.

"I'll do my best."

"It's strange that he should have asked for you."

"I suppose he couldn't think of anyone else. I'd met him that morning to get the ring and when he was trapped—"

"What was he like?"

"Small, consumptive. In his early thirties."

"Did he speak about what happened?"

"No."

I gazed out of the window at the lights of some sardine boats. My fingers found the place on the back of my neck, close to the cropped hair, where, four days ago, her nails had torn the skin. The marks had not healed, but the fever which had put them there was as dead as Scheele; had died with him. I had thought that I had lived for her body alone, but I was wrong: there are secret places in the heart to which stress and suffering give existence. Yet, though I had discovered the courage to accept defeat, I lacked stature. She had washed her hands of me: otherwise I wouldn't have held my tongue. If I had believed there was one chance in a thousand of winning her I would have told her everything I knew, filled her mind with all the filth of Gondra, gone without pity and searched for more wherever in Europe it might have been found. But she had finished with me. Scheele hadn't diminished as my vanity had once insisted he would. While he lived we had deceived him, but his death—and the timing of it—had made our deceit profane. I had been rejected in mind and heart; in the confessional and at the communion-rail.

Ilsa said : "You hated Erich, didn't you?"

Once more I remembered Zavella and his plea not to pass the disease on—"It will eat her away from the inside just as it's eaten me away. Why should she suffer, too?" And with anguish I thought : Amen.

"I love you," I answered, looking at her, enormously moved by the symmetry of her small, boyish face, wanting as never before to cup it in my hands : touch her soft, straight hair.

"You only imagined you did—and I am to blame for it."

"Since then. . . . Now."

"Please, Ty. I don't want to hear any more."

"All right," I said quietly. "You won't, I promise you. Never again. But I wanted you to know."

Nothing could shake her loyalty. "Only yesterday you were on the point of saying ugly things about Erich. 'He's best forgotten', you said."

I nodded, bitterness seeping in again; drawing the line at an apology.

"That isn't love, Ty," she said. "If you love someone you don't go out of your way to hurt them."

Imprisoned within myself I thought heavily : Why else am I sparing you? Then, because there seemed nothing else to say, I suggested we went in to dinner.

CHAPTER ELEVEN

THE Air France Constellation glittered on the oil-smudged apron and the runways pointed into the quivering distances. On one side were blue hills, their crumpled serrations hazed over with heat; on the other, invisible from the airport's departure block, the sea.

I seemed to have spent the greater part of my time with Ilsa in bars and restaurants and hotel lounges. Since Tuesday evening, in all our crises, we had invariably been besieged by other voices, other moods. Now, for once, I would not have wished it otherwise. I wanted every second peopled with activity; distractions.

"What time d'you reach Paris?"

"About six, I think."

"And you connect straight away?"

"I believe I will have to wait about half an hour."

I had asked her the self-same things on the drive from Bandaques, but one becomes repetitious as the minutes slowly dwindle away, filling each pause with desperate improvisations. Everything had been said that would ever be said, yet silence seemed a crime. Would she like something to read? Was she a good traveller?—or would she be happier with a pill? The very questions underlined how incompletely I knew her : and yet each tired gesture and response twisted in the awakened places of my heart. In seven hours or so she would be in Hamburg, but there was no comfort for me in the myth that the world is shrinking. We were already severed : Scheele's initials had mocked me for the last time when the porter unloaded his three matching travelling cases from the car's boot. There was nothing to be done except wait for the tinny announcement of her flight. The minutes stretched out elastically and I was torn between willing them to an end and staving off the final moment of farewell. But at last the disembodied voice clicked on : "Will passengers for Air France Flight Number 520 for Paris please make their way. . . ." And it was as if all the frontier posts everywhere had suddenly come down; like hearing a life sentence delivered.

"Good-bye, Ilsa."

How conventionally we behave in an effort to hide ourselves away : an onlooker might have supposed that we were no more than casually acquainted. But the truth was in our eyes, as frankly and fleetingly exposed as at the instant of our first coming physically together. For the minutest period of time I could have deluded myself that Scheele no longer seemed to be between us.

"Good-bye, Ty." Her hand was cool and she didn't falter. "Try not to think too badly of me."

I was numb; sealed off by the inadequacy of words. "Good-bye. . . . Safe and sound"—and the chance phrase gave life to a memory in her mind; in both our minds. I thought she was going to say something more, but she bit her lower lip, regret and disillusion re-possessing her. Like a stranger who'd asked me the way she turned swiftly and, without a backward glance, joined the group of passengers making for the numbered door. I could scarcely believe that I would never see her again or hear that quiet, slightly accented voice. There would be no letters, no telephone-calls. Whether she was going to a house or an apartment, I didn't know. Who would meet her, I didn't know. How she would spend tomorrow—all the tomorrows—I didn't know.

The door flapped to behind her and something inside me shrivelled away to nothing. I must have remained staring at the door for a long time because a girl in a blue uniform came and inquired helpfully whether there was anything I wanted. I heard myself answer, but have no idea what I said that could have made her look at me so strangely.

187

Then I went emptily into the dazzle of the sun and tried to remember where I had left the car.

About thirty miles south of Barcelona I had seen a plane go over; watched it as if it had been Ilsa's. Now, an hour later, the high, slim tower of the Church of the Incarnation pricked the skyline. She would be in Paris by the time I reached the villa.

The numbness had gone deeper. I was like a swimmer who had lost his strength and was being carried unwillingly on the tide. With the resignation of the powerless I told myself again and again that I had been right to allow her to go still believing in Scheele. But it made an unconsoling litany. A sign at a junction pointed towards The White Caves, and Zavella's words about time winning in the end were better suited to my barren mood. Sooner or later we were all losers; we all paid. Scheele had. Zavella had. Ilsa, despite the efficacy of the confessional, imagined she would eventually. And I was paying now, in the desolate sense of loss that Catholics will tell you is their understanding of Hell.

Bandaques gradually hemmed me in. I drove through the town's scabrous streets until, at the amphitheatre, I reached its central hub; then on past the España and the square where Romero's headquarters and the Bar Sinbad faced each other through the plane trees. There was going to be no escape. Gondra had left its livid stain along the beach and as I entered the house, Catalina was singing :

Por de bajo del puente
No pasa nadie....

I went into the living-room where Scheele's body had oozed water and Ilsa had come to identify him. She had left no souvenirs. Her wet footprints had long since dried on the tiles; the crumpled bed had long since been smoothed. And yet her presence filled the house—as did Scheele's and

Romero's, as did Zavella's from that other time. Dead or living they had all been here. I walked through on to the terrace and shut the doors against Catalina's singing. The cover on the typewriter was like a flag of defeat. Near the machine was an old copy of *The Oxford Book of Children's Verse* which I had taken out a few days earlier with the intention of giving to Joaquin, but which now I never would. Beside it, weighted down by the cigarette-lighter which had fooled Zavella, was the slip of paper bearing the words: *We are swords that spirits fight with. We never see the hands that brandish us.* . . . I screwed it up and tossed it away: the breeze of the sea chased it into the garden. True or false it made no difference.

I lit a cigarette, watching the day die behind the mauve sierras.

I'll have to go away, I thought. I can't stay here. I'll have to go home.

A BATTLE IS FOUGHT TO

BE WON

Francis Clifford

'Not only a fine novel as a novel, and the best novel about the war in Burma, but also one of the best novels about a soldier, or soldiers, that I have ever read'

Paul Scott BOOKS AND BOOKMEN

A civilian hastily enrolled in the British army, Tony Gilling was all too human. Fraught with complexes and humiliated by failure in a world that was not his own, he and his depleted company were thrown into the breach to stem the tide of fanatical Japanese for a few precious hours.

The pattern was relentlessly the same – demolish a bridge, deploy the men and repulse an onslaught of *Banzai* screaming enemy; retreat a few miles, blow up the road and face them again . . .

All the time losing men, all the time tortured by self-doubt but, in the end, Gilling was better than he knew.

'All of Clifford belongs on the connoisseur's bookshelf; he is unparalleled both in hovering suspense and distinguished style'

Book Week

CORONET BOOKS

ALL MEN ARE LONELY NOW

Francis Clifford

'It'll be a long time before we get another spy story as brilliant, gripping and satisfyingly written as this'

Sunday Times

'The best novel about counter-espionage that I have read'

Eric Ambler

Simultaneously and with equal impact, two things happened to David Lancaster.

First, he fell in love. Not a massively important piece of general intelligence. But for him it was the first time; and from him it demanded something that had hitherto remained hidden.

Second, he fell into the cold, dark well of intrigue and counter-espionage; an investigation that followed sharply on an East German's disclosures about a laser-guided missile. A talented amateur in a bitterly profes-sional world, Lancaster joined in the search to find out who was doing what to whom and why. Until finally he realised that a situation of his own making had led him into a callous and cold-blooded climax, in which the world of love and the business of hate were further apart than he had ever imagined.

'*A brilliant spy thriller*'

Sunday Express

CORONET BOOKS

ALSO AVAILABLE IN CORONET BOOKS

FRANCIS CLIFFORD

☐ 14983 3	A Battle Is Fought To Be Won	35p
☐ 15143 9	All Men Are Lonely Now	35p
☐ 02879 3	Overdue	35p
☐ 12505 5	Another Way of Dying	30p
☐ 04343 1	The Green Fields Of Eden	30p
☐ 17307 6	The Blind Side	35p
☐ 19486 3	Amigo Amigo	40p

OWEN JOHN

☐ 18993 2	The Shadow In The Sea	40p
☐ 19826 5	Sabotage	40p

BRIAN GARFIELD

☐ 17873 6	Deep Cover	50p
☐ 16786 6	Death Wish	40p
☐ 19672 6	Line Of Succession	50p